CHERYL BURMAN

First published in the UK in 2022 by
Holborn House Ltd
©2022 Cheryl Burman

Cover design Lauren Willmore
laurenwillmore.com

By Cheryl Burman

River Witch

Keepers

SHORT STORIES

Dragon Gift

GUARDIANS OF THE FOREST TRILOGY

The Wild Army

Quests

Gryphon Magic

Prequel

Legend of the Winged Lion

www.cherylburman.com

Dedicated to the memory of John Powell, who knew the river

The man was talking to the river.

Hester eyed him with piqued curiosity. Talking to the river was her job.

He was tall, and hatless under a hot summer sun. The same breeze which bent the grass of the field behind Hester wove strands of his black hair in the air above his head. He wore a long black coat which was shiny at the elbows. The coat made her suspect he was, or once was, a gentleman, because she had seen gentlemen on a rare trip to Shiphaven and they had worn long black coats. Hats too, so this gentleman must have fallen on bad times. Hester's mother had said this about a merchant family in the town whose boat failed to return from its annual pilgrimage and, fallen on bad times, they had to move from their townhouse and sell the fancy carriage.

The man spun about, as if suddenly aware of being watched. When he clasped his hands behind him, he displayed a yellow brocade waistcoat. A fine material, so it was a shame the buttonholes were frayed. Perhaps her mother could mend them, for money, as she did more and more these days. The farm was not enough, despite the long hours Father and her brothers worked.

'Hello.' The man touched his fingers to his head as if he had forgotten he was hatless. His hair glistened like raven feathers in the bright sun, and gold flecks glinted warmly in his dark eyes.

Hester needed to put her thumb in her mouth, but Mother had beaten the habit out of her, declaring that at eight years old Hester should have long outgrown thumb sucking. She agreed with Mother, so she folded her arms over her pinafore before the thumb could sneak its own way between her lips.

'You come here often, don't you?' the man said. 'I've seen you here, talking to Sabrina.'

Who, where, was this Sabrina? Hester turned her head so quickly her untidy curls slapped her cheek.

'Sabrina is the name of the river.' He gestured at the placid wide stream flowing at this moment down to the sea.

'That's not the name of the river.' She screwed up her nose. 'It's got another name …'

'You mean the name ordinary folk call it?'

'Yes.'

'You and I are not ordinary folk, little mistress. We are wise. We call the river by her goddess name, Sabrina.'

'God?'

'No, goddess.' He brushed strands of hair from his face. 'Did you know you were talking to a goddess?'

Hester's thumb twitched. She held it steady, pinned into her armpit. If she were honest, it wasn't so much that she talked to the river, as it talked to her. When the river was low it whispered, shushing its way over the sandbanks as the silks Mother sewed shushed over Hester's hands. When the tide came in, the waters swooshed and swirled while the swans hitched fast rides alongside shallow-bottomed trows.

The river told Hester she was a good girl, which was what Father told her when she found the eggs the hens hid or picked blackberries for Mother to make into jam.

She listened for the river's words. Today, it was silent, hurrying to the sea in a long smooth rush to collect the big ships and bring them up with the turning of the tide.

The man came nearer, his shadow falling over Hester's bonnetless head. 'May I walk with you?' He offered his hand for her to take, if she wished.

The hand was long-fingered and smooth, with pale lines across the palm. A gentleman's hand. When it didn't go away, Hester took it and the man led her alongside the hedgerows, away from the river, away from Sabrina. As they walked he told her the names of the flowers growing at the edge of the fields and sprouting from the hedges.

'Here is yarrow.' His fingers caressed the froth of fading lilac flowers. 'Cures colds,' he said. 'And toothache.'

He held a feathery cluster the colour of fresh cream to Hester's nose. Her eyes crinkled. 'Ah! Meadowsweet. Mother says I'll carry meadowsweet when I marry.'

'Marry?' The man raised a dark eyebrow. 'Does she now?'

Cheryl Burman

PART ONE

Chapter One

boisterous wind tangles Hester's hair and whips her back with its chilly gusts. She shouldn't be here, on the clifftop above the river. She should be hurrying back across the fields to milking – a task with which she was entrusted on her recent fourteenth birthday.

'Old enough to take on more,' Mother said, bequeathing Hester the roughest of her own tasks while adding that she herself needs to keep her hands clean for sewing, given the fancy merchants' wives of Shiphaven have no desire for streaks of pig muck on their lace collars.

Hester ignores the imagined lowing of the cows. Huddled in her thick, woollen shawl, she fixes her gaze on the waters. All life is down there. Fishing boats with their sails furled; barges sunk low with wood and coal and stone; the ferry with its passengers huddled close as puppies in a box, wanting the cold journey to be over.

Busyness and purpose.

While up here is Hester with a life of milking, unearthing eggs, playing housekeeper to pigs in their sties, and waking in the night to feed motherless lambs. Cows, lambs and hens are all well and good, and Hester understands she has much to be grateful for. Her mind roams across those families in the village where too little money and too many children mean constant hunger and cold. Yet, she has her own hunger. It's why she has sneaked from the farm to answer the call of the river nymphs, needing to feed the craving for their embrace which lives within her, the elusive memory of a dream.

She shivers, stamps her boots to get feeling into feet chilled by the wet, scrubby grass, and peers downstream. A low bore rears ahead of the tidal flow, a cavalry of white-maned grey steeds galloping away from the ocean with heads held high and steady. Small boats going down pull into the cliffs on the far bank to wait out the surging tide.

As Hester watches, she strains to hear Sabrina's voice.

Sabrina, goddess.

When Hester was a little girl, Sabrina murmured she was a good girl. Now the river whispers that Hester must be wise, and strong. And do what she must do, which is a puzzling demand.

Stretching towards the cliff edge, she searches—

There! The nymphs rise on the bow waves of the great barges before plunging beneath fishing boats, playing tag with nets and oars. Their bodies are as supple as spring's elvers which churn the shallows to a thrashing, black mass, but luminous, more graceful. Wrapped in mud-brown hanks of hair as thick as fishermen's ropes, they scorn November's cold.

'Join us, swim with us, learn with us.'

Their high sweet voices cleave the sailors' coarse shouts in mimicry of the wind from the fields slicing through Hester's shawl. They cleave Hester's heart too, filling her with a yearning to answer their summons, to ride the white horses far upstream, turning with the new tide to journey to the ocean. Hester has never seen the sea, felt only the tug of its salty call as she watches the nymphs on their downstream course.

'Join us, swim with us, learn with us.'

Sinuous arms wave above the waters, beckoning Hester as they always do.

Sabrina sings. *Be wise, be strong, do what you need to do.*

Hester's yearning is too much. Today, she resolves ... today at last, she will know the sea in truth.

Along the cliff she runs, scrabbling down the path to the water, digging her heels into the black soil, grabbing at stunted branches to push herself forward. She is a spawning salmon in her urgency to reach the rocks and mudbanks which will soon be drowned in racing water. Stretching out her arms, she begs the nymphs, seeks their wet touch, needing them to take her into the flow. She will learn with them, their strength will be hers. Their wisdom too.

Her boots are drenched as she wades forward to meet the oncoming wave and its soaring, plunging riders—

'Hey, you there, Miss!'

Hester ignores the call.

'Stop!'

A hand on her shoulder wrenches her from the swiftly rising flow. Hester's heart pounds. Cold, grey water swirls about her ankles. She stumbles backwards, is caught, is pulled and steered, breathless, up the path to the clifftop.

Her rescuer stands before her, breathing as hard as Hester breathes. A glimpse of faded yellow waistcoat, torn remnants of thread where a button should be, shows beneath his open greatcoat. Her memory stirs.

A frown slides across the man's forehead, as shadowy and fleeting as a night hunting owl.

'What were you thinking?' His dark eyes, with their glint of gold, narrow. Something hard, wild in them makes Hester squirm.

Her heart keeps its pounding rhythm. She presses her hand to her chest. Her hand is cold. All of her is cold.

'Sabrina called me … she wants me–'

He whips his head to the river. Strands of his too-long hair fly out from beneath his beaver hat. His hair is shrivelled at the ends, as if he has bent too close to his cottage fire.

'Talk to Sabrina from here.'

Hester winces at the harshness of his voice, drops her gaze to the stony ground, away from the man's cold anger.

'Far safer,' he says, waving at the river.

Hester peers up, blurts her excuse. 'The nymphs invited me.'

The man hisses a sharp breath and Hester dips her chin in embarrassment. He thinks her mad, or fey. She pulls a windswept curl across her face to hide the spring of ashamed tears.

'I have to go home,' she tells the ground, scuffing her soaked boot in the grass. 'There are cows to be milked.'

'Of course.' His tone is as coolly polite as if he and Hester are acquaintances passing on a busy street. He offers a stiff bow, reaches up to lift his hat. His fingers are blistered. 'Good day.'

Hester gathers her shawl around her shaking body and runs across the stubbled field, fleeing the river and the man. When she reaches the gap in the leafless hedge, she glances around. He's staring into the streaming tide.

She wriggles through the gap, hurries home. Her whirling mind picks at the unfolding memory. He is back.

Chapter Two

A frozen February brings Hester three lambs to care for by the kitchen fire. Tonight, the wind blusters the window panes and shrieks its frustration around the chimney like the too-soon dead. The flame of the tallow candle on the table bends and straightens in a draught, wafting its fatty scent across the room. Hester wriggles the empty bottle from the lamb's grip and squats on the cold flags of the floor to return the creature to its basket. It bleats a protest before butting the soft pink stomach of one of its bed mates and closing its eyes.

Hester should return to bed to close her eyes also, hope for sleep to find her before it's time to rise for milking. She hefts her shawl closer about her shoulders. It isn't worth the climb to her attic room.

The range has cooled. Opening the heavy cast iron door, she takes up the poker and attacks the coals which snap their irritation before falling in on themselves. She stokes the hissing flames, adds more coal, fills the kettle and sets porridge to cook before lighting a lantern and picking her way across the pre-dawn darkness of the farmyard to the byre.

The cow's flank is warm, the teats warm too, taking the chill from her fingers as she pulls and squeezes. The cow stamps a hoof and lazily chews fresh hay in the manger while the rhythm of her task sends Hester into daydreams.

The man on the clifftop. That's where her thoughts steal to more and more these days, whether scattering grain for hens, raking pig sties or milking cows. Before she falls asleep each night, too. She is unsettled, anxious; has been all the long, dark winter. It isn't about his rescue of her from the river that blustering autumn day. If he hadn't appeared, she would be with the nymphs playing in the green depths of the sea now.

No, it isn't how he wrenched her from the nymphs' welcoming arms. It was his coolness which was a disappointment. Very different from the first time. He didn't remember her, and why should he? It's been years since she met him by the river one summer day.

'Anyway, why should I care?' Hester says to the cat.

Heavy with pending birth, the cat scratches at the straw and nestles into the newly made bed. *Men,* she hisses. *You'll learn their casual ways. Best not to care.*

Hester breathes in the earthy scents of cow and warm milk and closes her eyes. At the time, she had considered him old. Now, however, she thinks maybe he isn't so old. Two or three years senior to her oldest brother Will, who is twenty, she guesses.

Except for his eyes. They are ancient, guarded, their gold flecks dulled as if scarred by unendurable images. Their warmth has cooled.

She empties the pail of bubbly milk into an urn and moves her stool along to the next cow. Pushing her head into its velvet softness, she summons the heady scent of meadowsweet.

'I know this one,' she had told the man, glad to display her learning.

'Marry?' The man had raised a dark eyebrow.

Hester smiles at the memory of the man's quizzical eyebrow. She pats the rump of the last cow and lifts the pail. There is milk set aside for cream, and for her mother to churn into butter for sale in the village.

Putting aside thoughts of the man along with her stool, she lifts her skirt above her pattens to pick her way around the frozen puddles to the house. An owl flies low overhead, swooping to its roost in the barn. The wind has ceased its howling, possibly comforted by the greying of the darkness across the river. Hester stops at the kitchen door to watch dawn's hesitant approach above the river.

Sabrina, goddess. She talks to a goddess.

In the days that follow, Hester takes the cat's advice and breezily convinces herself she doesn't care. There are times, however, when she's sewing, or scrubbing her big brothers' shirts, or scraping carrots – and not noting what she does, she could do these things in her sleep – she will relive the conversation on the cliffs. Tossing swill into the pig trough, peeling parsnips or carrying baskets of kindling, Hester will recall the man's narrowed eyes as he scolds her: 'Talk to Sabrina from here.'

He was angry about the nymphs, too. Remembering his hissed intake of breath, she grows hot with embarrassment. There is no-one Hester can talk to about the white-maned horses which carry the bore, about the horses' lissom riders.

When she told Father, he chuckled. 'A wild, beautiful mind, daughter.'

Mother arched her brows and muttered how her daughter's head was in the clouds and had she locked the hens up tight?

Washing dishes, Hester's worries carp in her mind. Was the man angry because he assumed she is lying, or does he think the nymphs belong to him? And to Sabrina.

The question grows with the cat's belly, reaching its niggling fingers into corners of her mind where it has no business being. When the cold abates, she will go to the clifftop and find him, risk his irritation and ask about the nymphs. She throws coals on the kitchen fire and draws on their heat to fuel her courage.

*

The weather defers Hester's need to be brave. A deeper freeze falls across the countryside. Father brings ewes and lambs into the sheds, cows too. Hester's brothers give up their attempts to dig the soil in the vegetable garden, the duck pond ices over and the sheets on the washing line are stiff as planks.

'River's frozen,' Father says over supper. 'No boats up or down. Quiet as the grave.'

Hester wriggles in her chair, anxious for the nymphs. How can they ride the white horses if Sabrina is frozen? Are they buried under the ice? She twists a strand of hair with her finger. No. They would have swum with the tide down to the sea to frolic through winter, splashing in the waves, combing the sandy floor for pretty shells. They won't return until the river warms.

Sim, the middle brother, waves his knife. 'It'd better thaw soon and get to proper spring, else there'll be no crops sown in time.' He glowers at Hester as if she has commanded the icy soil. She squints at him, defiant.

Silence follows. The farm is doing no better than it ever has. It's why Mother is taking in more sewing and Hester is expected to help with that as well as do farm chores. Her appetite for her bread and cheese slides away.

Mother clicks her tongue and gathers dishes, knives and forks. 'Come, Hester, help me clear up.'

It's a signal for movement. Will pushes back from the

table, shrugs on his coat and empties the remains of the kindling onto the hearth stones. 'I'll fetch more coal and kindling for the morning,' he says. 'Then I'm off into the village. Coming Sim?'

'No.' Sim curls his lips in contempt of the humble village. 'I'm into Shiphaven for real company.' He tosses Hester a sneer. 'After I've checked Hester locked the chickens up good 'n tight. Foxes are famished in this cold.'

Hester scowls. All is well with the hens. If Sim wishes extra work it's no worry to her.

'Our lass will have done right by the hens, Sim.' Father smiles at Hester and moves to the cushioned chair by the fire where he tends his pipe and puffs smoke into the air for the time it takes Hester and her mother to wash the plates and cutlery.

Reuben, the youngest brother and at sixteen the closest in age to Hester, takes up the butter churn lying by the door waiting for its handle to be mended. Mother places the kettle on the range, rakes the coals, and picks up her sewing. Hester perches on a stool beside the cat's basket.

'Her kittens will come soon,' she says. 'We have to make sure she stays warm.'

Mother gives a soft snort. 'Cats fend well enough for themselves, you needn't worry about her. Instead'–she hands Hester a worn brocade waistcoat with newly mended buttonholes and a paper packet of mother-of-pearl buttons–'you can sew these on, though why the young gentleman considers this garment worth pearl buttons I have no idea.'

The waistcoat is a sleeping pale yellow cat lying in Hester's lap. 'Who brought this?'

'Who? A gentleman, as I've just said.'

'What kind of gentleman?'

'What kind? Why, one with an ancient waistcoat and a fancy taste in buttons. What does it matter?'

'I–' The words stop themselves. 'Never mind.' Hester strokes the brocade as if it truly is a cat. She will sew the pearl buttons so tightly they will never come loose, whatever lengths of good thread she has to use.

Father taps his pipe on the grate. 'This freeze,' he says, 'reminds me of Grandmother's tales when I were a little one – how she kept ice from the pond and made the pump flow with her clever ways.'

'Silly nonsense.' Mother squints at the thread and needle she holds to the candlelight. 'If that woman had been alive two hundred years ago, she would've been burned for a witch.'

Hester giggles, shares a sly grin with Father. Mother makes this pronouncement each time Grandmother is mentioned.

'Lydia!' Father blows out a fragrant cloud of white smoke which momentarily disguises the greasy smell of the candles. 'Grandmother were no witch. She were a wise woman, good with animals and learned in the ways of the countryside.'

Reuben nods, concentrating on prodding the churn's handle with a tiny screwdriver.

Father settles in the chair. 'The animals were quiet and docile as lambs under her hand.'

Hester laughs. 'Lambs aren't always docile.'

'No more they are,' Father says. 'Except they were under Grandmother's care. The cows, the horses, the pigs – they all loved her.'

'Because she fed them and cleaned out their muck.' Mother sniffs. She pushes her needle and thread under Hester's nose. 'Thread this for me, please. The light in here is terrible.' She humphs. 'We need proper lamps, not these smelly candles.'

The daughter of a prosperous shopkeeper in the town, Mother grew up with lamps and a servant. Pretty and outgoing, wooed by the sons of rich merchants with tall houses and taller ships, she married the farmer's son, Stanley Williams, for love.

'I could have been a wealthy woman with a carriage,' Mother will say, with a small, resigned smile.

Father never has anything to say on the topic of his wife's provenance. His soft, proud eyes tell their story, however.

'No, it were more than cleaning out muck.' Father returns the conversation to Grandmother. 'The labourers and the cottagers would come for potions and herbs and go home happy.'

'Superstitious and uneducated.' Mother bends closer to her sewing.

'You'd never say so if you saw the time she cured the little girl of a deathly fever which had the child shaking hard as wheat in a wind, and the same colour too.'

Hester has heard the story many times.

'I would love to do the same as Grandma,' she says. 'To heal children with my cures.' Where did the thought come from? Expressed so vividly too, like a long-harboured wish abruptly set free. She strokes the waistcoat and her breath catches.

Of course. When she first met the man he told her about meadow flowers and how they heal fevers and colds. Asking him to teach her about flowers will surely make his hard eyes kinder. Better than asking about river nymphs. He can't tell her flowers come from her wild imagination.

Father nods, opens his mouth to speak, and is cut short by Mother.

'Your future is as a good wife and mother,' she says. 'What you need to learn are the skills and manners you need to marry well.' She glances up to ensure she has Hester's attention. 'There's enough to do here, Daughter, without you wasting time brewing futile potions.'

Hester hauls her thoughts back to the kitchen and

nods, obedient to the oft-stated idea she will be wooed by those merchant sons her mother spurned. Yet, the notion of following in Grandmother's steps, lingers, warming her stomach as the fire warms her feet. Picking up a pearl button, she positions it on the yellow brocade. There is a sadness to touching the stiff material. The man will wear it and be none the wiser Hester sewed the buttons. If he knew, he would understand she isn't fey, or mad. She is ordinary and does ordinary things like sewing buttons.

*

Aaron clasps the blanket around his shoulders with one hand while he shuffles forward from his seat on the low stool, poker in hand, to stir the coals into a hissing grumble. Flames stutter into life, wavering in the chilling draught which seeps through the gaps in the window frames and under the warped door. The candle flickers, and he sets his dog-eared Culpepper on the stones of the floor, eyes itching from trying to read its closely printed pages in the poor light. He's careful with it, as the frayed binding barely keeps the book in one piece. He will find a bookbinder, have it repaired once this freeze is passed.

All winter he has sought refuge in his books, studying, scribbling in margins, occasionally transferring the most illuminating scribbles to his newly purchased tooled leather, blank journal which will become his own published work on the healing properties of herbs and flowers.

However, despite the study, despite bouts of fierce concentration, winter brought no relief, failed to purge the demons. He spends too much time with his own head for company, too much time by the fire imagining the coals' modest flickers soaring to lick the beams in the roof and scorch the yellowed walls in tame imitation of the way the flames scorched the cliff. Too much time listening to the wind howling against the window in deadly mimicry of the shrieks of that awful night.

Fire leaping. Eyes lit with red. Dark curls, wild, burnished red and gold. A swarm of sharp buzzing like warring wasps… stinging … heat and wetness … the river rising, plunging …

The image of the girl on the cliff fills his mind. He shivers, pulls the blanket tighter.

The nymphs invited her. His stomach roils.

His thoughts scrabble deep into memory, a rabbit chased by a fox to its hole. A hot, sunny day and a child's sticky hand tucked loosely in his while he rambled on about yarrow and meadowsweet. Seeing the child talking to Sabrina, telling her she spoke to a goddess. Afterwards watching her skip through ripening barley, black curls flying, arms flailing as if she would take flight with the birds.

Does she remember?

The nymphs invited her. Of course she remembers.

He shakes his head, violently, his hair brushing the idea aside like a broom sweeping splinters of broken glass. He squeezes his eyes shut and summons a different, older, sunlit scene.

Himself and Marianne gathering flowers with bursting seed heads, following the instructions of Mother Lovell who totters bent-backed behind them, basket on her arm. He tries to let the memory soothe him.

All that blossoms is renewed agony.

Mother Lovell had been wrong. Aaron conjures the coldness of the old woman's bony claws clamping his twelve-year-old chin, her wrinkle-lidded eyes sparkling with a keenness which belied her apparent age. They had held Aaron's flickering gaze.

'You'll do,' she had said in a voice as fresh as spring.

And he had failed.

Chapter Three

he long dark days shrink into themselves, too weary to resist the light. A chill April brings showers, May warms the moistened ground. From his chair by the window, Aaron glances along a line of bouncing dust motes to peer through newly minted honeysuckle flowers threatening to obscure the grubby window. High clouds as fluffily white as lambs' tails frolic in a soft blue sky. He huffs out a breath, resenting the blueness of the sky, resenting the frolicking clouds. Winter better suited the darkness of his mood when he could put aside his books and drowse by a low fire, half aware of the whispering spirits which have taken to cluttering the tiny cottage. Their sighs are for each other, not for Aaron. Yet they are company of a sort, reminding him there is life beyond the stone walls of his sanctuary.

Life, yes …

He rouses sufficiently to inspect the row of phials and jars straggling over a shelf which stretches across one wall. With the exception of the recently distilled oil of primrose and a bowl of drying lavender from the bush by the cottage door, the glass phials are empty. He takes up a stone pot labelled Feverfew, lifts the lid and sniffs. The smell of stale dust confirms his expectation. He returns the pot to its place.

He should shake this lethargy, although why and for whom?

He peers out at the blue sky, imagining the sun on his face. Yes, he will wander across the fields and along the hedges, gather new hawthorn, yarrow, fat hen for himself and his potions. Experiment, write down the outcomes to fill the many blank pages of his journal, the leather covers of which remain stiffly new. Spring brings hope for redemption, if redemption exists.

He puffs out another heavy breath and fetches his waistcoat from where it lies on the chair. As he does each time he wears it, he runs his fingers lightly over the pearl buttons. The girl sewed them. Aaron senses it in the bare hint of warmth which brightens the buttons' soft sheen. He collects his coat from its peg, settles his beaver hat on his head, picks a hessian sack from the pile by the door and steps out of the cottage.

· ✳

Hester has taken Father his dinner in a far-off field and should be hurrying home to her own meal. She hasn't eaten since dawn and on the way to finding Father her gut had rumbled at the smell of the warm bread in her basket. She flushes with guilt, remembering how her fingers found their own way under the cloth to tear at the grainy loaf, popping the stolen crumbs into her mouth. She swallowed without chewing, as if her lack of savouring the morsel negated the sin of the theft. Father will have seen the torn bread and will tease Hester this evening.

'A little mouse nibbled my dinner before I could take

one bite,' he will say, all serious, and Mother will turn to Hester with a frown while Father laughs and pats Hester's shoulder.

The stolen crumbs have tempered her hunger, for instead of going back to the farmhouse she is making her way to the river, stealing time to assuage her need for Sabrina's whispers. It's not her first visit this spring. When the ice of March had melted, she ran to the river, apprehension somersaulting to delight at the sight of nymphs diving around fishing vessels as if the freeze had never been.

There had been no chance to listen for Sabrina's words, however. Sim appeared on the path.

'What you doing here, staring at the river?'

His mocking words drowned the goddess's whispers.

Hester frowned. 'Can't I have any time to myself?'

'Not when there's jobs to be done.' He caught her by the arm and tugged her about to face the farmhouse. 'Life tain't all about you, Sister. Get on home and help our mam instead of dawdling by the water.'

Today, Hester has the excuse of Father's dinner to take her from the house and its endless tasks. She hurries across the ridges and dips of a ploughed field and climbs the steps of a stone stile into a field where tall grasses warm themselves under the May sun.

She isn't the sole visitor to the field. She shades her eyes, furrows her brow. Not one of her brothers. Tall hat, long black coat, a glimpse of yellow waistcoat. He's walking along the hedge towards her, head bent, hands clasped behind him, trailing a hessian sack. A knot catches in Hester's throat, she hesitates at the top of the stile. The man looks up, and stops.

*

The sense of eyes on him lifts Aaron's gaze.

A girl pauses on the stile ahead.

The girl.

He considers turning aside except … his legs take him striding forward, lifting his hat in greeting.

'Hello, Mistress.' He touches her cloth-lined basket. 'Are you taking advantage of the sunshine to search out nature's own food and medicines, too?'

'Medicines?'

Aaron swings an arm to take in the length of the hedge and its white and yellow offerings. 'The hedge plants.'

'Oh, yes, of course.' She remains on the top step, eye to eye with him. A faint grief shadows her face. 'No. Mother says there's too much work on the farm to be brewing witches' potions.'

There's a touch of bitterness in the bald statement.

'Witches' potions?'

The girl blushes. 'Sorry,' she says. 'I didn't mean …'

Aaron's lips twitch. The girl's blushes grow pinker and a faint sheen dampens her brow.

'I want to learn,' she says slowly, chewing her lip. Then, in a rush: 'My great grandmother cured deathly fevers and the villagers went to her for cures. Father says she was a wise woman.'

Aaron raises an eyebrow.

'I want to be a wise woman too,' the girl says, bolder now, 'if I knew how.' The basket swings to and fro, her gaze intent on the bottom step of the stile. 'I thought, maybe …' She looks up, the request clear.

'Against your mother's wishes?' Aaron shifts the sack from one hand to the other. 'What are you asking of me? To encourage young girls to flout their parents?' His lips lift, to counter the sour plunge of his stomach.

'Father would approve, I'm sure.' Her eyes glint with fondness. 'He loved his grandmother, he loves old-fashioned ways. Yes, he'd approve.'

'Hmm.' Aaron struggles to keep his voice light. 'Your

mother would tan my hide if she found out.'

'She needn't find out.' A coy lift of her brows.

Aaron considers this girl standing on the stone with her swinging basket and flirtatious gaze. The autumn scene of her reaching for the river nymphs tumbles through his head. And earlier, of her listening to Sabrina's enticing songs. He leans towards her. There is no conscious thought as his hand lifts itself, palm up in offering.

She regards his hand, hesitates, decides it's trustworthy and rests her warm palm on his before stepping down, as light footed as air, from the stile.

'Will you teach me?'

Her young voice quivers. Her loose curls blow across her cheeks. She peers up at him. Is the tug of war battling deep inside him, reflected in his eyes?

Dark curls hiding cheeks flushed from the fire, mutters of incantation, white flames curling around the bubbling pot ...

Aaron snatches his hand from her grasp.

'... *a potion to give us power, Aaron ...*'

'No.' His voice is thick, rough. Cruel.

She jerks as if he's bitten her, crushing her hand to her chest. Tears smudge the cornflower blue of her eyes. He takes an awkward step back when she pushes past him and runs, her skirts slapping the tall grasses from her path.

Aaron stands with arms hanging straight, the sack limp, forgotten. A lump rises in his throat. He's frightened her. It's for the best, his brain decides. A deeper, visceral feeling disagrees.

The nymphs invited her.

*

Hester's heart is a bird trapped behind glass, beating at her ribs. Shame prickles her skin as if she's been caught in a wicked sin, yet what has she done? So much for her fanciful idea of the man warming to her if she asked about flowers.

She might have been a wolf springing to tear out his throat the way he'd recoiled from her.

The slim gap in the hedge forces her to a panting halt. The man will be watching her and she wants to wave, to call she's sorry, she'll never ask again.

Taking a long, shuddering breath she keeps her back to the field, squeezes through and hesitates. Her desire for Sabrina weighs on her as heavily as an unconfessed sin. She recalls the man's hissed breath when he pulled her from the nymphs' arms last autumn. Sabrina and the river nymphs are why the man hates her, and she cannot go there, not today. Lifting her skirts, she runs, breathless, to the mundane normality of the farmyard.

*

Aaron brushes his fingers along the pearl buttons. He will not give way, not this time.

He gave way to Marianne. The two of them had stolen all the hours they could from their schooling and homes to spend them in Mother Lovell's cluttered, herb and smoke-scented cottage under the contemptuous gaze of a ginger cat squatting on a settle by the inglenook. Marianne never tired of bending over the scorched table littered with chipped pots, part-burned candles and lidless jars holding greasy, lurid ointments.

'I want Mother Lovell to make a spell to fly.' Giggling, she crooked her arms and flapped them before flipping back her braid and pointing a grubby, nail-bitten finger at Aaron.

'What spell do you want?'

As if she was asking him what sweet he wanted: a sugar plum, a barley twist?

Aaron too, came to be entranced by Mother Lovell's age-spotted hands pounding the petals, the seeds and roots, mixing the juices, breathing words to bring power to the potions. He relives the smell of dried herbs and cat piss, inwardly chants the lessons: feverfew for strength, yarrow for fever and blue periwinkle to protect them – from what? Mother Lovell was never explicit.

'You will learn,' she told them.

A promise or a prophecy?

The girl disappears through the hedge. Aaron waits a minute, two, his fingers absently playing with a button. He climbs the stone stile into the field, his restless body taking him up the hill into the forest. Purple dog violets, patches of pale mauve bluebells and wood anemones flourish here between the leafless beech trees. He adds white wood sorrel to the contents of his bag. Later, he walks to the stream which feeds into the river close by his cottage to harvest handfuls of wild garlic leaves to eat with his plain supper. His collecting is desultory and in the early evening he sits by the fire and rests his head in his hands.

'Why wasn't it enough?' he cries to the unmoving air.

He and Marianne had learned, as Mother Lovell promised. Aaron was content. Escaped from the dreariness of their expected lives, travelling from village to village, bringing healing. And magic to join lovers, husbands to heel, and wives to successful birthing. Animals too: sick pigs to health, lame horses to walk and cows to give creamier milk. His contentment, however, wasn't shared.

As the fire sinks into carmine coals, the shushing of the spirits lull him into a restless sleep.

Chapter Four

er dreams are of fire and water. The river flows, shipless, bargeless, as unburdened as the gulls screeching above its fast waters. Red and yellow flames rise from the mudflats to scorch the rocky cliffs and throw fiery reflections across the racing river. She flies with the gulls, high, chasing the flames, the smell of smoke in her lungs, the heat of fire burnishing her bare legs …

Hester wakes in a tangle of damp sheets and rucked nightgown. Tugging at the bedclothes, she pulls herself up and swings out her legs, perching on the edge of the straw mattress. Her toes curl into the rag rug which partially disguises the boards. Usually she would be up immediately, splashing her face with water from the washbowl and reaching under the bed to draw out the chamber pot. This morning she continues to sit, hands tucked under her bottom, staring at the June sky outside her high window.

No red and yellow flames. A pearl dawn glows, serenaded by birds and the crowing of the rooster. She wraps her arms about herself and wills away the turmoil in her gut.

The vivid dream troubles her through her morning tasks. It's a dream she has dreamed before, slinking into nothingness on wakening. A memory catches as she pushes her head against a cow, hands pulling gently at the teats, hearing the swish of milk squirting into the pail. A memory of a story from across the river which Will and Sim brought home last autumn, of devils screeching and flames scorching the cliffs. Flames which leaped from the river itself – Sabrina alight.

Father, sitting in the cushioned chair by the fire, had been dismissive. 'It's just gone All Hallows Eve. Our friends on the other side of the river be in league with the fishermen, pulling gullible legs up and down the river, you daft boys.'

The mysterious tale had not been mentioned again, not in this house.

'What does it all mean?' she asks the cat, who slides between the legs of the milking stool in expectation of a missed drop or two.

You will know one day. In the meantime, I'm sure you can spare a saucer of milk from all this richness.

*

'Hester, I need you to run an errand in the village.' Mother holds out a brown paper package and a folded paper. 'Take this to Mrs Ellis – it's the dress for her youngest – with this bill, to be paid before you leave. Make sure you receive the coins. I've dealt with Mrs Ellis before.'

The afternoon is warm. Hester had hoped her short post-dinner break might involve doing absolutely nothing harder than lying in the grass under the apple trees with a book. The fairytales of the Brothers Grimm is her favourite, its pages creased and stained since Hester was able to read. Mother brought the old book with her, along with half a dozen others and a framed picture of Queen Victoria, when she married. The farmhouse had lacked an image of the queen, or any books, until then, apart from *The Old Farmer's Almanac*. More recently, a shiny pamphlet on cattle husbandry, left by their landlord's estate manager, has been added.

Father's reaction to the pamphlet had been to tut, and state no good would come of these fandangled notions of hurrying nature up or forcing her into giving more than she could.

'Can't people see how it will weaken her over time? The old ways are good enough for me,' he says. He's never opened the pamphlet as far as Hester is aware.

She walks slowly, glad of her bonnet under the afternoon sun. In the peaceful silence, her thoughts reach out to the man. Why did he shy from her that day in the field? The memory makes her pulse throb. She hasn't been to the river since, although she has longed to. The man might be there and she worries he will flee from her as if she is the devil come to chase him to Hell. In any case, she convinces herself, much as she craves it, she shouldn't waste her time talking with Sabrina, watching the nymphs taunt the fishermen by urging the salmon from the nets. Her farm duties fill the long days of summer and will keep her loneliness at bay.

She wanders along the short high street to the Ellis' bakery, the village quiet under the burning sun. The labourers are in the fields, the fishermen on the river and the children too hot to play in the dust. Two women stand on the step of a rose-draped cottage talking, heads close together. Hester calls a 'Good afternoon' and they nod brief acknowledgements before taking up their earnest chat. Another woman walks towards Hester, her gait far too fast for the heat, her hands clasped under her bosom. She is crying.

'Mrs Bilson, whatever's the matter?'

Mrs Bilson lifts her hand to her nose to hide her sniffling sobs.

'Hester! Why, dear, it's Annie, Mrs Ellis' youngest. So sick, they say'–Mrs Bilson draws in a sob–'the child will die.'

Annie, whose new dress lies in Hester's arms. Hester clenches the parcel tighter.

'Has a doctor been?'

'Yes. Expensive medicine and no change. White as newly washed sheets, coughing, fever; one minute burning, another shaking with such chills no number of eiderdowns can warm her.'

Fever. The child with the deathly fever which had her shaking like wheat in a wind.

'Your great-grandma would've been able to help.' Mrs Bilson's statement matches Hester's thoughts. 'A good, kindly soul. Had a cure for whatever ailed us.' Mrs Bilson wriggles her shoulders. 'Shame she had no one to pass her skills on to.' Her glare suggests Hester is the one at fault.

Hester diverts the accusation. 'You remember her?'

'Yes, despite I was a mite, younger than poor Annie, I remember her.'

The brown package is heavy in Hester's arms. 'This is for Annie,' she says. 'Her new dress made by Mother.'

'For their going to Gloucester for Mrs Ellis' sister's wedding.' Mrs Bilson shudders a sob. 'Now the angel will never wear it.'

What should Hester do? Take the dress home? No, going home assumes Annie will die.

'I have to go on,' she says, and walks past Mrs Bilson to the bakery. The door is closed, a sign warning customers of the lack of their daily bread due to an illness in the house. Hester makes her way down the narrow side lane and in through the gate in the fence. Hens peck in the dirt. The baker's cart is in the yard, the stable empty.

Hester knocks at the open kitchen door and waits. Mrs Ellis' oldest boy, Nathaniel, comes to her, eyes red-rimmed.

'No bread. Go away.'

'I'm not here for bread.' Hester holds out the package. 'I'm here to give this to your mother, and … to ask if I can do anything … anything … for Annie.'

Nathaniel doesn't take the parcel. 'Nothing to be done for Annie,' he hisses. 'Go home.'

Hester is left on the step, with the package.

The urge to help, any way she can, compels her. She steps into the dark, cool kitchen and crosses quietly to the opposite door. The sick girl is laid on a bed to one side of the small parlour, hidden beneath a pile of blankets. A fire burns, stifling the air with heat and coal smell.

Mrs Ellis, thin and round-shouldered, crouches over the blankets. At the sight of Hester in her doorway, she scowls.

'What do you want?'

'I … Mother sent me with this.' Hester offers the package.

'The frock?' Mrs Ellis jerks as if the brown paper is alive and snarling.

A cough comes from beneath the blankets on the bed, a dry rasping sound which tightens Hester's chest. Her need to do something is a physical pain clawing at her throat.

'What can I do? To help?'

'You?' Mrs Ellis peers at Hester. 'Can you stoke the range and prepare a honied tea?' She glances down at her daughter. 'It might ease her.'

Hester sets the package on the table and prepares the honied tea. While Mrs Ellis feeds the tea to Annie spoon by dripping spoon, Hester says to Nat, 'Have you and your mam eaten dinner?'

When Nat mutters no, Hester finds cheese and bread, a jar of onions and a cold mutton joint in the larder. She prepares the food, bids Nat to sit and eat and takes a plate and hot tea to Mrs Ellis, who waves off the meal but allows Hester to set the drink on a low table by the bed.

In the kitchen, Hester asks Nat, 'Where's your dad?'

'Gone to Gloucester to find another doctor. One what can do summat.'

A half day round journey, if he pushes his horse and doesn't rest. And finds a doctor able to come quickly. A doctor who can do something.

Of course! Hester rebukes herself for not thinking of it earlier. The man by the river. He might be able to do something.

If she could find him. She should have asked where he lives and if he didn't want to tell, she should have followed him. Maybe her mother could tell her, given he was a customer. Should Hester go home, find her mother and ask? Should she go to the cliffs above Sabrina and wait for the man to appear?

'Hester!' Mrs Ellis' call stirs Hester into motion.

'Yes?'

'Cold towels, Hester, to cool her.'

Hester draws water from the well and wets towels which Mrs Ellis uses to bathe Annie until the child shivers with chills and Mrs Ellis lays the blankets over her. Hester makes more honied tea which remains un-drunk, tells Nat to tend to the hens, sweeps the kitchen floor and sets a pot on the range with vegetables and what remains of the lamb.

'Remember to stir this from time to time,' she says to the boy.

He scowls as if he wants to protest, flicks his eyes to the blankets and holds his tongue.

When the shadows outside lengthen to a size where true night will have to erase them, Hester leaves. In the high street, she passes Mr Ellis leading the big cart horse, which has gone lame. There is no doctor with him.

Next morning, Father comes home from delivering eggs, milk and cream to the village. He finds Hester tossing fresh hay into the pig sty and gives her a look of such kind pity, her breath dries up as Annie's had.

'Poor Annie.' She exhales a shuddering sigh. 'And I could do nothing except make honied tea.'

'Mrs Ellis says you were kind and helpful. Gave me the frock your mother sewed, saying we should sell it.' He bobs his head at Hester. 'As payment for your kindness.'

Hester bridles. 'I don't need payment. Any decent person would've done the same.'

'I don't think she meant it that way.' Father places his sun-spotted hands on Hester's shoulders. 'It was meant as a thank you, I'm sure.'

Hester's eyes fill with tears. 'Mrs Bilson said Annie needed our grandmother, that she would have known what to do.'

Father holds out his arms for her to walk into them and be comforted.

''tis true. Grandmother would have done her utmost best to help the poor child,' he says above Hester's hay-dusty hair. 'A shame, so few of her kind left, hounded out by Church and science.' He gently puts Hester away from him and rubs his chin. 'Children die, and they call it progress.'

All day Hester stumbles about her chores, dry-eyed. A cow kicks out at her when she's clumsy, and the rooster pecks at her legs as if shooing her grieving presence from his sight. The cat follows her from task to task, watchful.

When she finally sleeps she dreams of fire and water, and of a girl the colour of wheat coughing out her frail breaths on a bed of fever-hot blankets. The bed floats on grey waters while flames flare all around. A frantic Hester hovers in the shimmering air, beating back golden flames which keep her from reaching the girl's side.

Chapter Five

er troubled dreams have pulled her here, to the place on the clifftop where the man hauled her from the nymphs' arms. Below her, stunted trees jut from rocks to spread their wind-twisted branches above the summer-glazed river. Sabrina's whispers rise and Hester strains to hear above the shouts of sailors, barge owners and fishermen all battling for space on the river's wide reaches.

Be wise, be strong, do what you need to do.

She breathes in the goddess's murmuring approval, uses it to shore up her precarious courage.

The tide is turning, and those going down pull into the bank to wait out the tug of the upstream flow. It's a high bore this morning. Although Hester craves glimpses of river nymphs playing in the spindrift, she closes her ears to their call. Today, she is here to confront the man.

Her need is a stony weight in her gut. She paces, and paces some more. He doesn't come, the farm's endless tasks prod her conscience, and she's uncertain she will find her nerve a second time. One more turn, and then …

He is there, his eyes wary.

'What does Sabrina say, Mistress?' He bows and doffs his beaver hat.

Hester's courage wanes, would flee from her. With effort, she hauls it back and wastes no time in the trivia of greetings.

'Sabrina wants me to learn the lore of herbs and wildflowers, of mushrooms and toadstools, of leaves and roots.' Arms folded, she forces herself to meet his eyes. Heat rises up her neck.

'Is that so?' He searches her face. She is afraid to blink. 'Why does Sabrina want this?'

Hester uncrosses her arms, crosses them again. 'She doesn't want children to die because I can't help them.'

'Ah.' He finds the streaming water of interest, following the high wave and its white riders. 'The girl in the village.'

'You knew? And you didn't go to her?'

He keeps his gaze on the water. 'I heard this morning.'

He doesn't say 'too late' or of course he would have gone if he'd heard earlier. Hester pushes down her disappointment, choosing to believe that if he had, he would have saved Annie.

Annie is beyond saving. This is about tomorrow's Annies.

'Will you teach me?' She can't help the desperate plea in her voice.

He raises an eyebrow, watching her face. 'Your mother?'

Brushing away a curl sticking to her cheek, Hester phrases her answer carefully. 'Father is happy for me to learn.' With his love of old ways, he would, she is sure, if she asked him.

'Hmm.' The man looks to the fields. 'If the doctor couldn't save the girl, neither you nor I could have. It was Annie's time.'

Hester ignores the kindness in his tone.

'Her time? She was five years old! The poor girl had no time, no time at all.' Tears wet her lashes. Her hands clench, rise up, wanting to beat the man's yellow brocade chest.

He catches her fists in his warm, smooth hands. 'No. I will not teach you. The path you want to tread is treacherous.' He pauses, closes his eyes. When he opens them, their glint of gold is hard and bright. 'Perils, disaster, crowd that path for such as you ...' He shakes her fists. 'Do you remember how you told me once, when first we met, how you knew meadowsweet because your mother says you will carry the flower on your wedding day?'

'Yes.' Hester is conscious of his hands around hers and of his eyes, their tinge of sadness with its intimations of deep regret. 'That is what you will do. You'll carry meadowsweet when you wed a lusty farmer, and you'll bear him dark-curled, blue-eyed girls and sturdy boys.'

He drops her hands as if they are fire-heated branding irons and strides away, matching his pace to the incoming tide below the cliffs.

Hester is left with tingling palms, stifling frustrated sobs.

*

Aaron doesn't slow his long legs until he has passed through the fields where the sheep graze unconcerned, over a stile and along a grassy track which passes his cottage to return him to the river. The cliffs are taller, steeper here and topped with a narrow strip of wind-dwarfed oak and ash. He breathes heavily, sticky with the sweat of exercise and the sultry air. Shades beneath the deep green canopy embrace him, leading him along the path to the cliff edge. They are gentle, as if he's a coltish horse which might startle, sighing their relief when at last they leave him in a dapple of sunshine.

The taller cliffs and heavy woodland mute the noises

of the river traffic. The river itself is a beaten silver sheet, unruffled.

He has never returned to this place, until today.

Fire leaping. Eyes lit with red. Dark curls, wild, burnished with heat. A swarm of sharp buzzings like angry wasps ... stinging... heat and wetness ...

Sinking to his knees, he casts around, searching out charred logs, blackened stones. The woodland has hidden it all, forgiving and forgetting. Lacy ferns, delicate daisies and pink mallow flourish in this place of death.

She will not be denied.

Marianne's voice is as clear to Aaron as if she is kneeling by his side.

He sits on his heels. 'I will not permit it,' he says.

What you allow or not allow is nothing to her.

'As it was nothing to you.'

She has the soul of a goddess. Sabrina will not be cheated, not a second time.

Nausea curdles Aaron's stomach. 'Haven't I given enough?' he cries.

A gull rises above the river to screech its affirmation.

Aaron closes his eyes, summoning up her image. Marianne laughs, as she always did. Except at the end.

*

Hester jabs the trowel into the earth and levers up the carrot, tosses it onto her flat basket beside the pods of peas, and moves to the next feathery green top, jabbing harder this time. Her frustration will not be calmed.

She carries the vegetables into the scullery and takes a bucket to the pump in the farmyard. When she goes into the kitchen, Mother has put aside her sewing and is chopping lamb, throwing the chunks into an iron pot.

'Bring me onions please,' she says, 'and then deal with the potatoes and carrots.'

Hester obeys and stands beside her mother at the long table, both with their own thoughts, scraping and chopping.

'Mother.'

'Mmm?'

'The customer who brought the yellow waistcoat, in the winter ...'

'Yellow waistcoat?'

'The pearl buttons, the ones you had me sew on.'

'Ah, yes! What about him?'

'Is he from here?'

Mother shrugs. 'I've no idea. I haven't seen him since.'

'Where was he living?'

Mother stops scraping and frowns at Hester. 'Why? What's this curiosity about a young man?'

'Hester's curious about a young man?' Sim is beside them. His sly grin burns Hester's cheeks.

'No I'm not,' she mutters to the potatoes.

'Our Hester, in love already.' Sim's grin widens. He pokes Hester's midriff with a dirty finger. 'Too soon for you, Miss.' He smirks. 'Don't want spoiled goods for our father to have to sell off when the time comes.'

The heat in Hester's cheeks flames, fanned by Sim's vulgarity and by her mother's angry, 'Stop it, Simeon. Speak nicely or not at all.'

'Come on, Sim, we're needed outside.'

Hester hadn't seen Reuben walk in. She's grateful, however, for the way he tugs at Sim's shirtsleeve until the older brother shrugs and slouches his way outside. Not without a final jeer over his shoulder: 'Best keep your daughter on a tight leash, Ma, else bear the consequences.'

Mother tuts. 'Coarse and vulgar. Simeon spends too much time in the ale house and not enough in church.'

Hester scrapes carrots and doesn't dare remind Mother about the man.

*

It's midsummer eve, cloudless, and the light is only now fading. Hester is at the kitchen table sewing a piped edging onto a small, Annie-sized frock. A lump forms in her throat. It must never happen again. She must learn. Her yearning to understand, to be confident in the ways of flowers and herbs, to raise future Annies from near death, battles to triumph over her fear of the man's anger.

Reuben, sat on a stool by the empty fireplace with the family Bible on his knees, stretches his arms and yawns. 'I'm to bed,' he says. 'Before I do, I'll check the hens.'

'I did it earlier, after supper.' Hester doesn't glance up from her sewing.

'I'd rather check.' Reuben taps Hester on the shoulder. 'Come with me. Then you can berate me for not trusting you.'

Glad of the excuse to put the small frock out of sight, Hester stands, brushes down her skirt and skips after her brother.

The hens are on their roosts and none-too-pleased about the interruption to their sleep. Reuben pulls the gate to, tests it is latched, and bolts it. Bending to the bottom of the fence to check for gaps, he says, 'I overheard you the other day asking Ma about the man with the yellow waistcoat.'

Hester's face grows hot. 'Yes, so?'

Reuben straightens. 'Why were you asking?'

Why was she asking? How can she answer without revealing the truth? Reuben is kind, her favourite brother. However, given he's destined for the Church, he won't countenance the idea of his sister becoming one wise in the ways of herbal lore. Despite their mutual admired great-grandmother, in these days of progress such women are frowned upon by the Church and by those who consider themselves civilised.

'Annie.' This might lead somewhere.

'The little girl who died?'

'Yes. I heard in the village,' she says, bending down and scratching her skirt to cover her lie, 'how he supposedly knows healing, same as our grandmother. I thought ... I thought ...' She examines her boots.

'He might have saved Annie?' Reuben's voice is quiet, conspiratorial.

'Yes.'

'Yet he didn't, so why are you interested in where he lives?'

'Because ...' Hester offers this warily. 'If another child, or anybody, falls ill, we should be able to find him.' Here is her way forward. She carries on, waving her hands in emphasis. 'Imagine if it was Mother sick, or you, or me? Wouldn't you want to fetch him, see if he can help?'

Reuben snorts. 'We can pay a doctor, a real doctor.'

'We can.' Hester calms her pleading, steers to another approach. 'There are many who can't.' A pause. 'Surely they'd be grateful for his help?'

Reuben strokes his chin. 'I see what you mean. *In extremis* ...'

'Yes, yes.' Hester nods so hard a number of curls escape the pins which have weakened their hold over the course of a busy day. 'Do you know something?'

'Not much.' Rueben's gaze is steady on her face. The shadow of the hen house will disguise her blushes. 'On occasion,' he says, 'he can be found at The Rope & Anchor and it's said he has use of Farmer Bree's old cottage, the near-ruined one not far from the higher cliffs, towards Gloucester.'

Hester hasn't seen this ruined cottage, but from the direction the man walked, she can picture where it might be. The clifftop path will take her there.

The knowledge kindles her frustrated desires, which boil over, unwilling to wait another moment. Yet caution is needed.

'Oh,' she says. 'Yes.' She runs a finger along the henhouse fence, pretending nonchalance. 'Thank you, in case there is ever need of him.' Her hand covers a yawn. 'I'm off to bed.'

She walks with Reuben into the house. Mother and Father have already made their way upstairs. Reuben says goodnight, takes the stairs two at a time. Hester holds her breath, counts to ten, slips outside and flees across the yard's lengthening shadows before her resolution falters.

*

The spirits this midsummer eve are as restless as at All Hallows Eve, as are Aaron's thoughts. He's given up any notion of reading, and his pens gather dust in a dry inkpot, as does the cover of his journal. There are hours of light left, and a need to fill them. He could go to the river to seek distraction in the twilit life on its waters, or he could join the fishermen and labourers at The Rope & Anchor where distraction will be easier. Easier still at the King's Shilling, further down the river and nestled on the overgrown bank of a steep-sided, narrow tributary. Any of these activities will mean moving, however, and while his mind buzzes, his limbs are too heavy to lift into motion.

He doesn't stir from his stool at the tentative knock, only stares at the door.

The latch lifts, as if by a spirit's hand, which may well be the case. The door opens with the rusting squeal Aaron has done nothing to cure, given he's not intending to stay much longer in Farmer Bree's decaying cottage.

'Hello?' A black-haired, unbonneted head squeezes into the gap, a bodiless silhouette against the deepening blue of the sky.

The tumble in Aaron's mind collapses into a bewildered tangle. What madness is this, so late at night? Or has her spirit come to haunt him for refusing her while her body is tucked up in bed where it should be?

The door opens wider and more of her steps into the room. No spirit this. Her cheeks are flushed and her chest rises, falls, as if she has been running.

She will not be denied. Marianne's breath is warm in his ear, teasing.

Aaron stands, makes no move towards the girl. He should return her immediately to her home.

The goddess has decreed it.

The goddess.

What will happen, will happen.

No. He won't risk her.

The flame of the lone candle on the table dies, and relights in a sputtering temper. The girl's eyes briefly widen.

Would you have the nymphs teach her? Marianne's murmurs shed their teasing tone.

The nymphs invited her.

See her there, embracing the nymphs. The cold waves ...

Once already she has given way to their siren calls. If once, then ... He is defeated. For now.

'You'd best come all the way in,' he says, lightening the mood, 'before the neighbours gossip.'

The girl doesn't appear to catch the joke, although she scuttles in, shoulders the door closed and stands with cheeks the colour of the blowsy poppies in Mother Lovell's garden.

They look at each other for a long time. Aaron remains by the stool, aware of his rolled up shirtsleeves, his waistcoat abandoned to the warm summer night. His braces droop at his sides. He is barefoot. She wears a clean pinafore over a blue cotton frock which does not reach the tops of her boots. A dark-haired Alice in Wonderland.

He does not know her name and he doubts she knows his. Yet empathy flows between them, a shared knowledge – vaguely understood in her case – of what this is all about. Perhaps redemption has arrived after all, a thief in the night stealing to his cottage. Wearing a blue frock.

A contented breath warms his ear.

'Well,' he says, softening his words with a gentle smile, 'is it too late to start lessons tonight, or do you have to be home for your mama to tuck you in and sing you a lullaby?'

PART TWO

Chapter Six

The meeting of workhouse guardians is as badly chaired as usual. Joseph Michaels would have thought Courtney-Brown eager to be riding out to his tenants, inspecting the progress of barley crops rather than spending time poorly chairing meetings.

Summer sunlight hammers at the tall, lead-paned windows like Joseph's namesake knocked on inn doors. It's achieving little inside the vast chamber, however. The distant shadowed ceiling, brown walls, and glass-fronted bookcases lined with sombre-hued tomes combine to swallow light as the whale swallowed Jonah.

A lost cockchafer buzzes at the closed window in competition with Reverend Jarvis' interminable droning about the lack of space within the workhouse and the need to be particular about the morality of those seeking shelter within its walls. Joseph frowns, fiddles with his pencil. He should say something, as he rather thinks physical need should guide their hand and the attribution of sin in all its degrees should be left to God. He also fervently wishes the meeting to end and one item remains on the agenda. He glances at his fellow guardians, some with glazed eyes, others fidgeting with papers, and understands any argument he might put forward won't be won today. He remains silent.

The topic passes and Courtney-Brown says, 'Gentlemen, we have come to the most satisfying agenda item for today.' The stern countenance required to discuss potential sinning applicants drops, replaced by a beaming smile. 'My desire,' he says, 'to ensure the highest, modern standards of cleanliness in our institution, both of the building and its inmates'–soft laughter around the table–'has come to fruition.' He pushes the tips of his fingers together. 'Our sanitation project is complete.'

The news raises a cheer. Joseph cheers too. Clean, running water to encourage greater hygiene among the inmates, and water closets which flush. The height of modernity.

'And on budget,' Courtney-Brown says. He turns to the clerk at his desk by the window. 'Mr Shill has prepared a detailed report.'

Cornelius Shill rises to place several pages of graphs and closely typed paragraphs in front of each guardian.

Joseph scans the report, impressed. Neatly done.

Courtney-Brown gives a brief summary before opening the meeting to questions, which he indicates the clerk will answer. Joseph is further impressed at the clarity and succinctness of Shill's answers. Meanwhile, Courtney-Brown nods and taps the ends of his long fingers together in the manner of a schoolmaster proudly showing off a talented student. It amuses Joseph and makes him realise it was likely the aristocrat's patronage which brought Shill into the role.

From time to time, the chairman directly answers a point of detail, highlighting his enthusiasm for the project. It makes sense. Rumours among the businessmen of

Shiphaven say the landowner works hard to impose up-to-date, more productive methods on his tenant farmers, as he has done here at the workhouse. Some farmers are less than enthusiastic, which Joseph considers a shame. Progress is progress and farmers as well as sea merchants like Joseph need to move with the times or suffer financially.

'Thank you, Mr Shill.' Courtney-Brown brings the questions to a close and soon afterwards the meeting itself, later than he should have done.

Joseph gathers his papers and walks to the stand by the great wooden door to collect his hat and coat. As he fetches them down, he catches sight of the landowner standing by the clerk's chair, patting the young man's shoulder in a 'well done' gesture. Shill remains intent on sorting his paperwork, and his dark skin deepens a shade. Joseph smiles.

The acrid smell of unwashed bodies and the rumble of voices from the workhouse refectory rise to meet his descent of the staircase. Passing by, he catches a brief view of rows of shirt-sleeved men at long wooden trestles, spooning up gruel and ripping chunks of grainy bread which they dip into the beverage to soften before chewing it. The women will eat later. Male, female, young, old, petty thieves or honest folk fallen on hard times are all distinguished by their dependence on charity. A few, especially the young ones, might be redeemed from any crime or immorality by their time in this God-fearing place. An opportunity not, it appears, to be given to future tainted supplicants.

The groom has Joseph's mare ready in the stone-paved yard. In a patch of shade, four women in shabby uniforms are lined up on a bench, dull brown birds on a leafless branch. Each is bent over a length of old rope, undoing it strand by strand, the piles of resulting oakum lying at their feet resembling dolls' haystacks.

Working for their scant food and unsanitary lodgings. Nothing is freely given, not even charity.

Two of the women glance up, eyes disinterested beyond Joseph's usefulness as a distraction in their long day. He raises a finger to his hat in greeting. Workhouse oakum doubtless caulks the joints of the timbers in his ship, the *Lady Catherine*, and acknowledging the women's labour is the least he can do.

At the end of the driveway, he pauses to glance through the vast iron gates which imprison the inmates each night. With its grimy windows and numerous chimneys, the dark brick building is humble enough for the worst of sinners. Whatever the vicar's view.

Already overdue for his household's midday meal, Joseph does not hurry the mare. The two mile journey down the hill to his home in Shiphaven is a pleasant ride despite the heat. On one side, elder and ash clinging to a steep bank cast cooling shadows over the road. On the other side, beyond a hawthorn hedge, a man in an inappropriate tall beaver hat and a girl of about fifteen years with loose, black curls, walk slowly through a rising, multi-hued meadow, stooping to pick flowers which they place in the girl's basket.

Joseph's mare comes to a sudden stop and faces the meadow just as the girl sets down her basket and throws both hands in the air. She lifts her face to the sun as if welcoming rain after drought and whirls about in a lone dance. In the midday stillness, the high notes of her laughter carry across the meadow and over the hedge. Joseph's mare whinnies a response and the girl ceases her whirling to blow the horse a kiss. Joseph's lips curl upwards in an instinctive response to this improbable shared greeting. He doffs his hat to the pair and the man returns the gesture. The girl dips a pretty curtsy which Joseph is unsure is meant for him or his mount.

He rides on, smiling, imagining Catherine dancing among the flowers, throwing out her hands and laughing. His smile melts. She would adore the experience and all of them would suffer the consequences of such energetic activity.

Ahead, the great arc of the Severn loops across his view to the yellow and green fields on the river's far side. Joseph takes comfort. He never tires of watching the river, in any season and in any mood. The waters have been good to him. As has life.

Mostly.

*

In the green-papered dining room, the mahogany table is set for one. Catherine, sitting in a brocade upholstered chair in the bay window with a book on her lap, hears the front door open, the clip clop of horses' hooves and jangling harness on the High Street beyond, before a click shuts the noises out once more.

'Papa, you're home at last!' She lifts her head for her father's home-coming kiss on her forehead. 'Aunt is resigned and Mrs Bryce tight-lipped over the state of the beef. We waited and waited and in the end my belly demanded feeding before I fainted.'

After the kiss, Papa steps away to appraise her better. 'Hmm.'

Catherine squirms. She wants to lower her eyes to her book, fearing the next question.

'Are you well, my dear? Not too warm?'

This is an old euphemism for, 'Do you have a fever?'

Catherine shakes her head cautiously, to avoid bringing on a dizzy spell. 'No, Papa. Really, you fuss too much.'

He lays a hand on her forehead. 'Hmm.'

'It's warm in here, that's all.' Catherine fans her face with her hand. 'Once I've kept you company while you eat, I'll take my book into the coolest corner of the garden and laze the afternoon away under the beech.' She smiles. 'Tell me all about the meeting and how dull it was and did you at least enjoy your ride home?'

'I did, enjoy the ride that is. You would have enjoyed it too, my dear. Yes, very much.'

*

His mother will have waited dinner, despite Cornelius' insistence not to do so. He walks briskly from the workhouse along the rutted road where carts and horses stamp dust to thicken the air. He passes a bakery which smells of yeasty bread, a grocer's which smells of sunburned tomatoes, and the dairy which smells of sour milk given it is well past noon.

Pushing open an iron gate, one in a row, he walks up a path bordered with pink and white hollyhocks to a red door. He opens it into a dark hallway with a flagged floor and two rooms leading off left and right ahead of a steep staircase.

'I'm home, Mother.' He removes his hat and coat, hangs both on a stand and enters the room on the left.

'There you are, dear. Dinner is waiting. I imagine you're hungry after having to listen to the gentlemen going on all morning.' Mrs Shill puts aside her sewing and stands. Her brown eyes, twins of her son's, sparkle their welcome.

'You shouldn't have waited. I told you I'd be late.'

Mrs Shill waves the objection aside, heads into the kitchen, and calls over her shoulder. 'Too dull to eat by myself. Besides, I'm longing to hear how the guardians took your excellent report about this fancy sanitation project, or'–the mischievous tug of her lips makes her appear younger than her near forty years–'is such a topic not fit for the dinner table?'

She brings through a platter of cold lamb and a bowl of mashed potatoes kept warm over the fire, and Cornelius holds a chair out for her before sitting himself. He waits for her to place food on her plate, serves his own dinner and says grace in a quick, abstracted manner.

'What's wrong, Son?' Mrs Shill raises a slim, dark eyebrow and sets down her knife and fork. 'Didn't it go well?'

Her mouth is set in a sympathetic line which she un-sets when Cornelius says, 'Not at all, it was fine.' He pauses, frowns. 'So fine, Mr Courtney-Brown went out of his way to make sure I knew it.' He squirms at his earlier discomfort of the chairman's hand laid familiarly on his shoulder as he tidied his papers, and at the overly grateful edge to the man's voice telling him he had done an excellent job.

Mrs Shill concentrates on her plate. 'Ah.' She picks up her cutlery and cuts through a slice of lamb. 'It was … good of Mr Courtney-Brown to employ you as the workhouse clerk. Today, I suppose, his decision is justified to his fellow guardians.'

'I suppose.' Cornelius wants to ask about the hesitation in her statement, if he could find the right words. He concentrates on his dinner.

'You're a good worker, bright and industrious. You could go far, especially with the … patronage of Mr Courtney-Brown.'

There it is again, that hesitancy. Cornelius nods. For a reason he can't articulate, the patronage of Cornelius-Brown is not a notion which makes him glad.

Chapter Seven

ong stems of sunny agrimony harvested from the forest, feverfew from the hedgerows, delicate pale yellow florets of Lady's Mantle and the green leaves of verbascum from the meadow spill from the basket which sits on the cottage table. Stems of fluffy white yarrow and the curling leaf stems of pink-purple vetch lie beside it.

'Can we sort them tomorrow?' Hester pours water from a clay jug into two mugs and hands one to Aaron. The brim of his hat is dusty with pollen. 'I'm supposed to be weeding vegetables and if Mother finds me missing she'll ask where I've been.'

Aaron shrugs, removes his hat. 'You must do what you must do.'

Hester grimaces, drinks the water down in one long swallow and sets the mug by the basket.

'You can sulk all you want. We've spoken of it too many times and I won't be budged. If Mother discovers this'– she waves a hand to take in the cottage, its crowded table and bulging shelves–'she'll keep me tethered to her apron strings tight as an ox to a millstone.' She tries to lighten his scowl, stomping around the table, back bent. 'Round and round I'll go, getting nowhere.'

His lips twitch. It's a start.

In the year she's been learning, Aaron has chided her from time to time about her insistence on secrecy. It's Hester who sulks then.

'Don't you want me as a pupil?' she will cry. 'Are you bored with me? With teaching?' She will run a hand over the rapidly filling leather journal containing the results of her lessons, together with delicate illustrations of herbs and flowers and neatly inscribed lists of their uses, mainly medicinal, some more spiritual.

'Don't you understand? I don't do this lightly, or only because it's fun. I'm not some bored daughter of a wealthy man who needs to fill her time.'

Aaron will soften, tut, explains he does understand. He understands too well. A frown will crease the skin above his nose before he clears his throat and takes up a jar of some concoction, opens it, wafts it under Hester's nose and demands she tell him its ingredients.

Today, she is delighting in her short encounter with the beautiful mare on the track down to Shiphaven. She can't sulk after exchanging greetings with such a valued and well-cared-for creature. Her mood is light, floating, despite the shadow of the afternoon's drudgery.

Aaron shrugs. 'Before you flee from me'–the twitch of the lips is more pronounced–'I've been meaning to give you this.'

His fingers dance among the detritus on the table to land finally on a small muslin bag hung on a cotton thread. 'Do you remember the feverfew we picked and dried at the beginning of summer?'

Hester sighs. 'Another test? Umm ... it's for nausea,

vomiting and … about everything else.'

'Hardly a specific answer. Besides, it wasn't the question I asked.'

'I do remember. What of this feverfew?'

'I've made a gift for you from it.' He loops the thread over her hair, commenting on how tall she has grown and she laughingly says she would have expected to grow in the past year.

'The feverfew will protect you.' He doesn't say from what. 'And make you strong.'

'Thank you.' Hester tucks the bag inside her dress, pats it, testing its place against her skin.

Aaron breaks the silence, picking up the agrimony. 'Now tell me what we'll do with this.'

'Use it on wounds, cuts, to stop bleeding,' Hester says immediately. 'And I really must go.'

She walks to the door, pulls it open and stands with her back to Aaron. 'The leaves – place them under our pillows to make sure we sleep well,' she calls over her shoulder, and escapes into the afternoon heat before he can answer.

Running across the fields to the gap in the hedge, Hester's thoughts shift from potions to vegetables. This year, she has planted marigolds among the carrots, parsnips, peas and lettuce. Mother approved, saying the flowers should deter slugs. Hester, happy for the approval, airily, unthinkingly, added how the bright yellow petals could be made into an ointment for rashes and burns.

'How do you know that?'

Hester, stumbling over her answer, eventually said it was a piece of lore she'd heard in the village, in the baker's, she thought.

'Old wives' tales.' Mother dismissed the ointment, and Hester breathed again.

Healing the Annies of the world is her dream and she won't be driven from it by Mother's intolerance. To keep her visits to the cottage secret, she works twice as hard to finish her work on the farm. In the evenings, she helps Mother clear the supper things before both of them bend to their sewing. Her mother assumes Hester's absences are due to work outside, especially in the summer months. Her father and her brothers are off doing their own work in different corners of the farm, so normally Hester is free to come and go with no suspicion. Which doesn't mean there haven't been times when her heart pounded at the possibility of discovery.

'Lazy Hester,' Sim said when he found her one time by the river. She was coming from the cottage and taking the chance to talk with Sabrina. 'Idling your time away.' He huffed. 'Our father spoils you, girl. There's weeds to be pulled and butter to be churned. You're not some fine lady, not yet.' He screwed up his mouth. 'Get back to your chores and earn your way.'

She had worried for days he might accuse her, when Mother was about, of time-wasting or, worse, ask why she was on the river path. Hester prefers her lies to be by omission.

Chapter Eight

The hot end-of-summer weather drains Catherine's energy to the point she can do nothing except languish on the sofa, feet shoeless on the ottoman, her back against a tapestried cushion. Her aunt brings her hot drinks of the best Indian leaf tea, saying if such drinks cool the natives of the searing Indian sub-continent they will assuredly cool Catherine. Mrs Bryce brings her elderflower cordial.

'Do you think that high and mighty Courtney-Brown would give us a chip or two of ice from his ice-house?' Mrs Bryce rolls her eyes at the impossibility of it.

Catherine laughs. 'It would melt long before it arrived here.' She takes the long glass. 'Besides, with this water straight from the well, the drink is perfectly refreshing.'

'Water from the other well is what you need, Miss Catherine.'

'Other well?'

'The sacred well. St Ceyna's.' Mrs Bryce folds her arms under her bosom. 'Powerful stuff. When my mam was ill with milk fever with the youngest, Betty, may she rest in peace, it was the saint's water cured her right off. Granny Williams, good woman she was and wise in the ways of herbs and wildflowers, used it in her fenugreek poultice. Showed me how to make it.'

'Surely it was the fenugreek which righted your mother. Did the water matter?'

Mrs Bryce arches her brows. 'It did, Miss Catherine, it did. And now I must attend to dinner before your father is home asking why he's waiting for his meal.'

Catherine sets the cordial on a side table which also holds an unread book and a lawn handkerchief she is supposedly embroidering. With her skull stuffed with sheep's wool, sewing or reading is impossible in the dry airlessness of noon. She lifts her legs onto the sofa, rests on the cushion and closes her eyes. Led by Mrs Bryce's comments, her mind wanders to St Ceyna's deep waters. Papa had taken her there when she was eight years old, to show her this place of local legend and general beauty.

It was autumn. Catherine's pony breathed frosted drops into the air while its hooves crunched the red and gold leaves carpeting the ground as richly as any of the Turkish rugs at home.

'Who was St Ceyna?'

'A Welsh princess, from long, long ago. A great beauty, yet she never married and lived as a hermitess at the end of her life.' Papa arched his brows. 'People say she talked with the spirits of the forest and the streams.'

Catherine had stared into the stone-walled, rectangular clear pool, conjuring a long-haired beauty bathing under a silver moon. They visited three more times, in the days before her wearying illness kept her tied to the house like a cow in its stall.

Her body relaxes, her breathing deepens as she sinks into the well's imagined, languorous coolness. Today, the leaves sheltering the pool would be heavy with the mature green of late summer. A penultimate taste of life before the final glittering display, a last burst of joy, heralds their death in the frozen nights.

How might it feel to glitter with joy before death? If she is dying – as she believes she is – Catherine badly wants to glitter first, instead of this lethargic fading away she can do nothing about.

She broods all afternoon, and as she plays with the chilled vegetable soup Mrs Bryce serves for supper to tempt Catherine's sparrow appetite. When the bowls are cleared and the family settled in the drawing room, Catherine sits up straight on the sofa, a finger marking her place in her book. While it takes effort to sit thus for any length of time, she has to demonstrate how strong, how well she is, otherwise her father will deny her immediately.

'Will you take me to St Ceyna's well, Papa?'

'St Ceyna's? Why do you wish to go there?' He puts aside his newspaper and frowns from his chair by the side of the empty fireplace.

Aunt Lottie glances up from the cushion cover she is embroidering with white lilies and golden daffodils. 'Why indeed?'

'Aunty! Papa!' Catherine puts desperation into her voice. 'I'm tired of staying in the house all day with only the garden for a change of scenery. I need to see somewhere different before winter locks us in forever.' She takes her finger from the book and clasps her hands beneath her chin. 'Please, Papa?'

He waves his pipe. 'I understand, my dear, truly. I'd gladly take you if it were possible. However, you're not strong enough to ride, and the carriage is impractical on that narrow, overhung track. I don't see how it can be done.'

'It can't.' Aunt Lottie snips a yellow thread. 'You're unwell, Catherine. Doctor Newton says you need to rest.

Gallivanting off into the forest is not resting.'

Catherine pouts. 'If I rest any longer I'll die of boredom long before I die of whatever ails me.'

'Catherine!'

Her aunt's horror shames Catherine's outburst into apologies. 'Of course I'm not dying. I'm sorry, Aunt, my words were in poor taste.' A bright smile will encourage Papa to say yes. 'It seems I'm recovering, aren't I, if I have this desire to go somewhere?'

'Not the well.' Papa lifts the newspaper and flicks over a page.

'I can ride Molly. I do remember how to ride, Papa. It's not far.'

He puts the paper down for a second time, along with his pipe. 'I'm sorry, my dear. You'll have to make do with the carriage and a short promenade along the river.'

Aunt Lottie eases stem-green thread through a needle. 'Far more sensible, if the sun isn't too fierce.'

All those people, jostling their unwashed bodies too close, greeting each other with loud cheeriness and banal chat.

'No thank you,' Catherine says. She surrenders her upright stance and wriggles her aching shoulders into the sofa. 'I'll stay here and dream of St Ceyna instead.'

And dream she does, while her longing to visit the well grows into an obsession through the last days of August. The imagined cooling freshness consumes her. In her dreams she floats on the waters, the wet caress soothing her arms and legs, sliding silken across her naked body. Her head thrown back, her light blonde hair trails its lengths on the glassy surface as St Ceyna's dark hair did all those centuries ago. She wakes in a knot of damp nightgown and sheets, flushing at the memory of her own dreamed nakedness.

She must visit. She must. At least to run her fingers

through the water, touch the drops to her face and eyes, to her arms. She will remove her boots and stockings and cool her toes. The waters cannot cure her body. She is certain they will refresh her spirit.

Catherine's desire, her desperation, can't wait on permission.

*

The rhythm of the mare lulls Catherine into a dreamlike state. The path weaves in leisurely loops between blunt-edged quarried stones, clumps of fern and stands of bracken up to a ridge. The coolness beneath the trees breathes like a living creature, as if ancient eyes measure her progress through the forest. Maybe the spirit of St Ceyna follows Catherine's journey to the well, encouraging her with whispers and the fluttering of a hand on her shoulder.

Molly tosses her head and snickers. Catherine keeps on, the rapid guilty thudding of her heart which has accompanied her out of the house, up the track and into the forest, quieting the closer she comes to the waters she thirsts for.

From the ridge, the narrow valley which was home to the saint falls away to a thin, straight stream which feeds the sacred well. The beech and oak are as Catherine remembers: thick with age, entwined branches shelter the rough stone rectangle which encloses the pool in imitation of elaborate trusses sustaining a church roof above a nave.

Catherine halts Molly at the trees' edge. Someone else is here. A girl two or three years younger than she is, and with a tumble of dark curls falling over her cheeks, kneels above the water to dip a pitcher. Mottled sunlight shimmers on her arched body as if she is attended by dancing water sprites.

Catherine watches, delighted. Has she been granted a vision of St Ceyna in her youth?

The girl sets the pitcher on the ground and turns to Catherine. No vision after all. Here perhaps is a sturdy farmer's daughter, or she could belong to a shopkeeper. She is dressed well, although plainly, in a blue calico frock with a white collar. A muslin bag on a plaited thread swings from her neck. Her feet are bare. A pair of black boots stuffed with white stockings are lined up neatly not far away.

'Hello,' the girl says. 'Have you come to collect water too?'

'No.'

'To bathe?' The girl jumps to her feet and comes closer.

The dappled sunlight follows her and Catherine peers closely, unsurprised if fairies really did play about her head and shoulders. When the girl reaches out to Molly's nose and strokes it, Catherine senses the mare relax under the caress, ears forward. A farmer's daughter?

'No, not to bathe.' Catherine grows hot, momentarily living her dreams. 'Perhaps my face and hands, maybe dip my feet, to cool them, to cool myself.'

'I bathed my feet earlier.' The girl brushes aside a wet strand of curls. 'The cold water makes your skin tingle.' She continues to stroke Molly's nose. 'You're beautiful, aren't you?'

Molly wickers in agreement and Catherine says, 'You've an excellent way with horses. I'd swear she understood you.'

The girl glances up, a smile tugging at her lips. Pride gleams in her cornflower blue eyes and Catherine is captivated, wants to ask: 'You can talk to horses?' She bites her tongue on the silly question.

'Are you going to bathe your face?' the girl says. 'Can you dismount by yourself?'

Catherine hesitates. It might be the flaw in her plan. The block at home meant she could mount Molly by herself, settling comfortably in the side-saddle as if it hasn't been nearly a year. However …

'I can. The trouble is, I'm not sure I'll be able to re-mount. And it's a long way to walk home.'

'I'll help you.' The girl squares her broad shoulders. 'I'm strong. It's all the farm work I do. In any case, there's that.' She points to a broad, uneven stump a few feet away.

Catherine hesitates no longer. She lifts her legs from the pommels, sits side-on and jumps to the ground, twisting to face the mare as she does so.

'Bravo!' The girl claps her hands. Then, 'Are you all right, Miss?' as Catherine sways, dizzy, and rests her head on Molly's flank.

'Yes, yes. I'm fine.'

'I don't think so. Are you faint? Here, lean on me and we can use the stump as a seat.'

Fuller-figured, the girl is strong as promised, easily able to support Catherine's slender body.

'Apple cider is what we need.' She lays her hand on Catherine's forehead where beads of sweat prickle. 'Good for dizziness. Or ginger tea and honey. For now ...' She gently pushes Catherine's head down. 'Stay there while I fetch you water.'

Catherine grips the edge of the stump, willing the dizziness to stop. Nausea rises in her throat and she swallows it down. And if she can remount, she worries she won't be able to stay in the saddle. Papa may well be right: she is not well enough to ride, not in this sticky air. His anger at her foolishness, his disappointment in her, worsens her discomfort.

A patterned clay mug of well water appears under her nose. Her hands tremble as she takes hold of it and sips. A liquid sherbet coolness fizzes in her parched mouth, tingling on her tongue. She gulps the rest with the passion of a lost, thirst-tormented soul falling upon an oasis.

'Are you feeling better?'

'Thank you, yes. It's silly, I have dizzy spells, my head is heavy. It'll pass soon.'

The girl lifts Catherine's chin and frowns into her eyes in the manner of Dr Newton. Catherine quashes a desire to laugh, not wishing to insult her young nurse.

'Your eyes.' She frowns. 'Aaron would …'

'Aaron would what? Who's Aaron?'

The girl steps back. 'No-one. At least, it doesn't matter. Are you better?'

Catherine searches her warm eyes. The notion a ghost or a spirit attends her, comes again. 'I am, and I'll bathe my face as I promised myself.' She glances over to the girl's boots. 'Unless we might be surprised by other visitors, I'll dip my toes too.'

'Few come here this time of day. We – I – rarely see a living soul.'

Catherine lets the plural pass. This Aaron she supposes, probably a young farmhand with a good countryman's rudimentary knowledge of basic ailments. The reference to a 'living soul' appeals to her, makes sense. Whether a ghost or a robust young girl, her helper belongs in this place, a living human spirit surrounded by careful, watchful souls; a vivacious foil to its deep shade and coolness.

Fanciful notions. Her aunt would tell her to read fewer novels.

She gives the girl a sly look. 'Let's hope we too have St Ceyna to ourselves.'

*

Over the time they spend sliding their bare feet through the cold water, Catherine's colour rises from waxen to the soft pink of apple blossom. Hester's new friend tells how she lives in Shiphaven, loves to read and hates to sew. Hester tells about life on the farm and how she would love to read more and also hates to sew. There's no choice though, because it's how she and Mother bring more money to the farm.

'It isn't doing as well as it should, despite Will, my oldest brother, trying hard to persuade Father to try more modern ways like our landlord insists.' She rolls her eyes. 'Father, bless him, says the old ways work and there's no reason to change them.'

Catherine reaches across and touches the little bag around Hester's neck.

'Is this something to do with old ways?'

Hester fondles the bag. 'Feverfew. Aa– It was a gift.' She lifts the muslin to her nose and sniffs it before tucking it into the collar of her frock. 'It's feverfew, to protect me and make me strong.'

'You and Mrs Bryce, our housekeeper, would get on well.' Catherine leans down to trail her hand in the water, giggles. 'She firmly believes certain herbs, spices, dried leaves, can cure all manner of things, all the more so if they're mixed with water from a sacred well.'

Catherine's giggles stop when Hester says, 'Your Mrs Bryce is right. My great-grandmother cured people with such *potions*, as Mother calls them.' She wraps a curl around her finger. 'I would love to help people the same way.' A peek confirms Catherine doesn't mock her ambition. 'I'm trying to learn this lore, from a … a friend, an older friend who understands it well, and Father would agree it's an honourable way of life. My mother …' She shrugs. 'It's why I haven't told Father, although I'd love to, I hate deceiving him.' The unquietness which lives deep inside her over the deception stirs, as it often does. 'He'd say I need Mother's blessing too, and she would never …' She lets the silence tell the story.

Catherine lays her fingers on Hester's arm. Her eyes are wistful. 'I'm sorry, and also happy for you. To have a purpose, a vocation, is wonderful. Me …' She withdraws her hand to press her fist into her breast. 'I'm useless, a mere decoration, a …'

'… star on a Christmas tree,' Hester fills in, laughing, sad for those wistful eyes. 'You're beautiful, a shining star, and that's purpose too, isn't it?'

She has made Catherine smile, if only for a moment, for Catherine peers up through the leaves, squints at the sun's lower position and frowns.

'It's getting late. Papa will be furious.' She pushes herself up from the stones and offers Hester a hand. 'I do feel much, much better.' Her voice is serious, thoughtful. 'Mrs Bryce could be right, about there being magic in the waters.'

Hester walks beside Molly and Catherine as they follow the winding path through the forest to the track. Catherine fascinates her. It's not just her extraordinary clothes, better than anything her mother sews for the town's ladies, or her exquisite mare, which Hester has fallen in love with. It's her delicate kindness, her high breathy laughter and the way she delighted in the cool freshness of St Ceyna's magical waters.

When they part, Hester strokes Molly's neck under the silken mane. 'Take care of her, won't you?' she says softly into the horse's ear.

Molly tosses her head. *I always do. When they let me.*

PART THREE

Chapter Nine

utumn is never Aaron's best time of year. As All Hallows Eve approaches, the memories – ever stirring in their shallow grave – disturb his days as well as his nights. He paces the cottage, re-orders the stone jars and glass bottles, chops firewood until the heap outside squeezes the eaves, and paces some more.

Will he stay in the cottage long enough to burn the fruits of his chopping labour?

What keeps him here?

You know what keeps you here. A teasing laugh tickles his neck.

Aaron jerks to a halt by the table and lays a palm over the open pages of his journal. It's his third, the first two filled with sketches and jottings recording the distillation of potions, unguents and teas; where the necessary herbs and flowers can be found in which seasons and quantities; and the efficacy of water from a sacred well versus rainwater stored in an oak barrel. They are a history of three years of Hester's lessons.

'Yes,' Aaron says. 'Except she's grown, a woman of seventeen. Will she be content with what I've given her? Will it be enough?'

Perhaps you should ask?

The teasing tone is spiked with harshness. Aaron ignores it.

'It would be in her best interest,' he says, 'if I flee as far as possible from here, take ship to the Antipodes and stay forever.'

Marianne's mocking laugh is accompanied by the fire's flames spiralling and collapsing. *You won't. Haven't I known you since boyhood?*

Since boyhood. Among Mother Lovell's herbs and flowers. 'You will learn,' she told them.

What has Aaron learned? He questions the roof beams. With no answers in the rough-edged oak, he is forced to dredge his own mind, and his heart too.

She will not be denied.

'Who will not be denied? The river? Hester?'

Her teasing laugh sours further and, as with the beams, contains no answer to Aaron's question.

'What should I do?' he cries to the air.

Silence, except for the soothing of anxious spirits.

'Marianne? Tell me? What should I do?'

In the shushed silence, Aaron slumps to a stool warmed by the softly hissing coals and holds his head between his hands.

Fire leaping. Sabrina rising, slapping at the flames. Eyes lit with red. Marianne's dark curls writhing in the heat, a gorgon's tendrils, wilder than any Medusa ... Torn between horror and wanting this too ... stretching his arms ... take me ...

Marianne's Church upbringing, her father the vicar, never dulled the demons in her. The vicar and Aaron's parents – his father a comfortably-off landowner, minor gentry – approved their children's friendship. Aaron snorts.

71

If Marianne had not found Mother Lovell fascinating, they could be sitting this autumn afternoon either side of a fire set and lit by an overworked housemaid in a gabled house on the outskirts of town. Aaron would be dandling a chubby toddler on his lap watching Marianne spell out the words to *Polly put the kettle on* in *Old Nurse's Book of Rhymes* to a rapt five-year-old who rests against her silk-smoothed knees.

He peers at the plain stool where she sat by this fire, set and lit by herself, scribbling notes about combinations of herbs, estimating quantities, spelling ideas out loud to Aaron who would tsk and suggest a spell to fly might have been better conjured three centuries ago.

He waits for her mocking chortle. Silence.

What comes instead is the well-remembered cold of Mother Lovell's arthritic fingers twisting Aaron's jaw to tell him: 'You'll do.' And how he had immediately seen himself as Hansel being bundled into the flames to assuage the witch's unnatural hunger.

He shivers, understanding how prescient his twelve-year-old self had been.

The latch on the door lifts with a click.

'Hello? Aaron?'

'Come in, Hester, and close the door tight. I've not long got some warmth into the place.'

Hester slides through the door. Aaron sniffs. Something in the basket his visitor holds smells of fresh baking, savoury. He takes the basket and eyes Hester over its handle.

'Lamb pie.' She removes her red woollen shawl and hangs it on a peg. 'Mother's too busy with orders for winter dresses to notice an extra pie in the oven.' She brushes aside the tendrils of hair which used the walk over the fields as an excuse to make a run for freedom.

'You don't have to feed me. You're not my cook or housekeeper.' Aaron sets the warm cloth-wrapped dish on the hearth stone.

'I enjoy it.' Hester shrugs. 'If it makes you feel bad, consider it payment for my lessons. Part-payment in any case.'

A generous spirit. Such generosity will be underlaid with strength of character. Aaron should know this and be consoled. With his mind still on Marianne, the idea leads him to hope Hester's strength is of a positive kind.

'Talking of lessons.' Hester eyes the table of pots and jars and crushed flowers. 'Instead of herbs and flowers, can we go to the river? Sabrina is missing me. I haven't been able to spend time with her for days.'

Aaron glances out the window. He wipes the top of his lip with his hand. He frowns.

'There's enough daylight left,' Hester says, misunderstanding the frown.

'It's not that.' Aaron puts his hands behind him and rocks on his heels.

'What then?'

'You shouldn't really, by all moral standards, spend time here in the cottage now you're a young woman.' He takes a step back to eye her up and down, a farmer appraising a mare he might wish to purchase. 'There'll be gossip if we're seen wandering by the river together.'

'Pooh.' Hester dismisses Aaron's moral concerns. 'No one cares, and who will come all this way to spy?'

'Your brothers?'

Hester squirms.

'They ask questions, don't they?'

'Sometimes. Not often.' Hester picks up a stone jar marked Valerian Root Powder and weighs it in her hand.

Aaron knows Hester's hands as he knows his own: the deftness of her fingers as they strip flowers from stems, seeds from pods, how she keeps her nails short and blunt for the sake of her cows. Strong hands, calloused and, today, scratched. Blackberry picking no doubt. Aaron wants to coax those hands to their natural soft whiteness with a balm gently massaged into the slim fingers, the palm held between his own ... He coughs.

'If they found you here ...'

Hester's cheeks bloom bright red.

'They're too busy.'

She exchanges the valerian for a glass phial containing an amber liquid. Aaron had intended to ask her what the liquid is, by sight and smell, and what its uses are. Now his uneasy spirits nag at him. This has gone on long enough. He should send Hester to her farm and tell her to stay there.

'Only Father and Will are on the farm,' Hester says, eyes on the phial. 'If I could tell him, I know Father would be happy for me to be learning all this'–she sets the phial on the table, dares to look directly at Aaron–'to be like Grandmother.' She glances away. 'Will has no interest in what I do as long as I get through my chores, and Sim is on the river all day, comes home stinking of fish, and irritable. Or drunk.'

'You have another brother.'

'Reuben doesn't count. He studies in Gloucester, rarely comes home. Theology, he's to be a priest.'

Pride warms this last sentence. A priest. Well, well. Absolution may be available after all.

'Hmm.' Aaron's uneasiness isn't lightened.

Hester lifts her chin in the manner she has when about to be particularly pig-headed. 'Besides, we're not ordinary folk to be worried by small-minded gossip. Isn't that right?'

Aaron grimaces. Hester, with her soul of a goddess, has gone to the core of the problem. He is damned whatever course he takes; has been damned since first he saw the child on the cliff talking to Sabrina.

'Very well.' He sighs heavily, surrendering, takes the phial from Hester and places it on the table. 'Come then.'

He wrenches his mind from goddesses to concentrate on matter-of-fact learnings. 'You remember the Beggar's Blanket we picked in the summer? In the meadow near the workhouse?'

'Yes. For coughs and hayfever.' Hester grins.

Aaron reaches for her hand, holds it carefully in his. 'Not this time. This time we'll make an ointment from the leaves, for your hands.'

He lifts her scratched hand, smiles widely to show this is all in fun, and blows a kiss to her palm.

She giggles.

*

Hester runs along the path, half-listening to Sabrina's songs which rise through the evening mist, heard above the noise of the river traffic.

She had forgotten how the days draw in faster. Will and Father will be on their way home from the fields, weary, hungry. Despite what she told Aaron, Will's bound to be angry, ask questions, if she's one second late for milking. And there was the day last spring when Sim, who had not yet turned to fishing for his livelihood, found her on her way to Aaron carrying a basket piled with wood sorrel. It was the direction of travel which lit his eyes with ready suspicion.

'Where you taking those?'

'Home, to dry and brew for tea to help Father's heartburn,' Hester glibly replied.

'Home's the other way.'

'Of course. Can't a girl enjoy the sunny day for ten minutes?' Hester scowled and hurried homewards, praying the threatening rain didn't add to the lie by falling on them both.

It's possible Father suspects something is afoot. Hester worries for him, for the greyness of his skin after a day in the fields, how he falls asleep earlier and earlier in his chair by the fire, neglecting his pipe, stumbling up the stairs to his bed while Mother grumbles how the work is too much these days and Sim should be here to help.

Heartburn, Father claimed, when Hester caught him wincing and pressing a hand to his chest. Which is why she gathered more wood sorrel, brewing a tea and watching him drink while his tired eyes thanked her with what sparkle they could manage, and her mother suggested a visit to the apothecary might be more effective. A suggestion Father ignored.

Aaron's unease at her visits prises open her own disquiet. At seventeen, she is fully aware how horrified Mother would be if she knew her daughter visited a man alone in an isolated cottage. Father too would baulk at the idea, however virtuous he deemed the purpose. Does she believe her own words – the words Aaron told her at their first meeting and which have never left her?

Slowing her pace, she whispers them into the evening chill. 'You and I are not ordinary folk, we are wise.'

She and her teacher are not ordinary people bound by the conventions of manners and moralities. They are wise folk. Aaron teaches her skills which her great-grandmother used to benefit the poor and ill. Hester will do the same, one day. What they do in the cottage is noble, good.

For the past three years Hester has worn these notions in the same way she wears her feverfew bag, trusting them, taking their power for granted. Today, they fail to soothe her agitation. Not because they are false. Something is different.

She lifts the hand holding the corner of her shawl to her cheek and strokes the skin. The touch of the creamy Beggar's Blanket balm is smooth and cool. Like the teasing breath of Aaron's blown kiss on her palm. She quickens her step, faster and faster, running. Dusk is shadowing the fields when she slides through the gap in the hedge into the farmyard. The line of cows turn their brown eyes on her and low their rebuke in unison. The cat stalks towards her, tail high.

I know where you've been. Haven't I warned you? To be wary?

Hester scowls, heart pumping. 'Don't be vulgar.'

The tail swishes, sharply.

A cat cannot be vulgar.

With her head against a cow's warm side, Hester's thoughts return to Aaron, as does her angry frustration. No, she will not give up her dream. All is well, this far. Whatever the cat says.

Chapter Ten

ester hurries past thinning hedgerows under a sun resting on rain-laden clouds. She is on her way to take Father his dinner in a distant field, where he is ploughing to plant winter wheat. As she walks, she thinks over yesterday's lesson with Aaron.

To mark a milestone in her three years of learning, he trusted her with brewing a potion of belladonna, the dried berries blended with water from St Ceyna's well which he carried down from the forested hills. They had harvested the shiny black fruit one hot summer day, stored them with care and Hester's hands bathed afterwards with honey-scented tallow soap.

'Belladonna,' Aaron told her with a lift of his dark eyebrow, 'aids in forgetting past loves.'

Hester laughed, ignoring the tingle of her nerves. 'It has other uses,' she said, too loudly, 'better ones.'

'They are?'

It was another of his endless tests. Hester has not been tested as much since she left the village school all those years ago. Yesterday she welcomed the normalcy of the question which banished her hidden awkwardness.

'To ease coughing, to help the patient sleep, to cure hay fever of certain types and to ease pain.'

'And?'

'When a woman's birthing pains start far too early, to save the babe being born before its time.' Hester has given up her blushes on such matters, mostly.

Aaron nodded and said Hester was a good student, at which she asked the question which she asks more and more these days: 'When and how can I use all this knowledge?'

Aaron had no answer, then or any other time. When asked, he rubs his beard and mutters the day will come when it comes, which is not an answer at all.

There are feverish Annies out there who need Hester's learning and she is eager to offer it. Visions of sweating children regaining their colour, their burning foreheads cooled, their mothers sobbing their gratitude, fill her mind. The question is, how can she bring the visions to reality when she's tied to the farm and no one is aware of her hard-earned skill?

She blows out a breath and hastens her steps, her frustration eased at the anticipation of Father's pleasure at seeing her, and his meal.

*

Aaron is planning to walk into Shiphaven to lunch at the Ship and buy a second mortar and pestle which will be Hester's own. As he pulls his greatcoat from its hook, the hovering spirits hiss and flutter, while at the same time a sharp tingling runs along his arms and across his chest. The sensation is momentary, uncomfortable rather than painful. He stands for a moment, one arm in the coat sleeve.

Urgent mutterings sound in his ears; an iciness chills his bones.

He pushes his arms into his coat and hurries from the cottage, his feet taking him to the river, to the cliffs where he rescued Hester from the nymphs' embrace. His head is in turmoil at this urgency he cannot fathom. Nerves taut, he walks the clifftop, smelling dampness in the air, listening to the wind in the sails of the boats below, the chugging of engines. He strains for the goddess's voice rising among the shrieking of gulls.

Go to her. She needs you.

How can he go to her? She has always come to him. The goddess cannot be ignored, however. Aaron strides across a stubbled field towards the farm.

*

When Hester reaches the field, the plough is motionless, halfway along a new furrow. The harnessed horse stands quietly, flicking its tail. Hester frowns.

Swinging around, she searches for her father across the partially furrowed earth. Nowhere. She quickens her steps, catches sight of a trousered leg lying on the plough's far side, and runs.

She flings herself around the plough and stops. A lump rises in her throat, she can't breath. Father lies spread on the dark, crumbling earth. His arms are flung wide and his eyes stare into the louring clouds. Hester drops the basket, crouches over him. Great gasping sobs claw through her throat.

Her strong father! No!

'Hester.'

Aaron is there, his dark eyes shadowed.

'Is he dead?' Hester says between sobs.

Aaron squats beside her, presses his fingers to Father's neck, lays his head on Father's unmoving chest.

'I'm sorry, Hester.' He stands, stretches out his hand, palm up.

Hester refuses the offer. She hunches lower over Father's body as if she would revive him with the heat of her own. She glares up at Aaron.

'Raise him!' she demands. 'You're a wise man … give him back to me!'

Aaron shakes his head.

Hester's mind gallops through her years of lore. 'Bergamot? Rue and rosemary?' She jumps to her feet to beat her fists on Aaron's chest. 'Tell me! There must be something! There must!'

Aaron clutches her fists, draws them to his much-faded yellow waistcoat. She buries her head against him and sobs her pain.

'No,' he murmurs into her hair. 'There's no tincture, no potion to raise the dead. Have strength. Remember, you're not ordinary folk.'

Hester reaches inside her gown to crush the muslin bag of dried feverfew. It doesn't make her strong, doesn't ease the pain which sears through her chest, her lungs, her throat, as if all air in the world has been sucked away.

'Go home, tell them.' Aaron glances up at circling ravens in the greying sky. 'I'll watch over him.'

*

The farmhouse fills with women laying out Father's body and comforting Mother. Hester makes tea and sees to her mother's tasks, glad to be active and not have to sit by the coffin. She forces herself to stay quiet when what she wants to do is scream and rage.

His heart, the doctor said, once Will unharnessed the horse, returned to the barn for the wagon and, with Hester's help, lifted Father's body in to carry him home. A misty rain fell to compensate for the tears Hester could not shed in her stony anguish. She walked behind the wagon, aware of Aaron's tall figure further along the clifftop, watching as any stranger might watch from a distance.

Her mind understands there is nothing Aaron could have done, not once Father was dead. Why didn't she appeal to him before? What might have helped? Foxgloves. None at this time of year. Hawthorn. There is dried hawthorn in Aaron's cottage which she could have used to brew teas, make tisanes, heal Father's ailing heart. And she'd done nothing. Except wood sorrel for heartburn. Heartburn! Father's death is her fault.

The brothers blame themselves.

'I should have been ploughing the field, not Dad,' Will said over their scant supper the first evening of Father's death.

'I should have been here to help.' Sim chewed the last of his bread, chin in hand, elbow on the table. Normally a sight Mother would scold, that night her eyes were drawn inward.

It was Reuben who offered comfort, after he was sent for and arrived home the next afternoon.

'Our father loved his alone time with the soil and the sky and the horses,' he said to his brothers and sister. 'God took him at his best.'

Hester bit her tongue. Why should it be up to God to choose when is best? Why not the Devil? The Devil would make more sense when young lives such as Annie's are felled through mortal illness, and strong men like Father fatally weakened when not far out of their prime.

When the women are gone, her brothers at their work, the cows milked, Hester grabs her red shawl and runs to the river. The tide is low and she scrambles down the steep, stony path to where wet boulders meet the bank.

River nymphs call to her, 'Join us, swim with us, learn with us.'

Grief, anger, frustration course through her. All her stolen learning has shrivelled to ashes at its first step. She failed Father, failed herself. She should be with the nymphs, learning from them as they have always offered. Yes, that is where she should be.

She takes a step onto the mudflats, her boots sinking into the ooze. Two squelching steps.

Sabrina's song reaches her above the river noises.

Be strong, be wise, do what you need to do.

'I am not strong!' Hester shouts to the river. 'And I'll never be wise.'

Her bitter guilt pushes her forward, the mud tugging at her boots. There's no Aaron to clutch her shoulder, drag her to solid ground. Three steps ... except ... her mother's swollen eyes, her brothers' sorrow. How will Hester joining the nymphs be strong for Mother? Will it help her be wise?

Her fingers go to the bag of feverfew, lift it to her nose. She inhales the faded musky scent, draws a deep breath of windswept misery, and takes a step backward.

*

The funeral service in the church in Shiphaven is made harder to bear by the freezing chill of the flagged floors and stone walls. Hester clasps her black-gloved hands together, more to warm them than in piety, and wriggles her cold toes to ensure they are attached to her feet. Her mourning dress of black bombazine, hastily sewn by herself with help from her distracted mother, falls stiff and cold around her. She's glad of the discomfort. It is right, with Father dead, that she should never again be comfortable.

Mother sits upright beside Hester, her newly sunken cheeks hidden by a veil made of dressmaking leftovers to disguise an old hat. Her Sunday best black gown has been sponged into cleanliness, there being no time to sew two new dresses.

In the graveyard, Reverend Jarvis intones more words to speed Father on his way to Heaven and offers comfort to the bereaved. Hester shrinks both from the comfort, which sounds stilted and false, and from the dark maw of the grave. She seeks her own comfort from Sabrina, flowing fast to the sea below the slope of the graveyard, her waters thick with sails and plumes of steam trailing like kite tails. A cattle boat is being hauled across by the ferry and the cows low their panic into the air. The goddess does nothing to soothe them. Instead, she reaches out to Hester, the damp wind carrying her message: *Be strong, Hester, be wise.*

Hester presses her hand to her chest where the feverfew lies.

Opposite, her brothers glare at the coffin as it is lowered into the earth and Mother throws the first clods onto the shiny wood.

Hester searches for Aaron among the crowd of villagers and townspeople come to say their farewells to their fellow toiler. He's not there. She brushes away different tears.

The funeral is over, the family is home and Reuben is not yet returned to his studies. Hester lays out a supper of cold meat and leftover potatoes. The fire is stacked with coal and burns as cheerily as ever, heedless of the missing man warming his field-chilled feet at its flames. Its light-hearted crackling does nothing to lift the mood. Hester stabs a slice of meat with her fork, lifts it to her mouth and sets it down with a lingering sigh.

'Well you might sigh, Sister.'

Will rests his hands on the table. He clears his throat.

'Mr Courtney-Brown spoke to me at the funeral,' he says.

'It was good of him to come.'

Will ignores their mother's sentiment. 'He needs me to come to the manor tomorrow. Business things.'

'Yes,' Mother says. 'He'll need to transfer the tenancy to you, Will. I should have thought of that myself.'

'No.'

'What do you mean?' Sim pays attention, having refilled his mug of small beer.

'Yes, what do you mean?' Hester's quick beating of her heart is faster than her head in anticipating more suffering to come.

'Mr Courtney-Brown tells me he has a buyer for the farm, won't renew the tenancy.'

Hester's heart lurches.

Mother sets down her fork with a clatter. 'What?'

'He can't do that!' Sim jumps from his chair and glowers at Will.

'He can and he is.' Will looks past his brother to his mother. She holds her hand to her open mouth.

'Why?' Reuben says.

'I asked, of course. Do you want to hear what he told me?'

'Don't make us guess.' Mother's voice is breathless, tight.

' "Your father," he said, shaking his head pretending he's sorry, "would never heed my advice on how to improve the farm, how to up the yields in the field, in the byre." ' Will mimics the pompous tones of their erstwhile landlord. ' "Therefore, I am obleeged to withdraw the tenancy." '

'Didn't you say you would farm differently, whatever he wants?'

Hester hates the desperation in Mother's voice.

'I did.' Will tugs his chin where the day's stubble lies dark on his tanned skin. 'He's no interest in how I might farm. He's set on selling, despite the generations of Williams who've worked this land. We're the least profitable and one of the smallest of his farms.' He bangs his fist on the table, causing Hester to jump. 'We're to be sacrificed to our betters' desire for capital in the bank as if we're no more than fatted pigs.'

'Not fatted enough.' Sim's indignation twists his lips and reaches his eyes.

'What will we do?' Hester's head is catching up. It tallies her world: the house, the pigs, the cows. What will become of them all? The chickens?

Themselves?

The meat and potatoes sour in her belly.

'Nothing we can do.' Will softens his voice and reaches over to pat Mother's arm. 'It's not all bad, Ma, we can work it out. It's just me needing a new livelihood. Sim is fixed with Mr Stokes on the river.'

Sim's mouth tightens. 'Yes,' he mutters. 'Salmon … and more.'

Will shrugs. 'I can hire myself out to any farm hereabouts, or go to fishing with Sim.'

Her big brother a farm labourer, dependent on the work needs of others? Hester's pride rebels.

'No,' she whispers. 'And me and Mother?' She sits up straight, the tips of her fingers dug into her breast bone, pinning the bag of feverfew.

'We'll find us all a house in town,' Will says, 'and you and Ma can do your sewing in comfort, without having pigs and cows t' worry about. It'll be better, you'll see.'

Hester can't see.

Mother finds her voice. 'Who will pay for this house in town?'

'Us.' Will waves a hand at his brothers, finishing with Reuben. ''cept him. Me and Sim, we'll pay.'

Hester sees her life as one long sewing session, buttons and buttonholes for eternity. She shivers. What about her other skills? Is this the moment that when it came, she would know it? Is there redemption in using them wisely, after all? A penance for her failure to save Father.

'I can–' she blurts and stops, unsure how to go on without bringing more upset to her mother.

'You can what?' The scorn in Sim's voice drowns Hester's desire to speak. 'Waste your time wandering by the river? You'll still be able to do your wanderings, easy in Shiphaven.'

'Nothing, never mind.' Hester stands and clears the dishes. Her head is light. It is too much news to take in, on top of everything else.

Chapter Eleven

he low ship making its way upriver is a shadowy silhouette in the starlight. At the point where a stream forms a muddy estuary in the bank, a shuttered lantern briefly signals. Jem Stokes stands beside the lantern-bearer, his eyes on the rowing boat hauled up onto the mud, a grey bulk in the outer glow of the lantern. An answering light flickers from the ship, something heavy splashes, and the ship's light dims, stays steady.

'Time, Jem?'

'Yes.'

The lantern is extinguished and the bearer and Jem push the rowing boat to the river, the mud sucking at their boots in reprimand of their purpose.

There is no talk as Jem rows with muffled oars to the ship, progress swift with the tide. No talk either as two crates and three barrels are slipped over the taffrail, steadied by Jem's companion while Jem pulls hard to keep the rowing boat from drifting upriver. The water tugs at his blades. He fights, slapping at the river with his oars. The water slaps its retaliation, and Jem curses under his breath.

'Bloody river.'

When it is done, he and his companion take an oar each to row against the tide, the boat sitting low. It's easier once they're through the entrance to the stream where they move quickly, steering between bushy banks to a small dock below the King's Shilling. Three men wait here to offload and carry away the crates and kegs by light this time provided by a sliver-moon.

The rowdiness of the Kings Shilling's tap room breaks the hushed strain of the evening. Nose taps and winks are used to pass the information to those who need to know that the night's undertaking is a success.

Jem relaxes into the settle. He packs and lights his pipe before lifting a mug of beer to toast his companion.

'Here's to a successful night, Sim.' He grins. 'You did well for a young 'un.'

'Hear, hear,' Sim says, loudly. 'There's a living to be made from the river, ain't there?'

'Yeah. One what don't mean stinking of fish.'

'That too.'

Jem grins at his young apprentice's faked knowledge of fishing, the legitimate trade Jem is responsible for teaching him. He'd been hesitant about introducing Sim to the hidden yields of the river. A lad from a respectable farming family isn't normally a candidate for a smuggler's role. It was Sim who brought it up, after his daddy's death.

'Losing the farm,' he told Jem as they mended nets in the chill October dusk. 'Good thing I took on the fishing.' His voice sounded too casual.

Jem sensed there was more. 'Why?' He inspected his work, frowned, dug the thick wooden needle into the rope.

'Bastard landlord, Courtney-Brown, him from Blaize Hall, kicked us off. Selling it, won't transfer the tenancy to Will.'

'Ah.' Jem concentrated on the net, squinting in the darkening light.

'Makes things tough, with Reuben at school studying to be a vicar. Will's got no job, he'll have to take up the fishing too, I reckon.' Sim straightened from his work, caught Jem's eye. 'Leaves me to keep 'em all.' A pause in which Jem nodded an encouragement. 'Need to lay my hands on more cash, soon.'

And here they are. Lad's a fast learner, he'll do well.

'It's good to get the better of the damn river,' Jem says, by way of passing on experience, 'when she fights like she bloody did tonight.'

Sim splutters his cider. 'The river be a fishwife.' He sniggers and lifts his mug to Jem, swaggering in the manner of a man who holds the secret to it all. 'Here's to taming the shrews, hey?'

Jem joins the sniggering. 'To the shrews!'

Sim props his arms on the table, elbow sunk in a cider pool. He winks prodigiously. 'Any luck with your cousin's girl? Caught you up at last?'

Jem snorts into his drink. 'Plain Jane?'

'Yeah, ain't her mam the laundry woman at bastard Courtney-Brown's place? Loads of daughters?'

'Yeah, yeah. Reckon *luck*'s the wrong word though, lad.' Jem puffs out his red, coarse-bristled cheeks. 'No way I'd take her, no matter how much her mam throws the skinny cow at me.'

'Anyone else you fancy?'

'Well, now you say ...' Jem winks. 'This business brings enough I've bought my own place.' He takes a long swallow, wipes his thick lips and sets the mug down with a thwack. 'A house needs a woman in it. Young 'uns too, before I get too long in the tooth to want to bother with rowdy brats.' He fiddles with the handle of the mug. 'But no laundry maids for me. Bit of class is what I'm aiming for, a bit of class.'

'And?'

Jem leans heavily on the table. 'Your sister, pretty thing.' He chuckles. 'Now, here I am, good earner, decent house.' He flicks his pale eyes to Sim, testing the waters, which don't immediately warm.

'Your sister ...' Jem pushes harder. 'Your pretty sister ... she's a choice any man'd be proud to make.'

Sim pulls at his chin. 'If they've got the manhood for it,' he says, and shouts his mirth into the smoky air.

*

Hester's new attic room is warmer than her farmhouse bedroom. It's the one part of her new life which is better, although her mother's blank eyes lightened when she saw the fancy range she will cook on. The house sits on the High Street, near the top of the hill opposite the church and graveyard.

The parlour boasts a tall window which welcomes the light for much of the day. This room is given over to dressmaking and customers, leaving the family to gather in the kitchen. With the house on the High Street, the shopkeepers' and merchants' wives find it easy to bring their sewing needs, to explain exactly how they want the dress draped or the shoulders shaped, and the size of the bustle, if bustle they want, and the width of the sleeves.

Reuben suggests their mother should have a machine for her sewing. Will says there is no money for machines and Ma has sewed by hand all her life. Their mother agrees.

Hester sits in the parlour and sews hems, seams, buttonholes and buttons, hating every minute. In between the endless needlework, she carries out her household tasks and tends the chickens, which have come with them into the town and soon settled after a day or two of fretful clucking.

To the outside world, Hester goes through her days with all the emotion of a dangling wooden puppet. Within, she

91

grieves for the life she has lost. She daydreams of her cows, imagining her head against their velvet sides, the scent of cow, dry hay and warm milk. She misses the pigs' snuffling demands for food, misses their small black eyes overseeing her mucking out their sties.

She misses Father. Her sorrow refuses to release her. No matter what images she conjures of him sitting by the fire telling tales of grandmother, of soothing the panicked moanings of a birthing ewe, or of rubbing his hands through his greying hair as he ponders the farm's accounts, it's the sight of his legs sprawled on the cold ground behind the plough which wins out in her mind. And Aaron holding her, telling her nothing can be done.

There are nights she doesn't sleep, hearing the random clatter of hooves on the cobbled road, listening to the wind off the river carrying Sabrina's urgings.

Be strong, be wise, do what you have to do.

Bitter reminders. If only she had been wise and known what to do when Father was not beyond saving.

She misses Aaron. She longs to be in his cottage, breathing the layered smells of rosemary, lavender, woodsmoke and steaming tisanes, stringing flowers to hang for drying, crushing haws to cure hearts not yet beyond curing. Does he miss her? What is he doing without his pupil? How is he filling his journals with no lessons to record? Her craving burrows deep inside, a trapped rabbit struggling for freedom.

'Am I to spend the rest of my life sewing?' she complains to the cat.

The cat had insisted she'd no time for the farm's new owner. She sprang onto Hester's lap as the wagon bearing what furniture they could fit into the new house set off on the track to Shiphaven. Hester, aggrieved with too many losses, stroked the grey and black fur and didn't look back.

'I wish, I wish … oh, to do something different, to have

a different life,' she cries to the buttonholes.

The cat sits in faded sunlight under the parlour window, licking her paws. She stops. *Be careful what you wish for.* And continues her ablutions.

To escape the house and sewing, Hester offers to go on any errands needed – errands which, in their almost natural way, take her down the steep laneway to the path along the river. Passing the church, she is sometimes rewarded with a glimpse of Father, a soft-edged shadow leaning on the fresh white stone which marks his resting place, casting about him as if his presence there bemuses him. If she can squeeze the time, Hester goes in, hoping to snatch a word. It saddens her that Father's shade is reluctant, melting into the deeper shadows of the tall church before she can reach him. In the spring and summer, she vows, she will leave armfuls of flowers on his grave to warm the cold slab. The scent of fresh flowers might lure him out, persuade him to stay and talk.

She dawdles on the river path, listening to Sabrina purling about the reeds and rocks, watching the nymphs ride the white horses of the bore, envying their free abandonment to the running water.

There are other visitors to the path. Some hurry, having business to attend; others are sturdy gentlemen in black coats who beat their walking canes into the dirt and touch their hats to Hester and to the ladies wrapped in warm capes going about their daily exercise. The strolling ladies and gentlemen exchange conversation, glancing sideways at Hester's unbonneted head and her concentration on the river. On occasion, Hester offers a nod, which is politely, quickly, returned before the person looks away.

Today, ambling by the river, a cold October wind whips Hester's hair about her face. Pins prick her scalp and she is determined to leave her curls loose for as long as her mother allows. She faces into the embrace of the wind, brushes the strands of hair aside and watches the tide swell Sabrina's waters from bank to bank. No cliffs here, the water swirls not far below Hester's boots. Sabrina whispers in her ear, telling her she is strong.

'Strong for what?' Hester cries to the goddess. 'To sew buttons?' She throws out her arms wanting the wind to lift them, to bear her into the air, to float free of her grief and her hopeless life. 'Tell me! For what?'

A lady and gentleman conversing a short way along swing their heads around.

She pays no attention. Her longing to be with Aaron is too much. She swivels on her heel, determined to be where she wants to be, despite the fading afternoon, the long walk and lack of any excuse to be absent from the house for so long.

'Hello, Hester.'

Aaron stands on the path. He touches the brim of his beaver hat to her.

'I was about to come to you,' Hester says. The trapped rabbit within her calms, sensing delivery.

'You mustn't.'

'Why not?' Disappointment sharpens her voice.

Aaron offers his arm, should Hester wish to take it. 'Walk with me,' he says. 'And don't look so earnest. We're casually met acquaintances and I'm escorting you home.'

'Home.' Hester ignores the injunction not to look earnest. 'Home is a place of drudgery, of brothers to feed and keep house for. And buttons to sew.'

She stops, withdraws her arm from Aaron's and faces him, head lifted. 'Do you know what I really want to do?' she says. 'I want to toss all those silks and laces spread over our parlour into the street and fill the space with tinctures and potions.' She sweeps her arms wide. 'I want to tell Mother to forget her wealthy merchants' and shopkeepers' wives and invite the poor of the town to knock on our door all hours to receive healing herbs!'

Hester sees herself in the kitchen, brewing teas in the kettle on the fancy range, crushing rue in the mortar and storing dried cornflowers in stone pots on the parlour shelves currently inhabited by packets of needles, spools of threads and glass jars of buttons. Her reputation as a healer, a wise woman, will spread. The poor, the rich too, will seek her out to ease their discomforts.

The rabbit quivers its excitement. Hester draws in a breath. The glint in Aaron's eyes is bright today, despite the lack of sun.

'You might think so,' he says, taking her arm again to walk along the path. 'Or you might consider you're a young woman who will soon want a husband and children.'

Hester snaps her head up. Aaron tightens his grip and carries on, his eyes on the way ahead.

'You have knowledge and skills to relieve your little ones' aches and fevers, to bring comfort to a thankful husband when his labour in the field brings soreness to his muscles, or concentrating too fiercely on his business accounts makes his head ache.'

'What are you talking about?' Hester's mind leaps to the time after Annie's death, when Aaron spurned her plea to teach her the ways of the fields and woods.

'You will carry meadowsweet when you wed a lusty farmer,' he had told her, 'and you'll bear him dark-curled, blue-eyed girls and sturdy boys.'

Now Aaron says, 'The time of learning must end, Hester. It's served its purpose and you have a future to embrace.'

'No!' She twists from his hold and glares, her hands clenched at her sides.

A delivery boy cycles behind Aaron and smirks over the top of his willow basket. Hester scowls after him and keeps the scowl going for Aaron.

'I have no desire to be ordinary folk,' she says. 'You know

what I've always wanted.' She stamps her boot. 'How can you tell me no, after the years you've spent teaching me? Am I such a bad pupil?' Tears spring to her eyes. A further loss, near as hard to bear as the loss of Father and harder than the loss of the farm. Her chest fills with a strangled knot of emotions: anger, exasperation, self-pity.

Aaron gazes down at her. His lips tremble, his eyes are dark, their glint faded. 'You are set on this path?' he says.

'Yes!' Surely he understands this is what Hester has craved all these years?

He searches her face. The question he finally asks, however, takes her by surprise.

'Will it be enough?'

Enough?

'Yes, yes it will.' Hester's assertion rings false in a tiny way she doesn't understand. Perhaps a response to the worry which Aaron makes clear in the shake of his head and narrowed eyes.

She faces the river, instinctively seeking Sabrina's view. Why this uneasiness? This is what Aaron has been teaching her these last years, this is what Hester wants, to be loved and sought after as great-grandmother was. To stop the Annies of the world from too early deaths. To cure the fatal illnesses of fathers whose daughters love them.

'It will be more than enough,' she says, and turns to Aaron.

He's no longer there.

Chapter Twelve

other.'

Hester broaches the subject mid-morning, when customers are not expected, the brothers are at work and her mother not yet weary. They sit side by side beneath the tall window to avoid wasting one ray of the greyish light which struggles to enter the parlour. The room is cool, the coals in the fire having sunk to a yellow-white glow. Hester hasn't refilled the coal scuttle this morning. She's been distracted, practising this conversation in her head.

She pats the last button sewn onto the child-sized silk-lined waistcoat, sets the garment on the dresser and turns to lean against it. 'I have an idea for bringing in more money,' she says, before she can think too hard about it.

Mother glances up from the lace she is attaching to the end of a sleeve. 'Yes?'

'Herbs, selling herbs ...' The words Hester rehearsed dry up like the wildflowers hanging from Aaron's beams.

'You mean lavender bags?' Mother's voice is raised in happy surprise. 'Sachets of rose petals to line drawers and linen chests? A lovely idea, we should do it.' She tips her head at the window, below which a narrow strip of garden lies between the house and the street. 'We could grow the plants there, harvest and dry the petals, make the bags from leftovers.' She waves her needle in the air. 'How simple, how clever!'

'Yes.' Hester tries again. 'I meant more ...'

'More?' Mother shifts forward on her chair, eager for Hester's clever ideas. 'Pin cushions? Sweet smelling pin cushions. Or antimacassars with tiny hems embedded with cloves.' She sniffs the air as if the cloves are already in the antimacassars, despite the smell being only of coal.

'No.' Hester relinquishes the dresser's comfort and sits, crossing her hands in her lap. 'I mean herbs to cure fevers, distillation of berries to help the sick, to ease birthing pains, to ...'

Mother's smiles fold in on themselves. Twin lines cut deep into her forehead above her straight nose. 'What are you talking about?'

'The same as great-grandmother.' Hester's pulse jumps in her neck. 'Remember what Father told us about his grandmother curing fevers, snatching mortally sick children from Death's hands?'

'We have doctors in these times, Hester.' Mother's voice loses its lightness. 'We have faith in medicine to cure the sick, not wizened old ladies with foul-tasting brews.'

'But–'

'Where in the good Lord's name did you get such a foolish idea?'

'I thought–'

'I suggest you think in a different direction, Daughter.' Mother picks up the lace. 'And concentrate on monogramming those handkerchiefs.' She nods sharply at a snowy pile of cambric on a low table. 'Mrs Samuels wishes to collect them this afternoon.'

Hester picks up a handkerchief, glares at it, sets it on the table and stands up. 'I need to fetch coal first.' As she walks from the room, the gust from Mother's frustrated sigh tickles her neck.

Will and Sim come home in the darkness smelling of fish, sweat and mud. Will's attempts to find work as a farm labourer are poorly timed given the main work of the year is over. Until spring demands endless attention from farmers, he will earn a wage as a labourer on the wharf rather than the soil, or take to fishing with Sim.

Hester's disappointment on her brother's behalf is intense. He misses the farm and the animals too. The knot of hostility towards their former landlord, tightens.

This evening, Mother sends her sons to wash at the pump and once they are sufficiently clean she ladles soup. Hester slices the thick loaf she baked in the afternoon.

The sound of her brothers' slurps has her wishing to escape to Sabrina. It is true night, however, and she can think of no excuse to be wandering the town in darkness. She lets her thoughts go there, hearing whispered songs, seeing silver manes and tails in the spray of wind-whipped waves.

'You should keep your daughter closer, Ma.' Will points his spoon at Hester.

Hester is jolted back to the kitchen. What's this about?

Sim's smirk heightens Hester's worry. She searches her past several days for remiss behaviour. There is nothing.

'I should?' Mother frowns at Hester.

'Folks telling how she's been talking to a man on the river path,' Will says.

'Arguing more like, a lovers' tiff.' Sim crows the news.

Will ignores his brother. 'Strange fellow. See him at the Rope on occasion, keeps to himself. A gentleman once, perhaps.'

Mother rests her spoon in her bowl of soup. 'What's this about, Hester?'

Hester's cheeks, already hot from the soup and the warm kitchen, burn harder. She wavers between guilt and indignation at being the subject of innuendo. Harnessing her wrath, she places her palms on the table and berates Will.

'Do you mean our customer, the gentleman with the yellow waistcoat?' She doesn't pause, or show any uncertainty. 'We happened to pass on the river path one day and he asked after our mother's health and how we're settling in town, and I answered civilly and we moved on.' She narrows her eyes. 'Do the good people of Shiphaven have nothing else to gossip about?'

'You never told me this.' Mother's complaint inflames Hester's cheeks further.

'I'm sorry. I completely forgot.' The last sentence is delivered at Will who shakes his head.

'Seems I need to worry about you.' Mother holds tight to the complaining voice. 'First the silly nonsense over herbs and potions, now this.'

Sim swallows a lump of bread. 'Herbs and potions?'

'Your sister tells me we should sell witches' brews to supplement our income.' Mother sniffs. 'Those stories your dear father told when you were young, about the supposed healing powers of his grandmother, gone to the girl's head. After all these years, when she should have more sense.'

'Why not?' Hester rises and takes up her empty bowl. 'It's a respectable way to earn a living, to be a wise woman, to heal people with herbal lore.'

'Be a witch, you mean.' Sim sinks his head between his shoulders and cackles. 'Watch out for the besom broom she'll be demanding next.'

Mother shakes her head, clasps her hands on the table.

Sim scrapes back his chair, wags a finger at Hester. 'All those times our mother told you to behave like a lady, so's one day you could marry a *gentleman* and be better'n the rest of us. A witch.' He sneers, turns away. 'I'm off to the Bargeman. Coming, Will?'

Will hesitates, peers from Sim to Hester, and says, 'To the Rope, I'll go there.'

Sim shrugs. 'Good night then.'

Hester glares at his retreating figure. His footsteps shift from loud to muted as they pass from the wooden boards to the rug in the parlour. There's the rustle of his heavy coat, and the draught as the front door opens and closes with a bang.

Will tilts his chair. 'This nonsense needs to stop, Sister. We can't have gossip. Folks'll be reluctant to bring Ma sewing if they think the household harbours a witch.' He crosses his arms on the table. ''specially on top of talk of consorting with strange men.'

'Consorting?' Hester laughs. 'Sounds too grand for Shiphaven, consorting.'

Will harrumphs. 'You need to settle. Be a proper woman.' He grimaces. 'Sim's jealous 'bout the way you got treated different, especially by our dad, but he's right.' He looks to their mother who nods along with his words. 'It's what Ma brought you up to be and it's time she enjoyed the fruits of her labour.' He rises from the chair, pats his belly. 'And I'm out too. I'll leave Ma to talk sense into you.'

Hester is left facing Mother. She waits for more lecturing, but all Mother says is, 'There's the lace to finish off on Mrs Jones' petticoat before I go to bed. You clean up here while I get on with that.'

Chapter Thirteen

ear your bombazine for dinner, Hester. We have a visitor.' Mother pulls the spitting lamb joint from the range and bastes it.

Hester scrapes potatoes. She has wondered at the extravagance of this Sunday meal.

'And you'll make an apple batter pudding with the Bramleys Mrs Wilson kindly gave us.'

'Who's visiting?'

'Your brothers' friend.'

It's more fuss than is necessary for a friend of her brothers, unless Mother means …

'Reuben? Is Reuben coming home? With a friend?' She waves the scraper in the air as if summoning her brother to her.

'No. It's Mr Stokes, Sim's master.' Mother slides the joint into the range's glowing maw and shuts the heavy door with a tea towel-covered hand. 'Water for the potatoes, please. And the carrots need scraping and peas to be shelled. You're too slow today. Off in your dream world!'

Hester wants to ask what is important about this visitor other than being Sim's master, which means he is a poor fisherman the same as all other poor fishermen begging favour from Sabrina to give up her riches. She will find out in time and isn't interested in any case.

The water buckets in the scullery are empty, so she throws on her old red woollen shawl and walks out to the pump in the courtyard. The smell of roasting lamb hangs about, tempting the neighbourhood cats.

Hester narrows her eyes at a scrawny ginger tom. The tom twitches his whiskers. *A scrap for a passing traveller?* he asks, politely for a tom.

'Hmm.' Hester exchanges the empty bucket for the full one and bends her strength to the pump. 'If anything's left. We have a visitor.'

Two, if you count me. I'll hunt a mouse in exchange.

'You do that. Make yourself useful. Our own madam has grown indolent with town living.'

Indolence suits her beauty. The ginger cat smooths his whiskers with an elegant paw.

The visitor is dressed neatly in dark trousers, a clean collar on his shirt and a brushed coat. His shoes are as shiny as belladonna berries. He twists his hat in fishhook-scarred hands.

Will carves the lamb, which causes Hester to swallow back tears, remembering Father doing the same each Sunday. Will keeps his eyes on the meat and says to the visitor, 'The fishing's been good to you, Jem. Bought a cottage, right?'

Jem accepts a plate of meat and heaps potatoes and carrots to fill what space remains. 'I do.' He grins at his hostess. 'Near good as landed gentry. Thanks to the river.'

Hester catches the slight lift of Will's eyebrow and Sim's smirk. What is there to raise eyebrows about? To smirk about? This Jem is old, far older than Aaron. He's had a lot of years of fishing and apparently no family to feed and clothe. Which is why he's better off than most of his kind. Lucky him.

'Business is good.' Sim waves his fork, earning a frown from his mother. 'Even you, Will, could make a living from the river if you chose. She gives up her creatures right willing.'

Hester glances at her brother. Not all her creatures, she silently corrects him.

The talk keeps to fishing and the price of elvers, keenly sought, and the price of salmon, and talk about a bridge or a tunnel to replace the ferry sometime in the future. Hester's mind wanders to her own future, and to her answer to Aaron and his strange question: 'Will it be enough?' Again, she has a sense the answer might be No. That's wrong. What she wants is clear, and if she can find a way to do it, surely it will be enough?

Afterwards, the fisherman scratches his thick neck and mumbles his thanks to Mother.

'Thank Hester more than me,' Mother says, with a fond smile for her daughter. 'Especially the apple batter pudding. She's an excellent cook, our Hester.'

Will nods his agreement and Sim strangles the retort Hester expects.

'Then thanks to you, Miss Hester.' The fisherman's eyes dart to Hester, stopping somewhere between her face and her breasts.

'Hester, give me a hand, please.' Mother collects dirty plates to carry to the scullery.

Hester takes up more plates and cutlery, and follows her.

'A pleasant, modest man, don't you think?' Mother fills the baking dish with water from the bucket and leaves it to soak on the bench. 'And comfortably off.'

Hester wraps an apron over the bombazine and sets the kettle on the range to boil for the washing up. 'And dull.' She scoops up a cold potato and carries it into the courtyard. Here she exchanges it for two dead mice which she buries in a garden bed.

'The visitor is a dull fisherman,' she says to the tom.

The tom hisses. *Fishermen, selfish with their catches. There's no sharing with them.*

Hester sniffs her agreement, strokes the tom and goes back to the scullery.

'Leave the dishes,' Mother calls from the kitchen. 'Mr Stokes has invited you to walk by the river, so fetch your bonnet and shawl. The fresh air will pinken your cheeks.'

Hester's stomach drops. Walk the river path with this dull fisherman? Why?

She stands in the doorway, a dish cloth in her hand. 'I was proposing to finish Mrs Burton's collar. Doesn't she want the blouse tomorrow morning?' Her face is averted from the visitor and her brothers, all of whom have taken a sudden violent interest in Hester's words and actions.

'I'll finish the collar. You young people enjoy yourselves while the daylight lasts.' Mother waves through the kitchen door towards the parlour window, which is full of afternoon gloom. 'There's sunshine enough for a walk by the river.'

The men scrape back their chairs. Sim fetches Hester's shawl and bonnet. When she glares he smirks. Will sets her boots by the door with a flourish of his big hand.

Hester bends to lace her boots. 'Am I the Queen of the May, despite it being October?'

She doesn't bother to keep the irritation from her voice. Something is off. Nevertheless, if she has to waste what remains of the day pretending to have fun, she will take the flattery and have fun for real, playing queen.

They stroll down the lane past the graveyard, Will leading, Hester on his arm. The wind has blown itself out and the air hangs heavy with the smell of coal fires and a creeping, chill fog off the river. Lights show in those house windows where oil lamps can be afforded, casting yellow glows to form a patchwork with Sunday's unlit shop fronts. Hester peers through the damp air to the graveyard to see if Father is watching his queen and her attendants. He is absent today. When they reach the river, the fisherman takes over from Will and lumbers by Hester's side with his gaze fixed on the puddled path.

He doesn't take Hester's arm, for which she is grateful.

Nor does he talk, which allows Hester to pay heed to Sabrina's whispers as the tide rolls out to the sea, the waters shushing past in the growing gloom and thickening fog.

You are wise, Hester. You are not ordinary folk. You are not for the likes of him.

For the likes of him?

Hester stops walking. Of course. How blind and foolish she's been. Will's talk of settling, of being a proper woman sound in her head. Mother's roast and her comments about the fisherman's pleasant nature and comfortable earnings. A warning as clear as any foghorn if she'd been listening. Angry humiliation burns in her gorge. She hurries her steps to outpace the fisherman. He lengthens his to catch her up, grasps her elbow through her shawl, tugs her around and lunges at her.

Hester stumbles backwards. Where are her brothers? Nowhere on the path, which is shrouded in fog.

The fisherman doesn't trouble to see if Hester's brothers are near. It's as if he's certain they won't be. He wraps his thick arms about her waist and kisses her, hard, on her mouth.

Anger escalates to fury, drowning Hester's humiliation. She shoves hard, pushing him away with a mocking laugh.

'Why?' she says.

'Why not?' The fisherman grins. 'We'll wed, and I'll kiss you whenever I wish.'

'Will you?' Hester's laugh is shrill with disbelief. When

he reaches for her, she's ready. She lifts her skirts and runs through the puddles, up the lane and into the street where the lamp lit windows light her way home.

*

The girl melts into the fog, her laugh echoing along the path. Jem chuckles, admiring her slim, sinewy form and the wild black curls she rarely covers, leaving a man to imagine the silkiness of them in his hands – or on his naked chest. A spirited maid, one to tame as he's tamed the river which bends to his will these days, and nights, unlocking its riches. It'll be the same with the girl.

He strides up into town and down the other side, to the Kings Shilling where he drinks a pint with his old friend, Ezra. His encounter with Hester has put him in an expansive mood and he needs to share his cheerfulness.

He takes a long draught of beer, wipes the froth from his beard. 'Thinking of adding some bits of comfort to the cottage,' he says, casually.

'Oh?' Ezra peers over the rim of his mug. 'Earnings pretty good, huh?' He winks.

Jem snorts. 'Yeah, but it's more about taking myself a wife.'

'You? Marrying?' Ezra's brows rise. 'Your Plain Jane caught you up at last, hey?

'No! It ain't her. No way!' Jem throws back his shoulders. 'Of course the girl's mad about me, can see it in her moony eyes. Her mam won't let it go, pushes her in my face whenever I'm anywhere near.' He guffaws. 'Like I don't have choices!'

'So who's the fortunate maid?'

'The Williams' lass,' Jem says. 'Sim's sister. The fey one.'

'Ah! Yes. Black curls all a'flying. Seen her by the river, dreaming along. Fey? Rumour has it she's touched in the head.'

'Been let run wild, spoiled by her dad, Sim told me. Strange since a little 'un, he reckons. Sneaking about on the farm and their dad or mam not caring what she was up to, while he had to pick up the work she didn't do.'

Ezra snorts. 'Sounds too strong-minded.'

Jem upends the last of his ale. 'Needs a firm hand, I reckon.' He sets the mug down with a bang, wipes his mouth on his coat sleeve. 'Besides, she cooks a tasty joint, is fit and young. Needs a man's hand, is all.'

Ezra sniggers. 'A man's hand, indeed.'

Jem's deep chuckles are so merry and loud, the tap room's drinkers join in with the unheard joke.

Excepting one man, sitting alone at the next table. His much-faded yellow waistcoat and a beaver hat which has seen better days, mark him as an erstwhile gentleman and unusual customer at the King's Shilling. Jem squints in his direction. His dark eyes with their glint of gold catch Jem's and hold them, with neither a narrowing or a lightening. Jem turns away first and when, having drunk deeply after his heady laugh, he looks to the table, it's empty.

*

'Well?' Mother sits in the candle's circle of yellow light. She puts aside the collar she is edging with green ribbon, and rubs her eyes.

'Well what?' Hester hangs her shawl on its peg and chafes her arms. She wants to go to her attic and scrub out her mouth with cold water and soap.

'When will you wed?'

'Wed?' Hester's stomach curdles at the echo of the fisherman's assured words. She throws out a hand. 'Him?'

'Yes, him. He has a name: Jem Stokes.'

'Why would I marry anybody, let alone him?' Hester's confusion is real. 'Why this haste to have me wed? I'm seventeen, hardly an old maid.'

'You should be aware, Daughter, there's more to the gossip than about talking to strange men.'

Hester moves to the fire, in dire need of its comforting warmth. 'More?'

Be strong. Sabrina's calls echo in her ear.

'Yes.' Mother's voice is weary. 'They ask me if you're sickly, if you suffer from visions. They see you walking by the river talking to yourself.'

'To myself, or to men I'm not supposed to be acquainted with? Which is it?' Hester's agitation reveals itself in the strangled shrillness of her voice. She breathes, deeply, stands before the fire, hands clasped behind her in a stance which copies her brothers. 'Is one not allowed to walk by the river?' Her voice quavers. 'The gentlemen stroll there with their ladies every sunny Sunday—'

'Don't be clever with me. I thought it was grief for your father made you stranger than you normally are.' Mother massages her temples, closes her eyes. 'Until you talked of brewing witches' potions. The townspeople are right to be concerned. I'm grateful for their interest.'

Hester holds her tongue on her desired reply that nosy prying is not concern. She calms her voice, reaches for strength. 'And what do you tell them?'

'I tell them what I once believed and hope is the truth, how you grieve for your father. I tell them you're a spiritual young woman. I tell them a sturdy husband and lusty babies will settle you. The sooner the better.' Mother rises from the chair and takes up the candle. 'The problem is, few men will take a mad wife who wanders by the river talking to herself.'

'I see.' Hester tilts her head towards the door. 'And he's willing to solve your problem.' The memory of his cold mouth on hers raises bile in her throat.

'Yes, thank the Lord.' Mother shields the candle's flame from the draught through the window frame. 'And he's well enough off, with his house near to the King's Shilling. A good income, enough to keep a wife and children.'

'What about the merchants' sons you would have had me marry?' Hester clutches at the straw. 'You were always on at me to sit straighter, to speak nicely, to behave as if I was a gentlewoman.' She brings her toasted hands around to her front, holds them in prayer to her chin, radiating earnestness. 'Have you forgotten, Mother, your ambitions for your daughter? Am I to be thrown to the first man who comes asking? Because he has a house?' This last said with a raw bitterness which has Mother shaking her head at Hester's lack of understanding.

'You've wasted those opportunities through your own behaviours.' Mother touches Hester's arm. 'I blame myself for not taking more care. Except, your father's death, losing the farm, all this change unsettled me. I'm sorry, Hester.'

'Do I have any say?' Hester's mind is suspended in disbelief. Father would never have allowed this nonsense. Nor would the mother she used to know. Stern, yet loving, wanting the best for her daughter.

Mother withdraws her hand. 'No. You will marry Jem Stokes.'

Marry Jem Stokes. This is what Mother has determined is best for her daughter. Hester aches with new loss, new grief.

The candle's light goes with Mother up the stairs, leaving Hester abandoned to the ebbing flush of the coals.

The tabby rubs herself against Hester's skirts. *Marry the fisherman? He might be a sharing kind after all, despite what the tom says. I'll come live with you if he is.*

'No, no and no.' Hester falls into a chair and grasps her icy cheeks with both hands. The chill she carried from the river settles deeper into her soul, refusing to be warmed by the cat's weight in her lap.

She sits until the fire sinks to ashes, mourning anew all

she has lost. And will lose. She thinks of Aaron. Can he, will he help her? Is now the time which she would know when it came, to put her learning into practice? Somehow. With no money, nowhere to go … unless Aaron …

The cat squirms, opens one eye, shuts it, and settles in Hester's arms to be carried up the stairs to bed. Hester lies with blank, dry eyes filled with darkness, her window latched open to the cold river draughts and Sabrina's muted calls.

Chapter Fourteen

From her bedroom window Hester watches the flames of the All Hallows Eve fire cast the glowering clouds in pink. A heavy wind offers the noises and smells of the celebration to her like an unwanted gift: the townsfolk cheering, fiddles screeching, the smell of flames and woodsmoke with undertones of beer and cider.

Her mother and brothers are there, excepting Reuben in Gloucester. Hester believes Reuben would take her part. He would tell their mother his sister cannot marry this lumpen fisherman. Hester refuses to name him as if, nameless, he might prove to be a figment of her nightmares, an ephemera to melt in the morning's wakefulness. She should write to Reuben, beg him to come home. He could be here inside two days, talk sense into her family.

Soon the fisherman will knock on the house door, confident, brash. He will grin his fish-breathed grin and demand Hester take his oar-stiff arm and dance joyfully around the fire as any maiden about to be married with her posy of meadowsweet.

Her breath catches. She cannot see Sabrina from the window, only imagine the river flowing serene, untroubled by the chill blowsiness of the night. Hester listens past the All Hallows celebrations, muting them, needing the goddess's urgings.

The words ring in her ears as if Sabrina had trumpeted them. 'Be strong,' she whispers. 'Do what I need to do.'

Abandoning the window, she runs down the stairs into the parlour, lifts Reuben's old, heavy coat from its peg and shrugs it on, pulling it around her rather than lose time fiddling with buttons. A lantern and tinder sit on the flags by the door and Hester takes them up. Her hands shake so badly she needs three tries to give herself light for the dark journey.

She carefully pulls the door closed and runs through the lanes down to the river, her booted feet skipping over the cobbles in her rush. The lantern swings like a call for help as she takes the sliver of path out of the town, through the tall reeds. Hatless, her curls tug at their roots, demanding the freedom of gulls. Behind her, the sky glows with the All Hallows fire. The wind blurs the noises of the merrymaking and the smell of burning is replaced by the smell of water and marsh.

Hester stops, the lantern at her feet, breathing deeply, breathing in the river. Sabrina's soft calls rise on the bow waves of the ferry gliding on its massive cables.

'Yes,' Hester tells the river. She takes up the lantern, sets her jaw, and walks swiftly along the path, towards the fields and Aaron's cottage.

*

If autumn is never good to Aaron, All Hallows Eve is the worst of all nights. He has determined to stay indoors, to compound a tea to relieve the symptoms of coughs and colds. Something harmless to fill his brain, to keep the devils out.

He searches his shelves and pulls phials and jars which he lines up on the table, first clearing a space among the litter of papers, cups and bottles. He rests the fingers of his hand on first one, then another, of the phials and jars, lingering over some before moving on. He puts four aside: Lady's Mantle, to reduce an inflamed throat, the dried leaves holding their soft grey-green colour, the flowers a paler yellow than in their living state. Secondly, dried lemon balm to breathe into the lungs to calm a fevered or anxious body. He pauses a moment before lifting down a slim glass phial from a higher shelf. Essence of hawthorn flower. Finally – here he hesitates for a long minute – a jar of poppy seeds. To ease a cough.

Lady's Mantle, lemon balm, hawthorn. Poppy seeds.

Every flower, leaf and seed has more than one function. Aaron has drilled this fact into Hester from the beginning. Flowers and herbs to cure the body's afflictions, and flowers and herbs to cure the soul.

Or afflict it.

And once afflicted, there is no cure. This last lesson is one he hasn't yet instilled in Hester and when will he do so? He hasn't seen her since the meeting in Shiphaven. There have been no lessons since her father's death. And now she is to be married, if what he heard from the boisterous fisherman in the King's Shilling is true.

He pushes down hard on whatever emotion he feels about this. It's as he said to her, she should marry, have children, take her place in ordinary life. Yes. He reaches over the table, moves a saucer containing the stub of a candle to one side, slides it back.

He will leave, before winter makes it impossible. Hester is gone from him. Saved. Saving Hester is what Aaron has desired, has needed, all along. This is his redemption.

Saved for whom?

It's a whisper in his ear. He flicks it away. He has tried not to dwell on that, taking up his journal at night, scribbling and annotating, remaining wakeful until near dawn when he takes what rest he can.

'Does it matter?' he says, roughly.

Tell me anyway. Marianne has abandoned her teasing tonight. *I'm curious.*

Aaron sighs his indulgence. 'For a fisherman and smuggler, by name, Jem Stokes. Not a particularly successful fisherman.' Other fishermen, Aaron has learned from tactful probing in the Rope and Anchor, mutter how the river fights Stokes, gives up its natural harvest to him after mighty struggles and in miserly quantities. It's Stokes' success — and this too is hard won — at reaping a different harvest from the river which allows him to live comfortably, and tolerated by those who benefit from these harvests.

Ah. Sabrina has no fondness for the fisherman.

'So it seems.' Aaron casts an eye over the phials and jars set out on the table, places a finger on one. 'And it's none of our business.'

The fire leaps, crackles. A rush of wind tickles Aaron's cheeks and he glances at the door. It's shut firm. The window too, which is caulked with oakum in readiness for winter.

You choose hawthorn? For you or for her? Who needs to open their heart to love? Who needs courage? Marianne's questions are taut with repressed fury.

Aaron doggedly pursues his adopted indifference. 'Hawthorn eases tired limbs and opens the lungs,' he says. 'It will make the tea more efficacious. Have you forgotten?'

He waits for mockery. Instead—

She needs you.

'It's best this way.' Indifference is impossible, better to take a moral approach. Not that morals were ever Marianne's strength. 'I won't let it happen a second time.' Aaron slides a finger through the leaves of Lady's Mantle, takes a large pinch and drops it into a clay cup.

What you wish to let happen or not happen is neither here nor there. It will or will not happen.

'She should marry, be ordinary folk.' He adds the lemon balm to the Lady's Mantel. 'She should have children, grow old with grandchildren to comfort her.' A draught tickles his neck. He shivers.

She is not ordinary folk. You told her so yourself.

'It was a mistake.'

There are no mistakes. There are different destinies.

Aaron's finger moves from the Lady's Mantle to the jar of poppy seeds.

Yes. Poppy seeds for wise folk. As Mother Lovell taught us. You see, I remember well.

'And I remember how much more magic you wanted from these seeds.'

Perhaps this time the seeds will do what they can do.

'No! This is not for her.' His words ring false. 'I won't risk it.'

The fire brightens, fierce as a hellcat, spits golden sparks across the room to singe Aaron's trousers. He brushes at the sparks.

Yet you will risk her with that oaf. Close your eyes, see it, see them.

The image Aaron has been denying since the night at the King's Shilling insists on rising before him. It shimmers in the firelight, bright and gaudy as a circus dancer, and as mesmerising. Hester willing or unwilling he cannot tell, because the fisherman's body, white and cold as the underbelly of a fish, splays itself across her slim form. Only her dark curls show, tangled damply across a yellowing pillow. Aaron chokes on the nausea which rises in his throat.

She needs you. Go.

Aaron clamps his eyes shut.

Go.

He lets out a long breath and swivels on his heel, taking three fast steps to the wall where his greatcoat hangs. He struggles into it, leaves the beaver hat on its peg, wraps a muffler around his neck, pulls on his boots and lets himself out of the cottage. Dusk has given way to a full moon, and, being All Hallows Eve, the spirits have wandered down from the forest and St Ceyna's well and risen in the fields and leafless hedgerows. Aaron has ample company to guide him to the town and down to the river.

The air fills with their susurrations, their whispered, *She needs you.*

*

'Hello, Hester.'

Hester has not gone far beyond the last houses of the town when Aaron emerges, lanternless, from the darkness ahead.

'I was coming to you,' she says, lifting the lantern to his face.

He gently pushes it aside and she sets it down. Her urgency is appeased by his presence, the knowledge he has come to her in her need. It will be all right.

'What does Sabrina say tonight?' Aaron gazes across the waters, standing close by her side. He smells of lemon and fire.

Sabrina is as low, grey and swift as the sky, where a fat moon sculpts shadows in the scudding clouds. Boats nestling by the far bank to wait out the tide are defined by their swinging lamps, while the ferry lights quiver on the undulating surface like nerve-raddled stars.

Hester listens. The river sings to her, straining through the wind to be heard.

'She's sorry for my unhappiness.' Hester is unsure of this. Sabrina has never been a consoling goddess.

'Unhappiness?' Aaron keeps his eyes on the river. 'I

believe you're to be married. Surely marriage is a cause for celebration?'

Hester tugs her brother's coat tighter about her. Is she wrong about why he's here?

'I won't marry him,' she hisses. 'He's crude and ill-mannered, and he stinks.'

'Ah. I'm sorry.'

Hester blanches at his even tone. Aaron, her friend, her teacher, her rescuer, has no sympathy for her fate in the hairy arms of the fisherman? Her urgency resurges, the lump of grief she carries within her grown so heavy it threatens to force her to her knees. She turns to seek solace in the river, if solace is to be found, and pushes out her chin.

Struggling to adopt the same neutral tone, she says, 'Sabrina tells me to have courage, as she did when the soldiers threw her into the waters and the nymphs blessed her with divinity.'

Aaron has taught Hester more than herbs and potions.

'Should I follow her?' She takes a step closer to the water. Her legs are shaky. 'I should throw myself into the river, answer at last the nymphs' calls to me.' She takes another trembling step.

Aaron's fingers dig into her shoulder, his hand clutching a handful of coat to wrench her from the waters. He releases her, stands apart. Close enough, however, for the moon to reveal a reflection in his eyes of Hester's own troubled, tangled thoughts.

He tugs at his chin. 'That's one path. You're stronger than that.'

Hester waits, the trembling in her legs matching the roiling in her stomach.

It's an age before he offers his arm for her to take, if she wishes. She lays her hand on it.

'Come then,' he says. 'There's another learning waiting

for you. The way you desire.' He remains on the path, unmoving. 'I would warn you … you should understand … this way comes with sacrifice, and with hardships I would've spared you.'

Hope flickers, a tiny spark. She tightens her fingers on Aaron's arm. 'You'll teach me everything? Not send me away?' Aaron will save her after all. He won't allow her to be surrendered up to the fisherman and his house by the King's Shilling.

'*Everything* is a substantial word. I can offer, and if you choose to embrace what I offer, you'll take a different path. A harder path.' He covers Hester's hand with his own, ungloved one. 'It's a way I hoped for you to avoid, to leave it untrodden. You don't, can't understand …' He seeks her eyes.

She holds his gaze. 'No, I don't. But believe this. I would rather die than marry the fisherman.' Aaron's cold hand tightens on Hester's. 'It's my choice.' Her heart thumps. 'Let me choose, Aaron, let me choose.'

He glares across the river as if waiting for a sign, or expecting help. There's no sign as far as Hester sees and, finally, he leads her away, slowly.

The thumping of her heart threatens to strangle the air from her lungs.

*

Aaron opens the cottage door. He raises his eyebrows, silently offering Hester the chance to return to town, to the All Hallows fires, to dance with the fisherman. To be ordinary folk. He's aware what she will choose, and guilt strolls beside the knowledge. Or is it as Marianne insists, that what he wishes is of no matter? It will or will not happen.

Hester walks past him, chin up, and he closes the door behind her. The latch falls into place with a soft click.

A cheerful light is cast by the fire, which burns brightly despite Aaron's absence. Tongues of flame curl into beckoning fingers and Hester is drawn in, hot-cheeked and laughing as if greeting an old friend. A warm draught brushes Aaron's cheek with the softness of a sigh. After it passes, he feels the stillness of absence.

Hester shrugs off her overlarge coat, drops it on a chair and, her laughter gone, waits for whatever is to happen. Her tongue touches her top lip and withdraws behind her teeth.

Aaron takes the kettle steaming above the fire and pours its boiling contents into the cup holding the Lady's Mantel and lemon balm. He takes up the phial, uncorks it and spills two drops of hawthorn flower essence into the mixture. He lifts the lid from the jar of poppy seeds, otherwise lets it be. He is keenly aware of Hester watching him, his hands, his face. Beyond her, outside the window, the spirits jostle each other, keen to embrace a kindred soul.

Nothing happens for a long moment.

'I'm ready,' Hester prompts.

'Yes, I believe you are.' Aaron's voice trembles. 'You must know …'

'Know what?'

'I do this to bring you knowledge, to bring you courage for what lies ahead. Your destiny is set. The stars and moon, the river nymphs, Sabrina – they've understood this long before you did, before I did. I would have changed it, wish it were otherwise with all my tainted soul.' His voice catches. 'My wishes don't count.'

Still he hesitates, fingers spread over the jar of poppy seeds. Hester points at the jar, eyes fever-bright.

'Those too,' she says, and the strength of her voice compels Aaron to tip the seeds into the cup.

He offers the potion to her.

'Will you drink?'

*

Aware of the flecks in Aaron's dark eyes glistening as bright as polished amber in the firelight, Hester takes the clay cup eagerly, holds it close to her nose, breathing in the grassiness of Lady's Mantle, the citrus tang of lemon balm. Youth and beauty, the giving and receiving of love; these are what he wishes for her. And these he can bestow on anyone, a gift to a happier life. There is the hawthorn too, for courage. Yes, Hester needs courage.

A potion of love and courage.

And more.

Over the lip of the cup she eyes the open jar of poppy seeds sitting by the mortar among dried yellow flowers and curling leaves.

Other magic crouches in the hot liquid – magic to carry her into the shadowlands, to commune with spirits, to soar with them as gulls fly with the winds. She lets out a shuddering breath and drinks from the cup, one long swallow.

Aaron's eyes widen, snatch at Hester's heart. She gives it, willingly, happily.

She hands the cup to Aaron, who stares at it with a greed Hester has never seen before. A lava flow of heat boils through her veins. She pushes the cup into his face and his hands reach for it as if by instinct. One heartbeat of hesitation and he too drinks, deeply.

She bubbles with delight, throwing her arms wide, leaning into Aaron who draws away, his arms pushed forward, palms up to ward her off. Hester will not be denied. She falls against him, wraps her arms around his neck.

'Courage.'

Which of them whispers it? Aaron holds her and Hester is a gull wheeling into its nest on the cliffs, untouchable.

The leaping, flickering fire mocks the tawdry village flames and heats their sweat-slicked arms and legs tangled on the hearth mat. The wings of his hair brush Hester's burning face and her tongue seeks the sulphurous odour which settles on her lips. She grasps the power, savouring the dizzy joy.

Afterwards, there is the night sky, a white moon chasing tempestuous clouds. Flying above the river, gleeful, her heart pounding against Aaron's, holding each other close. Below them, a shower of red and gold sparks erupts from the cottage chimney in a celebration of fireworks. The wind whirls her hair into the silvered darkness and the spirits press close, gabbling their exultation.

From the star-dusted waters below, a triumphant Sabrina calls, *You are strong, Hester, you are strong.*

Chapter Fifteen

he sun wakes her. She is in her own bed. She half-opens her eyes, lazily closes them, and pulls her knees up, her arms hugging her legs.

Remembering ... a thrill courses through her, her heart too large to fit her chest.

She throws off the blankets and peers down at her body. It appears to be the same as yesterday, clothed in chemise and drawers. Her dress is folded on the chair under the open window. Reuben's coat is laid over it, a puddle of heavy wool falling to the floor. Sitting up, she swings her legs over the side of the bed, and winces.

She pushes the blanket to the floor and stands. A spot of blood stains her sheet.

Hester stares at the spot and licks the taste of sulphur on her lips. Her pulse quickens. Her path is chosen.

*

Aaron's cottage has cooled. The fire is reduced to grey ashes which he sweeps into a pan and scatters outside on the frosted ground. A pre-dawn wind lifts the finest of the ashes to swirl them about in ghostly imitation of Hester's hair swirling in the moonlight. He stands for a moment, pan in hand, before treading slowly inside.

He strips the blankets from the bed and rolls them into a cylinder which he ties with a belt. He weighs the bundle in his arms, unties the cylinder, takes one blanket and re-rolls it. The other he leaves, folded, on the bed. He searches along the shelves, ignoring his books to concentrate on choosing pots, bottles and phials which he sets at one end of the table. He lingers over some before passing on. When he has finished, he divides those on the table into two groups. He pulls a Gladstone bag from under the bed, shaking his head at its sorry state. He wipes the outside with a damp rag, promising the dry leather a refreshing tonic of dubbin at the earliest opportunity. He lifts the clasps, wincing at their stiffness and scraping a fingernail over the flecks of rust visible on their dull surfaces, and opens the bag. Inside, wisps of straw show how his medicines were once packed. With no straw to hand, Aaron cuts strips of hessian from his collecting bags to wrap the glass bottles. He packs his journals then carefully stows the jars and bottles into the bag. He hefts it to judge its weight. It will be manageable.

Four items remain on the table. Aaron touches each one. Hester will know.

Finally, hesitantly, he retrieves a slim glass phial with a rounded stopper from the Gladstone bag. Holding it between thumb and forefinger, he tips it upside down to loosen the tiny black seeds.

… a potion to give us power, Aaron …

He replaces the phial on a shelf, tucks them behind a brown stone bottle of plain vinegar. It is all the help he will offer Fate.

He packs his spare shirt, undergarments, tooth mug, shaving brush and razor into a small, scuffed valise also rescued from under the bed. When done, he pulls on his greatcoat, drapes his muffler loosely about his neck and sits on the bed to wait for full daylight.

You're leaving us?

Aaron doesn't want this conversation, but in death as in life, Marianne will be heard.

'Us?' he says, expressionless. 'Doubtless you will continue to haunt me.'

No. I cannot leave.

'Cannot leave what? Sabrina?'

Silence. Aaron thinks she has gone—

Why do you flee like a thief in the night?

'You of all people should ask?'

She is not me.

'She is not you.' His voice hardens. 'Which gives me hope.' He gets up from the bed, clasps his cold hands behind him and paces the four steps to the other end of the cottage. 'Last night was not meant as it happened. I can't stay, can't tempt her to come to me any more. What will that do to her? How will she find the way she wants if she is tainted with gossip and rumour?' He paces the four steps of the return journey and stands by the grimy window. Outside, a rain-misted dawn calls. It is time to leave. 'I've given her what she needs. Now she must find her own path.'

Given her what she needs? What seeds have you planted within the girl, Aaron?

'Courage, knowledge, desire. Those are the seeds I've planted.'

Think how much more she could be, under your wing.

Aaron relives the heat of the potion in his throat, Hester wrapped about him, laughing at the pure elation of the night flight. Feels also the pull of the river, calling to them.

It wasn't what he had wanted. Or rather, wasn't what he'd planned.

'That's why I cannot stay.'

He steps, fast, to the shelves, takes one last jar down, wrenches off its lid and scatters the dried creamy florets around the phials on the table. A sweet scent, hinting of almonds, rises. He breathes it in, gagging as if he is tasting rotten eggs, hating himself.

'Clear enough?'

As you wish. Marianne's whisper is cool on Aaron's cheeks. *As you wish.*

*

Hester dances down the stairs to whirl into the kitchen, kissing her mother on the cheek and exclaiming what a beautiful day it is before waltzing into the yard to fill the water buckets.

As she pumps the handle, her skin tingles with glorious memories, barely believing they are real, thinking perhaps they were visions arising from the potion she and Aaron shared, and if so, will he brew another? Except … the spot of blood on the sheet, the ache between her legs, waking in her own bed. Hester's stomach is liquid. She lifts her arms high and opens her mouth to the rain, her shawl slipping from her shoulders. Water spills over the lip of the bucket to splash her skirts. Giggling, she jumps away, and carries the buckets into the kitchen.

'Why didn't you answer the door to Mr Stokes last night?' Mother frowns at the pastry she is rolling.

Hester's happiness palls at this reminder of the fisherman. 'I had no wish to dance with him,' she snaps, 'or any other callow youth, bonfires or not.'

'You weren't here when we came home.'

This isn't a question, so Hester feels no need to reply.

'If people discover you were out on your own, in the night …'

The pause is meant for Hester to fill.

'You missed seeing me in my bed, Mother. I forgot to

empty my chamber pot and needed the privy.'

'Really?' Mother's sarcasm emphasises her disbelief. 'What do I tell Mr Stokes when he calls, asking where you were? Your reputation isn't improved by such goings on, innocent or not.' She throws out her floury hands, imploring Hester to understand. 'You're not a child wandering free across the fields, not any more. You shame me! I hear mutterings, avert my head from pitying glances. People gossip, say I can't keep my daughter under control.'

Mother's voice quivers and Hester badly wants to put her arms around her, tell her nothing is amiss, she behaves in the way a good daughter should. Only ... she is certain that boat has sailed.

Besides, the quiver in Mother's voice strengthens to a strangled sob and a heated, 'Your father's to blame, spoiling you, giving you too much freedom. Then leaving me to deal with the consequences.' She snatches up the wooden rolling pin lying beside the pastry and brandishes it at Hester. 'I should beat it out of you, as I beat nasty habits out of you when you were a child.'

Hester steps backwards, sympathy fled, nerves jumping.

The tabby leaps onto the kitchen table and stalks to a jug of cream near the edge. Mother flashes the rolling pin at the cat and Hester's nerves jump higher.

'Shoo, you dirty cat, get off the table!'

The cat flicks her tail, headbutts the jug to send it crashing to the flagstones. She jumps down after it, scrabbling in the thick yellow mess and covering her paws in the seconds before Mother lifts her by her scruff and tosses her through the scullery into the yard.

'No!' Hester cries. 'She's pregnant, you know she is!' She runs after the cat.

Mother's shout follows her into the cold. 'Hussies, the pair of you! I should cast you both from the house.'

In the yard, the cat sits under the bare shelter of a

rosemary bush, licking her paws.

Hester strokes the silky black ears. 'Did she hurt you?'

Did I do well?

Hester sinks to the cold pavings and hefts the cat into her lap.

'I suspect we haven't heard the last of being hussies,' she says, 'or of the stinking fisherman.'

Chapter Sixteen

No, Hester. Sim will collect the thread on his way home this evening. There's no need for you to go out.'

There is never a need for Hester to go out. Despite Mother's attempts at subtlety, Hester is aware she is a prisoner in her home. As with any prisoner, she yearns for freedom. More, she yearns for the river. She goes about feeding the hens, searching out eggs, sewing buttonholes and hems and her mind is filled with memories of the night wind lifting her hair, of the glitter of boat lights below her, of Sabrina's exultant cries and the spirits' joyful whispers. In her bed, she wraps her arms about herself, closes her eyes and imagines the licking heat of the cottage fire on her nakedness. She yearns to see the nymphs play among the trows and to talk to Sabrina. She longs to go to Aaron.

There is no chance to leave the house.

'Why am I kept hidden? Am I a mad woman?' she says to the tabby, heavy once more with a belly full of kittens. The tom, grown nicely rounded on Hester's handouts, hasn't been seen since All Hallows Eve.

The tabby rubs herself on the leg of the table where Hester is plucking a hen, one from the farm grown too old to lay.

You're a mad woman. And we're both hussies, remember?

Hester snorts and throws the tabby a scrap of skin.

As autumn moves towards winter, Hester is kept busy helping Mother, whose sewing business thrives. The townswomen bring their gowns to reshape to new fashions, and breeches and frocks to let out for growing children. They cast sidelong glances at Hester sitting in the light of the parlour window concentrating on her sewing, and ask Mother about the girl's health.

'We heard it was some affliction kept her from the All Hallows fires,' they say, eyeing Hester's robust glow.

'How sad she missed the fun. I understand Mr Stokes was most disappointed, although chivalrous of course.'

'Was it walking by the river in the damp, and so often, which gave her a chill?'

'And no bonnet, either, which could not have helped.'

Hester sews, listening to Mother's too insistent claims that, yes, it was sad, especially for Mr Stokes, when Hester was suddenly indisposed on All Hallows Eve. Thank the Lord she is recovered. Besides–

'Hester and Mr Stokes will marry in the spring,' Mother tells the visitors. 'A sturdy husband and lusty babies will soon settle her, keep her from her river wanderings.' Mother's lifted lips indicate she, at least, sees no harm in this indulgence. She gestures at her daughter. 'She cannot wait.'

Hester bends closer over her needle, horror roiling inside her to match the windswept waves of the river. She closes her ears to her mother's simpered conversation and takes herself to Aaron's cottage, to the table with its dried flowers, stubbed candles, his journal open as he scrawls notes about this concoction or that. Or, more often, summons the strength of his arms about her as they flew beneath the moon, listening to Sabrina's calls.

How long must she suffer this imprisonment? Why doesn't he come for her, as he did the night of All Hallows Eve? Doesn't he yearn for her as she does for him?

*

In the weeks before Christmas, the fisherman visits for Sunday tea. He shuffles his chair close to Hester's as they sit in the parlour's window bay. Mother pours from the big brown teapot and asks questions about the progress of work in the house by the King's Shilling.

'Hester will find it comfortable, when all's done,' the fisherman says with glowing eyes.

When he faces Hester, the great slice of lemon cake he's shovelled between his wet lips fails to shield her from his foetid breath. She shuffles away. He shuffles with her. His eyes rake her face, her neck and down to her breasts. His thick fingers open and close secretly on Hester's thigh. She stands to pick up her cup from the low table and nudges her chair with her foot when she sits, putting distance between them. His indulgent, lustful grin suggests he interprets these as the actions of a shy maid. He will bide his time, his curled lips say, although not patiently.

Rain falls heavily beyond the window, drowning the iron ring of horses' hooves on the cobbles and doing nothing to disguise the lack of conversation in the parlour.

When the fisherman has gone into the winter darkness, wrapped in his heavy woollen coat, cap pulled down over his ears, Mother draws the curtains and picks up a petticoat she is hemming.

'You will learn to love him,' she says.

'What is there to love?' Hester stoops to the coal bucket, desperate for the flames of a fire to thaw the icy block clogging the breath in her lungs.

Mother snorts. 'What about all this effort he's putting into his house to make you comfortable? He does well for a fisherman, and he's not unwilling to spend his earnings on his bride.'

'He smells of fish.'

'As do your brothers,' Mother responds with asperity.

'I don't have to lie with them.' Hester stirs the fire with the poker. The heat which flushes her face makes no difference to the chilled weight behind her ribs.

Mother puffs out an exasperated breath. 'You've brought this on yourself. A girl with your prettiness, with your quickness of wit, well, you could have set your cap at more than a fisherman.'

Hester has set her cap at more than a fisherman. She can't say this to Mother.

On those Sundays when the rain and sleet are recovering their strength for the next onslaught and watery sunshine reflects off the cobbles, the fisherman will latch his fingers onto Hester's arm and walk her through the town and along the river path. A smirking Sim accompanies them.

While the fisherman doesn't try to kiss Hester, his salmon breath falls hot on her cheek when he pulls her close to his side. His arm brushes her breast.

The conversation is one-sided.

'Put in one of those new ranges,' he says, adopting the air of one bestowing diamond tiaras. 'A cushioned chair too, covered in brocade, under the front room window for your sewing.'

Hester pulls her cloak closer to defend against the biting wind off the water, lowers her head to hide her smiles at Sabrina's whispered mockery, and doesn't ask if this sewing is meant as a means of income or for her own entertainment.

It doesn't matter.

Later, alone in the kitchen, Hester tells the tabby, 'When the weather warms, we'll go to Aaron.'

The tabby, stretched in her basket by the fire with her kittens at her teats, twitches her ears.

Chapter Seventeen

hile Christmas cheer brings a bloom to Catherine's cheeks, the days following leave her tired beyond weariness. Wrapped in the softness of a deep green cashmere shawl, she lies on the brocaded sofa in the drawing room with book and sewing at hand and rarely attended to.

'It's these long, dark days,' she complains to her aunt. 'How I wish for sunshine and blue sky!'

Aunt Lottie fusses and insists Catherine eats the broth Mrs Bryce makes, full of tender white chicken, carrots, potatoes and brown onions, and guaranteed to bring colour to Catherine's white face.

'Is it made with water from St Ceyna's well?' Catherine asks Mrs Bryce, willing the housekeeper to say yes, for then the broth's goodness would be enhanced by the water's magic. The tingle of sherbet fizziness on her tongue is as real now as on the summer day two years ago.

'If only it was, Miss Catherine, if only it was.'

When Catherine dozes, she dreams of the well. Hester

sits on the low stone wall alongside her, both of them wriggling their bare toes in the cold clear water, delighting in newfound friendship and, for Catherine, the audacity of her adventure. Despite, or perhaps because of her constant imaginings, the afternoon has taken on the quality of a dream, a painting hazily recalled or a piece of music remembered for its cadence rather than its individual notes. Her first notion on seeing Hester bent over the well, that here was a vision of a youthful St Ceyna, has firmed into conviction. Hester and her sacred waters imbued Catherine with a wellbeing she hadn't felt for years. She craves its return.

Catherine would love to learn more about this girl who did so much good for her, to visit her if she knew where to find her, and to go to the well. She doesn't, however, have any idea where to start. Whom can she ask? The dreams remain dreams and Catherine wearies her way through the dark days believing her eyes will never again gaze on birds flying in an azure sky.

This grey afternoon, Aunt Lottie has a visitor. Catherine is well enough to sit on the sofa, swallow a mouthful of tea and run her cake fork through Mrs Bryce's sponge filled with red jam and cream. The conversation turns to gowns once the state of the weather (cold), the state of the roads in and out of Shiphaven (frozen mud) and the state of the country (abysmal) are dealt with.

'I'm thinking of having one of my winter capes re-lined,' Mrs Allan says, picking up her black China tea in its violet-patterned cup. 'A more fashionable colour, possibly a cheerful red with gold trim.'

'How lovely!' Aunt Lottie appeals to Catherine. 'Don't you think so, Catherine?'

'Oh yes, beautiful.' Catherine glances to the window where the greyness is deepening to an early night. 'We need cheer in all this gloom.'

'Will you ask the Misses Stanleys to do it for you?'

The Misses Stanleys are Aunt Lottie's preferred seamstresses when local rather than Cheltenham or London skills are acceptable.

'Normally, yes,' Mrs Allan says. 'However, I've recently been told such good things of Mrs Williams' sewing, and of the daughter too, I've decided to try there. After all, how much damage can they do re-lining a cape?'

Aunt Lottie sets her rose-patterned cup on its matching saucer. 'Mrs Williams?'

'Yes.' Mrs Allan tuts. 'Such a sad tale. Mrs Williams, her three sons and a daughter, had to leave their farm when the father died. The oldest farmed, could have taken over.' She leans as far as her tight bodice allows. 'Only, my husband tells me Mr Courtney-Brown was keen to sell. Wouldn't renew the tenancy.' A sorrowful shaking of her head. 'Not profitable, is what my husband says.'

Sewing? Farm? Catherine pays closer attention. There can't be too many farmers' wives who take in sewing. Is this Hester's family? It troubles her to think of the girl suffering like this, and Catherine not suspecting.

'The daughter,' she says, 'do you know her name?'

Her aunt looks at her curiously.

Mrs Allan frowns, puzzled. 'No idea. I do believe, however, that while she's nimble with a needle and thread, she's also … well, to be kind … strange. A little too bold.'

This could be Hester.

'Strange? Bold?' Aunt Lottie takes the bait of gossip.

'Spends more time than she should on the river path, by herself.' Mrs Allan lifts her forefinger to her lips. 'It's said she *talks* to the river.'

It is Hester, Catherine is certain. Smiling, she returns to her study of the window, her fingers playing with the fringe of the cashmere shawl.

Aunt Lottie puts her hand to her throat. 'Doesn't her

mother keep her in hand?'

Mrs Allan raises her eyebrows as if the impossibility of mothers keeping their daughters in hand is something she understands and pities. 'Difficult, although poor Mrs Williams has help in that direction these days.' She simpers over her tea. 'I believe the girl is to be married. To a local fisherman. Older, settled, has his own house down by the King's Shilling.' She shifts forward with an almost-wink of her eye. 'And not all paid for by salmon and elvers according to what folks say.'

Aunt Lottie raises an eyebrow. 'Haven't such going-ons long passed in these regions?'

'Seems not, Miss Michaels. It's still there, on the river at night, when respectable folk are abed.'

'It would take a strong, foolhardy man to tackle the river at night, in pure darkness, surely?'

'Not sure about foolhardy, Miss Michaels. Strong, yes, which is what the Williams' girl needs. A strong hand to tame her.'

Catherine's chest tightens. Hester being tamed by a strong, old fisherman and a smuggler to boot? She wants to believe it isn't Hester after all.

Their guest hasn't finished with her tale.

'Mrs Williams has had much to bear.' She shakes her head strongly enough to send the ribbons from her swept-up hair swaying about her shoulders. 'Which is why I believe it my duty to give the woman a try. I believe she's been sewing for people in the village for some time, and more often now in town, and her reputation is solid.'

Here is a way to discover the truth. Catherine puts her hands together.

'We should do the same, Aunt, try Mrs Williams' skills,' she entreats. 'I have … I have … a jacket which needs taking in. We can see how well she does with it.'

Mrs Allan bows her head at Catherine. 'I'm sure she'd be highly appreciative.'

*

As it is, Aunt Lottie needs persuading to allow Catherine to walk the two hundred yards up the hill to Mrs Williams' dressmaking shop and home.

'It's too cold.'

'The sun is shining today, Aunt! Please let me take advantage of it, please.'

'The road is muddy.'

'No, they swept the cobbles not two hours ago and laid fresh straw.'

Her father is called upon, and to Catherine's astonishment, sides with her.

'The girl needs fresh air from time to time and the sun will do her good, bring a spot of rose to her cheeks. Make sure she wears her warmest coat over her warmest clothes, and Mrs Bryce has hot food and tea waiting your arrival home.'

On the slow walk, Catherine see-saws between excitement at the prospect of meeting Hester and consoling herself that this girl who is to marry a smuggling fisherman won't be Hester. She wriggles her gloved fingers inside her fur muff and tries not to let her anxiety seep into her breathing.

Hester opens the door to admit them. Her wide, surprised smile lights Catherine's heart despite her worries. Hester appears to capture Catherine's warning flicker of her eyes to her aunt, and her greeting is polite, not at all effusive.

Catherine and Aunt Lottie decline tea because Catherine is not fully well and their visit needs to be short. Catherine dons the too-large jacket and moves in a slow circle in the weak sunshine filtering through the parlour windows.

'A beautiful colour.' Hester tilts her head to one side. 'The colour of late summer leaves on old oaks,' she breathes in Catherine's ear as she pinches in a side and pins it. 'And this lining!' she says aloud. 'As smooth to the touch as a pony's brushed mane, don't you think, Miss Catherine?'

Catherine holds in her giggles until Hester asserts, 'I do believe the ripples in this lining remind me of sunlight on sacred water.'

Catherine's irrepressible snort earns a frown from her aunt and a flustered, 'Don't be fanciful, Hester. Miss Catherine is not here to listen to your nonsensical talk,' from Mrs Williams.

Miss Catherine is, however, there expressly for that purpose. Already Hester is working her magic on Catherine's wellbeing, without the aid of sacred water.

'My daughter is too easily excited these days.' Mrs Williams is all apologies. 'It's the excitement over the wedding. She's going to be a spring bride and she can't wait.'

Catherine catches Hester's eye as she helps her out of the pinned jacket. The idea of this beautiful, bright girl living the life of a fisherman's wife in a cottage made dank by river fog, makes her nauseous. Yet her unease doesn't appear to be shared, for Hester lowers her eyes, her lips lifted in a modest smile.

A date for completion is agreed. Money isn't discussed. The housemaid will collect the garment and the bill to be paid at the same time.

When they are done, Hester helps Catherine into her long coat before holding the fur muff for her hands. She brushes Catherine's fingers and smiles – a different, conspiratorial smile this time – and Catherine fancies Hester's eyes are bright with secrets. More secrets than the shared harmless deception they had played. Something has changed in the girl. No, not a girl. A young woman.

Catherine mulls it over on the short journey home. Yes, Hester is a young woman, with a secret. She yearns for it to be a happy secret and hopes she will soon be able to learn more. She will contrive to visit again, somehow.

Chapter Eighteen

atherine dreams of Hester. Not the Hester who peered intently into her eyes the summer day by St Ceyna's well. She dreams of Hester dressed in a stained, drab, shapeless gown, alone in a chill, bare cottage waiting for the old fisherman's damp return from his night's endeavours on the river. Will he bring Hester a gift from his illicit booty? Perfume? Silks for a new petticoat? Ribbons for her hair? Catherine finds it hard to dream these luxuries. Instead, Hester is a fragile shadow of her robust self, worn out by scrubbing fish scales from putrid trousers and river mud from flagstones, from bearing child after child and peeling vegetables for a pot which contains poacher's meat, if any meat at all.

Her dreams worsen with fever. She cries out, shifts her aching limbs from place to place in sweaty sheets which need to be changed hourly. Her head fills with a kaleidoscope of images, all centred on Hester.

'I knew it was a bad idea to take you out.' Aunt Lottie bends over her with a cool flannel smelling of lavender.

'Joseph is to blame.'

Papa comes home from work and lays his warm, dry hand on Catherine's wet forehead. 'Dr Newton is on the way, my love. He'll give you something to reduce the fever. You'll be well soon.'

'Hester,' Catherine mumbles. 'Hester ...'

'Who?'

'I think ... yes, I believe it's the name of Mrs Williams' daughter, the dressmaker,' Aunt Lottie says.

'Williams? Mrs Stanley Williams?'

'No longer.' Aunt Lottie dampens the flannel, folds it and places it across Catherine's forehead. 'Why?' she says. 'Are you acquainted with the family?'

Acquainted? Catherine's heated mind takes the word in and rolls it around until it gathers substance, like rolling a snowball on a winter morning.

'Yes, barely, many years ago.' Papa takes out his pocket watch and examines it with a frown. 'What could be keeping Dr Newton?' And then, 'What do you mean by no longer?'

'Mr Williams died. Gossip tells Mr Courtney-Brown sold his farm, so the widow and her children, all quite grown, had to move into town. She's the dressmaker, the visit you allowed your daughter to go on, with this result.' She gives a sharp shake of her head, lifts the flannel, dips it in the cool, scented water. 'Yes, Hester is the daughter. Catherine took a liking to the lass.'

Catherine's lips move to shape the word, Hester. Acquainted with the family. Hester. Her fleece-filled brain catches the words, holds on to them. Hester ...

'What do you say, my love?' Aunt Lottie bends closer to listen to Catherine's whisper.

'Doctor is here, sir.' Mrs Bryce is at the door.

'Good, good, send him in, don't dawdle.'

*

While Dr Newton attends Catherine, with Lottie present, Joseph stands before the red glow of the drawing room fire and lets his mind pick over his sister's scant information.

Mrs Stanley Williams. Lydia Bennett, as she'd been. Daughter of a well-to-do draper in Shiphaven and a single child. Lydia's burnished chestnut curls, teasing eyes and ready laugh had captured his young and vulnerable heart. He said nothing, however, too poor in those days to aspire to a wife who would expect a measure of comfort. He badly underestimated Lydia Bennett, who broke his vulnerable heart (and Joseph suspects other swains' hearts) by marrying the popular Stanley Williams and becoming a farmer's wife.

No longer. Joseph has heard rumours of Courtney-Brown's recent high-handed dealings with his tenants. While he has some sympathy for the landowner having to deal with recalcitrant old farmers resisting modern ways, he believes there are more ways than one to skin a cat. The stories of Courtney-Brown threatening evictions and non-renewals irritate him. This particular story, however, angers him. There were sons who could have carried on after their father's death? Grown sons, who surely could have been persuaded to take a more progressive view? It was scandalous of Courtney-Brown to throw them off. And all for the sake of profit. Although Joseph is fond of a profit, he prays he makes his without damage to others.

He tuts quietly. What business is it of his? He has more than enough of his own problems.

Lottie's lips are set in a straight line when she enters the drawing room ahead of Dr Newton. The doctor's features are set in their usual non-committal blandness.

'Well?' Joseph takes a step closer.

'As I've said to Miss Michaels, keep her cool and when she can take it, light broth.'

'That's for now.' Joseph is at pains not to sound peevish.

This is an old conversation with Dr Newton, and with other doctors too, more expensive ones from further afield. 'Can't something, anything, be done to address this long-term weakness which my daughter suffers?'

Dr Newton gives a slight shake of his head. 'There seems to be no physical cause beyond a general lack of robustness. Good food, rest, and when the weather allows, fresh air and sunlight.' His smile suggests there's no real need to fret. 'She'll recover in time, I've no doubt.'

'Forgive me, sir. You doctors have been saying the same thing these last several years.' This time Joseph doesn't bother to keep his annoyance under control. He could be a doctor too if this is all the prescription required. 'Admit it, sir, no one of the medical profession has any idea what ails her.'

'My dear Mr Michaels—'

Joseph walks to the door, holds out his hand to the doctor. 'Thank you for your time, and for your assurances. I wish you a good journey home.'

*

In the night, the fever breaks. Catherine sleeps. Her dreams remain with Hester – a younger, happy Hester, perched on the stones of St Ceyna's well, her bare feet kicking up water which glitters in the shafts of sunlight between the beeches. Water sprites cavort about her head and shoulders, pearly wings flashing. They touch their tiny feet lightly to her face, her neck, her bare arms before springing into the air to ride the sunbeams eddying like gold-lit whirlpools.

'Imagine,' Hester says with teasing eyes. 'Imagine bathing with St Ceyna in her well. Imagine …'

Catherine sighs in her sleep, luxuriating in the soothing coolness of the water suffusing her limbs; her hair loose, drifting on the clear surface.

Chapter Nineteen

s winter strengthens its grey hold on the countryside, Hester becomes aware of changes in her body. In her bed at night, she touches her swollen breasts and counts back.

Sitting under the parlour window edging a handkerchief and listening to the wind bludgeoning the glass, she eyes the fire and wishes the room was less stuffy.

Mother glances up from the cape she is lining with new silk. 'Didn't I say you'd learn to love him?' She puts her fingers to her mouth. 'Because surely it's love making you bloom. You'll be a beautiful bride with your posy of meadowsweet.'

Hester flushes and shrinks into her chair.

Later, pleading the need to finish Mrs Bailey's son's breeches, she sits alone in the parlour, the breeches untouched on her lap. The wind has wandered off to bother other folk and taken the clouds with it. Moonlight streams through a gap where the curtains refuse to meet.

Putting the breeches aside, Hester kneels before the fire

to stoke the ashy coals into a last burst of heat. She stares into the flames, breathing in the imagined scent of Lady's Mantle, remembering gold-flecked eyes and the night wind in her hair. She wraps her arms about her, closes her eyes and summons a lover's hot breath, not mere coals, to heat her cheeks.

Her mother's words about love and blooming have harried her all day. Soon, Mother will be speaking less of love, and questioning Hester about her lack of monthly rags. Her stomach grows nauseous at the thought of the shame she will soon pile on Mother's long-suffering head.

'Aaron loves me,' she whispers to the cat. 'He'll take me in, I can go to him.'

Males. They're all tomcats, wanting one thing. You shouldn't rely on him.

Hester ignores the warning. 'We'll marry and be wise folk together, healing children, caring for poor, sick folk.' The image shines like a bright star in the heavens.

What about the fisherman?

Hester conjures scarred hands and stinking breath. A shudder runs through her.

She climbs the stairs to her room, prepares for bed. When sleep evades her, she wraps a quilt about her shoulders and gazes through the puckered glass at the darkened windows of the shops and houses opposite. Those snowflakes which have not settled on the roofs, the cobbled lanes or the narrow gardens have been herded away by the wind like sheep before a shepherd's dog. A white stillness smothers the town. The cottage will be blanketed too, with Aaron sitting by the fire, reading, writing in his journal ... dreaming of Hester, wanting her. Her skin prickles with longing, and fear.

Courage. Sabrina's call rises from the river, slides through the gap in the window frame. *Be strong.*

Hester clutches the muslin-wrapped feverfew around

145

her neck. She is strong. She has courage. Waiting is over, has already gone on too long.

She throws off the quilt, and with trembling hands snatches a dress from its hook, struggles into it over her nightgown, pulls on stockings.

The household sleeps. Hester creeps down the narrow stairs, hand to the wall to lighten her footsteps. In the last of the firelight, she takes Reuben's old coat from its hook, wriggles into it, pushes her feet into her boots and unlatches the front door. It creaks as she opens it. She holds her breath.

Only the soft stir of the cat in her basket.

Outside, the night is lit with frozen stars lorded over by a full moon. Hester has no need of a lantern. She hurries past the graveyard, where she searches in vain for a glimpse of Father, wanting his blessing to bolster her shaky bravery; past the Bargeman, where the sailors' and fishermen's bawdy songs stagger drunkenly into the road and she prays the lustful singers won't decide this is the time to seek their boats and huts; and across the fields where sheep glimmer white against the moonlit blue of the snow.

When she lifts her coat and frock to cross a stile, her boots slip on the icy wood. She catches herself on a thorny bramble, winces at the stabs into her palm. A hunting owl calls encouragement, steadying her breathless worry. She blunders on, moonlight shimmering on water below her on one side, blue-tinted fields on the other.

Wind from the river lifts Sabrina's voice to wrap her in damp comfort.

'I am strong,' Hester echoes.

By the time she reaches the place where Aaron delivered her from the river nymphs, the chill in her feet matches the cold of her glove-less hands. With frozen fingers, she wraps Reuben's coat tighter about her, reaches for the feverfew and trudges on. The moon guides her into the darkness, across the fields, past the sheep, to Aaron.

His cottage shows no light. He'll be sleeping. She doesn't knock. Instead she tries the latch. The door swings wide, welcoming her as it has a thousand times.

She is met with a cold stillness. There are no ruby-flecked ashes left by the evening's fire, let alone flames leaping to redden the cast iron pot which hangs on its tripod. There is no scent of lavender or rosemary, no yellow candle flames burnishing glass phials and copper bowls.

The moon continues to be her friend, sending a stream of shifting beams through the window to light the table and the shelves, the stripped bed with its one folded blanket, and the two chairs by the swept fireplace.

Hester stands in the doorway, her arms wrapped about her waist. Her breathing, already fast from the floundering journey across the fields, quickens. Her frail courage frays.

There's no rescue here.

'No!'

Behind her the rising wind carries Sabrina's muted voice from the dark waters. *You are not ordinary folk, Hester. You chose your path on All Hallows Eve. You are strong.*

'I am strong.'

Her trembling legs carry her inside. She closes the door and pushes her back into its solidity while she glances about.

The shelves which held the results of her lessons are as thick with dark gaps as an old man's gummy smile. She walks across, recalling what had once filled those gaps. Dried yarrow, Beggar's Blanket, other leaves, seeds and various potions which could cure much of what ailed the common folk and their animals. She turns to the table where she has spent countless tranquil hours. Usually covered in iron weights, clay measuring cups, scraps of paper scrunched up beside dried-out ink pots and old saucers holding candle stumps, the table is as tidy as the bed and the hearth.

It isn't bare, however.

She picks up a glass jar of dried leaves labelled Raspberry Leaf, tipping it side to side to watch the leaves fall into each other. She presses the jar to her belly, a cry gathering in her throat.

Does Aaron know, or guess? Does he think she might seek to rid herself of this – her, his, their – babe? Or has he left it to ease her birthing pangs when the time comes, a surrogate for his inability to offer practical comfort? She swallows down her pain, sets the jar in its place and moves her fingers over the mortar and pestle he has left for her, to a stitched muslin bag. A new gift of feverfew?

More courage is needed. Greater strength too.

Hard by the feverfew, the milk-coloured stone bottle of belladonna potion gleams in the moonlight. Its lightness when Hester lifts it tells her about half remains.

'To forget past loves.' Bitterness wells in her gut.

Finally, she runs her finger through the dried flowers, the colour of stale cream, scattered between the jar, the stone bottle, and the pestle and mortar. Meadowsweet.

His desertion screams its message into the grey room.

'You will carry meadowsweet when you wed a lusty farmer,' he had told her, 'and you'll bear him dark-curled, blue-eyed girls and sturdy boys.'

He is telling her – despite what passed, despite the gift he gave her – that she must marry the fisherman, have his babies, make Mother happy. He is telling her she must assure the townspeople she is ordinary folk after all.

The bitterness rises from her gut into her throat, where it combines with a grief as great as the sorrow she suffered for Father. She clasps the new muslin bag to her stomach and breathes, deeply, slowly, reaching for the fury which lurks in her anguish.

How dare he? Has he no belief in her strength, her determination? Has he no belief in his own strength?

She returns to the shelves, pushing the remaining jars

aside, fingers scrabbling in the dust. A brown stone bottle throws itself to the flagstones with a crash to wake the dead and Hester jumps. The biting tang of vinegar overwhelms the meadowsweet.

And there it is, behind where the bottle had stood.

She pulls the phial with its rounded stopper from the shelf and walks with it to the window, showing it to the moonlight. The tiny black seeds glint like polished onyx. Hester runs her hands through her curls and laughs.

The shadow of another laugh echoes in the cottage, and Hester is glad.

*

There is only the night sky, the white moon sailing the tempestuous clouds as smoothly as the ferry gliding on its great cables across the river. Above it all, Hester rides the wind, joyous, her hair whirling into the silvered darkness. The muslin bag is warm on her skin, her clothes warm against her body.

Sabrina reaches up, calling: *You are strong, Hester.*

In the moonlit cottage, the jar of raspberry leaf sits unopened on the table. On the wet flags of the floor, the shards of the bottle of belladonna potion mingle with the fallen brown bottle's vinegared remains.

Chapter Twenty

he tabby is smug and offers no comfort, reminding Hester of her warning she could not rely on Aaron. Not once he'd had his way with her.

'Had his way with me?'

The cat is wrong about Aaron's intent. Hester is certain this was no seduction. The puzzle, the thing which grieves her deeply, is why, the night of All Hallows Eve, did he offer her this gift, far beyond what she ever knowingly wanted? Then thrown her into the oafish fisherman's bed.

Where she will not go.

The cat is right on one count. Hester can't rely on Aaron to save her.

'Mother.' Hester puts aside the sewing she has just taken up. Her hands tremble too badly to thread a needle.

'Yes?' Mother keeps her eyes on the jacket she is embroidering.

'I will not, cannot, marry Jem Stokes.' Hester sits straighter in her chair, fingers clasped on her lap.

Mother looks up sharply. 'What are you saying? I thought

you were learning to love him, at least accept him, with love to follow, as I said would happen.'

'Love him? Accept him?' Hester's fingers tighten. 'Never.'

Mother huffs. 'I understand the fisherman mightn't be your first choice—'

'Whichever choice he is, I cannot marry him.' Hester's voice cracks. 'I … I … I'm bearing someone else's child.' While heat burns her cheeks, something hard lodges below her breastbone. It might be courage.

Mother lets go of the jacket and slaps her hand to her chest. 'A child? You're having a baby?'

Her voice rises on the last word as if Hester has said she's bearing a devil-horned monster. She might be.

'Yes, Mother. So I can't, with any integrity, marry Mr Stokes.'

'Integrity?' Mother chokes on the word. 'How dare you talk of integrity.' She pushes the jacket aside and stands, swaying as if considering fainting.

Hester stands also. In the small, dim parlour they glare at each other.

'Who is he?' Mother's tone is as icy as the cobbles outside.

'I won't tell you. And it doesn't matter, for he's no longer here.' Hester tries to keep acrimony from her voice.

'Used and abandoned, like a … a …'

'I'm not a whore, Mother. I was glad, and I'm glad still, to be bearing his child.'

'Glad? Glad?' Mother spits the words with such venom, Hester shrinks away. Her pulse beats loud in her ears.

'I should throw you into the street, where you belong,' Mother hisses. One eyelid twitches in its own fury. 'Your father will be spinning in his grave.'

Hester blanches. She will try to find out what Father has to say. She rather believes he would offer kindness and comfort, despite his undoubted disappointment.

Mother clenches her hands together, unclenches them, searches the parlour as if inspiration hides in its distempered walls. 'We'll bring the wedding forward. Mr Stokes need never be aware the child isn't his, if we–'

'I will tell him myself.' It would be a sweet moment.

'No!'

'You can't stop me.'

Mother slaps Hester's cheek, sending her lurching into a table. They glower at each other like warring tomcats and Hester determines she will win this war.

*

'You old dog. Couldn't wait, hey?' Sim is hunched over his tankard of cider, his unshaven face close to Jem's. He winks.

Jem breathes in the boisterous fug of the Bargeman and grabs the lifeline with no less relief than if he was overboard on the river. Hester's news, given to him yesterday when he made his normal visit for Sunday tea, had stunned, then infuriated him. She showed no shame, simply a straightforward confession. No, not a confession, a bald statement. His instinct had been to beat her. He had raised his hand, and she had glared in a way which said: I dare you. Jem had lowered the hand and stamped from the house with Mrs Williams' gabbled pleadings following him into the street.

His fury is a tightly coiled rope ready to spill into untamed tangles if he loosens his grip on it. Another man has taken the cherry from this sweet cake and Jem Stokes is left with crumbs. Worse, he is left with egg on his face. He can plead morality and cast the bitch off. That won't stay his fishing brethren's jeers. Sleepless in the dark night which followed, he heard their mockery, scorning old Jem for not being quick enough, man enough, to get to this lustful beauty first. If he plays the saddened, benevolent betrothed and marries her, they will snigger through all the years to come, point out how the child in no way resembles his 'father', poke fun at the cuckold.

If they find out.

'Ha!' He echoes Sim's wink. 'Playful lass, your sister. Knows how to set a man on fire.'

Sim grimaces. 'Seems so,' he says. 'Family's got your back, Jem. Ma won't let Hester out of her sight until the wedding, if wedding it's to be?'

In last night's restlessness Jem also imagined the tainted, sinful Hester beneath him. He savours the hot memory and decides crumbs can be tasty too.

'Why wouldn't there be? The right thing to do and all.'

Sim grins and raises his tankard. 'Welcome to the family.'

*

'Whose is it?'

If Hester is her mother's prisoner, the fisherman is the prison guard. Her brothers are at the Rope and the Bargeman. Mother keeps to the kitchen.

Hester winces at the tightness with which Stokes clutches her arms. His thumbs press her skin to the bone.

'You're hurting me.'

He squirms closer, pale eyes slitted. 'You've hurt me, girl, hurt me bad, and I swear to you I *will* find out who's the daddy of this bastard, and when I do–'

'It's useless, Mr Stokes. The daddy is nowhere hereabouts.'

'Threw you off after he'd had his taste, hey? Poked you and left you to carry the consequences?'

Hester lets the words float through the coal-scented air. She is a snail curled in its shell, twitching a long-stemmed eyeball out from time to time to have more vitriol poured on her. Within her shell, her refuge is memory. The fire dancing, licking her arms and legs with its warm tongues. Her ecstasy, the laughter, the moon on the clouds.

Sabrina's joyful: *You are strong, Hester.*

'I am strong,' Hester whispers to herself.

'No worry to me.' The fisherman tugs at Hester's arms to force her forward as if she's a recalcitrant cow at milking. 'I've a lifetime to learn the truth.' He thrusts his chest into hers and kisses her.

Hester has suffered this trick before. She jerks her head aside and it is her cheek which receives the wet smack of his blubbery lips. He growls and shoves her away.

'Not long, my love, not long.' He grins, strides to the door, collects his hat and coat and walks into the street. A freezing draught marks his departure.

The wedding is set for the beginning of February.

'Mr Stokes is very keen.' Mother titters at the customers. 'And as Hester cannot wait either, we must indulge love and bring the marriage forward.'

The customers hmm and hold their teacups close to their mouths to hide their sniggers.

Hester keeps to her sewing and marvels at the strength of pride which can make a barefaced liar out of her hitherto righteous and respectable mother. A mother whose affection she has never before questioned. When Mother nagged her to sit straight, speak properly and walk with grace, she did so with her own gentle grace. There was loving goodwill behind the admonishments; this was all for Hester's ultimate benefit. A visceral need to be accepted, however, has triumphed over loving goodwill. Hester hardens her heart against this further loss.

Will is sad.

'Sad on two accounts.' He sits with Hester at the kitchen table late one night. Their mother has taken herself to bed and Sim is at the King's Shilling with Jem Stokes.

'Two accounts?'

'I don't think much of Jem Stokes.' Will taps his fingers on the table top. 'You're aware what they say of him, Sister?

How he's come by much of his money by smuggling, in cohorts with the landlord of the Shilling?'

'Smuggling?' The notion of the fisherman defying the respectability of ordinary folk holds a moment's glamour for Hester.

'Yes.' Will folds his arms. 'Allowing the Courtney-Browns of the world to buy their brandy cheap.'

Hester's fleeting admiration dissolves into disgust, one more provocation to wrestle her way out of this tangle.

'And the second reason?'

'I don't need to spell that out. What I don't understand, given your dislike of Jem Stokes, is why not give up your lover's name and marry him instead?'

'Because, as I tell Mother, as I tell you, a hundred times, he's not here to marry.'

Will pats her hand and breathes a gusty breath.

Reuben comes home for a short time to pour oil on the troubled waters. He expresses neither sadness nor disappointment despite his religious vocation.

'You will have to make the best of it with Mr Stokes, Hester. Mother tells me he's comfortably off and is taking this with dignity. That speaks well for him.'

Hester doesn't tell of the smuggling, or show Reuben the thumbprint bruises on her arms.

In her attic room at night, she inspects those bruises by candlelight. Thumbs are a small weapon compared with an open-fingered palm, or a boot. Hester is afraid to the point of nausea for the baby. The fisherman will have no regard for its tiny life. This, more than her own fate, feeds her desperation. She gazes into the night. A freezing wind hammers at the glass, snow flurries whirl the chimney smoke into wild dances across the roofs. Sabrina calls on the wind: *Be strong, be wise, do what you must do.* The goddess is with her. Hester steels herself to do what she must do.

While Will avoids his sister's eye, Sim catches it as often

as possible. He gives Hester straight-lipped smug grins which suggest he's in on a mighty joke at her expense. More than her mother's frequent weeping, those smirks trouble her and fortify her resolve.

Once, when she is alone in the parlour, Sim comes home earlier than normal. The tabby lifts her head from her basket to bask in the odour of fish. Sim hangs his coat on the peg.

'Someone asked today about the young so-called gentleman you used to see by the river.' He gives Hester a supercilious leer. 'Not been spotted hereabouts since before Christmas, this someone remarked.'

Hester gazes directly at her brother. 'I spoke to him once.'

'T'aint speaking I'm meaning.' Sim's grin broadens.

He takes three long steps to stand over Hester, clasps her shoulders with dirty hands. She tries to shrug him off.

'Shame our dad ain't here to see what all his spoiling did to his precious daughter.' He lifts his hands, pats Hester's hair as if she is a pet dog. 'It's our mam I feel sorry for, trying to make a *lady* out of you, and look now. No better than the rest of us after all. Worse in fact.' He wanders off, chuckling.

Hester pinches in her lips and addresses the tabby.

'We'll see who has the last laugh, won't we?'

Chapter Twenty One

he hardest part about leaving the sleeping house is persuading the tabby that a journey in the darkest hours of the night in a winter storm, with the wind blustering snow against the window, is a good idea. Or does Hester use the need to persuade the cat, to convince herself?

It's the night before the wedding. After tomorrow, she'll be in his hands. Her fear, her indignation, mean the decision is right, whatever storms she has to struggle through. Her mother's sure humiliation weighs heavily, balanced against the suffering this same mother would force on her. Hester hardens her heart.

'I'm going to carry you in this bag,' she whispers to the cat. She opens the hessian sack and peers in. 'See, my blanket's in there, you'll be warm. It's me who has to make my way in the dark, in the snow.'

Why are we doing this?

'Because I will not marry the fisherman.' Sleeting snow and freezing darkness are warmer than Jem Stokes' mouth.

Hester layers her clothing – two chemises, two petticoats, two pair of stockings, two pair of drawers, a summer frock under her winter one, until she begins to understand the clumsy slowness full pregnancy will be hers to bear in the months to come. She shuffles down the stairs, breath catching at each creak, and into the scullery. She feels about in the near pitch blackness for the bag she hid earlier, with candles, matches, a few torn sheets of newspaper and a small cooking pot. She adds this to the sack where the cat curls in the blanket. Mother will notice the pot's absence and doubtless imagine the witch's brews bubbling inside it. Hester sighs a joyless smile.

A second sack holds flour, a handful of winter-stored carrots, apples and potatoes. And, in a show of optimism, seeds of thyme, camomile and parsley to plant in the spring. She will forage for food. Even in winter the fields and forest will provide. She shuffles into the parlour, squeezes into Reuben's coat, ties a muffler around her neck and pulls a hat close over her curls.

Listening for a moment for any stirring in the bedrooms above, she hears only the wind. She swallows down her fear, lets her resentful anger rise in its place and leaves the house, carrying a shuttered lantern. The night is too dark, the shadows of the church too deep, for any hope of glimpsing Father. Hester prays he sees her, imagines the touch of his rough farmer's hand on her shoulder, urging her on.

Her breath comes in short gasps as she slips and slides on the dark cobbles making her way out of the town, afraid some sleepless person peers from their window at the moment she passes. Burdened with the bags looped over her shoulders, awkward with the lantern, she leaves the path through the reeds by the river to wade across dark fields in calf-deep snow. Her boots and skirts are sodden, her feet chilled. With her light showing no more than a step or two ahead, she can only hope she stays true to her path. She sweats with the exertion and when the sweat chills on her body she shivers as in a fever.

One step after another, heart hammering.

Lumbering over a stile, tripping on its stone steps, her snug bed in the attic room looms in her mind like a vision of the holy grail. Should she turn back?

The attic room, the snug bed – after tomorrow, they will no longer be hers in any case. She tramps on, breathing hard, arms and shoulders aching from the load she carries.

The white whirling wind from the river, somewhere to her side, carries Sabrina's calls: *Courage, Hester, courage.* She struggles on, panting, hot and cold, clammy, and glad of the tabby's complaining mewls which tell her the animal has neither frozen nor suffocated.

Dawn's late wintry glimmer hasn't yet pierced the storm-bleared horizon when she reaches dry sanctuary. Snow heaped by the door drifts with her into the cold cottage, along with whirling flakes. She sets the lantern on the table, a pool of welcome yellow within the utter darkness. Heaving the bags to the floor, she frees the cat, who flicks her tail.

Remind me why this is necessary?

'You know why.'

She eyes the bed with its one blanket folded at the end, thinks of the cat-warmed second blanket in the bag and is tempted to put all aside and sleep. No. A fire is her first task, while she is warm from the trudge across the fields and able to stand. She lifts the tabby, who narrows her eyes in further protest.

'You lie on the bed and warm it for us and I'll get a fire going.'

The cat kneads the blanket and settles, watching Hester venture into the snow.

Aaron has stacked chopped firewood hard against the

side least affected by the weather and sheltered under wide eaves. Nevertheless, much of the small pile of kindling is wet. Hester eases out the driest lengths and carries them inside to lay in the fireplace. She adds paper and lights it with the matches she brought. The damp wood resists the burning paper, threatens to collapse in smoking futility. She feeds in more paper, feels for the driest of the twigs. The paper burns to ashes, the kindling smokes, refuses to catch.

Hester watches anxiously, the cold of the cottage seeping into her clothing, chilling her, when … a sudden strong draught, like a hot breath of summer, fans the stuttering sparks into instant, glorious flame.

Hester jerks back on her heels. The same breath tickles her neck and is gone. She glances around, unafraid. Something or someone friendly keeps her and the tabby company. They won't be alone in the cold, dark days and nights to come.

*

Jem has made a surly gift of the wedding feast laid out at the King's Shilling to anyone who cares to pass by. It has to be eaten given it's paid for. His own appetite for solid food took flight hours ago. He and Sim have passed the day there, which is where they expected to pass it, in different company. Their best coats are hung over their chairs, unfamiliar buttoned waistcoats abandoned and sleeves pushed up to elbows. Jem's good shoes pinch his toes. The pinching and the drink have exacerbated his bad humour to the point where one wrong word will have him at the speaker's throat.

The memories burn, and no number of tankards of ale can dull the humiliation. Only yesterday, the drinkers in the Bargeman nudged him, winked, raised their ale and saluted his virility and easy conquest of the fey girl with the wild hair. He'd dug a deep hole to bury his fury, lifted his chin along with his drink and returned the winks, chuckling. Once or twice he hinted at his betrothed's hidden charms, revelling in the jealous jibes of his listeners, happy as a pig in a wallow. And then–

Standing this morning beside Ezra in the big, cold church, thinking on how, soon, those hidden charms would be his to truly enjoy. Visions of a naked Hester, his own at last, warming him despite the freezing air.

The church bell rang the hour, ten o'clock. She'd be here on the instant, the organist would squeeze his dirges from the old instrument and Jem would watch his young bride walk the long aisle to be delivered up to him. Impatience propelled him around to face the door through which Hester, on Will's arm, would come.

He relives his unsuspecting puzzlement at the empty front pew, where the bride's family should sit. She was going to keep him waiting? He sniggered. Petty and futile. She'd be his after today. He'd have her when and where he wanted.

Then Reverend Jarvis disappearing, Jem grumbling to Ezra who said something about Sim summoning the vicar to the vestry, and Jarvis returning, his high brow furrowed above his spectacles. Jem's unease, the feeling that, somehow, he was being made a fool of, and Jarvis plucking at Jem's elbow, about to destroy his world.

'There's a message, from Mrs Williams.'

A frown as deep as the vicar's etched above Ezra's brows as he put a hand on Jem's arm.

'I reckon she's fled, Jem, gone,' he said. 'Your pretty bird has flown the coop.'

Red fury exploded in Jem's head, and there it rages still.

'Needed a hand to her backside and never got it.' Sim slams his tankard hard onto the wet table. Ale splashes over the edge. 'Fey since a young 'un, thought herself above us all, and now she's covered us in shame with her hussy ways.'

He wipes his hand across his mouth.

Jem catches the young man's eyes, angry slits either side of a creased forehead. His mortification is mirrored in those eyes.

He growls, deep in his throat, a vicious dog dragged from its victim's leg. 'Humiliating, totally humiliating.'

Older humiliations rise up to bait him, to feed his rage. He thought he'd buried them good and proper when he buried his harridan mam and her sneering, jibing mouth. Always drunk, taunting him, telling him nothing good would ever come of him, he's stupid, worthless. It's back, a gut punch he hates, making him tremble with fury.

Women. Scratch the surface, have 'em too close, and they'll find ways to belittle you every time.

Sim waves his tankard. 'Embarrassing. Making idiots of us all over Shiphaven.' He stretches across the table. 'Can't help thinking it might be a good thing if Will and the others don't find her. Folks might forget if she's gone for good.'

Jem stares into his drink which blurs under his fixed gaze. 'Made a fool of me.' Being made a fool of was supposed to have disappeared from his life forever. He grits his teeth. He'd planned on being drunk today, on more satisfying terms. With a more than satisfying end to what should have been celebrations. His mind goes to the newly furnished house nearby, sees himself carrying his bride to the big, shiny iron bed with its feather mattress that cost a month's earnings, honest and dishonest. There he is, throwing her onto the blankets, crouching over her, tugging at her gown's ties and bows and laces until her luscious nakedness is spread before him. He goes hard at the vision. The tumescence is brief.

'Hussy ways is right.' He glares at Sim, who jerks his head like he's surprised at having his own accusation thrown at him. Jem snorts. 'Tempted me, she did, with those hussy ways. Drew me in, lured me sure as a fish on a hook.'

He brings his tankard down with a crash. The babble in the King's Shilling momentarily quiets. All eyes glance his way. Pitying, mocking eyes, with greedy mouths below them content enough to gorge on Jem's wedding feast.

He widens his glare from Sim to all around him, his head reeling with everything he has done for the hussy. His fury burns bright. Duped by blue eyes and dark curls.

Bedsteads, feather mattresses, food and booze, golden rings and fancy clothes. The witch did her best to impoverish him before her unsuspected flit, leaving him with more than egg on his face.

Witch. Talking to the river. Fey.

'Fey since a young 'un?' He squints at Sim who grimaces. 'She's more'n fey, that black-haired, black-hearted sister of yours.' He reaches across the table to grab Sim's arm, squeezes tight. Sim flinches. 'She's a witch, she is,' Jem snarls. 'But she got the wrong man when she tried bewitchin' Jem Stokes.'

Chapter Twenty Two

 oseph peers at his sister over the scallop soup. 'Fled? Mrs Williams' lass?' He glances through the window at the snow-laden ledge. 'Fled into the storm? Have they found her?'

'I don't believe so.' Lottie rests her soup spoon beside her bowl. 'As you say, Brother, into the storm, in the darkness.'

'Papa, we have to do something.'

Catherine's soup is untouched. She is paler than usual. Joseph would give a fortune to ease those tight lines around her eyes.

'Do something?'

'And what are we to do?' Lottie says. 'Do you suggest sending your father into the snow to search? Half the town is out, in any case.'

'There must be something!' Catherine's eyes glint with tears. 'Poor Hester. What horror drove her to flee? The man must be a beast. She'll be in great distress and cold, freezing, sheltering somewhere, God willing.' She sniffs a sob. 'I can't bear to think of it.' She brushes at her tears.

Joseph is beaten. 'Catherine,' he coaxes, 'I'll go immediately to Mrs Williams after dinner and offer what help I can. Will that satisfy you? And tempt you to take a morsel of this excellent soup?'

*

His daughter's extreme concern for the Williams' girl nags at Joseph as he hurries up the High Street. He has no time for this. A young clerk has recently left his employ and he's had no chance to find another. Right when a large shipment from the Far East waits to be unloaded and inventoried. This girl could not have picked a worse time to run away. Yet he has to do something to alleviate Catherine's obsession. Based as it is on one meeting, it's unhealthy and he fears her anxiety over this headstrong escape will worsen her health. Hopefully, the girl will soon be found, preferably alive.

Although the wind has eased, the snow is heavy enough to muffle the normal clatter of horses' hooves on the road. A besieging army of black clouds has taken up position above the town. A fitting day for a drama.

A young man answers Joseph's thumping of the lion-headed door knocker, asks his business and allows him in when he claims an old friendship with Mrs Williams. Lydia sits in front of a window, wintry sunlight picking out silver threads in her piled chestnut braids.

Her hand goes to her chin when Joseph steps into the room. She stands, takes a step forward. 'Joseph!'

'Lydia.' Joseph gives a small bow. 'It's been a long while, and I'm reluctant to disturb you at this difficult time.'

Lydia's gaze searches out the rug at her feet. Joseph pretends not to notice. He coughs.

'It's my daughter, Catherine. She met your daughter here before Christmas and my sister tells me she took a strong liking to the lass. I've been sent with strictest instructions to offer what help I can in finding her, if she's not already found.'

'Sadly, no.' The young man offers his hand. 'I'm Reuben, Hester's youngest brother.'

Joseph shakes the hand, noting its smoothness. He says he is pleased to meet Reuben and gives his attention to Lydia.

'Is there any clue where she's gone, and why?'

Colour rises in her cheeks. She sits down heavily, avoiding Joseph's eyes. 'I knew she was unhappy at this marriage, but to run away! Mr Stokes is, as can be expected, angry and disappointed. As am I.' She lifts her chin and gives Joseph a look of such defiance he immediately understands there is something shameful at the bottom of this tale.

'My sister is pregnant, sir.' Reuben offers the statement in a matter-of-fact tone. 'Which makes her flight into the cold all the more distressing.'

'Reuben!' Lydia purses her lips, her cheeks deepening to scarlet. 'Mr Michaels doesn't need the full sum of our shame.'

Joseph, moved by her distress, steps closer. He lifts Lydia's hand from her lap. 'We're old friends. Tell me, what can I do?'

'Thank you, Joseph.' Her colour fades. 'You were always a kind man and I'm glad to see wealth hasn't changed you.'

She withdraws her hand and Joseph moves apart, aware of the son's careful attention on him.

'My brothers are out searching, along with others,' Reuben says. 'We pray to our good Lord we find her safe and well.'

'Does she have money with her?'

'We don't believe so. She took a few clothes, food, and the cat.' Reuben smiles briefly.

Joseph's eyebrows rise.

He hands Reuben a visiting card. 'I won't impose on your worry any longer. If you need anything, anything at all, or if you hear word, please let me know, day or night.'

He bows to Lydia. 'While the circumstances are sad, I'm pleased to have seen you, Lydia. And, given my daughter's feelings, I trust at some stage she and Hester will be able to take up their new friendship.'

Words tritely said and truly meant, and which do nothing to fill the hollowness behind Joseph's ribcage as he utters them. An aching worry for both daughters.

*

'Well?' Catherine has sped into the hall at the sound of the door opening. She is there before Papa can remove his coat. 'Have they found her? Is she safe?'

'Let me take my coat off, and please go and sit by the fire.'

Catherine sits on the sofa, tapping her fingers on her knees. Papa's serious demeanour suggests the news is not good.

'Well.' Papa sits beside her and takes hold of her hands.

Catherine holds her breath.

'So far, she's not been found.'

Catherine exhales. The worst is not the case, so far.

'Her mother is extremely distressed,' Papa says. 'Her brothers are searching for her and I pray that later today we'll have news.'

'Poor Hester!' Catherine releases one of her hands to brush at her tears. 'What madness, what desperation drove her to do such a thing?'

Joseph reclaims her hand and squeezes it gently. 'Her mother says the girl was unhappy about the marriage.' He pauses, draws in a breath.

'There's more, isn't there?'

'Yes.' Another pause. 'She took the cat with her.' It comes out so abruptly Papa appears surprised at his own words.

'The cat?' Catherine claps her hands together. 'Then all is well! Hester would never put an animal in danger.' The lightness of relief makes her giddy. 'She knew where she was going, knew there would be warmth and shelter.'

Papa's eyes widen briefly, before he smiles and nods. She can't be sure he totally agrees with her or whether he is simply glad she sees light in this whole dire mess. It doesn't matter. Catherine is comforted, a little.

Mrs Bryce comes in with a tea tray. 'Is there any news of the lass, sir?'

'No, Mrs Bryce. We can only pray she is found safe.'

'And her with child too.'

Papa's eyebrows fly to his forehead.

'With child?' Catherine frowns.

'Oh, Miss Catherine, I do beg your pardon, and you also, sir.' Mrs Bryce rattles the tea cups onto their saucers. 'I should have put my thinking hat on. What with Miss Catherine not going out, she wouldn't know.' She lifts the lid from the sugar bowl, sets it on the tray. 'It's common knowledge the Williams' girl is with child which is the reason for the wedding done in such a rush. Or not done.'

Catherine's brain spins. Pregnant? 'Papa? Is this true?'

Papa squirms. 'Yes, yes, it is.'

'Jem Stokes avows the child is his,' Mrs Bryce says brightly, 'though many in the town wonder. Especially now the girl has fled. Why flee–?'

'Thank you, Mrs Bryce.' Papa is gentle, and firm. 'Catherine will pour and you may attend to your tasks, we have no wish to keep you further.'

Mrs Bryce blushes, arches her brows and leaves without seeming to take too much offence.

Catherine pours. Papa takes his tea from the tray, sits straight and sips.

'My dear, I have to say I'm curious about how deeply you care for this poor young woman. When you were last ill you called her name constantly. Now there is this wretched worrying all on the basis of one short meeting in a dressmaker's parlour. Is there something I'm missing?'

Now it's Catherine who blushes. However, it was a long time ago and no harm was done.

'The dressmaker's wasn't our first meeting.'

She tells him of her visit to St Ceyna's, of meeting Hester there, of the instant bond they formed. 'Hester has a wonderful way with animals,' she says at the end. 'I could tell by the way Molly immediately loved her. Which is why I'm sure she's fine, because of the cat.'

She'd like to tell Papa about bathing her feet in the sacred pool, about the sherbet fizz of the water on her tongue and how vital, restored, she felt that day. She can't. He would lovingly assure her it was all in her mind, and worry further.

Papa strokes her hand. 'Your faith in the girl does you credit. I pray it's rewarded.'

'And meanwhile,' Catherine says, 'you'll help however you can, won't you, Papa?'

'I promise, my dear, I promise. For many reasons.'

His gaze strays to the fire. Despite Catherine's curious gaze, he doesn't say what those many reasons might be.

Chapter Twenty Three

The tabby mews about Hester's legs.

My kill. Tasty raw.

Hester glances down, one hand on the rabbit's white belly, the other positioning the knife for the long straight cut. 'At least let me skin it, then you can have a leg for your supper. And thank you.'

Her decision to steal the cat the night she fled Shiphaven continues to make her glad. As well as being someone to talk to, the cat has proved her use in hunting rabbits on more than one occasion. What else she hunts and keeps to herself, Hester doesn't ask. Certainly, the cat is round and sleek. Which Hester is not.

The snow which threatened her escape thickens during the remainder of February, and freezing winds batter the window panes. On many nights, Hester is sure they will crack. They hold, thanks to Aaron's earlier repair work. The nights are eternal. Hester wraps herself in her shawl, tucks her legs under her in a chair by the fire and tells out loud the lessons Aaron instilled in her over the years. She drinks

170

dandelion tea made with last summer's dried leaves and lets the lessons trail off, leaving Aaron's voice in her ear.

Aaron amused, shaking his head, pretending to be shocked at Hester's inability to distinguish agrimony and verbascum ('Grey for one, green for the other.' 'It's too hard when they both have long flower stems and yellow blossom.'). Aaron irritable, snapping at Hester for insisting she will visit Sabrina in the evening, she doesn't care if Aaron comes or not, and what is it about the river which sends him into these morose moods?

Aaron searching her eyes, asking, 'Will you drink?'

And what came after.

She lurches like a rudderless boat on wind-chopped waters from exultant memory to fury at his betrayal to grief at his absence.

'Where has he gone?' she says to the cat, curled in the diminishing space of Hester's lap.

The cat opens a sleepy eye. *You will know in time.*

Hester screws up her nose. 'Which is your favourite answer to everything and leaves me as ignorant as before.'

During the short days, she forages for food, digging under the snow for sodden nettles, chickweed and horse parsley. Buried in the snow below a crab-apple tree, Hester finds wrinkled windfalls, not too spoiled. She boils them into a sweet-smelling mush. Her mother would once have strained the juice through muslin overnight to make a clear red jelly for flavouring gravies and stews. Hester eats the pulp and is grateful. When at last the snow recedes, she tramps into the forest to gather last year's chestnuts to dry by the fire before laboriously grinding them into a flour of sorts to knead with water and bake in the pot over the fire.

She thinks of Mother and her brothers less often than she thinks of Aaron. Her thoughts of her family are spoiled with acrimony at how they threw her at the fisherman, a bloodied sacrifice to appease respectability. And how the fisherman would have taken her. And taken her, and taken her. Hester's stomach curls at the years she might have spent under the fish-stinking weight of Jem Stokes.

She thinks of Father too, and does he miss her since she can't pass by his grave to glimpse his kindly shade. Is he resting, or does he worry for her?

Worry, worry, worry, the spirits sigh, and one, clearer than the others, shushes them. Hester is warmed by the same breath which brushed her neck the night she came to the cottage.

Be easy, Hester, be easy. For the babe's sake, be easy.

Who is this spirit which accompanies her nights and often her days?

Hester asked it once what it knew of Aaron's whereabouts. She was met by silence. She hasn't dared ask again in case the spirit abandons her as her father, her mother, her brothers, and Aaron have.

Spring brings relief, with sunshine, occasional days which suggest summer is not a figment of imagination, and easier pickings in forest and fields. At last summer truly arrives, the days lengthen and foraging becomes easier. Finding food and having less need to fuss about the shrinking wood pile should comfort her, if it isn't for the fact that as her stomach swells, weariness comes upon her more often. She frets about the birth itself. The cat is unsympathetic.

They come out.

'It's fine for you, you've had dozens of kittens. This is my first and it's more difficult for humans.'

The cat lifts her tail and strolls outside. At least she isn't pregnant. No toms have ventured this far.

Hester gains more comfort, though equally impractical advice, from her unseen companion.

We are here, Hester, to help. You must not worry.

The question niggles: who is this helpmate? Has Sabrina come to her, since Hester dare not go to the river since leaving Shiphaven? Walking along the cliffs or clambering to the mudflats and rocks would make her too visible to any river fisherman who might pass the sighting on. Her longing to be close to the river, to watch the beckoning of the nymphs and hear their calls, carves a hollowness in her gut which matches the one where her sorrow for her lost family and lover lives.

With the warmer nights she determines to go at the next full moon. For now, she has to be content to listen to these souls who have come to her in her need.

You have strengths, powers, the whispers say. *Use them, use them* ...

Power. Hester's mind fills with the sights, sounds, the exquisite pleasures of those nights, both with Aaron and by herself. The moon riding the clouds, the vanity of the stars reflected in the mirror of the river, the lights from the ferry – and Sabrina calling, *Courage, Hester, courage.*

She wraps her shawl closer, rests her hand on her stomach where the babe sleeps. She worries the babe should be more active. Is that right? What does she know about bearing children except its many dangers? It's a lesson Aaron did not teach beyond which herbs ease the pains. Hester has gathered what remains on the shelves – the jar of raspberry leaf, glass phials of rose, camomile and lavender oils, and a clay pot of dried willow bark – and put them together on the table. She worries at their lack of freshness, hoping the baby will wait until she can gather and prepare more. Soon at least, she will be able to harvest more belladonna, for her labour.

Belladonna and poppy seeds ... power to heal, power to fly ... the spirit croons.

All well and good, if she believed the power to fly would help her when the time comes. Hester is alone. Aaron should be here. Will he return in time to be by her side in her need, as he has before?

Fever curdles Catherine's dreams. The once cooling waters of St Ceyna's bubble as hot and fierce as a witch's cauldron to scald her bare toes. She doesn't think to lift them. Instead, she watches the skin redden and blister with no sense of pain or concern. A skeletal Hester, her stomach a small mountain, perches beside her waving bottles of bilious green and lurid blue potions and grinning inanely in Catherine's face.

The lavender-scented dampness of a cloth on her forehead soothes the dreams away. The cauldron-well melts into its own steam and a rosy Hester stands by Molly, stroking the mare's nose and murmuring into her flicking ear. Catherine's limbs are heavy, a languorous heaviness which carries her into sleep, the fever vanished, dreamless.

Today, she is well enough to leave her bed. Mrs Bryce tuts as she sets a tray with tea steaming from a cup beside the sofa.

Catherine, lying among cushions wrapped in a light, silk shawl, smiles a thank you. 'Why the tuts, Mrs Bryce?'

'The new maid, Jenny.' Mrs Bryce runs a finger over the table top where June sunshine lighting the drawing room exposes the housemaid's lack of dusting expertise. 'Useless as … well, never mind Miss Catherine, the girl is useless.'

'She's very young.' Catherine has tried to talk to the maid, a child no more than thirteen, she guesses. Her delicate strength, however, has not withstood the stammering responses and constant curtseys. These days she says a soft thank you, deferring conversation until the girl is less terrified.

'Young as may be, no younger than I was when I first went into service.' Mrs Bryson pours the China tea and nudges cup and saucer closer to Catherine. 'A slice of lemon cake, Miss Catherine?'

'No, no thank you. Tea is enough.'

Mrs Bryce withdraws her hovering hand from above the cake.

'I expected better of her, being Mrs Collins' youngest.'

'Who?'

'Mrs Collins. The laundry woman at Blaize Hall. Hard worker, respectable, all her girls are in service and never heard a complaint to this day.' Mrs Bryce pauses. 'Her eldest has done all right, or so her mother believes. Married Jem Stokes not a month after the business with the Williams' lass.'

Catherine shifts on the sofa. Talk of Hester has subsided in the Michaels' household, with Aunty blaming the 'whole sorry tale' for Catherine's long bout of fevered illness. Papa too has been tight-lipped, saying simply Hester has not been found and no one is searching.

'He mustn't have been too upset at being left at the altar.' Catherine hopes the oblique approach might yield information, if any is to be had.

Mrs Bryce clasps her hands under her bosom and sniffs. 'Seems so. Also seems the Williams' girl might have been wiser than many believe.' She taps the side of her nose.

Catherine happily rises to the bait. 'Why? Is there something amiss with Mr Stokes?'

'Amiss? One way of putting it.' Another sniff.

Catherine waits. She has all day. Mrs Bryce doesn't.

'Some say'—the housekeeper lowers her voice and glances at the doorway—'as how Jem Stokes' fondness for drink has grown somewhat since the winter and, rumour mind, no proof, he raises his hand to his bride.'

Catherine draws in a short breath. 'I see,' she says. 'Let's hope for his wife's sake the rumours are ill-founded.'

Mrs Bryce arches her brows, wrinkles her nose and leaves Catherine to the untasted lemon cake.

She takes up the tea and blows gently on the hot surface.

If the rumour is true, Hester has indeed made a wise choice. Assuming she is well and safe somewhere. Of course she is. Catherine can't believe the girl's bright spirit is dulled in any way, and certainly not extinguished. Still, with a baby well on the way it will be hard for her, wherever she is.

Catherine sets the undrunk tea on its saucer. She will beg Papa to search out whatever news there is, further afield than Shiphaven if he can. If Aunty objects, Catherine will plead she needs to find out for her own peace of mind; worrying might make her ill.

Chapter Twenty Four

he workhouse meeting is endless. Joseph's mind wanders to the list of tasks awaiting him in his office, a list as long as this midsummer eve day. He shifts in his seat and scribbles pencilled notes on the agenda which are nothing to do with the increasing average length of stay of female inmates and what can be done to ensure these women are virtuously occupied.

'We know the truth of the devil making work for idle hands,' Reverend Jarvis intones.

Joseph's own hands can never thus fall foul of the devil. He grimaces, inwardly berates himself for thoughts akin to blasphemy.

The tedious meeting isn't helped by Courtney-Brown's ineffective chairing. The landowner allows discussions to carry on far beyond their value, while he taps his fingers on the table and examines the ceiling. He will finally stir, cough, and attempt to summarise a conversation he clearly hasn't heard. When he fails to do so, he asks the clerk if he has sufficient for a decision to be recorded? His tone is brusque and poor Cornelius Shill, struggling to make sense of things, is reduced to babbling various views until one gentleman or the other suggests a resolution. Shill dips his pen and scribbles hastily.

At last it is over. Courtney-Brown stands, mutters a curt thank you to the room and strides through the door. Others are nearly as fast. Joseph would have joined the general exodus except, as he rises from his chair, he knocks his document case to the floor. Papers spill all over.

'Clumsy fool!' he exclaims.

Shill rushes to help. 'There you go, sir.' He sets the untidy bundle on the table and bows.

'Thank you. More haste, less speed, hey?'

The clerk smiles. Joseph expects him to return to his own sorting. Instead, he bites his upper lip, opens his mouth, closes it.

'Yes sir, as you say.' His fingers flutter as he takes a step away. 'Sorry sir, you're bound to be in a hurry, being such a busy gentleman.'

Joseph is a busy gentleman, true. He is also kind and he admires Cornelius Shill.

'Is there something I can help you with?' He glances from the door to the clerk. 'Life should never be too busy to help a fellow Christian.'

Shill hesitates and Joseph waits for the denials. Then it comes out, in a quick spew of nervous words.

'Mr Courtney-Brown has done me a great honour, sir, asking me to work for him at Blaize Hall, to understudy Mr Freeman's position, learn to be estate manager in time.'

'Oh!' Two images collide in Joseph's mind. One is of Courtney-Brown resting his hand on the clerk's shoulder at the end of the meeting where he reported on the sanitation project. The other is of Lottie telling how the aristocrat had needlessly thrown Lydia Williams and her family off their farm, and how angry Joseph was.

Cornelius Shill understudying the apparently ruthless estate manager? Subjected to the influences of the callous landowner?

He covers the tiny lurch in his gut with an automatic, 'Excellent news, congratulations.' A hesitant pause before saying, 'We'll have to find ourselves a new clerk and you're concerned. Is that what worries you?'

'Um, yes, sir, of course.' Shill swallows. 'If I accept, finding a replacement will indeed be a task to concern myself with.'

The tiny lurch repeats itself, this time with a cautionary glee.

'If you accept?'

'Do you think I should, sir? Would it be entirely foolish to refuse such an honour?'

Joseph packs papers into his document case. 'Tell me, what makes you think of saying no?' He keeps his voice neutral.

'I can't see why Mr Courtney-Brown would consider me, sir. I'm young, have no farming experience. Why does he ask me?'

This is a puzzle to Joseph too and he says so, adding, 'It's likely your proven intelligence and industry in this role is all he needs as a starting point. A bright pupil.'

'Hmm.' Shill twists his hands together, his neatly cut pink nails square against his broad fingers. 'I don't want to offend a man of Mr Courtney-Brown's standing,' he says. 'Only—'

'Only this is a huge decision and you need time to think on it.' Joseph's workload looms large. He moves to the door to fetch his hat.

'Yes, sir, that's so.' Shill gives Joseph a bow. 'Thank you for your time, sir, I'm most grateful.'

'Do feel free to seek me out if you wish to talk further.' Joseph nods, and hurries into the hall. He has no time to spend worrying about Cornelius Shill, admire him or not. It's none of his business and he trusts the young man will come to the right conclusion himself. Although, the question of why Courtney-Brown would bestow this life-changing presumed honour on a young workhouse clerk is a riddle Joseph cannot solve.

He thanks the groom waiting with the mare, mounts and clatters out of the courtyard, his thoughts firmly on work matters. As he trots down the lane beneath the arch of dappled greenery, he reflects on how his guilt at spending time away from the business battles with more guilt at not heeding Catherine's renewed pleadings to seek out information about the Williams' girl. His long hours continue and he sees no quick ending, given the search for a satisfactory clerk has yielded nothing. Shiphaven is close to Bristol, so any young man with ambition and the capacity to achieve it is lured to the big city. Who can blame them?

Joseph is also reluctant to see Lydia. It could be more guilt – remorse at not having pressed his suit all those years ago. If he had, the lively Lydia Bennett would have had a much happier life. These thoughts lead to another bout of guilt, of how he can think such things when his marriage to his dear, dead wife gave him such contentment. It also gave him Catherine.

And it's Catherine who raises the topic of the Williams girl as Joseph smokes his pipe in the drawing room after supper. He experiences a prick of irritation. He wants to relax for an hour before dealing with letters needing signature and documents needing checking which he's brought home with him.

'I've been thinking about Hester,' Catherine says, and Joseph rolls his eyes. 'Remember how I told you Hester has some knowledge of herbs and wildflowers, to use for healing? I think it would help Mrs Williams to know Hester can take care of herself, if she doesn't already know.' She wriggles forward in the wing chair, her book slipping to the edge of her knees. She catches it before it falls to the Turkish rug. 'It might give her comfort. Surely, after all this time, she needs some hope to lift her spirits, especially as the baby must be near due?'

Joseph's burden of guilt has grown weightier over his quick dismissal of Cornelius Shill's dilemma. He can do nothing about Shill. He can, however, ease the greater guilt of not responding to his patient daughter's unselfish request. He knocks the pipe on the edge of the ashtray.

'You are right, my dear,' he says. 'It's not too late to call tonight. I'll go immediately.' Procrastination is over, action is required.

*

Lydia answers the door to Joseph's knock. A shaft of midsummer evening sunlight highlights the etches of worry on her drawn face and blanches colour from her faded dress. Tendrils of hair, more grey than chestnut, hang loose below a bun which seems to have been hastily pinned and without benefit of a mirror.

Joseph hopes he transforms his instinctive frown into a warm smile before she notices.

'Evening, Lydia.' He doffs his hat and bows slightly.

'Joseph!' Her hand goes to her mouth. 'Do you have news?'

'Ah, no Lydia, my apologies. It's news I come seeking, not giving.'

She bites her top lip. 'Then we are both out of luck.'

Joseph puts out a hand, anticipating she might shut the door. 'I do, however,' he says, 'have information which you may not have, and which may partially ease your worries. It's from my daughter, Catherine, you remember her?'

'Yes. Come on in and tell me.' She steps aside. 'My son Reuben is visiting for a day or two, meeting with Reverend

Jarvis who is kindly helping with his studies.'

Joseph removes his hat and gloves and places them on a table by the door. 'He's to be ordained?'

'In a year or two.' Lydia is thin-lipped. 'At least one son is working with their brain and not their brawn.'

Joseph shakes hands with Reuben, asks a question about his studies and says Jarvis is a knowledgeable vicar and Reuben is fortunate to have his help. Secretly, he prays the vicar's views on the deserving poor might not influence this young man with kind, intelligent eyes. He takes the offered chair in the window bay. The parlour is more cluttered, less organised than on his first visit, as if his hostess has no energy to replace the buttons and threads in their rightful place as she has no energy to dress her hair properly. On this warm evening the fire is unlit, yet the ashes have not been swept. A faint smell of old coal dust hangs in the air.

'How does the dressmaking go?' he says.

Lydia clasps her hands in her lap and draws herself up straighter. 'Not well.' Her voice is caustic. 'Once my customers ran out of gossip about Hester, they became reluctant to entrust the mother of a so-called witch, and certainly of a fallen woman, with their capes and petticoats.'

'A witch?'

'It's a story being spread by Jem Stokes,' Reuben says. 'He claims my sister enchanted him to fall in love with her, all for the purpose of casting him aside for her own perverted amusement.' He blows out a soft breath. 'A sick story and untruthful. Sadly, though, people love to believe a witch tale.'

'Ah.' While Joseph is certain this story has not reached Catherine, now what he has to say becomes an uncomfortable burden.

'What is it your daughter has to tell, Joseph, to ease a distraught mother's worry?' The acid in Lydia's voice deepens his discomfort.

He plunges in, praying to the good Lord to guide his words. 'Catherine and Hester had met before,' he says. 'In the summer, about three years ago, at St Ceyna's well.'

Reuben and Lydia frown at each other.

'Why St Ceyna's well?'

'For Catherine's part, it was to remind her of visits from her childhood, when I had taken her to the well as a pretty place in the forest.' He grimaces. 'She shouldn't have gone there alone, not being strong enough to venture anywhere alone. And thus it proved, as when she arrived she was overcome with dizziness.' He pauses. How to put the next part of his story? 'Hester was there, collecting water and cooling her feet. She helped Catherine.' There, it's all he needs to say. 'They talked, found a mutual liking.'

Lydia lifts upraised palms. 'Two girls meet and talk and enjoy each other's company. How does this ease my worries?'

'You said Hester helped your daughter, sir.' Reuben fixes Joseph with an unblinking stare. 'May I ask how?'

Joseph clears his throat. 'She helped her sit, and ...' Reuben cocks his head to the side and Joseph has to carry on, with the truth. '...questioned her about the dizziness, a true young nurse!' He smiles, hoping the mention of nursing will cover his tracks. 'And suggested to Catherine harmless natural concoctions which might ease her condition.'

'Such as?' The creases in Lydia's brow deepen.

'I think ginger tea with honey was mentioned.'

Lydia folds her hands in her lap, purses her lips before speaking. 'Do you remember, Reuben, how Hester had these strange notions about wanting to set herself up as a healer?'

'I do.'

Joseph twists to face the young man, who stands by the fireplace.

'She learned those notions from our father's tales of

his grandmama,' Reuben says. 'We hadn't understood how deeply they'd embedded themselves in her mind.' His voice is steady and, to Joseph's ear, without condemnation.

Lydia looks to the ceiling. 'Did she pursue her desire, learned things, somehow, without our awareness?' She clicks her tongue against the roof of her mouth and gazes at him. 'This must not be spread about, please. It's fuel to nourish Jem Stokes' wild stories and will be the end of us as a family in Shiphaven. Certainly, the end of my living.'

Her chin quivers and Joseph wishes he'd gone on ignoring Catherine's pleadings.

'There's one other thing,' he says. He has debated whether to offer this piece of information. It might help.

'Yes?'

It's Reuben who asks. Lydia's head is down, her eyes on her hands in her lap as if contemplating their future enforced idleness.

'My daughter tells me Hester mentioned the name Aaron, and then retracted it, hastily, as if it was a secret she should not speak.'

'Aaron?' Lydia brings her head up. 'Who might he be? Which speaks volumes. Hester! What secrets has she kept from us, and for how long? What wickedness has she been hiding?' Her voice catches and Reuben steps to her side, lays a hand on his mother's shoulder.

'I can't believe wickedness of our Hester,' he says. 'Foolishness, romantic nonsense, yes. Not wickedness.'

'And without her here to prove otherwise, all Shiphaven believes the worst.' Lydia pats Reuben's hand on her shoulder. 'It's you I feel for. Your chances of getting a good parish, indeed any parish, are at risk because of your sister's shameful doings.' She huffs out a breath. 'Wicked, selfish girl!'

Joseph stands, uncomfortable at Lydia's distress, wishing all the more he had left well alone. He bows. 'My apologies,

Lydia, for being the cause of new distress. Catherine will say nothing of this, nor will I. And please, if there's anything I can do, in any way, my offer stands.'

A greater heaviness of spirit lies on Joseph when he leaves the house as when he entered it. He needs to walk, to think, to clear his head before facing Catherine. Her friend accused of being a witch! He clamps his hat to his head and crosses the road, making his way into the twilight-shadowed graveyard with the idea of allowing its view of the river and its thronging traffic to restore his normal, practical self. As he enters through the lychgate, he glances at Lydia's house, setting his mouth in a grim line at the further sorrow he has caused.

Reuben is coming out of the door, in a great hurry. He doesn't go down into Shiphaven's centre. Nor does he cross the street to the church, as Joseph might expect. He heads up the track which leads to the Williams' old farm.

Joseph has an urge to follow the young man. He re-crosses the street, dodging a wagon stacked with rattling empty milk urns, and starts up the same road. He stops. Whatever is he doing? He remembers the docks, and the inventory to be counted and stored, and the lack of a clerk. He ignores the letters and documents waiting his attention at home and hurries towards his offices. He will tell Catherine all about it later, when his own distress has been subsumed by practical and necessary tasks. Wherever Reuben is going is no business of Joseph's.

Chapter Twenty Five

The spirits are restless this midsummer's eve. As is Hester. At dawn, she risks a visit to St Ceyna's. Not her first since coming to the cottage. Her visits are made at dawn or dusk when the possibility of finding others there is low. Other people, that is. Hester is never alone at St Ceyna's.

Struggling with the added burden of her pregnancy, she climbs the short steep path from the track to gain the view of the stone rectangle and its clear waters. A pale, golden stillness steeps the little valley. Hester steps from the sheltering beech and oak to move carefully down the slope, the hand not carrying the clay jar snatching at low branches to help her uncertain balance. As she walks, she gathers a press of whispers. They might have been the breeze in the leaves, except the leaves are as motionless as the rocky outcrops dotting the valley walls.

Reaching the well, Hester fills the jar and wedges it between two stones while she bathes her face and arms. The longing to remove her gown, shoes and stockings and immerse herself in the water is strong. She resists, as alert as any deer to the crackling of old leaves or the snap of a twig which might herald visitors. She removes her shoes and sits on the stone surround, her belly a protruding ball which prevents her seeing her toes sliding through the cool wetness.

Her mind goes to Catherine, the two of them sitting here side by side trailing their feet in the water, refreshing their bodies and spirits that sultry afternoon. It had been lovely to see the young gentlewoman, the time in Mother's parlour after Christmas. Catherine was far too pale and far too thin, but her eyes sparkled in response to Hester's silly mutterings about beech leaves and ponies' manes. Their shared secret. Hester laughs out loud.

Her laugh is ousted by a sigh. What must Catherine think of her? A fallen woman, a hussy, a runaway from her husband-to-be. No doubt she's glad Hester hasn't ventured into her life, if only to take in over-large jackets. Catherine would be ashamed to acknowledge her in the street. A heavy sadness weighs on her. Friends have been a rarity in her life. She enjoyed Catherine's company that one time – how many years ago? – and wondered, the day in the parlour, if it might be possible to do so again, despite their different social standings. Dead dreams.

Hester sighs again and lifts her cold feet from the water. Leaning back on her hands, she stretches her legs out straight before her and wriggles her toes. Tiny dancing sprites ride the water drops sparkling in the bright early light which reaches through the leaves. She hauls herself upright, holds her hands up, fingers curling to scatter the diaphanous veil of sparkling sunlight. The luminous air beneath the green canopy fills with murmurings.

Life, the souls whisper, *we bring life.*

A sharp twinge shoots through Hester's stomach. She bends over, gasping, holding a hand to her belly. It can't be.

Far too early. She has done her sums. The baby will come at the end of July.

The lance of pain passes. Hester straightens. It might be something she ate or the way she was sitting. She dawdles no longer, however. Collecting the water jar, she walks as swiftly as she can up and over the ridge to the track, where she heaves herself across the stile and hurries through the fields to the cottage.

*

All day the pains come and go. Despite the warm evening, Hester wraps a blanket around her shoulders and huddles, shivering, in the chair by the unlit fire. It is set with kindling and dried furze. More kindling has been piled by the hearth and small logs are readied there for longer-lasting heat.

She should have a blaze going, to heat the big pot on its tripod which she keeps filled with water. She can't. The last pain has just passed and she needs to rest.

Strike a match, Hester. I will do the rest.

She will do the rest, the rest. Rest Hester, she will do the rest …

The spirits fill the cottage with their sympathetic murmurings. They flow in and out the open doorway, swirl about Hester's chair, reach out to touch her hair and her cheeks with fingers as soft and fluttering as moths' wings. Hester barely takes note of them, intent on the life inside her and its insistence on birth.

Too early.

She pulls herself from the chair, keeping the blanket around her shoulders, and stumbles to the table where she fingers the ingredients put aside for this moment. Here is a motivation to have hot water on hand – the raspberry leaves Aaron left for her in the winter will come into their own. The fresh leaves Hester collected from wild raspberries in the forest aren't sufficiently dry. Still, there are oils and willow bark.

She takes matches from the mantel and squats, awkward and heavy, before the laid fire. The instant the match is lit, a breath of hot air from over Hester's shoulder fans the tiny flame high to send it tumbling into the furze. The kindling crackles, sparks catch the wood and the fire burns as if it has been lit for hours, not seconds.

Hester mumbles a thank you to this ever-helpful spirit and falls to her side as agony wrings her bowels. She curls into a ball on the stone flags and breathes short, rapid breaths. When the contraction passes she drags herself up, grabbing at the mantle, head down, steadying herself.

Be easy, be easy, the spirits urge.

'You said babies just came,' Hester gasps to the tabby, which jumps onto the bed and kneads the blanket. 'You can't sleep!'

Warming the blanket for the babe and for you. You will need to lie down at some point.

Hester can't lie down. She watches the pot and, too soon, steeps the willow bark in warmish water and drinks it greedily.

Outside, the twilight lingers. Inside, the spirits linger too, giving what comfort they can. The pains come faster, tighter, bands of hot iron strangling her gut to make her want to die. She takes to the bed and its mattress of lady's bed straw – the best for birthing mothers, she told the cat when she stuffed the freshly washed calico cover with a yellow froth of flowers not three days ago. How it's best, she doesn't know and doesn't care. The agonising twisting of her insides goes on and on, until she has no memory of it ever being otherwise.

'Mother! Mother, help me!' she wails, wrapping her arms about her middle, folding into herself.

She may as well cry her anguish to the mice in the roof.

Between the wrenching pains, coming in ever shortening gaps, Hester's eyes stray to the belladonna berries on the table, not yet prepared. The spirits dance, agitated. *No.*

No. Hester cannot take them as they are, as Aaron has told her over and over. She falls back, writhing, hands clenched into her stomach to squeeze the hurt away.

'Aaron! Where are you?'

Where is he? All Hester's life, he has come to her in her need. All Hester's life, until the last time. Doesn't he feel her terror? Doesn't he know the stabbing hurt which has her screaming into the dark?

The tabby jumps up, brushes her head against Hester's and stalks to the end of the bed where she curls up, eyes on Hester's legs as if waiting to see what will emerge.

Full night finally vanquishes the long, long day. The spirits eddy through the darkened room. Hester senses their anxiety, their frustration at their uselessness. She calls to the river.

'Sabrina, comfort me! Tell me I am strong!'

The spirits swirl faster. *Be strong, Hester, be strong,* they whisper, and Hester finds a crumb of solace in their faint mimicry.

She labours by the red glow of the fire which burns brightly despite the pile of logs remaining high. She cares not a whit how this trick is done, grateful for the homely flicker and the heat. More pain-killing willow bark might help, if she had strength to rise from the bed to prepare it. Her back aches as if a dozen horses have stampeded over it and she looks to the oils on the table. An angry snort, overtaken by another caught breath, escapes her. Who is there to rub oil into her back?

At last, in the darkest hour, a high, animal scream fights its strangled path up her throat to blast through lips raw from hours of panting.

And there it is – the force of life slipping, sliding, finally, yes, finally, from her aching womb. And the pain is over, done with.

A moment of calm, eyes closed, panting.

The spirits hover, their touch cool on her sweating skin. *Sweet so sweet.*

Aaron's babe.

The murmur carries tones of humour and longing.

Taking up the slime-caked tiny creature, Hester holds it aloft and gives it a sharp slap on its skinny bottom. The baby breathes weakly, but breathes. Hester lets out a long, grateful breath of her own. A tiny, bony girl with thick black hair and dangling limbs. She lays the child beside her while, shaking with exhaustion, she cuts the cord with the knife she sharpened days earlier and kept wrapped in a clean cloth. The afterbirth is placed in a bucket to bury later, and then she swaddles the mite in the linen sheet she's had ready by the bed for weeks, and holds her close. The baby is quiet, barely moving.

There is a susurration of encouraging sighs and a light breeze stirs the thick hair on the baby girl's head. She flutters open her eyes and purses her tiny, dry white lips.

She needs feeding ... you have strength, use it ...

Hester pulls open her sweat-soaked chemise and puts the baby to her breast. After much encouragement, she latches on to the teat, her sucking desultory. Hester rocks her until both fall asleep to the lullaby croonings floating in the cool air of the cottage.

Chapter Twenty Six

Hester!'

Hester jolts awake and the baby, lying in her arms, gives a startled twitch. The voice is one she knows.

'Aaron?' She struggles to pull herself up against the iron bars of the bedhead, wincing at the pain between her legs. She squints at the figure standing over her. The summer dawn barely lightens the shadows inside the cottage. Her pattering heart falters.

'Reuben?'

'Yes, me. What in the good Lord's name …?' Reuben bends to shift aside the cloth covering the baby's head. The cries gather strength, though far from lusty.

'Oh, Hester,' Reuben exclaims. 'Is this baby newborn?'

'Early this morning.' Her head is stuffed with wool, her whole body aches as if she's been thrown into a wall time after time. The baby's insistence and her own painful breasts force her to pull herself fully upright and lift the child into her arms. The effort leaves her dizzy and she briefly closes her eyes. She wants desperately to sleep.

When she pulls at her chemise and puts the baby to her breast, Reuben jolts as if scalded. The cat, washing itself at the end of the bed, gives a contemptuous sniff.

With the baby sucking tentatively, Hester takes in the sight of her favourite brother who stares out the window into the growing light. She's unsure how welcome the sight is, to either of them.

'How did you find me?'

Reuben half-turns. 'Mr Michaels visited Mother yesterday evening. He told about your meeting with his daughter at St Ceyna's and your learning about herbs and such.' He dares to face her, his eyes finding refuge in a spot high on the stones of the wall above the bed. 'It jolted something in my memory. I went to the farm, hoping being there might jolt it further.' He shrugs. 'It wasn't until I was home in my bed it finally came to me.'

'Mr Michaels?' Hester's pulse quickens. 'Catherine's father?'

'Yes.'

'Why did he come? What does he have to do with anything?'

'Nothing, except his daughter nags at him for news of you and he obliges her by coming to our mother and upsetting her with tales which would entrance the gossip mongers.'

Reuben clears his throat.

'Gossip? Still?' Is life in Shiphaven so dull?

Reuben sets his mouth in a hard line, finds something else of interest in the stones of the wall.

'Tell me?' Through her fogged mind, Hester senses his struggle.

'Stupid nonsense,' he blurts. 'It's Stokes.'

'Ah.'

'He goes around accusing you of putting a spell on him, then abandoning him. Tells all and sundry you're a witch.'

Hester is too tired to care what tales the stinking fisherman spreads. She savours the tiny bubble of happiness Reuben's other news caused to well in her chest.

'Catherine Michaels? She asks after me?'

Reuben takes up the change in topic. 'Yes, as I said. Seems she took a liking to you, albeit she has seen you twice in how many years.'

Hester drinks it in. The baby has fallen asleep and Hester wants to do the same while relishing the thrill of knowing Catherine respects her–

'She's aware ... of my ... of my ... condition?'

'Of course. The whole town is.'

'I suppose ...' Hester's eyelids have become leaden, she cannot keep them open. They close and she mumbles, 'Mother ... must be ... angry.'

'Hester.' Reuben steps to the side of the bed, carrying Hester's shawl. He covers her shoulders, draws the shawl across Hester to envelop the sleeping baby, and sits on the edge of the bed. 'When did you last eat?'

'Eat?' Hester shakes her head. 'Let me sleep, Reuben. Please.' She opens her eyes long enough to watch him take in the bare cottage, the cold fireplace, the few items on the shelves which might be food.

'You can't stay here, not with a baby,' he says. 'I'm going to fetch help, bring Mother, she'll help.'

'Mother won't come.'

Grief bites into Hester's morsel of contentment. Mother didn't come last night when Hester cried out for her. She won't come now. She falls into sleep.

*

'Sir, that girl's brother is here to see you, sir.' Mrs Bryce is at the dining room door, arms akimbo.

Catherine, dressed in a morning gown, her feet stuffed into slippers and her hair twisted in an untidy knot, keeps her father company at his early breakfast. It is better than lying wakeful in her room listening to the birds chorusing their blithe freedom outside.

'The Williams' girl?' Papa says, laying down his white napkin and rising from his chair.

'Hester?' Catherine cries. 'Oh, Papa, I hope all is well.'

'Well, bring him in Mrs Bryce. It must be urgent, this time of the morning.'

Mrs Bryce has no need to obey. Hester's brother has already made his way to the dining room door. He hovers, squashing his hat between trembling hands. His forehead is tight across eyes bruised with the bags of lack of sleep.

'Has your sister been found? Reuben? Do I remember correctly?' Papa says. 'My daughter, Catherine,' he adds, gesturing to Catherine.

'Is Hester safe? Is she well?' Catherine pushes back her chair and hurries across the rug to stand in the doorway beside Reuben. She touches his arm and he jumps as if accosted by a ghost.

'Yes, sir and yes, Miss Catherine.' He looks at Papa. 'I'm sorry to disturb you at such an uncivilised hour, sir—'

'Please, tell us,' Catherine begs. 'What news? Where is she?'

Reuben glances from Catherine to Papa, returns his gaze to Papa.

'After you left yesterday, sir, something you said about the herbal lore, Hester being interested in it, reminded me of a time at our farm, years ago, when Hester asked about the whereabouts of the man who rented Farmer Bree's cottage. Not been seen since nearly a year. Word has it he knew about herbs and—'

'Aaron?' Catherine asks.

Reuben shakes his head. 'I don't know.'

'Is she there, at Farmer Bree's cottage?' Papa says.

'Yes.' Reuben's brow creases.

'You've been to this cottage, you've seen her?' Catherine continues to tug at Reuben's arm. 'Is she well?'

'Yes, Miss Catherine, I have.' He speaks directly to her, as if he cannot hold in the news any longer and here is a sympathetic ear. 'She gave birth last night–'

'Gave birth!' Catherine clamps her hand to her open mouth.

'–and she and the babe are weak. She needs help. I ...' He studies the rug, his ears pink, and Catherine assumes he is embarrassed to have spoken of births and babies in her presence. 'I ... went to our mother, to fetch her, to go to my sister.' He raises his eyes to Papa's face, lowers them. 'She won't go to her.' He gives his unfortunate hat another squeeze. 'I sought aid from Reverend Jarvis ...' His colour rises.

Catherine is shocked, saddened too. She has no time for Reverend Jarvis whom she considers a pompous bore. Mrs Williams is another matter. A mother who will not take in her own daughter at this dire time?

'Hester will come here.' Catherine snatches her hand from Reuben's arm to lay it on Papa's, encouraging his agreement.

'What's all this disturbance? At this hour?' Aunt Lottie, dressed in a long-sleeved gown and cap, joins the crowd in the doorway.

Catherine speaks, Reuben speaks. Papa holds his hand up.

'Let's move into the drawing room and decide what to do, for whatever it is, it has to be done quickly.'

Catherine trails the others across the hall, clenching and unclenching her hands. Hester might be dying and the baby too, and they want to talk? Papa, Aunt Lottie and Hester's brother sit, but Catherine can't be still. It bursts out of her–

'Papa, Papa. It's crystal clear what should happen. I'll go with Mr Williams to bring Hester here and have a doctor tend her and the baby.' She swivels to Reuben. 'Can we get close with the carriage?'

'Bring her here?' Aunt Lottie frowns and puts her hand to her chin, slowly shaking her head.

Catherine frowns too. 'Why yes, of course, Aunt. Papa?'

Papa joins in the frowning – at Aunt Lottie – and Catherine waits for him to say, yes, naturally Hester will come here, and her baby, and we'll make sure she rests and recovers. Catherine's hot brain dances with images of herself fussing over Hester as Aunt Lottie fusses over her, and, later, of a healthy, glowing Hester walking beside her as Catherine wheels the baby's high pram in the sunshine along the river path. And later still, the child – is it a boy or a girl? No one has said, Catherine will ask – will learn to ride on gentle Molly while Hester whispers thank yous in the mare's twitching ear. It will be as if they are sisters. Catherine will be like an aunt to the child, a godmother. It's heaven, it's perfect.

'Is it a boy or a girl?' Catherine demands of Reuben, whose eyes widen.

'I … I'm sorry, Miss Catherine … I … didn't ask.'

Catherine lifts her eyes to heaven. Men.

'Catherine.' Aunt Lottie's voice carries its familiar steel. 'We cannot take in an unmarried girl with a baby, particularly one accused of being a witch. Think what the townspeople will say.'

'Papa?' Catherine waits.

It is Reuben who speaks. 'Miss Michaels, Mr Michaels, please believe me when I say I did not come here to seek charity. I can't bring my sister and the child here, not under the circumstances.' He blushes harder. Shame, hurt? 'I came to seek advice from you, sir, and to tell you my sister has been found, as you asked.'

'And the advice,' Catherine says, too loudly, 'is that she will come here.'

'The girl cannot come here.' Aunt Lottie lifts her chin. 'I'm sorry, Catherine.' She nods at Reuben. 'You will excuse me when I say this to my niece.' She fixes her gaze on Catherine. 'You have met this girl twice and while your attachment is charming, it seems to be much misplaced.'

'I know her!' Catherine is mulish. She understands the rational nature of her aunt's argument, yet it is wrong, wrong, wrong. 'Papa, please show your Christian charity.'

Papa speaks slowly. 'I'm sorry too, my dear. Lottie is right. I can't risk your reputation, or hers, or, to be blunt, the business, by acting hastily and later regretting it. However'– he raises a hand to stop Catherine's splutter of outrage–'I will go immediately with Reuben in the carriage and we will fetch Hester to the workhouse.'

'The workhouse!' Catherine throws her hands out in horror. 'No!'

Papa holds up his palms. 'Remember, my dear, I'm a guardian there. I promise you Hester and the baby will be well cared for.'

Reuben stands, presses his palms together. 'Thank you, sir. I wouldn't wish the workhouse on any poor wretch, except I can't see any alternative. My sister can't remain where she is, not with a baby.'

'It will give her time to recover,' Papa says, 'and also … time for your … family to decide how to go forward.'

'Papa! Please!'

He steps across the room, bends down to put his hands on Catherine's shoulders. 'You care too much, my dear. Let this one go. It can't do you any good.' He straightens, says to Reuben, 'Let me fetch my coat and we'll be off.'

Catherine sinks into the sofa, fighting tears.

Chapter Twenty Seven

here are mutters and mumbles. Her brother and a stranger, not Aaron, an older gentleman. The baby's reedy cry, her own confusion, being lifted, a horse snickering with gentle concern, the pitching of a cart or carriage over rough tracks, hot sunlight on her head.

The carriage stops in a place shaded by high stone walls with many windows. Hester, supported by Reuben, is awake enough to walk inside. The damp chill is sudden after the heat of the road. Women dressed in ragged, dull clothes point and whisper. A well-rounded woman with keys at her waist takes over from Reuben; another, much younger, takes the baby. She lays her by Hester's side once Hester is settled in a narrow iron bed, one in a long row, each inches from its neighbour. She plucks at the coarse scratchy blankets, leans against the flat pillow encased in carbolic-smelling linen. A hospital?

The woman with the keys has left. The girl remains, part of a handful of women of all ages, dressed in identical faded brown dresses, greying pinafores and caps. They stare at Hester from the foot of the bed with blank faces. One, wrinkle-faced and with her greasy hair stuffed under a torn cap, squeezes between the beds and pokes gingerly at the baby.

'Lad or lass?'

'Lass.' Hester wriggles with discomfort. 'What is this place?'

'The workhouse.' A scrawny-necked woman with a hollow-cheeked child on her hip steps closer to the end of the bed. Hester shrinks from the heady perfume of old sweat. The child is intent on the baby, stretching out an arm as if he (or she) would stroke the pale, crumpled face. Hester draws her baby closer.

'They brought you here.' The mother jerks her head at the doorway.

'Reuben? My brother.'

'Brother?'

'Yes, and the gentleman?'

'Mr Michaels, one of the guardians.' The woman shifts the skinny child to her other hip. 'He's pleasant enough. Never seen him take a personal interest in one of us before.'

Hester, in her fogged state, doesn't understand why the woman leers, until–

'No, no. It's not–'

'What they always say, love, what they always say.' A salacious chuckle. The others join in.

Hester is more wakeful. She gazes at the sleeping baby, strokes the downy head.

'Her father had to leave,' she says, 'before he knew ...' Her eyes fill with weary tears.

An ancient woman whose face and throat appear to be made of the same stuff as her rumpled brown dress, pushes the scrawny mother aside.

'Not all is here because they sinned.' She scowls. 'Can't you see the babe t'aint twenty-four hours born? Girl needs rest, food, not your nasty gossiping jabbering.'

The mother tosses her head, sending her uncombed loose locks into her child's white face. The child screws up its eyes and bawls.

Hester closes her own eyes. What perverse kindness persuaded Reuben to bring her here? And why with Mr Michaels? Catherine's father.

'Here.' A girl about Hester's age squeezes into the gap on the other side of the bed and places a wooden bowl in Hester's hands. 'Matron says to eat it all.' She glowers at the others, hands on her bony hips. 'And you lot are to get on with your chores afore Matron comes here herself and makes sure you do.'

'Who d'ya think you are, Missy? The bloody queen?' The scowling mother ignores her wailing child to glare at the girl, who shrugs.

'She'll be along here soon, she told me.' She stalks from the room, reminding Hester of the tabby in contemptuous mood. The tabby! Hester, for the first time in how long, finds a morsel to be pleased about. The cat will see to herself, will be there when Hester returns. Which – Hester sniffs at the contents of the bowl, takes a tentative sip of its watery, lukewarm contents – will be as soon as she can walk unaided through the door.

*

Joseph stands on Lydia's step. In his office an Everest of papers craves his attention and he is meeting with a potential new clerk in a half hour. Yet he has to do this, before matters go beyond his reach. For the moment, he has reassured Catherine that Hester and the baby, a girl, are safely tucked up and comfortable. He passed by any mention of how the baby is weak and may not be long for this world.

Catherine begged to be allowed to visit.

'Impossible,' Lottie said.

Joseph agreed, standing firm against his daughter's weepy pleas. His objections are not for reasons of propriety. As the daughter of a workhouse guardian, Catherine would be seen as fulfilling charitable duties by visiting inmates. What troubles Joseph, more than if the baby dies, is what will happen if she survives. Hence his mission.

None of his business, Lottie would sniff, and Joseph agrees with this also. Except, for some reason he believes it is his business. Because he promised Catherine he would do all he could for Hester. Is this his reason?

Lydia opens the door. She runs her hand through her untidy hair and drops her gaze to the step. Not before Joseph sees the red swellings of her eyes.

'May I come in, Lydia?'

She leaves the door open and walks ahead of him, seats herself on one of the chairs in the bay. The sunlight slanting through the window is muted by the film of grime on the glass, inside and out. Joseph sweeps off his hat, holds it in his hands and stands by the fireplace. The room is in greater disarray than on his earlier visit.

'You know, of course, that Hester and her baby are at the workhouse,' he says.

She squints at him. 'Yes. Reuben told me.'

He coughs, speaks gently. 'Your daughter needs your help, Lydia, your love–'

'She survived this past frozen winter with no help. Earthly help in any case.' Her voice is tart, as if she is speaking of a bare acquaintance. 'Mr Stokes may have more right on his side than we believe.'

Joseph's eyebrows go up. 'And you have a granddaughter–'

'Devil-spawn.'

'Lydia!'

'Don't *Lydia* me, *Joseph!*' She huffs. 'You cannot understand, you with your big house and pretty, dutiful daughter, your business and your big ship, a man of success and substance.' She slaps a hand to her chest. 'I'm a poor widow, of low esteem and station. These last months, after Hester's shameful behaviour, I've had to claw my way back to respectability, to convince myself I can hold my head up when walking in the street, to be able to look the shopkeepers in the eye and believe they'll serve me.'

For one moment Joseph glimpses the loss, the sorrow, which has dulled the sparkle he recalls in her eyes from years ago. Old emotions creep from their buried hiding places. He wants to wash away the sorrow and the loss, to relight the sparkle.

He tries to resuscitate his mission. 'If you don't help, if you don't come forward, your granddaughter—'

Lydia stiffens. 'I have no daughter, I have no granddaughter.' Head bowed, she gestures at the door. 'Please leave, Joseph,' she says quietly, 'and do not trouble yourself further.'

Chapter Twenty Eight

The deep night snuffles, snores and groans of eighty women infiltrate Hester's dreams. Here they metamorphose into the shouts of river men, the creaking of taut ships' planks and the slap of water on hulls. She shifts on the straw mattress, unconsciously drawing the baby closer; and now she drifts, weightless, above the river in the place where Aaron pulled her from Sabrina's embrace. A cool night breeze lifts her hair, undone from its night time braid. The river men fall silent and the nymphs call, their outstretched arms shimmering in the glaucous moonlight.

Join us, come join us ...

Hester holds out her hands, accepting the nymphs' invitation.

Sabrina murmurs: *Have courage, Hester, be wise.*

Courage, the nymphs echo. *Join us.*

The baby whimpers, her tiny fist clawing at Hester's dishevelled braid lying on the flat pillow. Hester wakes, struggles to sit up and lifts the baby to her breast.

Surrounded by grunting night noises, she takes shallow breaths to negate the foetid odours while she strokes the baby's head and stares at the moon-whitened rafters in the high ceiling. She mourns the loss of her dream, searches for courage, for wisdom. She will need both if she and the baby are to have any future worth having.

Hester has named her daughter Ellen, after her great grandmother. It's a joke on herself, given Reuben's mutterings about Stokes spreading stories of witches and spells. For Ellen's sake, she forces down the gruel which passes for meals in this grey, depressing place. It's not working.

Ellen spurns Hester's offering and lifts her own curled fist to chew on. Her eyes are screwed tight, her too-thin face wrinkled like an un-ironed shirt. If she will not feed, Hester's poor milk will dry up and then where will they be? She bends her head close to the baby's, uses her forefinger to open Ellen's mouth and guide it to her teat. 'Feed, little one, you need to grow strong,' she urges.

'Yes, and pretty.'

The muttered statement is from Missy, the young woman who helps Matron and who sleeps in the bed beside Hester. Missy stretches an arm across the gap and sleepily pats the blanket.

'Because the prettier and stronger they are,' she says, yawning, 'the easier to sell 'em off.'

Hester is encouraging Ellen and takes a moment to hear Missy's words. When she does, she frowns.

'What are you talking about?' she hisses.

'Talking about how babies are supposed to have a mammy and a daddy both and the good people here making sure this happens.' She grins. 'Of course, if there really is a daddy about …'

Hester, uncomprehending, instinctively tightens her arms around Ellen.

'The people here make sure what happens?'

Missy rolls her eyes, the whites gleaming in the shadowy dormitory. 'Those what shouldn't have had a babe in the first place, if they'd kept their legs together like respectable folk, well, those types get relieved of the object of their shame.' She wriggles out from under her blanket, accompanied by the crackling of straw in the mattress. 'Here's my advice.' She pulls her uniform over her chemise, scrambles under the bed for shoes. 'Feed her up, make sure she goes to a good mammy and daddy, ones what can afford to choose the prettiest.'

'Choose?' Hester's mouth is dry. She swallows. 'The mother has to allow it, surely?'

'Ha! You think you get a say?' Missy's grin broadens. 'You'll see.' She shrugs and wanders down the empty aisle, one hand trailing silently along the bed ends.

Ellen has fallen asleep, her head pressed into Hester's breast. Hester's stomach churns with fear. She curses Reuben, and Catherine's father too. Did they know this would happen? Ellen whimpers and Hester cuddles her.

'We leave tonight,' she vows.

*

Sleeplessness comes easily. Hester waits until the darkest hour, wraps Ellen in her shawl, tiptoes between the rows of beds with their snoring, restless inhabitants and slowly, slowly eases the knob of the dormitory door. Locked. A sob rises in her throat. Imprisoned, a felon.

She slips into her rustling bed, listening to the dull, sensible voice inside her which asks: 'Where would you go? How would you live, how would you give your baby what she needs?'

All questions with no answers. Living in the cottage is impossible, given some well-meaning person is sure to have now told Farmer Bree of its habitation, and Bree is unlikely to allow a purported witch and her bastard baby on his farm, even if she could pay rent. Besides, while Hester can live on foraged food, Ellen will need milk and eggs and where is she to obtain those? She's penniless and who would employ her?

Her family too have abandoned her. Hester is aware she's being unreasonable, given she abandoned them. It hadn't stopped her, however, from inspecting every visitor – those well-meaning gentlewomen doing their good deeds – with hope pumping through her that one might be her mother. A forgiving mother, embracing her daughter and granddaughter with warm love. Hope's flame quickly died. Her brothers too, including Reuben, have failed her.

As she has been since All Hallows Eve, Hester is alone. With a baby, although that is a fragile thing.

*

A ray of hot sunlight through the dining room window lights the remains of the cold chicken on the dinner table. Catherine should rouse herself and pull the heavy drapes fully closed, sink the room into further airless shadow. She traces trails of condensation on her tall glass of lemonade. Her thoughts are on Hester and the baby in the workhouse, as they are on an hourly basis. She frets, despite Papa's assurances both are well.

'Happy?' she asks.

'My dear, no one is happy in the workhouse. Let's be content with your friend having food and shelter.'

'How long will she be there?'

'Catherine,' Aunt Lottie says, laying down her knife and fork, 'your father has far too many worries, is far too busy, to seek out the comings and goings of unwed mothers.' She huffs a heat-tired breath. 'This obsession of yours needs to stop. Forget this girl, who doubtless has forgotten you.'

'Yes, quite possible.' Papa picks up his napkin and dabs

at his moustache. 'Your aunt is correct, as ever. I have a mountain of work to deal with and need to pray a bright, talented clerk miraculously appears at my door one day.'

Catherine is ashamed when she thinks of Papa donning his coat and hat and confronting the shimmering heat. She frowns at the dark rings under his eyes, worries at the sallowness of his skin above his neat, dark beard. He pushes back his chair and comes around the table to give her a farewell kiss on her forehead.

'Of course I'm correct.' Aunt Lottie stands and walks to the bell pull. 'The girl will move elsewhere, hopefully take up a suitable livelihood or marry, untainted by these unfortunate happenings. The baby will be adopted out and raised as a good Christian–'

'Adopted?' Catherine throws out her hands. She swivels to meet Papa's wide-eyed gaze. 'What does she mean?'

'Please, Catherine, stop making a fuss.' Aunt Lottie gives the bell pull a solid tug. 'Your father has done what he can for the girl and what happens next is none of his, or your, concern.'

'You knew the baby would be adopted, Papa, and you never told me?' She leans away from his kiss. 'Does Hester agree to this?'

Papa frowns at Aunt Lottie. 'Yes, I knew, and it really is for the best. Whether she agrees or not, I'm not aware.'

Catherine stands to faces Papa. A fierce fury wells inside her, matched by an equally fierce desire to cry. Of course Hester doesn't agree. The kindly, good-humoured girl of St Ceyna's well, the poised, secret-sharing young woman at the dressmaker's – neither of these Hesters would willingly part with her baby.

She grasps Papa's arms, challenges his sad, wary eyes. 'It's too bad, all too bad! You can't allow strangers to come along and … and *steal* … babies from their mothers with no agreement from them.'

Papa pats Catherine's arm. 'What else is there to do? This way there can be a future for both mother and child. Otherwise ...'

Catherine releases him. She holds her head high and juts out her chin. 'I will ride there today and talk to Hester myself.' Her voice breaks. 'You must let me do this, Papa. I won't eat or sleep until I have.'

She waits for Aunt Lottie's horrified exclamation, for Papa's headshake. Determination burrows deep inside her.

Both come as expected. Then Papa says, slowly, 'Very well.'

Catherine's mouth opens, shuts.

'You will go in the carriage, not ride in this heat.'

Chapter Twenty Nine

ester settles a sleeping Ellen on the coarse blanket and buttons her chemise, readying herself for the tedious labour of the sewing room where turning sheets is her allocated occupation. Worry teases her gut. The baby refuses to feed despite Hester's long, persistent attempts. Her limbs are fleshless, her cheeks sunken, she grizzles constantly and chews her wrinkled fist. Neither of them will flourish in this dismal place. Worse ... Hester blanks the horrific notion from her mind.

Her yearning for her cottage with its pots and phials, for the cat, for the spirits which drift fog-like in and out of the open doors and windows, hurts her with its intensity. She yearns too for Sabrina's songs and the plashing of the river nymphs as they call to her. She plays their teasing cries over and over in her mind while she sews endless seams. Her soul is with the river even if her body is in this foul building.

Nothing has been said about taking Ellen from her. Hester dares hope Missy played a cruel joke. Or else they are waiting to see if the baby lives.

She adjusts her dowdy workhouse dress and bends to pick up Ellen. Her attention is caught by the far door opening, pushed ajar by a hesitant hand. Hester squints. Her eyes widen.

Catherine Michaels creeps into the long dormitory, peers around with the reluctance of a mouse gathering the nerve to leave its hole in the skirting board, spots Hester and scurries forward. A basket covered with a snowy cloth bangs nervously against her skirts. Her pale blue dress with its creamy lace collar and cuffs, her dark blue hat with a single yellow feather and her white gloves dazzle Hester. In the fuggy gloom of the colourless room, Catherine is a glowing peacock.

'Hello, Hester, do you remember me?' she says in one breath. Her face is flushed, her eyes too bright. She sets the basket on the bed.

Hester grins. 'Remember you? With … what was it? Oh yes. Your jacket the colour of late summer leaves on old oaks.' Discomfited at being caught in the workhouse uniform, seeing herself an underfed peahen to Catherine's brilliance, she fingers her uncombed hair, fallen from its cap. She's glad of the hasty cold wash she undertook early that morning.

'Of course I remember,' she says. 'I'm more amazed you remember me, and'—Hester glances at the baby as heat rises in her cheeks—'have come here at all.'

'Pooh,' Catherine says. 'You sound like Aunt Lottie. I do confess, however, to being here under sufferance.' She giggles; a sharp, high note which causes Hester to briefly frown. 'Papa and Aunt Lottie were dead against it until I threatened to ride here, by myself. It was amazing how soon the carriage was prepared.'

Ellen whimpers and Catherine gently touches her fingers to the baby's damp head. Her high colour is fading, she appears more relaxed.

'What have you called her?'

'Ellen, after my great grandmother.' Hester smiles into Ellen's wrinkled face. 'A wise woman. Villagers sought her out for healing, for themselves and their animals.'

'Ah.' Catherine taps the basket. 'I've brought you Mrs Bryce's chicken soup.' She blows out a breath. 'Papa says the food here is *adequate*. I can imagine.'

Hester's belly rumbles. How is she supposed to eat this bounty before it's stolen from her or taken to the kitchens to be 'shared'?

Catherine appears to guess Hester's worry. The dormitory is empty, so she pulls off her gloves, removes the basket's cloth and brings out a covered bowl. 'It might be warm enough to be edible.' She uncovers the bowl, plucks a spoon from the bottom of the basket. 'Give the baby to me and you eat. If the mother has good nourishment, the baby will thrive.'

Hester does as she is bid, encouraged by Catherine's stronger tone. The soup is warmish, filled with tender carrots, celery, peas and fat morsels of white chicken. Catherine paces between the iron beds rocking Ellen while Hester eats.

'How do you know what new mothers need?' Hester says when she has scraped the last pea from the bowl.

'Mrs Bryce, our housekeeper. She's full of such wisdom.' Catherine carefully hands the baby to Hester, and this time Ellen feeds. She's unenthusiastic, but Hester, full of chicken soup, is content.

Catherine places the bowl and spoon in the basket, covers them with the cloth. With her hands resting on the handle, she watches Hester and the baby. Her lips move, soundlessly. Her fingers tighten.

'Yes?' Hester says.

'Is it true?' The way Catherine blurts it, Hester

understands the question has been top of her mind since her arrival.

'Is what true?'

'They'll take her from you? Give her to a *respectable* family to raise, over your objection?' She wrings her hands. 'If you do object, of course. I shouldn't assume … I'm sorry … it's why I came. I made Papa let me so I could ask you myself …' Her words run themselves out.

Hester's soup-induced contentment slides away. 'Who told you Ellen would be taken away?'

'Aunt Lottie let it slip. I'm sure Papa had no intention of telling me, not until it was done.' She releases the basket handle and pushes her fists into her ribs. 'I want you and Ellen to come home, stay with me until you're properly well and can take care of Ellen yourself.'

Hester blinks, startled at the abrupt statement.

Catherine throws out her arms. 'Aunt Lottie forbids it, for all nonsense reasons. Papa agrees with her. I'm sorry, Hester. I pleaded, I really did.'

Hester allows herself to imagine it for one beat of her heart. Through her own renewed turmoil, she holds out her hands to Catherine who takes them and plumps heavily onto the straw mattress. Ellen sleeps in Hester's lap, her eyelids twitching with whatever dreams babies dream.

'I wasn't sure if it was true or not.' Hester's voice quivers. 'I'm glad you came. For you, for the soup, for this confirmation.' She lets go of Catherine's hands to stroke Ellen's cheek. 'They won't have her,' she says fiercely. 'Never. I'll fight them, somehow.' She swallows angry tears.

'You'll come home with me. I'll make them agree.'

Catherine's passion makes her eyes glitter in a way Hester doesn't believe is healthy. Her skin is mottled pink and perspiration glints on her forehead. It's too cool in the long dormitory for Catherine to be perspiring.

'Your aunt and papa are right.' Hester can't help her

bitterness. 'I'm a fallen woman and supposedly a witch too, which doesn't make me the most respectable of house guests.'

'Stupid, ignorant people.'

Catherine's face is white and Hester fears she will faint. Moving the sleeping Ellen to her side, she tucks the sheet over the tiny form and tenderly strokes the dark thatch of hair. When she looks up, she sees Catherine watching her with matching tenderness. Hester's tumult eases. At this moment, she can do nothing about Ellen. She can, however, help this kind, generous young woman who has befriended her and takes her part.

Which is what Mother should be doing.

The thought sneaks into her head, stirring up resentment like a broom stirs dust. Hester pushes it down, concentrates on Catherine.

'You aren't well,' she says. 'Come closer, let me see your eyes.'

Catherine shuffles along the bed and stares into Hester's face.

'Mmm.' Hester wrinkles her forehead, summoning Aaron's teachings, imagining dried seeds, petals, the mixing of potions. 'You're often weak? Don't sleep well?'

'Since I ... I ... reached womanhood.' Catherine's blushes raise a spot of colour in each cheek. 'Doctor Newton says it will pass, in time. It hasn't. It goes on and on, and I'm not allowed to do anything without Papa and Aunt Lottie fussing like mother hens. Constantly resting.' She bites her bottom lip. 'Sometimes I believe it's pure boredom which causes my malaise.'

Hester frowns. 'Can your Mrs Bryce make up a tonic for you if I tell you what to do?'

'I'm sure she can. As long as it has water from St Ceyna's, she'll believe it'll work miracles.' Catherine grins, briefly.

St Ceyna's. The beech and oak will be heavy with summer

green, sheltering the spirits drowsing in their shade. Hester's heart is sore with longing. She sniffs and concentrates on Catherine.

'Your Mrs Bryce sounds very sensible.' She holds up her hands and counts on her fingers. 'Liquorice juice, for one. And two, a tea made of ginseng with royal jelly to sweeten it.' She smiles. 'More effective of course if the tea is made with St Ceyna's water.'

'Liquorice, ginseng and royal jelly.' Catherine ticks them off on her own fingers before grabbing hold of the basket. 'I have to go. Papa's waiting and I've a great deal to say to him.' She hesitates, puts out her hand to Hester, withdraws it and bends to give her a sisterly kiss on the cheek. 'If I'm allowed to come again, I'll bring something for Ellen. A nightgown with embroidered roses, or daisies.' She touches a finger to the baby's tiny ribs and sidles out from between the iron cots. She clasps the bed end with one hand. 'They won't take her from you. I promise. Whatever it takes.'

Tears blur her eyes. She squeezes them dry and hurries down the dormitory. Three women are coming in and she stands aside to let them through. They stop, their chatter frozen, to stare at this blue apparition. Catherine blushes bright red and slips into the corridor.

Hester prays her delicate friend has the power to keep her promises.

'If not, we'll work it out,' she tells Ellen's pink ear. 'Do you suppose your mama can conjure a spell and magic up a cottage, a cow and chickens?' She grimaces.

*

As Catherine comes to the turn in the corridor leading to the entrance, she hears a man say, '... a well-respected family from Gloucester. The child will benefit greatly.'

And Papa saying, 'Good, good, all for the best.'

Catherine clutches her skirts and throws herself around

the corner. 'Which child and what's for the best, Papa?'

The stranger steps backward, dark eyebrows raised. Catherine glances at him and for one half second is distracted by eyes the colour and shine of the brown, smoky quartz of Papa's favourite cravat pin.

'My dear, this is Mr Cornelius Shill, clerk to the workhouse guardians.' Papa indicates Catherine with a small wave. 'My daughter, Catherine.'

Catherine holds out her hand, which is taken up in a gloved one and gently pressed. The man is her senior by two to three years, neatly and plainly dressed. He has thick dark hair under a tall hat, which he removes when he bows.

'A pleasure,' she says, and with the formalities done, repeats her question. Her heart thuds with anticipated wrath. 'Which child are you talking about and what's for the best, please?'

Papa twists his hat in his hands, coughs. 'Hester's child. Mr Shill has found her a pleasant home, where she will–'

'Not have the love of her own mother.' Catherine's voice trembles.

'Daughter, we've been through this.'

'And we will go through it again, Papa. Can't you see? Please.'

He doesn't see. 'It's for the best,' he repeats. 'For both mother and child.'

Catherine, shaking, appeals to Mr Shill. 'Do you have a mother, sir?'

'Why yes, Miss Catherine, I do. A good and patient mother.'

'Count yourself blessed.' Catherine has no idea how this spirited version of herself has been conjured. A deep sense of injustice drives her on. 'Yet you would deny the same to this child?' She taps her gloves against one palm and purses her lips in a manner copied from Aunt Lottie.

Mr Shill's skin deepens another shade while he seeks

voiceless help from Papa, who raises his eyebrows and returns his hat to his head.

Catherine shares Mr Shill's gaze. She wills her angry tears to remain unshed.

'Cornelius,' Papa says, frowning, 'I'm sorry to ask this of you after your efforts ... Could you please try to delay for a day or two without risking losing this excellent offer?'

'Yes, sir.' Mr Shill pushes his hands together and addresses Catherine. 'If I may say, Miss Catherine ...' He hesitates. Catherine tips her head to the side. Mr Shill stammers the rest. 'If I may say ... excuse me if I'm out of bounds ... it's ... your sympathy for this poor young woman is ... is to be commended.' He breaks off, lips slightly parted. If there is more he wants to say, it refuses to emerge.

Catherine wants to retort that sympathy is not what Hester needs. She needs practical help and not to have her baby stolen from her. She has no chance to speak. Papa takes her arm and guides her to the heavy front doors where the carriage waits in the courtyard.

'Thank you, Cornelius,' Papa says as he walks. 'And may this business with Mr Courtney-Brown resolve itself beneficially too.'

From the carriage, Catherine watches the clerk walk from the shadowed building and across the sun-heated courtyard. He slows his pace to say a few words to women lined up on a bench in the shade, picking oakum. Whatever he says makes them grin and two stop their picking to wave him on his way. Catherine wrinkles her nose. Mr Shill might not be wholly a wicked baby snatcher.

Chapter Thirty

The June heat aspires to August temperatures. By the time Cornelius reaches home he is sticky, dusty and thirsty, all of which serves to magnify his worries about Mr Courtney-Brown. He needs to make a decision, one he can stand by, and will stand by him, for a good many years. Common sense urges him to accept the landowner's offer. Who in their right mind would pass over this rich opportunity? He doesn't understand his own reluctance, which is plentiful.

Inside, he hangs his hat and jacket on the hallstand and peers into the parlour. His mother smiles at him from her chair by the window, resting the shirt she is mending on her lap.

'Afternoon, Son. You must be weary.'

'I am, Mother.' He lowers himself into a chair by the fireplace and exhales noisily.

'Troubles?' Mrs Shill sets the shirt down.

'It's this business with Mr Courtney-Brown.' Cornelius taps his fingers on the chair's arm and frowns. 'He's asked me to visit him at the Hall this Friday. To discuss my future, he says.'

Mrs Shill waits, her eyes on the shirt rather than on Cornelius.

'I've been given long enough to think over his offer to understudy Mr Freeman. His patience is done and he demands an answer.'

'And what answer do you wish to give him?' Mrs Shill looks into Cornelius' eyes. The creases in her smooth forehead are deep and Cornelius appreciates anew how serious the question is.

'Wish is an interesting word.' He pulls his lips in, releases them with a small smacking sound. 'What I *wish* is for Mr Courtney-Brown never to have asked me, because if he hadn't, I'd not be in danger of losing his goodwill if I refuse.'

'You wish to refuse?' There's no judgement in her voice, no surprise, no hint of encouragement either way.

Cornelius huffs a breath. 'I should be wallowing in gratitude, shouldn't I? I should be prostrating myself at the great man's feet and devoting myself to the profitability of Blaize Hall for the rest of my unworthy life.' A faint smell of coal from the cold, swept fireplace tickles his nostrils.

'Is that how it feels? Prostration?'

Cornelius peers at her, brow furrowed. 'Yes. As it should be, given our respective stations in life. He's the master, I'm the servant.' The resentment in his voice surprises him. He has never been bitter about his life. Loving parents, a roof and food, a good education.

'He is not a great man,' his mother says, and Cornelius is surprised at the hostility in her voice. 'There's been enough prostrating at his feet. Your life is not unworthy, nor ever will be.' She hesitates, clasps her hands together, prayer-like. 'And it was me who was his servant, not you.'

Cornelius' frown deepens. He lets the earlier sentences

pass over him to concentrate on the last. 'You were his servant? You never said you were in service at the Hall.'

'I was. Very young, very naïve.'

A cold discomfort lodges in Cornelius' bowels. What is she saying?

'He was the young master, not yet inherited. Handsome, always a good word for the servants, a wink and a pat for the little maids.' She brings her hands down and folds them on top of the shirt. The dark wood dresser, rather than Cornelius, takes her attention.

'Did you never think'—she still doesn't look at him—'how Mr Shill and I afforded your schooling? How we afforded this house, him on a miner's wage, me not working? Did you never think'—and at last she turns to him and her eyes are bright with unfallen tears—'why you, above others, were chosen as the workhouse clerk? Where the money for your new clerk's clothes came from? Not that you don't deserve the position, but were you unaware there were no other applicants and none sought?'

She is willing him to understand – something – without it having to be said. The cold discomfort inside Cornelius surges, a flooded stream straining to break over a weir. The hand on his shoulder, the possessive glances, the stifled pride.

'What are you saying?'

She brings her fingers to her lips.

'Are you saying … Courtney-Brown …?'

'Is your father, yes.' Mrs Shill's tears lie in her eyes waiting for the signal to fall. She sits straight, her chin up.

Sunlight continues to dance on dust motes through the open window. The jangle of harness from carts, shouts of drivers, a child calling for his mother, are all borne on the hot air as they ever have. But Cornelius' world tilts.

'Did Father know?' It's all he can think to ask. A double-deception would be impossible to deal with.

'Of course. He delivered coal to the Hall. Courtney-Brown saw us talking together, and when ... when ... my condition became apparent, he summoned Mr Shill.' She raises her glistening eyes to the ceiling beam, brings them down to him. 'Offered him a bargain he found impossible to refuse.'

Cornelius' mouth falls open, his eyes widen. 'Courtney-Brown sold you? The same way his forebears bought and sold slaves of old, our kin?'

'I suspect the irony was lost on him.' Mrs Shill snorts. There is the barest trace of humour in the sound. 'Though not on Mr Shill or myself. A good man, Mr Shill, a true father to you, and in time I loved him. It could have been worse. Much worse.'

Yes. It could have been denial and thrown into the street, unmarried, bearing a child. His thoughts slide to the girl, Hester, in the workhouse. Would his mother's baby have been taken from her, adopted into the family of a stranger? His mother's baby, him, Cornelius. Taken away, never to know her precious love. He tightens his grasp on the arm of the chair.

'Surely you see why Courtney-Brown,' Mrs Shill says, 'childless in any way meaningful to his society, has an interest in you?'

Cornelius does and doesn't see. He is a tightrope walker, wavering over a raging torrent of emotion. He wavers one way, leg metaphorically outstretched, toes pointed. 'Surely he would prefer me out of his sight?'

'He is a man, you're his son. If he had borne other sons, he would have let you slip away.'

Slip away, a pleasant interlude hazily remembered. A youthful 'mistake' buried in future successes. There are no other sons. Cornelius understands there is a daughter or two. He's unsure and doesn't want to ask, to learn he has sisters. Sisters who will never call him 'brother', whose affection he has no call on.

He recalls what else his mother said, about the house, his schooling, his clothes.

'He's spent his money, helped me. Doesn't his generosity put me under an obligation?' The cold lump in his stomach hardens. To be forever in the man's debt, compelled to repay the advantages he has been given. Forever, and with no acknowledgment why.

'I believe, Son, the obligation is on Courtney-Brown's side.'

Her tone is tart. She puts aside the shirt and goes to him. She rests her hands on his shoulders and squeezes gently.

'You owe him nothing. You should follow your good heart and make your decision accordingly.'

He gazes up. Her tears remain unshed, bringing a shine to the love he has experienced all his life. Something else shines too from the depths of her eyes. Bravery.

Cornelius badly needs his own bravery. For himself.

He conjures Catherine Michaels' sparking fury, although it is not for her he needs bravery at this moment. Certainty flares as clear as a match in the dark. It's for a young mother he barely knows, and whose happiness is dependent on his actions.

Chapter Thirty One

*oby Dick* cannot hold Catherine's attention. She closes the book, places it on the side table by her neglected embroidery and stands from the couch to seek distraction in the scene through the window. The recent heat has decided enough is enough. This afternoon a chill rain smudges the glass to blur the figures of men and women hurrying past with heads bent under their umbrellas.

The dank day viewed between the heavy drapes suits Catherine's mood. All is gloom and misery. She rejects the grey outside and moves to the low-burning fire, bends to scoop the scuttle into the coal bucket and tosses the contents onto the embers. Sparks spit and she replaces the tapestried fire guard before slumping to the couch with a groan Mrs Bryce possibly hears in the kitchen.

Hester is relying on her and here she slouches, as useless as a cart without wheels. Her friend, who put aside her own suffering to help Catherine, needs her. Mrs Bryce was complimentary when Catherine described the new tonic.

'Whether the girl is or isn't a witch is not for me to say, Miss Catherine. She's well versed in her herbs and flowers though.'

No mention was made of the waters of St Ceyna. Catherine worries that her first sherbet tingling experience was made possible only by Hester's presence, somehow, and she steers away from disappointment by drinking water which prosaically flows from the household's pump.

She is, however, determined to regularly imbibe liquorice, ginseng and royal jelly because she needs her strength to do her best for Hester, to persuade Papa to do the right thing.

Why can't he see how wrong he is?

Yesterday, the carriage had not passed under the great stone arch of the workhouse courtyard before Catherine spoke.

'I do understand the practical benefits to the child, Papa.' She placed her hand on her father's dark-coated arm. 'It's Hester's distress which makes me despair. You should see her with Ellen. She–'

'Ellen?'

'Hester has named the baby after her great grandmother, who–' No good could come of going down that path.

Papa took no notice of the aborted sentence. He gazed through the window across the fields to the flowing golden crops and a sparkling kaleidoscope of wildflowers.

'Well, Papa?'

He gave her a sad smile. 'You're too sensitive, my dear. Lacking a mother yourself has made you believe in the all-importance of a mother's love.'

'Yes!' Hope beat a tattoo in Catherine's chest.

'And it is important.'

Hope danced a jig.

'However, the child will be loved by her new family. She'll have a comfortable upbringing, which Hester, sadly, can't give her.'

Hope faltered and slunk into hiding.

'How can you say she can't? Has she had the chance to show she can? No! She—'

'Catherine, please, I'll have no more said on the subject. We're doing the right thing. In due course, when you're more experienced in the ways of the world, you'll understand. Until then you should trust my judgement.'

For the rest of the short journey, the view of the fields and flowers blurred through a smear of Catherine's bitter tears as the men and women today blur with the rain. She and Papa have never seriously argued, not over one single issue, and this quarrel pierces her to the core. She steels her heart. Papa is wrong. Simply wrong.

The rain brings an early twilight. Jenny comes into the room, curtseys. 'Shall I do the lamps, Miss Catherine?'

The young maid's nervous fear has barely diminished over the time she has been in the household. Catherine dresses her face with her brightest, kindest smile. 'Yes, please, Jenny, very kind of you.'

Jenny's face suggests kindness is an odd word to apply to her paid-for task, which she goes about proficiently and silently. As she does so, Catherine hears the front door opening.

Papa is home. The tightness beneath her ribcage squeezes harder. She stops herself from running to greet him. She sits straight on the couch, knees and ankles together, and takes up *Moby Dick*, opening the book at random.

'Thank you,' Papa says from the hallway. 'A miserable evening, Mrs Bryce, miserable indeed.'

'June weather, sir.'

Catherine imagines Mrs Bryce folding Papa's wet coat over her plump arm, readying to dry it before the master needs it in the morning.

'Supper in a few minutes, sir.'

Her footsteps sound on the patterned floor tiles.

Catherine bends to her book.

'Ah, there you are, my dear.' Papa places himself in front of the mantelpiece, side on to the fire. He gives Catherine a quick sideways glance before copying her earlier action of scooping coals onto the flames, despite Catherine's coals blazing gaily.

It will never be the same between them. Catherine's despair is as deep as she imagines Hester's to be. She turns a page with stiff fingers. She won't give in to it, won't abandon her friend.

'Papa …'

'Not now, Catherine.' Papa's voice is tender. 'I'm cold, damp and weary. We can talk further after we've eaten.'

Talk further? About this subject which is never to be raised? Or does Papa mean talk as in talk about nonsense things such as the state of the weather?

Clarification is delayed by Aunt Lottie peering through the door. 'Mrs Bryce is serving supper.'

At the long, white-clothed table, Papa pulls his napkin from its silver ring and lays it in his lap.

Aunt Lottie does the same. 'How has your day been, Joseph?' she says. 'Any luck finding a clerk? It's been weeks, months. Surely it's not so difficult?'

Papa picks up his fork, studies it. 'You would think not, wouldn't you? Young people today …' He sets down the fork. 'They want to do too little work for too much money and if they're any good at all they're off to Bristol, Gloucester, Plymouth or London. I lose any hope of finding a good man.'

Catherine's heart defrosts at the edges. This is not about Hester and Ellen. This is a different matter. Here she can show her deep felt sympathies.

'You can't keep working so hard, Papa.' She rolls her napkin into a tight bundle, unrolls it at Aunt Lottie's frown. 'If I was a man, I'd help you, learn what you do there day in and day out. Not be the idle burden I am now.'

'Tsk, Catherine.' Aunt Lottie pokes at the cold lamb with her fork. 'Besides not being a man, you're also not well enough to work, and certainly not such hours.'

Papa slowly shakes his head. 'And you are never to think of yourself as an idle burden.'

Another icicle drops from Catherine's wavering heart.

They eat in silence. Jenny collects the plates and carries them from the room.

Catherine waits. Is this the time to talk further? She battles her urge to start the conversation, ashamed at piling more pressure onto her father's overworked shoulders. Yet her task is urgent. She wriggles her shoulders, opens her mouth.

Papa holds up a hand. 'I had a visitor today,' he says. 'Cornelius Shill – you remember meeting him yesterday?'

The possibly not-very-wicked baby snatcher. Catherine's mouth goes dry. *A respectable family in Gloucester.*

'Yes.' Her lips quiver. No tears. She will argue, plead, beg.

'He told me a tale which I've given my honour not to repeat to a living soul.'

Aunt Lottie arches her brows. 'Then why tell us about this visit, Joseph?'

'The tale has a bearing on whether or not I involve myself further with the girl Hester, and her child.'

What do secret tales have to do with Hester's baby?

'Catherine.' Papa places his fingers on the edge of the table with a soft slap. 'You are young, inexperienced with the ways of this world.' He pauses.

Best to let the pause go undisturbed, for she has no idea where this is going.

'However,' Papa says, 'your judgement of character has been formed by your upbringing, by your good aunt and myself, and therefore I believe, I hope, you wouldn't easily be taken in by someone seeking to exploit your innocence.'

Catherine rushes to the defence. 'Hester has in no way, ever, sought to exploit me, as you put it.' She lifts her chin, glowers. 'In fact, all the kindness has been the other way, as I've told you.'

Papa again raises his hand. 'The tale Cornelius confided has caused me to rethink my opinion on the value of a mother's love. In fact, his errand was to persuade me to do so.' He gives Catherine a wry smile. 'Your impassioned plea impressed the young man. When added to this story he learned yesterday, you have brought him to your view, my dear.'

'Mr Shill wants Hester to keep Ellen?' Catherine imagines the clerk greeting the workhouse women, how they reacted to his friendly cheer and how her opinion of him had been tempered by the exchange. Mr Shill might prove something of a knight in shining armour, with Hester the damsel in distress.

And herself as Rapunzel? She squirms at the sudden thought, discards it.

'What romantic nonsense is this?' Aunt Lottie peers anxiously at her brother. 'Surely you aren't suggesting this girl, this unwed mother, comes here with her baby after all, Joseph? I must object.'

'No, Lottie, for the reasons I forbad it earlier.'

'What are you suggesting, Papa?' Catherine leans across the table as if drawing physically nearer to her father will allow her to see into his head.

He strokes his beard. 'There may be another solution. It depends on Hester.'

Catherine holds her breath, daring once more to hope.

Chapter Thirty Two

If she doesn't escape from here, she'll need the madhouse, not the workhouse. Hester longs for the cottage, for her rows of phials and jars, for the cat. She misses the spirits which have been her strength and helpmate during her months in the cottage. And one in particular. This spirit's comforting warmth would be greatly welcome in this dismal place.

Mostly, she yearns to walk by the river, to whisper with Sabrina, hear the river nymphs call, and delight at their antics teasing the fishermen. To let the river breezes play with her hair, to breathe their warm scents. Given she's not hiding anymore, she can walk where she wants. If she can escape this misery. If she can find a way to provide for Ellen. If she is allowed to keep Ellen. Her stomach flips.

Stepping around piles of crumpled sheets, Hester makes her way along the row of iron beds, stripping each and turning the straw mattress. Every few feet, she bends to gather the soiled linen into tidy bundles. She tugs another sheet from a mattress, revealing old, and new, stains. She screws up her nose.

Two women strip sheets at the far end of the room. Hester ignores them. Constant bickering and petty thievery – as if any one of the inmates owns a trinket worth stealing – the noise and stench, wear her down far more than the dreary sewing, the tasteless gruel and the grime which smears itself over everything and everybody. Ellen, asleep in their bed, tucked around with pillow and blanket, doesn't thrive, and Hester fears for her.

She pushes down the helpless anger rising in her gorge. Several unwashed curls escape the cap which fails to save her hair from dust. A mewling cry comes from the bed and she hurries to the baby, fingering the buttons of her brown dress as she goes. Sitting on the bed, she holds Ellen to her breast, letting out a breath of relief when the baby takes the teat and sucks, albeit with a lack of enthusiasm.

Hester strokes Ellen's cheek and thinks of Catherine and her promise to make sure Missy's horrifying revelation doesn't become fact. Three days since her visit, and nothing has been said or done. Is Catherine fulfilling her promise? Or do those who decide these matters wait to see if Ellen lives? Are they searching for parents who won't be fussed if the baby is scrawny and grizzles? Will they take her and sell her on to a baby farmer? Hester's terror gnaws at her gut. Sold, re-sold and then …? Rumours fly in here about these wicked women who promise to care for an unwanted child and instead 'deal' with it. Her violent shudder disturbs Ellen's feeding and Hester is absorbed in getting the child to suck again when a soft, polite voice says, 'Hello, Hester.'

Catherine stands at the foot of the bed, another basket covered with another snowy cloth on the boards at her feet. Hester's stomach growls.

'Catherine!'

'Did I startle you?' Her visitor grins and Hester envies the carefree nature of her grin.

'Has your father—?'

'I have news—'

Their sentences collide.

Catherine laughs. 'Yes, yes!' She pushes her gloved hands together. 'Papa has an empty cottage, the tenant left all of a sudden and poor Papa has no time to do anything about re-letting it and he says you can have it for six months, see if you and Ellen can manage.' Her grin widens, excitement overtaking her words.

Hester stares. A cottage? Ellen? Is Catherine a fairy godmother who waves a wand and pumpkins magic into cottages and potentially 'dealt with' babies into princesses?

She gives up encouraging Ellen, holds her to her shoulder and rises from the crackling straw. From the corner of her eye she glimpses the two women watching, whispering. Their heads go down, coveting the basket, and up to Catherine.

'Isn't it wonderful?' Catherine's beam reveals a neat row of white teeth. Her eyes glitter in a healthier manner than last time.

Hester starts with the most important of these tidings. The one which, if she understands it correctly, will be the beginning of the end of the nightmare.

'Ellen? Me and Ellen? They won't take her from me?' She doesn't blink. The baby's fragile weight lies lightly on her body and Hester prays to whatever god will answer her.

'Yes, yes. No, no!' Catherine nods, shakes her head. 'No more nonsense about adoptions.'

Hester sinks to the mattress. The terror lying in the pit of her gut spins itself into a whirling cloud to rise through her chest, her throat, and into her mouth; a foul thing needing to be spat out to die in the living air of Catherine's statement.

'Are you well?' Catherine slips between the beds, sits beside Hester. She pats Hester's arm. 'Poor, poor thing,' she murmurs. 'The anguish you've suffered.' Her eyes blur with tears. 'Such wickedness, to take babies from good, loving mothers.'

Hester forces herself not to give way to the light-headedness which wants to overtake her. There's a second part to this news, and this one worries her.

'You said a cottage?'

'Yes.' The tears dry, the beam shines once more.

'Your papa is kind, too kind, but where am I to find rent for a cottage? I need employment. And who will take me on? Ruined as I am.' Disappointment deepens her bitterness.

'No rent, not for six months.' Catherine giggles. 'Papa is a businessman, he'll have a contract, I'm sure. And it's in Barnley, not near here.'

Downriver, four or five miles from Shiphaven by the road which hugs the river's curve. It should be far enough for Hester to avoid the slurs and witch accusations. Her whirling mind spins possibilities. She could pass as a widow. Be respectable. Perhaps Mother will – no.

'Are you going to sit there all day, and us do all the work?' The women have reached the middle beds.

'She might have servants,' one mutters, pointing at a blushing Catherine. 'You don't and I'll tell Matron you've been slack.'

Hester draws in a lungful of muggy air. 'They'll get done, don't fret.'

'Need to get done right now and taken to laundry.' Both women push their fists into skinny hips.

'Come on, I'll help.' Catherine wriggles out to the aisle and waits while Hester places the sleeping baby on the blanket and follows her.

Hester jerks a sheet off a mattress, throws it onto the pile. Catherine copies her, struggling with the linen in a way which makes it clear she has never made or unmade a bed in her life. The women cackle. Hester wants to slap them.

She moves on, stripping beds and flipping mattresses. Catherine ties the sheets into bundles. They work in silence and the women move to the far end of the dormitory to carry on their gossip.

With the beds done, Hester says, 'I can't thank you enough. I'm forever indebted, me and Ellen, to you and your father. Please tell him I won't disappoint him. Somehow, I'll repay this debt.'

Catherine unbends from tying the last pile of linen which has spread across the floor to mix with the dust under the beds. 'Papa is not the first person to thank.' Red spots appear on her pale cheeks. 'It was Mr Shill who persuaded Papa, not me.'

'Mr Shill?'

'The clerk here.'

Hester recalls him. Amiable, pleasant to the inmates. Some recent gossip. 'Oh,' she says. 'He's not here anymore. He left.'

'Left?'

'The story is Mr Shill had to go all of a sudden, no notice, nothing. It's a mystery.' She stops to tear off a pillow case missed the first time round. 'Rumours are he displeased Courtney-Brown and was forced to resign.' The name of the family farm's uncompromising landlord is sour in her mouth. 'I'd thank him if I knew how.'

A startling thought comes to her. 'You don't think his troubles arose because he spoke up for me and Ellen?' It would be too sad if her own happiness had come at a high cost.

'I've no idea. It would've been Papa who told the board he'd give you and Ellen a place to live. I don't see why Mr Shill should have been mentioned.'

'Let's hope not. I'd hate to think so. He seems a nice man, Mr Shill.'

'Oh yes, indeed!'

Hester hears unexpected enthusiasm for a possibly disgraced workhouse clerk. She tilts her head. 'Is Mr Shill a friend of yours?'

Catherine's eyes widen. 'No, no. I've met him once, here. Papa speaks highly of him though, and I …' She trails off, looks around as if she has misplaced something. 'Papa and Mr Shill …'

The women at the other end of the dormitory stop their chatting to watch. One jabs the other with her elbow and mumbles something. Her friend sniggers.

Hester opens her mouth to berate them for their ill manners at the moment Ellen wakes with a whining, high wail. She drops the pillow case and hurries to the baby.

Catherine ceases her searching and walks after Hester. 'I have to go,' she says. 'I need to talk to Papa.' Planting a quick kiss on Hester's cheek, she walks rapidly from the dormitory.

The women at the far end hoot.

'Couldn't last the work, hey?' one calls. 'Might soil her white fingers.'

Hester scowls. How much longer will she need to bear this awful place?

A cottage. She upends the scowl into a smile and beams at the puzzled women.

*

Cornelius, wearing an old straw hat to protect from the noon sun, is in his shirt sleeves in the narrow front yard pinching out dead rose blooms. He's cut the lavender bushes, retaining the long, scented stalks for his mother to dry. Later, she will sew them into sachets for her linen chest, as she does annually. In the three days since his meeting at the Hall, Cornelius has washed windows and walls, repaired cracks and holes in wooden sills and frames, scraped them of old paint and applied fresh. The outside toilet has been refreshed with whitewash inside and creosote outside. Later today he will erect new shelving in the scullery off the tiny kitchen.

'What's on the list today, Mother?' Cornelius asks each morning, and Mrs Shill has obliged, clearly happy to keep Cornelius occupied, 'until you start your next position, dear.'

His next position.

The scene in Courtney-Brown's grand, book-lined study plays over and over in Cornelius' head. At the time, it was akin to watching the slow capsize of a fishing boat on the river – seeing how matters would unfold yet hopelessly unable to steer the course of events. When his domestic labours fail to distract him, he agonises over whether the outcome is for the good, or the extreme bad. And how long will it be before he can judge?

Sweat drips from his face, he's thirsty, and he decides it's time for the shelves to rescue him from the heat. He gathers up his secateurs and trowel from the stone path and is about to move inside when a lad calls out.

'You Cornelius Shill?'

Cornelius walks to the gate. 'Yes, why?'

'Letter for you.' The lad is puce in the face, his lank hair wetly sticking to his head. He holds out a skinny, freckled hand bearing a cream, sealed envelope. 'Gen'l'man says urgent, and if I wait for a reply, I get another sixpence.'

'A generous gentleman.' Cornelius takes the missive. 'Would you like a lemonade?'

'Ooh, yes, thank you.'

Cornelius opens the gate and gestures for the boy to come in. He leads him into the kitchen where Mrs Shill is chopping vegetables. She raises her eyebrows at her shabby visitor.

'He brought a letter which needs a reply. I've promised

him lemonade.'

'A letter?' Mrs Shill moves to the dresser to fetch a mug. 'From whom?'

Cornelius waves the envelope. 'Haven't opened it.'

'You deal with it, and I'll entertain our guest.' She smiles at the lad whose own grin reveals an alarming lack of front teeth. 'Where have you come from?' she asks him.

'Shiphaven, ma'am. Got a lift in a wagon. Hope to get one going t'other way too.'

In the parlour, Cornelius goes to the writing desk and takes up a paper knife to slit the envelope.

'My dear Mr Shill,

I understand you are no longer in the employ of the workhouse guardians. If your future plans are not settled, I would be interested in meeting with you. If you are free to visit me at my office in Shiphaven at 3 pm the day after tomorrow, please advise the bearer of this message.

Faithfully,
J Michaels

Not settled. Cornelius traces the letter's straightforward, strong handwriting. No fancy curves and loops. Mr Michaels doesn't have that kind of time to waste.

Cornelius sits at the desk, brings out ink, a quill, and a sheet of the watermarked notepaper his mother jealously hoards for letters whose importance warrants its worth.

Dear Sir … he writes.

His affairs are far from settled.

*

'Found? In Bree's crumbling shed of a place?' Jem Stokes frowns at Sim over the net he's mending.

''bout a week ago.'

Jem squints into a sun which has beaten the low tide to a glistening series of shiny lakes circling polished copper mudflats. All along the small coves fishermen have sold their morning catch and are mending and stowing gear for the evening's fishing.

Sim lifts a corner where the rope is frayed, near to breaking, and examines it. Jem watches him. His friendship with Sim has cooled over the last months, a perpetual reminder as it is of his mortification at the hands of the witch. The witch …

'Kept herself alive, hey? Through the winter we had?'

Sim kicks at a stone. 'Reuben took her to the workhouse. Our mam wouldn't have her at home.'

Jem tosses the piece of mended net to the ground. The shrieks of gulls, the chugging of steam engines, the noises and smells of the river embrace him in their familiar way, yet without comfort. He hasn't forgotten the slut, the temptress. It's not his wife's face he sees when he lies with her, not her body he penetrates. Each time he lifts her heavy cotton nightie, she is as rigid as an oar on the feather mattress. Jem's imagination needs to strive hard to conjure Hester's moans, grasp Hester's bare breasts and resist the arching of the witch's body as he rides her as a stallion rides a mare.

He grinds his teeth. 'What's it to me?'

Sim puts his hands in his pockets, slouches against a wooden upright wedged in the sand. 'Nothing, of course. Thought you should know.'

'Ta. I know.'

'It's a girl.'

'What's a girl?'

'The babby.'

Jem growls, irritated by Sim's twitching lips. 'Be a witch too, mark me.'

'Yeah.' Sim wanders off along the cove, to his own work.

Jem grunts, and takes up his net repairs, hacking through a recalcitrant knot with his gutting knife rather than waste his limited patience unpicking the bloody thing. She lives, and the bastard baby.

Devil-spawn. 'Cos that's what witches do, don't they? Jem knows the tales, knows how witches fornicate with the devil. Should have worked it out earlier. No wonder she couldn't produce the father, say who it was.

And now the witch and her devil-spawn are in the workhouse. He hugs the image, gleeful. No feather beds and upholstered chairs in any workhouse. She can rot in there the rest of her life for all he cares. Teach her to mess with Jem Stokes.

PART FOUR

Chapter Thirty Three

A wobbling Ellen grabs a handful of fading purple aubretia cascading from the garden wall and plumps to her clouted bottom. Hester waits to see how her daughter will take this defeat. Sanguine, choosing to examine the flowers rather than persevere. After all, at not quite one year of age, she has plenty of time to master the art of walking. The tabby, resting on the top of the wall, flicks her tail across Ellen's head and casts Hester a supercilious look.

Obsessed with flowers, same as you.

The tabby has settled well. When Hester went with Catherine to the cottage to retrieve her few belongings, she asked the cat whether she wished to accompany her and the baby to their new home.

Provided no sacks or snow storms are involved.

Hester shrugs at the tabby's observation about flowers and continues planting up the zinc tub with various mints. She straightens, stretches, and gazes along the sunlit lane, over the bed of deep pink poppies with their black hearts and crinkled sage-coloured leaves.

'Here's Catherine, come to visit us,' she tells Ellen. 'And Molly.'

She picks the child up and points her at the approaching horse and rider. Ellen wriggles in Hester's hold, stretches out her arms and coos like an excited dove.

'My precious Ellen!' Catherine dismounts, shaking out the long skirt of her riding habit before looping Molly's reins around a picket and opening the gate. 'Come to me, there's a good girl.' She tucks her riding crop under her arm and lifts the grubby baby from Hester, matching her own coos to Ellen's.

Hester laughs. Catherine visits often, keeping an old dress and heavy shoes in Hester's understairs cupboard to save her fashionable habit and shiny shoes from the black earth smears of toiling in the garden.

'I'm glad you've come today.' Hester leads the way around the side of the cottage to the pump. 'I've saved all the rent money for you to take to your father.'

Catherine, Ellen on her hip, sniffs. 'It's far too early! It's not a year since you came here. Papa will think you a poor business woman if you pay debts early. That much at least I understand.'

Hester hauls the iron handle up, forces it down to release a gurgling stream of water into a wooden bucket. There's lye soap in a dish on the paving and she scrubs her hands clean. 'Who's been teaching you about business?' She gives Catherine an arch look and smirks when her friend's cheeks blaze the colour of the deep pink yarrow blooming nearby. 'Has he asked for your hand?'

Catherine sighs. She sits on the stone wall edging the path and dandles Ellen on her lap.

'It's hard, Hester.' She pulls the little girl close, murmuring into her black curls. 'I'm sure Cornelius feels the same way I do, yet he never says a word. I catch him gazing at me, such tenderness in his eyes, my heart races … then he mumbles a *pardon me* and hurries off.'

Hester is distressed to see tears welling in Catherine's eyes. 'He loves you, I'm sure. Who could not love you?'

Catherine's lips curl, self-deprecatory. 'You are, as ever, too kind. Tell me, what am I to do?'

Hester wipes her fingers on the piece of cloth hanging from the pump handle. She plucks Ellen from Catherine's lap and says, 'I suspect your Cornelius believes it isn't his place to seek the hand of his master's daughter.'

'I can't let love wither into dust.' Catherine gestures at a dug-over bed where seedlings cast green shadows. 'Love needs sunlight and showers to grow. The same as your flowers and herbs.' She swings about and Hester worries at the depth of sadness in her friend's eyes. 'Here I am, being selfish. At least Cornelius is about and there's hope. For you, Hester …'

Hester's shrug covers the jolt of her heart. 'I can't mope about waiting,' she says, too sharply. 'I have a living to earn, my own way to make.'

Catherine stands, wraps her arms around both Hester and Ellen, mumbles an apology.

Hester steps away to offer her own apology. 'At least I don't have to bear the horrors of the lumpen fisherman.' Her theatrical shudder makes Ellen giggle.

Catherine's smile is fleeting. 'I worry how it goes with his wife.' She purses her lips. 'I saw her, a few days ago, in the haberdashery.' She hesitates, sits on the wall. 'I feel for her, I truly do.'

*

'Thruppence, please, Missus.' The draper counted out six big black wooden buttons, tipped them onto the paper laid on the counter, folded the paper and twisted the ends.

'Thruppence?' the woman repeated. She puffed as if

the price of buttons was beyond her understanding and fumbled for her reticule, awkward with the baby she carried in her arms.

'May I hold the baby for you?' Catherine stood to the side, waiting to be served.

The woman glanced at her, pulling the infant closer. Catherine smiled, bright, friendly. She extended her arms and this time the woman's lips tentatively edged upwards, exposing a tooth missing at one side of her dry-lipped mouth. Her sallow skin was drawn, her cheeks sunken. A faint purple bruise showed on her chin.

Catherine pitied whatever hardship or illness the woman suffered. She took the sleeping baby, gazing into its sweet face while the mother delved into the reticule for her pennies. The pink-cheeked child was wrapped in a cream knitted shawl which smelled faintly of soap and lavender. It fluttered long-lashed eyelids and wrinkled a rosebud mouth. Catherine was enchanted, and, given the haggard mother, concerned.

The commercial transaction was done. The mother reclaimed her baby and Catherine said, 'A girl? She's very pretty.'

'Yes, Miss, a girl.' The mother's pale eyes softened.

'What's her name?'

'Rose.'

'Ah! It suits her.' Catherine kissed her own forefinger and transferred the kiss to Rose's frowning forehead. 'You take care, little Rose, and you too, Mrs …?'

'Stokes.' Her terse pronunciation made it a curse.

Stokes? 'I'm Miss Michaels.'

'Yes, Miss. Thank you for your help. I must be going.'

'Of course. Thank you for trusting me with Rose. I hope we meet again.'

The quick up and down of Mrs Stokes' scant eyebrows showed her disbelief in such a hope.

Two days later, Catherine was reading in the drawing room. The hot weather had fatigued her, she was listless and bored, with no energy to visit Hester. Besides, Papa had invited Cornelius for supper and Catherine wished to be rested for the evening.

'Can I dust the books, Miss?' The maid, Jenny, peered into the room, waving a feather duster.

'Of course, Jenny, go ahead.'

Catherine idly watched the book dusting while daydreaming about Cornelius and marriage, and possibly children, a pretty baby Rose of her own. And poor, haggard Mrs Stokes.

Her mind dredged up a vague memory.

'Jenny.'

Jenny bobbed a swift curtsy. 'Yes, Miss?'

'Mrs Stokes, with the baby ... married to ... Jem Stokes, is it?'

Jenny's eyes hardened, something Catherine never thought the girl capable of. Her own ill-defined concern for Mrs Stokes reasserted itself.

'She's a relative of yours, I believe?'

'Yes, Miss.'

'I met her in town a few days ago.' Catherine was unsure how to go on. 'Rose is a sweet baby.'

'Yes, Miss.'

'It's clear to see how beautifully Mrs Stokes cares for her.'

'Yes, Miss.'

Catherine decided to play it straight. 'Is Mrs Stokes well, Jenny? She appeared to be not in the best of health. Is something wrong?'

The hardness in Jenny's eyes solidified into rock. 'No, Miss. Nothin' wrong.'

*

Hester mulls over the story of Mrs Stokes and baby Rose while she and Ellen wave their goodbyes to Catherine, who rides down the lane with the rent money in the reticule at her waist. Neither Hester nor Catherine concern themselves with the notion of robbery – it's barely evening, the summer light bright for hours, the road to Shiphaven busy with riders, carts, pedestrians. Besides, the peppercorn sum is insufficient to tempt any except the meanest of beggars.

Setting Ellen on the path, Hester idly deadheads choisya, pinching off browning white flowers and letting them fall into the earth. She picks a leaf, scrunches it and lifts it to her nose, enjoying the slight tang of basil. Her garden is the reason she's glad to have paid this debt, gladder to have had the chance to earn money to do so.

Here in Barnley, Hester lets them believe she is a widow. Bearing her great-grandmother's maiden name, Haycroft, there is no reason for any to connect her with jilted, or witch-cursed, fishermen, even if they've heard the story. Initially taking in sewing, she allowed her skills with herbal cures to be known gradually: an offer to a neighbour of thyme oil to ease toothache when chewing cloves was ineffective; of agrimony to anoint a particularly nasty outbreak of skin blemishes; or of dandelion root powder to aid digestion. Despite her youth, she is earning respect for her skills and her willingness to help at a price villagers can afford, sometimes in goods rather than coin – she has a little flock of mismatched chickens courtesy of various customers – and sometimes for no price at all.

She is doing what she aspired to, when she first plagued Aaron to teach her the lessons of the field flowers and herbs. It's what she's always wanted, to carry on great-grandmother's work, to be there for the wheat-faced Annies and the fathers with heartburn which kills them. The old ache surfaces. She misses Father, misses his shadow in the churchyard. Misses more than that.

Her gratitude to Catherine and Mr Michaels runs deep. She and Ellen thrive in the cottage with its narrow sloping beds where she grows her herbs and flowers, and where she has only to cross two stiles to find meadows vibrant with wildflowers. Below the garden a shallow stream bubbles over stones. Hester loves the overhung, root-strewn, mossy path which keeps the stream company on its journey to the river where at low tide shiny brown mudflats stretch between forever damp boulders. From the sparse grassy bank, with Ellen hushed to sleep on her lap, she watched the wriggling elvers mass black in the spring and ducks nest in the reeds higher up.

It's a life she loves, earned through harsh struggle and cruel sacrifice. A life she would never have had if she'd surrendered to her mother's designs. Poor, unfortunate Mrs Stokes, and her baby.

'Supper?' she asks Ellen, who lifts her head from tracing the erratic journey of an iridescent beetle thwarted by pebbles, and grins. Hester picks her up and cuddles her tightly. She rubs their noses and Ellen giggles and pats Hester's cheeks with her fat fingers.

Resting Ellen on her hip, she walks inside where the smells of drying lavender strive to overcome the newly picked rosemary spread on a bench under a window. The mild evening is too tempting to be inside, however, and Hester needs to ease her sudden restlessness. Supper can wait. She walks through the tiny kitchen and out the door, taking the gravelled pathway between borders where bees and butterflies hover above London Pride's froth of white flowers, to the stream and the river. Sabrina's purling waters will soothe her. The river nymphs, should they be there, will entreat her with their songs which beat in time with her heart as if they are her lover, they are the ones who want and desire her. If Hester didn't have Ellen to care for, there are days when she would wade against the tide, into the embrace of the nymphs.

This bright evening, the river flows wide and smooth. The traffic is thick, fast, riding the waters down to the big port and the sea. Ellen stretches her body forward, arms outstretched to the flow. Hester shifts the child to her other hip and searches among the boats. No nymphs rise on the bow waves of the barges and the shallow-bottomed trows, none plunge beneath the fishing boats to play tag with nets and oars.

Sabrina murmurs: *Do what you need to do, Hester. Be strong. Be wise.*

Hester should be happy. Yet …

She holds Ellen close and shields her eyes from the silver glare. She cannot shield her soul from the seed of grief which has taken root there and which, from time to time, burgeons like the river broiling under storm clouds, drowning her small contentment.

Chapter Thirty Four

In the nearly two years since fleeing Shiphaven, Aaron has avoided returning home to his parents, and Mother Lovell. He frequently scolds his cowardly self, but what would he say about Marianne? How could he tell any version of that terrible night? He instead tries to regain some morsel of the happiness of those early days when they travelled together, healing, putting things to rights with and without the aid of magicked potions. He constantly tells himself all will be well, eventually. While he will never forget, the memories will fade and the good he does will count towards his redemption. Purgatory might not last forever.

Perhaps.

And when he thinks of Hester – every day, most hours – he's comforted that he has saved her, that she won't suffer like Marianne suffered. Hester will be married to the fisherman by now, with her posy of feathery meadowsweet, likely carrying her first child, being ordinary folk. More to count towards Aaron's redemption.

And so it has gone on, up and down the country, through villages and towns, all the time half-conscious of a need to avoid the river, for she is Sabrina her whole length, of course.

Until he's summoned by a wealthy merchant to Shrewsbury, to use his healing on the man's favourite horse which is wasting with an illness the London college trained and certificated veterinarian can neither diagnose nor cure. As it is, the poor animal passes before Aaron can tend to it, which gives rise to his melancholy, frustrated mood when he leaves the grieving merchant and begins to cross the ancient Welsh bridge on his way out of the town.

The voice is faint, yet clear, but turn this way and that as much as he likes, none of the other persons on the bridge admit to being the speaker.

It comes again.

It is time. Soon, it will be time.

Understanding at last, Aaron steps to the stone railings of the bridge and peers down – into a floating tangle of rope-like hanks of hair wrapped around a pair of sinuous arms which reach from the water as if inviting him into their embrace.

'She will join us, swim with us,' the nymph sings, before diving beneath a pleasure boat which maintains its steady pace downstream.

Aaron steps sharply back, into the path of a fruiterer's boy pushing a barrow of apples. The boy swerves, cursing as the topmost fruit bounces to the cobbles. Apologising, Aaron helps with the collection of the bruised produce, offers payment, which is quickly accepted, and strides away.

It is time. Soon, it will be time.

Panic replaces his melancholy frustration.

'She will join us, swim with us.'

The message weighs on him, as heavy as the memory of Marianne. Has he failed, after all?

Soon ... whatever is to happen is still in the future. He turns his path south, urgency driving his steps. However, while he should be hurrying to Hester, a compulsion that this might be his last chance to see his parents, and Mother Lovell, drives him to make the short detour.

*

Mother Lovell's cottage retains its smell of cat piss tempered by the lavender in early bloom outside the open kitchen door. Curled on the settle in a spot of sun is a new cat, grey and white, plump and sleek. It blinks lazily at Aaron's arrival, foregoing the additional effort of lifting its head. Aaron sits at the cluttered table watching Mother Lovell pour boiling water from the kettle into an over-large teapot. Her fingers twine around the wooden handle like the knobbled stems of an aged vine cling to their supporting trellis. Aaron sniffs the scent of bergamot steaming from the pot.

'You've been home?' Mother Lovell's squint fastens on Aaron's eyes.

'Yes.'

'Hmm.'

His mother, joyful at her son's homecoming, and tearful at his insistence he won't stay, not one night. His father glowering below heavy eyebrows, saying nothing.

Neither asked about Marianne.

'The vicar?' Aaron says.

'Gone.' Mother Lovell pushes aside a saucer of wrinkled seeds to set down two tannin-bruised mugs. 'Not a month after you and Miss Marianne left.'

Her voice has lost its impossible youthfulness and is cracked with age. She peers at Aaron with those black eyes which terrified him at their first encounter. The tell-tale sparkle in them has faded.

'Gone where?'

She pulls out a chair opposite Aaron. The scrape of the

legs on the flagged floor is interrupted by the crunch of something being crushed – a fallen splinter of bone, a dried moth husk?

'No messenger hurried here, lad, with a forwarding address.'

'A new church posting?' Maybe Marianne's vicar father was called to a new ministry. Or volunteered for one, leaving memory to deal with its sorrows alone in the high-ceilinged rooms of the rectory.

Mother Lovell lifts her mug to her wizened lips, blows on the tea to cool it, sets it on the table without drinking. She shuffles on her chair, leans towards Aaron. 'Where is she?'

Dark curls hiding cheeks flushed from the fire, mutterings of incantation, white flames curling around the bubbling pot ...

Aaron snatches in a breath, tasting smoke and heat. He bends his head, elbows on the table, fingertips pressed to his damp forehead. He is hot, nauseous.

Mother Lovell reaches across to tap the mug of tea. 'Drink,' she says.

'Drink this, Aaron ... a potion to give us power ...' Marianne demanding, her eyes greedy.

'I failed her, Mother.'

Aaron dares to glance up. She has lost interest in him. She's following the dust motes lit by the sun through the grimy window, studying them with the same intensity she once studied the entrails of the mice which the ginger cat of years ago brought to her.

'She never would leave well enough alone.' Mother Lovell's voice, sharp with regret, sounds young once more.

Aaron persists. He needs to say out loud what he has never said out loud before.

'Your faith in me was wrong. I failed her, I wasn't good enough, strong enough. When it came to the time ...' He returns to pressing his fingers to his wet brow, muttering into the bergamot tea cooling in its dirty mug. 'When the time came ... when I should have followed her ... I couldn't ... If there'd been two of us ... if there'd been twice the power ...' He slides his fingers from his temples to his cheeks, rubs the skin above his beard.

Mother Lovell grunts, turns from whatever the dust motes tell her and reaches a bony hand out to Aaron, who clasps it. The hand is hard, unyielding, and Aaron is grateful. He hopes – believes – is certain – there is strength enough in her twisted hand to haul him from the pit he's floundered in these past years.

'If there'd been twice the power?' She tightens her grip. Her eyes snap shut. 'The river ... wind-whipped, screech of gulls, cliffs and fire ...'

Aaron's memories garnish her words with white light, molten heat and cold, angry waves beating searing flames. He's chilled, he's feverish. He wishes he had not come. Did he expect comfort? Salvation?

Mother Lovell releases his hand, half rises, stretches across the table and cups his cheeks with clawed fingers. 'The river witch, the goddess's darling. She will have her.' She releases him, plumps onto her chair, hands folded in her scrawny lap.

The nymph's song plays in his whirling mind.

'She will join us, swim with us.'

Aaron's nausea rises. He swallows it down, gulps a slurp of bergamot tea. The grey and white cat leaps to the table, its yellow eyes on Aaron. He should have ignored the compulsion to come here. What if he's delayed too long?

'You must not fail her,' Mother Lovell says, in her ancient voice.

Aaron stands, legs tremulous, the nausea climbing through his gut to fill his throat.

Unlatching the wooden gate in the crumbling stone wall, he pulls it wide and steps through. He pushes his beaver hat firmly to his head, leaves his coat unbuttoned, and walks quickly away.

The old woman's last words are flailing acrobats somersaulting in his head.

Chapter Thirty Five

'**I**'ve persuaded Mrs Bryce to make a cake with iced flowers,' Catherine tells Hester. 'I'll bring it on the day, together with my present.'

'More presents?' Hester thinks of the velvet rabbits, spinning tops and soft balls which fill Ellen's tiny bedroom.

She and Catherine kneel opposite ends of a bed of camomile, thyme and basil, weeding and harvesting. Fat hens dart in to grab exposed worms, and Catherine shoos them off.

'Yes, she'll love it! A doll decked out in a pink gingham dress with frilled petticoats.' Catherine breaks off a stem of thyme and sniffs. 'Merely a rag doll. I thought a porcelain doll for later, when she's old enough to care for it.'

'I'm sure she won't care one whit what it's made of.' Hester waves her weeding fork. 'You spoil her.'

Catherine sets down her secateurs and tidies the herbs she has placed in a shallow willow basket. 'She has no one else to spoil her.' And, in a rush: 'Ellen should be celebrating her first birthday with her grandmother and uncles.' She throws out her hands at Hester's quick upward glance. 'Can't you try? Surely any mother appreciates the precious bond between themselves and their child?' Her eyes drift across the buzzing garden, maybe in hope of conjuring her own lost mother. They return to gaze earnestly at Hester. 'A mother can forgive, and wouldn't any grandmother want the chance to love her grandchild?'

Hester sits on her heels. 'If she wouldn't come to me when I was birthing Ellen, when I truly needed her …' She draws in a sharp breath. 'The hurt runs deep and I'm sorry for it. I simply couldn't do it, not for all the houses and feather mattresses in the world, I couldn't marry that man.' She shudders at the memory of the fisherman's salmon breath and blubbery lips, his rope-calloused fingers digging into her arms.

'Of course you couldn't.' Catherine stands, the basket on her arm. 'Don't you think enough time has passed? I believe your mother is busy with patronage from the town. She might be happier, more willing to forgive.'

Hester suspects much of this patronage is from Catherine, who also forces her aunt to take her small sewing needs to Mother. If Hester has learned anything of people, Catherine's Aunt Lottie will need to confide to her respectable friends how perfectly Mrs Williams sews and how reasonably priced she is, and they should make use of her services too. There is safety in the herd.

'Memories fail quickly.' Catherine persists in her mission. 'If the gossip has died, your mother might be in a mood for reconciliation.'

A robust, hungry cry sounds from Ellen's open bedroom window.

Hester looks to the window and back to Catherine. 'Tea?'

After tea, Catherine holds Ellen before her on the

saddle and trots a short distance down the lane, the little girl squealing her delight at the treat. Lifting her daughter down, Hester murmurs her thanks to the patient Molly, who shakes her mane and snorts.

She'll be able to ride on her own soon.

Hester kisses the mare's nose and waves her friend farewell.

Once the tea things are cleared, Hester perches Ellen on her hip and makes her way through the garden to the stream. They dawdle through a scented rainbow of pink, white and red blooms where bees take their time, idling from one flower to the next, sipping and testing. Multi-hued butterflies hover and dip, and Ellen stretches from Hester's side to reach out to them, fingers waggling. Hester's free hand meets the waggling fingers and plays with them and Ellen crows at the game.

How could Mother not be swayed to love this beautiful, happy child? She makes her decision.

*

Sweat from the smithy's black-smudged brow drips hissing onto the orange iron as he beats and shapes it to fit the naked hoof. Aaron watches from his place at the horse's nose, holding the halter. The animal shows no sign of nervousness. It stands stolid, reflecting its inability to be moved by whatever surroundings it finds itself in. Aaron hired the horse to speed his journey to Shiphaven. It's proving a poor bargain.

The horse's refusal to be hurried was made worse by the loss of the shoe, accompanied by a limping gait which meant Aaron had to walk in any case. He was caught between villages, and the first hamlet he came to offered neither a smithy nor a hostelry capable of hiring him a new animal.

'Two mile on, sir, to Oakden. Smithy there, sir.' The

urchin's information was worth the penny Aaron gave over.

Once the horse is shod, he'll leave it at the hostelry he passed in the High Street, and, he hopes, hire a more enthusiastic means of transport. He needs to be moving, to ease the worry curdling in his gut.

*

They are admitted to the house, Hester certain the invitation is issued to swiftly remove her and the baby from public scrutiny. On their way through the parlour to the kitchen, Hester glimpses fabric folded neatly on the tables and colour-matched jars of buttons and shelves displaying spools of thread in serried rows. A red winter jacket, its lining exhumed, sprawls on a chair under the bay window, lit by the strong summer light streaming through the speck-free glass.

Nothing has changed. Hester imagines herself sitting with a silk blouse on her lap, sewing on buttons. Pearl buttons? The memory is a tiny, sharp pierce of sorrow. She sniffs. Lavender scents the air, coming from a wooden box filled with colourful, ribbon-decorated sachets. Hester is torn between weeping and laughing.

In the kitchen, Mother pushes her backside into the dresser and crosses her arms. The blue and white serving dishes, plates, saucers and cups which Hester grew up with, are ranged behind her like the gentlemen of a jury. The scent in here is of freshly made bread, the loaf set on the workbench covered in a linen cloth. Hester's hunger wakes.

Mother frowns. There's no offer of fresh bread or any other refreshment. No acknowledgement of her granddaughter either, who peers at this stranger from the cocoon of the heavy cotton sling holding her to Hester.

'Why are you here, Hester?'

'May we sit down, please? It's a hot walk with a child, from Barnley.'

'You should have walked it earlier in the day. Or not at all.'

Hester gazes at this woman whose love she was once sure of. Mother's chestnut hair, piled in tidy braids, is marked with grey which Hester has no memory of. Guilt pricks at her. She pushes it down and takes a seat without invitation, unbundling Ellen from the sling. Ellen twists about to continue gazing at her grandmother. She grins her one-toothed grin. Mother's eyes flicker to the child, and away.

'Ellen will be one at midsummer,' Hester says, all matter-of-fact. 'I thought it was time you met her, and she you.'

Ellen gurgles at hearing her name. She waggles her fingers at Mother, pulls them back and buries her curls in Hester's shoulder. Mother uncrosses her arms, re-crosses them.

'Does she want milk?' She gives a sharp nod at Ellen.

'Yes please, and I would love water, if I may.'

Mother goes into the scullery, brings back a small mug of milk and a larger one of water. She sets both on the table and takes up her post by the dresser.

'You're living in Barnley?'

Hester holds the small mug to Ellen's mouth, tipping it carefully for her to drink. 'Yes,' she says. 'We have a cottage, with a garden down to the brook. It's very pleasant.'

'How do you pay for such luxury?'

Hester listens for the deprecatory assumption. There isn't one. The question carries curiosity, not condemnation.

She meets her mother's gaze. 'I provide the villagers with cures for their aches and ills and they pay me in coin and kind.' She gives a soft smile. 'I have quite a flock of chickens these days, which keep me and Ellen in eggs and the occasional chicken broth.'

Mother squints. 'They accept your witchcraft?'

Hester bristles, forces herself to calm. 'They don't think

of me as a witch.'

She would deny the accusation altogether, if it weren't for the memories of the night sky, of stars reflected in Sabrina's black water, of soaring above the river with the wind whirling her hair into the darkness, her heart beating against Aaron's.

'Mr Stokes is married,' her mother says, linking witch accusations with the fisherman, 'but Sim tells me he's not forgiven your humiliation of him, how he insists you bewitched him.'

If this accusation is meant to shock, it falls short of its mark.

'He's an ignorant fool.' Hester dandles Ellen on her lap and scowls. Whatever magic she might have, she never cast any spell on the fisherman. If she had, it would have been one to make him find her undesirable.

'Married with a new babe.' Mother's eyes slide to Ellen, who is giggling as Hester bounces her on her knee.

'I've heard.' She doesn't pass on what she heard from Catherine about the bruises on the wife's cheek. Mother wouldn't believe her and it's none of Hester's business, sorry though she is for the woman.

'Would you care to hold her?' She thrusts Ellen at her mother, who pushes herself into the edge of the dresser, hands held up, palms out in rejection.

Ellen waves and grins. Mother's lips twitch before settling into their thin line. It's something, that twitch. It's a beginning.

'Do you understand the distress you caused your family, you caused me?' Mother says with a sharpness Hester assumes is meant to erase unwanted sentiment. 'It's taken me this long to believe I might have a life here which isn't tainted with gossip and insinuation.' She lifts her chin. 'People don't forget easily.'

Hester wants to shout: 'What about my distress, bound

to that stinking, lewd man?' Instead she says, 'What you asked of me was too much.'

Mother tuts and there's something of a letting go in the quiet hiss, as if she has no energy left to fight a now unwinnable battle. The fisherman has his bride and his babe, his male pride amply restored. The cause of his humiliation has been banished, sentenced by the townspeople as one not worth wasting pity on, an outsider.

Hester's pulse jumps at the understanding. Compassion, loss, might fight for her mother's acceptance, might pull her to her daughter and granddaughter. Yet there will be a price for yielding, a high price, and the scars of the last battle haven't healed sufficiently for the price to be accepted.

She stands and moves close to Mother, Ellen between them.

'I know your love for me is tarnished.' She bends her head to drink in her daughter's smell of milk, warm skin, and sweaty curls. 'I also know you are too good a woman, too caring of family, to deny this child a grandmother's love.'

The silence thickens the air like fog on the river, hanging heavy, and cool. Hester prays for it to lift, for Ellen at least to be allowed to revel in clear, warm light.

Mother swallows, lifts a hand as if she would stroke Ellen's cheek. She stills it, averts her head. Not before Hester spies the shining dampness of her eyes.

'Forgiveness is not bought with the fruits of sin.' Mother's voice cracks. She walks into and through the parlour and opens the front door to encourage Hester and her fruits of sin to leave.

Eyes blurring, Hester stumbles onto the hot, narrow footpath, waits for the slam of the door behind her. A gentle click comes instead.

She straightens, struggles to lift Ellen into the sling. She will talk to Father. He'll want to meet his granddaughter.

She takes a step into the street, and jumps back.

'Hey there, Missus! Mind out!' The wagoner's shout carries above the snort of his great horse.

Hester bobs an apology, dashes to the far side and stops, taking in deep breaths. Ellen whimpers and Hester soothes her as she walks, heart beating fast, through the lych gate. From the edge of the graveyard, she stares dry-eyed at Father's resting place. If she stares hard enough, she can see him stretched out in the chair by the farmhouse fire, legs crossed at the ankle. If she listens hard enough, she can hear the crackle of the flames, the clink of Mother washing the supper dishes at the kitchen bench. She draws a breath through her nose, smelling pipe tobacco and coal smoke.

Ellen quietens as Hester walks slowly to the grave. There are few words on the stone: Father's name, the years of his birth and death, and the short inscription: *Beloved husband and father.*

'Here's your granddaughter, Father.'

Hester takes Ellen from the sling and holds her facing the grave. The sun shimmers over the headstone and Hester is certain she sees Father in the wavering light. He's hatless, dressed in old trousers and shirt, his farm clothes. Not the suit they trussed him up in to bury him. Ellen stretches out her arms and coos, as she does for anyone new she meets if they make a fuss of her.

Hester's mood lightens.

She cuddles her daughter close and stands before the grave for a long time. Would it have been different if Father lived? It's still raw, losing the farm and the wildflower meadow. Her cows too, their musky warmth on a frozen January morning. And the pigs with their greedy, beady eyes following the scraps piled into their trough each day, moving aside to allow her to muck out their sty, grunting their approval of the housekeeping. She craves the certainty of the work the seasons brought.

She misses Aaron.

No, it wouldn't have been different if Father had lived. Hester's feyness, her wildness, would have emerged somehow, sometime. Some version of the lumpen fisherman would have claimed her.

Chapter Thirty Six

em peers blearily into the bowl. 'Call this fit fer a working man?' He uses his finger to prod at a lump of gristly meat swimming in brownish liquid between grey cubes of potato. 'Where's me chop, same as t'other night?' He lifts his head to scowl at his wife, too quick, and has to clamp the top of a chair for support. 'Least a chop starts out proper food,' he snarls, 'even if it don't end up that once you been at it.'

He wants to plump into a seat, take the weight off his unsteady legs. He doesn't. What's the bloody point? He's not going to swallow this rubbish. He'll have to haul his weary legs to the King's Shilling, hope there're victuals left to feed his roaring hunger. Righteous indignation fuels his rising anger.

'I'm sorry, Jem.'

Jane hunches in front of the range, red-faced, hair its usual mess, rocking the squalling baby in her arms. Jem scowls harder, irritation welling in counterpoint to the pathetic watering of his wife's eyes. The stupid woman is soft and daft as a day-old kitten, and as much bloody use.

'Sorry don't put a decent meal on the table.' He shunts the bowl away, splashing its unappetising contents onto the table's greasy wooden surface.

'No chance to get out,' Jane blathers on. 'Baby's been fussing all day, not given me a moment's peace. I'm sorry, I'll fix summat else, right off.' She looks about wildly, as if the summat else will magic into being.

Magic.

Jem has an involuntary vision of the taste, sight and nose-tickling smells of Hester's roasts. He takes a too fast step away from the table, lurches, grabs the edge.

Damn that extra pint Ezra forced on him. Damn this idiot woman and her feeble uselessness. He should've tracked the witch down, dragged her to the altar, tethered her to the kitchen, and the bedroom. A brood mare in a fancy stable.

He should have done that, instead of covering his mortification with the first woman shoved at him.

His rage bubbles, boils over. He raises his hand, pitches his furious body at the cowering Jane. She ducks, pulls the screaming baby closer. It don't help her.

'Shouldn't have married you, stupid cow!' Jem has to shout over the baby's racket and Jane's sobs. His open-palmed clout to her cheek wrenches her neck around. She staggers into the range.

'Stupid, stupid!'

If she doesn't get out of his sight, he'll kill her. He slaps his hands to her shoulders, squeezing the bones, wanting to snap them in his fury. He shakes her, watching her skinny neck toss her ugly head like a fingerless glove puppet. The baby wails.

'Go an' find me a meal worth eating,' he screams into her tear-bloated face. He tugs her about, smelling scorched cotton, and shoves her to the door. 'Go, go, and get home right quick, if'n you don't want more of where that come from.'

Jane lurches into the door frame, uses it to keep from falling. She stops, slowly turns to face him, all a'tremble.

What the hell?

'We're going,' she says, gasping heavy as a landed salmon. 'And we ain't coming home, Jem Stokes.' Her voice wavers, scared of its own words. The baby's bawling wears itself down to stuttering sobs.

Jem snorts. No way would she have the guts.

'I know you hanker after the witch.' Jane sets her shoulders firm, rocking her body as if trying to steady herself. Her breathy voice is clouded with hate. 'Clever girl, running off.' She titters, high, shrill. 'Musta seen you was a brute.'

Jem's had enough. He snarls, takes one long step towards her, arm raised, fist clenched.

She leans away, holds firm for a heartbeat. 'A brute what ain't fit for fathering.' An hysterical sob explodes from her scrawny throat. 'Not for husbanding,' she shrieks, pulling the babe close, 'and not for fathering.'

Jem growls, lurches forward and Jane whirls, scuttling down the path like a rattled crab, scorched skinny bum swaying, legs pumping.

She'll be back, Jem's sure on it. He stands on the flagged floor, legs astride, hands clenched at his sides. What's she mean not fit for fathering? His brain is soggy, he can't think on it right now. He fixes his wavering gaze on the open door while his seething melts into self-pity. Don't a man deserve peace and a proper meal at the end of a working day? He bangs his fist on the wall hard enough to scrape his knuckles. He'll have to go back to the King's Shilling to fill his empty cave of a belly. His legs are leaden, won't carry him out the door.

The silence is a relief. Makes him realise he needs rest

before food. He slumps his heavy body into the chair by the fire, head lolling, eyes closed.

*

Twilight falls stealthily, restraining full night for as long as it can. Ellen is fretful. It could be the silver light, or perhaps she is ailing, or simply exhausted by the journey to and from Shiphaven. Hester has tried warm milk, cuddles and stories. All to no good. The little girl will not settle, whimpering, clinging to Hester in a way not normal for her newly independent small self.

Hester shifts on the chair by the open window, places a palm on Ellen's damp forehead. 'At least you don't have a fever.' Her voice is bright, cheerful, at odds with the anxiety knotting her insides. 'It's warm in here, isn't it?'

She carries Ellen to the hooks by the door and pulls down a light woollen shawl which she twists into a sling.

'Let's go and watch the water. That might send you to sleep.' It's worked in the past, a short stroll along the path by the stream, the water hurrying over stones, burbling its lullaby on its way to join the river.

Ellen quietens as they walk through the dusk-shadowed garden. Hester glances at her daughter, whose eyes are wide. She's grinning her one-toothed grin, cooing as she does when pleased with the world. This shift to contentment is a relief, although sleep remains elusive.

Hester stops when they reach the stream, her arm around the sling, swaying gently with the rhythm of the flowing water. Birds trill their goodnights, a frog croaks its loneliness, a squirrel rustles its way to a nest high in the willow overhanging the water. Despite these soothing sounds, despite the balmy freshness of the air, Ellen grows restless. She strains away from Hester, wriggling, threatening to escape the shawl, as if wanting to be somewhere else. Hester holds her tighter and walks towards the river. Ellen hushes immediately.

'The river?' Hester says, and Ellen giggles her agreement. 'Oh.'

Uneasiness besets Hester. Until now, Ellen has been a passive participant in their outings to the river. While she has appeared entranced by the boats, the gulls and swans, waving and gabbling in her own mysterious tongue, Hester does not think her daughter sees the nymphs with their rope-like hair and glowing limbs as they ride the white horses of the bore. She has chosen not to point them out. Not yet.

She gazes at her child's serious face with her widened eyes set to the river, her head tilted as if listening to a distant voice. Hester listens too, hearing Sabrina's murmurings, carried in the warm breezes of the summer night.

*

Jem wakes with a parched throat and heavy eyes. The kitchen is dark, the range cooling. He's alone. She ain't crawled home yet.

He grunts, pulls at his unshaven, greasy chin and heaves his unsteady bulk from the chair and out of the cottage to wander along the twilit track to the King's Shilling. Hunger grabs at his belly, driving his ill temper up several notches. He'll teach the bloody woman a lesson or two when she comes skulking home.

Same he'd love to teach the witch, should he ever get his hands on her.

*

The path ends at a short, steep cleft which falls into the river. At low tide, Hester could clamber down and search in the shallow mud between the rocks for freshwater mussels. At this moment, the tide is ebbing, the cleft filled with swirling water.

Ellen jiggles, gurgles, and strains into the shawl, wriggling around to face upriver. Hester squints, trying to see what is exciting her daughter. Stars are claiming the dusk, colouring the whorling froth around the sandbanks to glittering white, and lighting a darker mass which floats steadily downstream. The mass stays close to the bank, cutting across the tossing water in a deliberate, sure manner.

'Here they are,' Hester whispers into Ellen's curls.

Ellen reaches out her arms, wriggling to escape the sling and Hester is afraid. Her daughter sees the nymphs as clearly as she does.

Do they entreat Ellen as they do her? Already? She grips the baby tightly, steps away from the cleft, considers running home. Ellen wails her distress and Hester's feet still themselves.

'Goddess, help me,' she cries, eyes fixed on the river nymphs.

∗

The King's Shilling is too quiet. Jem steps through the door and is stilled by stifled mutterings and head-shaking. There is absolute silence for a heartbeat, two. Jem's own heart pounds, for no reason he understands.

'Jem.' Ezra walks towards him, his tanned forehead wrinkled, eyes mournful.

∗

The nymphs surround a bundle of rags, keeping it afloat, steering it to the rapidly emptying cleft. Ellen waves her arms, wriggles in the sling, noisy with giggles.

Hester peers at the bundle, gasps, and slides down the short, muddy slope to lift it from the nymphs' wet embrace.

∗

'Sim seen her go in.'

Jem is given a glass of whiskey which he gulps in one. He gapes at Ezra who sits beside him, telling him how Jem's wife stood rocking back and forth on the river bank as the tide flowed out to sea. How Sim was heading to the King's Shilling where he never normally drank, not these days anyway. Sim tells Jem he wondered at a woman with a baby, close to the water's edge, rocking, rocking, and, all of a sudden, wading into the water, steady and certain, and Sim sees it's Jane and he ran, he says, earnest as a vicar at a funeral, he ran, fast, but she was gone, the waters closed over her head. The baby floated, a second, two, until the water took the mite so swift, Sim's sure it couldn't have survived long. He'd raced to the pub, thinking Jem would be there, as this couldn't have happened if Jem was home with his missus and baby.

Ezra is sorry. He was about to come to Jem, tell him. Sim is sorry. The patrons of the King's Shilling are sorry.

Jem drinks another whiskey. It's not true. It's a stupid joke they're playing on him. A cruel joke. The downcast eyes, the mumblings, Ezra's hand on his shoulder patting him like he's a lost dog, all tell Jem it ain't a joke.

Drowned. Drowned herself. Walked into the river. Disbelief erupts into fury. He smashes the glass to the bar. Ezra's hand flies off Jem's shoulder, he starts, cries out in shock.

A suspicion grows inside Jem, billows, coalesces into certainty. This evil is the witch's doing. Hadn't addle-brained Jane called on her, right afore she went and did what she did?

Drowned herself. The babe too. His babe.

Hatred burgeons in his gut, thrashing hard as a salmon in a net, strangling the breath from his furious body.

'*She* done this.' He spits it into the sobered air. 'This is witch's work, devil ways.'

Jem turns, ponderous as a laden barge, rakes the room with slitted eyes.

'Witch's evil,' he hisses. 'She'll pay.'

It's time he found the witch. Time he sorted her and her evil, devil-fornicating ways once and for all.

Chapter Thirty Seven

hen Hester lifts the sodden bundle from the nymphs' arms, it is unmoving, cold. She fears death has already come, but once out of the water the baby opens deep blue eyes and purses its mouth searching for succour. When none is available, it makes its frustration loudly clear.

Ellen giggles, her fingers gently playing on the baby's face as Hester hurries home, one child in the sling, the other lying awkwardly in her arms. Something about Ellen's touch, or the jogging movement of Hester's racing footsteps, soothe the crying, for a time.

The infant girl is about two months old. And when her face isn't redly contorted with impatient cries she's a pretty child, with long lashes lying black on pink cheeks and a rosebud mouth. The wet clothes and the shawl she came wrapped in are of medium quality, plain, suggesting she is the daughter of a craftsman or small shopkeeper. Hester aches for what the mother, and father, are going through.

How could she have strayed into the river? Someone

must have carried her there. The notion appals her.

And why did the nymphs bring her to Hester? Or rather, to Ellen. There's the real puzzle.

She spends an exhausting night alternating between trying to coax the baby to feed and carrying her about in the hope, unfulfilled, she might sleep. Ellen finally falls asleep on the small sofa, having protested at being separated from the baby each time Hester placed her in her cot.

Now, this morning, the three of them are on the sofa.

'Hush, hush, please drink.' Hester nudges a feeding bottle of warm goat's milk into the baby's reluctant mouth. Ellen pushes into her side, as intent on the baby's face as Hester is.

'Until we find mama, you need to take this, I'm sorry, that's simply the truth of it.'

'Hester, are you in?' Catherine taps at the open front door and walks into the parlour. She stops, raises her eyebrows. 'What have you got there?'

Ellen babbles, waving her arms at Catherine, patting the baby and cooing.

'I pulled her from the river last evening at dusk.' Hester has managed to persuade the child to take the bottle's teat and she is gulping goats' milk as if it was all she ever hungered for. Hester breathes out a loud whoosh. 'At last, little one, at last.'

'You pulled her from the river?' Catherine moves closer, picks up a delighted Ellen and peers into the baby's face. 'Oh, Hester!'

'Yes, indeed.' Hester grimaces. 'How on earth did she get there?'

'That I can tell you.' Catherine shifts Ellen, who is reaching for the baby, from one hip to the other. Ellen wriggles and babbles more loudly.

'Yes?'

'It's all the gossip in the town. Jenny, our maid, came to

the house this morning with red eyes and cried constantly until Mrs Bryce sent her home. She was no use to anyone and I was so sorry for her.'

'Jenny? Is this her babe?' Hester has never met Jenny. From Catherine's infrequent mentions of the maid, she believes she is a mere girl, too young to be a mother.

Catherine squashes onto the sofa beside Hester, allowing Ellen to reach over and gently stroke the baby's face, making breathy fussing noises.

'No, no. It's her cousin's, Jane Stokes. Mrs Stokes'– Catherine's voice wavers–'Mrs Stokes walked into the river, with baby Rose.' She draws a ragged breath. 'Can you imagine?'

'Mrs Stokes? The fisherman's wife? This is *his* child?'

'Yes. I recognise her. Remember how I told you I came across Mrs Stokes at the haberdasher's, and such a sweet, pretty baby? I held her to help Mrs Stokes find her pennies to pay, and Mrs Stokes herself …?' Her voice wavers. 'Skinny, haggard, frightened-looking.'

Hester keeps her eyes on the baby – Rose is her name – while a lump grows in her throat. 'The mother? What happened to her?'

'Drowned. They found her body early this morning far down the river, left by the tide among the rocks. It's a tragedy, Hester, a tragedy.' Catherine's voice is an anguished whisper. 'Why would she do such a thing, and take the baby too? Why?'

'That,' Hester says tartly, 'is too easy to understand. The fisherman is a lascivious brute, ill-mannered and cruel.'

'Oh.' Catherine strokes Rose's golden fuzz of hair. 'I knew you detested him. I had no idea, not really.'

'You've been blessed, my dear friend, with a loving family. How could you have any idea?' A warm, light breeze ruffles the curtains on the open window, yet Hester's body is cold as winter. Driven to drown herself, and her baby. She glances at the tabby, sitting upright in a pool of sunshine, tail flicking.

Yes, you were right. Sacks and snow and freezing cottages … I did understand.

Catherine doesn't hear the cat's confession, and talks over her.

'Poor Jenny! It explains her unease when I asked after her cousin, having met her and being concerned.' She stands abruptly, taking Ellen with her. Ellen kicks her legs at the interruption to her adoration of Rose. 'Oh, Hester! I should have insisted on finding out what was wrong! I might have been able to do something to prevent this awful, awful tragedy.'

'Catherine, sit down.'

Catherine obeys. Her lips quiver and her eyes fill.

'You can't take on everybody's problems,' Hester says sharply. 'Besides, you didn't know Mrs Stokes.'

'No, no, you're right. It was the way she acted … it touched me, I felt the poor woman's need and I ignored it.' She buries her face in Ellen's dark curls and the little girl leaves off giggling over Rose and wraps her pudgy arms about Catherine's neck.

Hester's own eyes well.

'Rose is safe.' Catherine lifts her head to gaze at the baby. 'A miracle. How didn't she drown?'

Hester is too tired to be evasive. 'The river nymphs brought her to me, no doubt by the wish of the goddess. Or they brought her to Ellen.' And she tells Catherine of the evening's strange happenings and Ellen's insistence they go to the river.

Catherine's eyes grow wide. 'River nymphs, goddesses? Is it true?' she says. 'You really are a witch?' She appears more curious than worried or frightened.

Hester laughs softly. Rose finishes the bottle and Hester lifts her to her shoulder, to burp her. 'I've seen the river nymphs since I was four years old. It's how I met Aaron, when he caught me talking to the river, watching the nymphs.' Her voice breaks on a sob. Weariness, the emotion of the night, discovering whose child she has lying against her, are jostling each other for space to grow and engulf her feelings as the white and grey horses of the bore engulf the rock-strewn mudflats.

'What will you do? You need to give Rose to her father.'

Hester raises her eyebrows, peering at her friend over the baby's sleeping shoulder.

'How can I give over a tiny babe to a monster?' She rocks back and forth, once, twice, stills herself. 'Sabrina brought her to me. I'm meant to care for her.' Her voice is firm, despite the doubt clawing at her conscience.

Catherine bites her top lip. 'The baby isn't yours to keep, Hester. Besides, whatever you think of Mr Stokes, he must grieve the loss of his child.'

'I'm sure he does, publicly.' She lifts the baby from her shoulder and cradles her. Asleep, she is cherubic, and Hester embraces her as surely as she embraced Ellen at her birth. Doubt crumbles under the force of her love for this foundling.

'Who's to know?' she argues. 'He'll never be able to love Rose, to cherish her.' She is fierce in her own defence. 'At best she'll grow up wild, neglected, pressed too early into laborious work, a slave to the fisherman's demands. At worst'–Hester shivers at the remembered repulsion of the fisherman's thick fingers digging into her thigh–'at worst …' Her tears fall, silent and heavy.

Catherine places her arm across Hester's shoulders, draws her and Rose in close, pressing Ellen to her chest. The four of them sit, comforting and comforted, until Hester's tears run themselves out. The tabby watches from her spot of sunlight on the flagged floor, her tail wrapped about her legs.

He's a half day's ride from Shiphaven. The young gelding is more willing than the beast which went lame and Aaron has trotted steadily forward on the baked roads, where the thickness of traffic allowed. He is approaching Gloucester. Dust hangs red in the late summer evening, coating humble carts, proud carriages, pedestrians, and horsemen alike. A farmer's wagon jolts in the ruts ahead of him, sending straw raining down. The air is stained with the smell of horse sweat, the stink of unwashed, over-hot bodies, and the manure piles which steam every foot of the way. Aaron steers the gelding around another pile, past the hay wagon and onto the bridge into the city.

Sabrina narrows here. There are a few miles yet in her journey to the sea before she sprawls across the low, flat landscape where the horses of the bore ride the incoming tides. Aaron glances over the low stone wall which edges the single arch, and down into the water where a cluster of vessels mimic the jostling of the traffic on the bridge. He imagines the young Hester scrabbling down the cliff face to embrace the nymphs. His longing for Hester, for the cottage, billows in his chest like a sail in the wind.

Soon, soon, he will see her soon.

See her soon, soon …

Aaron starts at the faint voice. He tugs at the reins and the gelding tosses its head irritably. He looks around. His fellow travellers are wrapped in their own worries, none have eyes or time for him.

Soon … soon…

There's an urgency to the faint whisper hewing a path through the noise of the city traffic. It's come from the river. He peers down. All he hears is a wagoner's shouted, 'Mind there, Missus,' as an old woman stooped under a heavy basket staggers into the wagon's way.

The urgency preys on Aaron's dusty weariness as he picks his way through the clogged, darkening streets. He finds an inn where he can rest for a short time. Mother Lovell's ageing voice creaks in his ear: 'This time you must not fail.'

Chapter Thirty Eight

or all Hester's brave words to Catherine, she has spent a disquiet night. Today is midsummer eve and the air is sultry, oppressive. She sits with elbows on the table and rubs her throbbing temples to ease a headache willow bark tea will not shift. Ellen, dressed in a loose cotton gown, has crawled to Rose's cradle which is set on the flags near the door to catch any breeze. She waves her arms at Hester, wanting to be lifted to see the baby. Hester stands and does as she is bidden. A babbling Ellen stretches down. Rose's tiny lips curve in her sleep, eyelashes fluttering on her cheeks.

Hester hugs Ellen close.

'What are we to do, hey? Do we hide her, pretend we never claimed her from the river nymphs?'

As Aaron once claimed Hester from those pearly, enticing arms. She lets out a juddering breath, exhaling the image of Aaron in his faded yellow waistcoat and beaver hat, letting go the memory of his long-fingered touch, the sound of his voice as he teased her over her lessons. It's too much emotion. She tries to be rational.

It will be hard to hide the sudden appearance of a baby in this small, tight community. When the tragic drama of poor Jane Stokes' drowning, and of her baby, reaches Barnley – doubtless it already has – suspicious minds will calculate, weigh possibilities, prattle theories.

Hester lowers Ellen closer to the baby, allowing her to stroke the sleeping cheek. 'We can't let the brute of a fisherman have her, can we?'

Rose is Sabrina's child, as is Hester, given up by the river for whatever purpose. They belong with each other.

The tabby strolls by, brushes her arched back against Hester's skirts.

We've run away before. At least it's not snowing.

Hester glances down. 'I'll need more sacks this time.'

*

A two hour journey has been drawn out into twice the time. Aaron is hot, ill-tempered, and the charged humidity of the air saps his energy. He tries to put the distress of the last hours behind him.

It's hard. He had whispered to the great horse, placed comforting hands on its neck and prepared it for death as it lay on its side, tangled in harness, stabbed with the shafts of its own dray. He had cursed the wagoner who piled the wagon with kegs beyond stability, keeping the curses under his breath for the man was distraught over the loss of his animal, and not, Aaron sensed, for purely commercial reasons.

He has done what he can there. It's the task ahead, whatever it is, which calls to him in sharp, high notes of urgency.

River witch … goddess's darling …

Mother Lovell could be wrong. The old witch's visions might be of Marianne, after all.

…will *have her* … will …

Hester wading into the oncoming tide. Cold, grey water swirling about her ankles, drenching her boots. … *the nymphs invited me* …

The gelding weaves through a cluster of dust-grimed travellers limping, footsore, along the road.

Hester will be married and busy with domestic chores.

'… *I won't marry him* … *He's crude and ill-mannered, and he stinks.*'

Her mother and brothers were determined, the groom too. Aaron hurries over images of the groom. Regardless, it would be better, yes, better. He stamps on his jealousy, for isn't marriage what he always urged her towards? Wanted for her? Truly?

No doubt she rarely thinks of him, and then as the man in the beaver hat who taught her the lore of forest, field and hedge.

He baulks at remembering what else he taught her.

At last he reaches Shiphaven and stops at The Ship to stable the horse and organise a room so he can refresh himself. He splashes water on his face, combs his black beard into a semblance of neatness and brushes his hat. The beaver hat is gone, replaced with a low top hat, black wool, red-silk lined. He takes the brush to his trousers, and his summer waistcoat where Hester's pearl buttons have been re-used, sewn on to pale cream linen. He wipes his high riding boots with a cloth. The cheval mirror on top of the tallboy is all he has to see if his efforts have resulted in respectability.

Outside, the sun skulks behind grey, louring clouds. The lethargic air settles on his shoulders, heavy as a sleeping cat. Aaron walks up the hill, seeking the dressmaker's house. It's close by, at the top, opposite the church. He draws a deep breath, and knocks.

*

The garden offers a pretence of cool under the beech and Catherine has taken herself there to sprawl, inelegant, on the cushioned wicker chaise longue. A jug of lemonade drips condensation onto the glass-top table beside her and Mrs Riddell's novel, *The Mystery in Palace Gardens*, lies open on her lap. *The Mystery* is insufficiently mysterious to engage her. Hester's dilemma gains far more of her attention. And worry.

If Hester insists on keeping baby Rose, the consequences are unthinkable. At the least, the citizens of Barnley will be curious about this unexpected arrival of a babe to a supposed widow. What explanation does Hester offer? No truths can be told. The river nymphs brought the child! Catherine puffs out a breath. Any such tale will entirely and rapidly unwind all the goodwill Hester has built in the hamlet. What lies will she tell? A cousin dying in childbirth, the father unable to care for this last of ten children – ten being a good round and easily remembered number? It could work, if it never becomes known whose baby it is. If it did? What are the penalties for child-stealing?

Catherine sees Hester in pitiful state in a dank, stinking jail, sleeping in rat-infested straw, and Ellen in the care of a loveless, cold orphanage. No. Catherine will fight the devil to ensure Ellen never lacks for love and comfort. She wriggles on the long cushion, fiddles with the book's pages, seeks a way forward from the heat-silenced birds resting in the green depths of the tree. Papa will be home for dinner soon and she will talk to him, seek his advice. Guilt flushes her hot face at the idea of giving up her friend's secret. She rationalises it away. Hester can't do this to herself, or to Ellen.

'There you are, dear.' Aunt Lottie's silent approach startles Catherine. 'Mrs Bryce tells me dinner is in fifteen minutes, which gives you time to freshen up.' She lays a cool palm on Catherine's flushed forehead. 'Are you well, dear?'

'Yes, yes, Aunt.' Catherine slides her feet from the chaise longue to the ground and stands. The effort brings on a faint light-headedness. She steadies herself, takes Aunt Lottie's arm and they walk slowly to the house.

'I hope Papa won't rush off the moment he's eaten,' she says. 'There's something I need to talk to him about. Something urgent.'

Lottie pats Catherine's hand. 'I'm sorry, dear. Whatever it is will have to wait for supper. Your papa has been summoned to Blaize Hall to discuss workhouse matters with Mr Courtney-Brown. He sent a message to say he would lunch there.'

Catherine's already poor appetite for lunch becomes nausea at the prospect of a whole afternoon to work herself into a deeper worry.

*

Further up the High Street, Aaron asks a question of the neat, once-pretty woman who opens the door. The shape of her face, the firm set of her jaw, are twins of Hester's face and jaw.

'Yes, I'm Mrs Lydia Williams. What can I do for you, sir?'

Aaron removes his hat, tells her his surname and he is seeking information about the whereabouts of her daughter, Hester.

Mrs Williams' eyes are stone.

'I have no daughter.' She closes the door before Aaron can blink.

He stands on the step, pondering. She has no daughter. She has no daughter she is willing to acknowledge. Is Hester disgraced?

' *…I will not marry him … He is crude and ill-mannered, and he stinks.*'

No happy marriage with meadowsweet posies, a grandchild on the way for Mrs Williams to cuddle and spoil? Aaron's mind, and soul, go to the place at which they baulked earlier.

Hester's heart pounding against his, their arms entwined. And afterwards, soaring above the river, her starlit hair a dark wave shimmering in the moon's glow, Sabrina singing approvals while the river nymphs leaped and dived among the night-lit boats.

Whatever the reason for the mother's disavowal, he is at fault. Somehow. He pulls at his beard, casts about in vain hope of reassurance. There is no one in Shiphaven he can ask about the dressmaker's daughter, not without aggravating whatever problems she faces. He walks to the Ship, collects the rested gelding and rides out to the cottage. It's all he can think to do.

The last length of path is overgrown with thick, thorny brambles fortifying the dogwood hedge. It puts Aaron in mind of the princess sleeping her one hundred years in her tower room. He finds it hard to imagine the quicksilver Hester motionless for one hundred years, or himself as the prince come to rescue her. He clenches his jaw. Mother Lovell's words, the nymph's song, urge him, unhappily, into the role.

Perfumed honeysuckle reinforces the stone walls and crumbling slates of the cottage's roof, its scent pervading the breezeless air. The faded door peers through the pale yellow blooms to seek a last glimpse of the world before being buried forever. The weather-stained windows also strain for a view. Their worn cotton curtains hang listlessly inside, having given up any notion of being drawn.

A rosemary bush entwined with honeysuckle clings to the wall beside the door, grown straggly with under-use. On the other side, lavender spikes, their heads bountiful with unharvested seeds, reach high. A patch of parsley spreads from the lavender across the dry earth, fighting the thyme in its effort to strangle the camomile which bravely resists the onslaught of both.

Aaron never planted herbs here. Whoever did, however, has gifted them to the butterflies which hover, indecisive for a second before landing, folding their wings and supping. The bees too are grateful for this undisturbed banquet.

The door is unlocked. Aaron finds the heavy iron key on the inside when he steps into the shadowy cool. He stands with his back warmed by sunlight and takes it all in. The fireplace is swept, a basket of kindling and a handful of logs on the hearth inviting someone to set a new fire, raise the flames once again. The table is bare, as are the shelves he built all those summers ago. The bed is stripped of sheets, the blanket he left behind folded at one end with a pillow sitting on top. The cottage has been left tidy, as if the occupant expected a new tenant to arrive. Or themselves to return.

He wipes a hand along a shelf, collecting dust and – he is sure – a frisson of a presence. He sits on the straw mattress which, surprisingly, has not become home to mice, and tries to work it out.

The herb garden. The missing phials and pots he left behind. Has Hester been here, living here? Determined to follow her dream without his guidance? He sees her pounding dried feverfew in a pestle, carefully measuring belladonna seeds, or adding essence of vanilla to some concoction she has formulated. Her smooth forehead is creased, her tongue poking between pink lips. Aaron shakes the image from his mind. It hardly matters whether she has been here or not. She is gone and Aaron has no means of finding her.

I knew you couldn't stay away.

Aaron rests his palms either side of him on the bed. A weariness, a feeling of coming full circle with nothing achieved for all the arduous journey, bears him down.

'You knew?'

Yes. I also know it's not for me you've returned.

'I'm glad to hear your voice, Marianne.'

As I'm glad to hear yours, Aaron.

These pleasantries out of the way, Aaron says, 'Was Hester here?'

Until the birth.

'Birth?' Aaron's weariness flees.

I asked you, remember, what seeds had you planted in her?

His heart thuds as if he's galloped from Shiphaven, no, from further afield, to this quiet cottage. 'Hester has born *my* child?'

A girl.

It's not real.

Except, there is Mrs Williams' bald statement: 'I have no daughter.'

Aaron walks to the empty fireplace. He stares into it, remembering. Hester's limbs golden in the firelight, her arms about his neck, the gentle murmurs of the spirits as bridesmaids and groomsmen tending this ever-fated reunion.

Mrs Williams is explained. And Mother Lovell also. Is this the tempest the old witch dreamed?

'Where are they?' He's already at the door.

Marianne's breath is a summer whisper on Aaron's neck. *The workhouse. Men came and carried her to the workhouse.*

*

Aaron rides through the great workhouse doors into a courtyard where drab, bonneted women perch on benches picking rope. The soupy air in the enclosed space stinks of unwashed bodies and sewage. Men in shirtsleeves, hands on hips, heads shaking, surround a broken downpipe in one corner which oozes brown sludge.

Reining in the gelding, Aaron addresses the women, none of whom have lifted their heads at his approach.

'Is there a Hester Williams here?' he says. 'With a baby, a young child?'

A sallow-faced girl glances up. 'No.'

'Was she here, last summer, say?'

'Last summer?' An apple-wrinkled woman lays a length of rope on her stained, aproned lap. 'Hester.' She closes her eyes. 'Babby too.' She opens her eyes and squints at Aaron, claws folding, unfolding. 'Mighta been.'

Aaron reaches into a pocket, pulls out a penny and bends from the gelding to hold it in front of her. When she grabs for it, he moves it a fraction, far enough she can't take it without standing.

'What can you tell me, Mother?'

A black-gapped grin greets his question. 'Mr Michaels, God-fearing genl'man, had a fancy for her, I reckon. Took her away.'

No, it cannot be, not Hester.

'Who's Mr Michaels?'

'What you want with Mr Michaels?' A warder appears on the other side of the gelding, frowning up at Aaron.

'I believe he might have news of someone I seek. Do you know him?'

'Everyone does.' Aaron is obviously an ignorant stranger. 'One of the guardians here, merchant in Shiphaven.'

It's all Aaron needs. He gives the penny into the ancient's arthritic fingers.

'Thank you.' He nods to the women, who eye the exchange with jealous interest, and to the warder, wheels the gelding about and trots out of the foul-smelling steam of the courtyard into the fresher air beyond the high walls. He sets the horse's head in the direction of Shiphaven and urges it to a canter.

Chapter Thirty Nine

y mid-afternoon Hester's headache is worse, her turmoil not helped by the air which hangs heavy as a foreboding of the end of the world. If the tension in her neck doesn't ease, she will take something stronger than willow bark tea.

During the morning she dealt with two villagers wanting relief from toothache and an itching rash respectively. She worked hastily, an ear out for Rose – asleep in the crib in Hester's bedroom – worrying the infant would wake and cry. Rose did wake, squalling hungrily, less than a quarter of the hour after the second customer retreated down the lane with her jar of extract of aloe vera.

Hester latches the front door against afternoon visitors, encases Rose in a light shawl to hold her to her body and hefts Ellen to her hip. She walks through the kitchen to the garden.

'A walk by the water is what we need, there might be a breeze off the river.'

Ellen giggles, squirming on Hester's hip to watch

Rose. If Hester is forced to give the baby up, Ellen will be heartbroken.

The muddied ruts on the path alongside the stream have hardened. The white froth of cow parsley blooming along its edge is powdered with dust, discouraging the butterflies which flutter ceaselessly from flower to flower. Hester walks steadily towards the river, drawn by her need to talk to Sabrina, to listen to the whispered wisdom of the river. She is burdened with two babies and her headache. Breathing the sultry air is like breathing water.

When she reaches the cleft where she rescued Rose two nights earlier, she searches the river. No nymphs call, or cavort about the boats. Hester remains motionless, closes her eyes, listening. Her head throbs, her neck taut. Sailors on a barge shout their warning to a trow to stay clear of their coal-laden weight, their gibing curses cleaving the air.

Sabrina whispers: *Be wise, Hester. Be strong. Do what you need to do.*

What she needs to do. Hester opens her eyes. She glances at the babies. Both of them gaze at the beaten-silver water. Ellen giggles. The baby gurgles.

*

When the office door opens, the papers on Cornelius' desk stir in the cross-breeze from the wide-open window. He twists on his high stool.

A tall man steps through, bringing with him the clatter of horses' hooves on the cobbles and the peremptory shouts of a man on horseback swerving around a pedestrian. The man appears to be a gentleman, although his clothes, while of good quality, are well worn. He removes his low top hat and brushes back his too-long black hair.

'I'm seeking Mr Michaels,' he says. A gentleman's voice.

'Mr Michaels is absent.' Cornelius slides off his stool to stand before the visitor. 'Can I be of help?'

The man measures the worth of Cornelius' help through narrowed eyes. 'Perhaps,' he says. 'I'm seeking the whereabouts of Miss Hester Williams. I went to the workhouse which was the latest information I had of her. There I was given to understand Mr Michaels may have knowledge of her.'

Hester? Cornelius knows where she is, because he manages Mr Michaels' properties. He's also aware her presence in Barnley is to be kept in confidence.

'Mr Michaels may or may not, sir.' Cornelius offers a small, helpful bow. 'May I pass your request to him and ask you to return tomorrow for an answer?'

'You're not expecting him today?'

'No sir, I am not.'

The man squeezes shut his eyes, opens them.

'Is there anyone who might have this information?'

Cornelius bristles. He's not a gossip. Besides, he is aware of the sisterly closeness between Catherine and Hester, and Catherine's extraordinary generosity to her friend, despite Hester's apparently poor morals and reputation as a witch. He smiles, having to admit the only witchcraft he sees practised on Catherine is the ability to make her bubble with laughter when telling him, or her aunt or her father, of little Ellen's antics.

'No, sir.' He sits on his stool, takes up his pen. 'I'm afraid I don't. And now sir, if you will excuse me.'

The man clamps his hat to his head, mutters a curt goodbye and leaves. The papers on Cornelius' desk rustle in the cross-breeze.

*

Frustrated, hot, and hungry, Aaron rides to the cottage bearing the improbable hope Hester has heard he is seeking her and has rushed there to meet him.

Well?

He plumps on a chair, long legs stretched to the cold fireplace. The cool of the cottage has dissipated and inside is as sultry as out. His coat sticks to his waistcoat and his linen shirt is limp with damp.

Tell me. Marianne is insistent.

'The workhouse sent me to a gentleman in Shiphaven who may or may not know her whereabouts. Sadly, he's absent today and his clerk not forthcoming.'

Aaron believes the clerk simply refused to divulge information he assuredly had. He can't blame the young man. Not given what he's heard.

We are to sit here and wait? Insistence balloons to impatience.

'We are to sit here and wait. Until tomorrow in any case.'

Tomorrow is too late.

Mother Lovell's whispered warnings fill Aaron's head. His brooding ill humour, his anxiety, his tiredness at riding to and fro in the heavy heat, boil over. He shunts the chair back with a clatter on the flags, waves his arms.

'Why do you say that?' he shouts. 'Why is tomorrow too late? What is to happen? Why now?'

The goddess has decided.

The goddess? The river?

Mother Lovell's words: 'The river witch, the goddess's darling. She will have her.'

Aaron's chest tightens, his mind conjuring old nightmares.

Fire leaping. Eyes lit with red. Dark curls, wild, burnished with fire. A swarm of sharp buzzings like angry wasps... stinging ... heat and wetness ...

That was autumn, All Hallows Eve. Today is midsummer's eve.

'Why today?'

The strength of the spirits will be with her.

With whom? Hester? The river? Aaron dare not ask.

He paces from fireplace to window, window to fireplace. He will go to the cliffs above the river, to the place he pulled

Hester from the embrace of the nymphs. Sabrina might whisper the answers he needs. Hester might be there. He grabs his hat and strides from the cottage.

The river is sullen under the reflected weight of the black clouds broiling above. The tide is low, sandbanks revealed, mudflats glimmering between dark grey rocks. Fishing boats crowd the deeper channels, moving sluggishly up and downstream, enervated by the damp heat. The smell of thunder is in the air.

Aaron scrambles down the path from the clifftop to the rocks, digging his heels into the black soil, grabbing at stunted branches to push himself forward. He reaches the mud, steps onto a rock and balances there, listening. Above the fishermen's cries he hears the river. The whisper floats in the hot air, a challenge and a command:

You must not fail this time.

*

'My dear.' Joseph places his palms flat either side of his finished meal. He's unsure he should raise this subject, but curiosity prevails. 'I'm wondering if you might be able to shed light on a strange visitor to the office today.'

Catherine runs her fork over her cold salmon. 'Strange visitor, Papa?'

'Cornelius told me of it when I stopped by on my way home from the Hall. I'd intended coming straight here but my conscience pained me leaving the poor man there all alone at this busy time.'

'Cornelius, I mean Mr Shill, would not blame you, Papa.' Catherine's neck glows rosily, more than the warm evening warrants. 'He's such a generous man, devoted to you and to your business–'

'Yes, yes.' Joseph indulges in an exchange of minutely raised eyebrows with Lottie. He wishes Mr Shill would declare himself given his devotion clearly extends beyond

Joseph and the business – to Joseph's daughter. The way Catherine blushes each time Cornelius is mentioned suggests such a declaration would be welcome. Joseph would also welcome it. He much admires Cornelius Shill. However, this is not the time for that conversation.

'A tall, slim gentleman, youngish, came enquiring about your friend Hester. Specifically, could I advise him of her whereabouts.'

'Tall, slim?' Catherine's hands clasp the edge of the table. 'Did Cornelius, I mean Mr Shill, notice anything more about this man?'

Joseph shrugs. 'Dark hair, over-long. Piercing eyes. Dressed well, albeit shabbily, as if he can't afford new.'

Catherine's hands come together in a soft clap. 'Dark hair. Piercing eyes. Hmm. Could it be?'

'Who could it be?'

'Aaron. Is Aaron here for her at last? Oh.' Vertical lines appear in her pale forehead. 'Will she welcome him?'

'Aaron?' Lottie dabs at her mouth with her napkin and nods her thanks to Jenny, who is collecting plates and cutlery. 'Who's Aaron?'

The rosiness deepens in Catherine's neck and ears. 'Ellen's father.'

Joseph's eyebrows rise. 'The blackguard who seduced and abandoned her?' Rage thickens his voice. 'Far from directing the scoundrel to her door, I shall send him on his way tomorrow with a stern word to never again set foot in Shiphaven.'

'No, Papa! It's not what you think.' Catherine throws out her hands in defence of the seducer. 'Let me talk to Hester before you drive him away, please.' She draws in a breath, glances up at the intricately worked cornice and down to her salmon remains. 'Something else has happened, which I need to talk to you about, to do with Hester.' Pleading eyes are turned on Joseph. 'If Aaron is here, it might help, or hinder. I'm at a total loss what to do for the best.'

Joseph is at a loss too. What drama is the young, so-called witch about to put them through this time?

*

Catherine's mind buzzes like a pollen drunk bee. Is Aaron's timely appearance, his seeking out Hester, a means to solve the problem of baby Rose? He can take them all from here, leave Barnley, go far from Shiphaven. A bereft Catherine will have to be brave. They needn't go so far they will be lost to her for all time. Not to Australia or Canada. She shudders.

'Excuse me, Mr Michaels, Miss Catherine.' Mrs Bryce sets the pudding on the table: a pile of glistening jelly encasing apricots and cherries. The jelly sags in the warmth of the room.

'Yes, Mrs Bryce?' Papa says.

'It's about Miss Catherine's friend, Hester. As you mentioned her, sir, I thought you should know ...' She pauses, glances at Jenny who is setting out dessert bowls.

Catherine frowns. 'Know what, Mrs Bryce?'

Mrs Bryce draws a breath. 'It's all about the town, and Jenny tells me it's true, how Mr Stokes ... well ...'

A cold finger slides down the nape of Catherine's neck. 'Mr Stokes what?'

Mrs Bryce flicks a sideways look at Jenny. The girl has moved to the dresser to collect the serving spoon. Her mouth is pinched.

'He's telling everyone who'll listen and most who won't, how it's all the witch's fault, how she cast a spell and drove poor Jane to–' She stops. 'Jenny, fetch the cream from the scullery, will you? Put it in the brown jug, make sure the jug is cold, run water from the pump over it.'

Jenny carefully places the serving spoon beside the pudding and walks from the table. Her eyes are expressionless, fixed on the doorway, but her pinched mouth curls into a sneer which, Catherine believes, none of them were meant to see. Is the sneer for Jem Stokes and his ignorant belief in witches or is it for the purported witch who supposedly drowned her cousin and baby?

Catherine winds her napkin into a tight roll, clutches it in her hand. 'He's stirring up trouble for Hester?'

'He is, Miss Catherine. Says he believes the witch can't be far, someone knows where she's hiding and he's going to ferret her out like a rabbit from its hole.'

The cold finger on Catherine's neck turns to ice. 'Papa.' She crosses her hands over her chest. 'Papa, I need to tell you, except I made a promise and now I need to break it for Hester's sake. Oh dear.' She swallows.

'Break a promise? Hester?' Papa's forehead creases. His eyes are troubled. 'What do you need to tell me?'

'Hester has the baby.'

The confession should be a relief. Papa will know what to do, how to persuade Hester to give Rose up, restore her to her father.

Except, having said it out loud, Catherine has a Damascene moment.

Too late, Mrs Bryce's warning crystalises Hester's distrust of the fisherman. His hatred, his bullying ways, the purple bruise on Mrs Stokes' face. Of course such a man cannot be allowed to raise that sweet child. It's why the nymphs carried her to Hester. It is meant. And – Catherine's breath freezes – what will the man do to Hester once he discovers she has Rose? Should she survive him, her reputation won't. All his talk of witchery will be proven, her friend will be spurned, her livelihood lost to rumour and acrimony. Her certainty Hester mustn't keep Rose cracks, splinters into shards like a dropped vase.

What has Catherine done, blurting it out? Papa, Aunt Lottie, Mrs Bryce all know and where three people know there will be more in an instant. She's a foolish, foolish woman.

'The baby lives?' Aunt Lottie's fingers fly to her throat, her eyes widen.

'How?' Papa says.

Mrs Bryce fans herself with her hand. 'Stokes will be on the warpath when he finds out about this!'

Catherine swallows. Warpath is one word for it. 'Hester pulled her from the river,' she says, not mentioning river nymphs or goddesses. 'The baby was floating, alive.'

'A miracle!' Mrs Bryce collapses onto a dining room chair, fanning herself harder.

'And she's unwilling to return the child?'

Catherine is no longer surprised when Papa wings straight to what this is all about. She bites her lip. 'The baby, Rose, will have a dreadful life with Stokes. The river brought her to Hester and she is meant to have her.'

'What romantic nonsense!' Aunt Lottie says. 'Joseph, you will go to Barnley tomorrow with Catherine and retrieve the baby, take her to her father before there's trouble. Won't you?'

Catherine opens her mouth to protest it's not romantic nonsense, it's the truth.

Papa speaks first to Aunt Lottie. 'That's not my role, Lottie.' And then to Catherine. 'I will if I must. First, however, Mrs Williams needs to be told her daughter might be in danger, whatever her feelings.' He clicks his tongue. 'Sentiments will run high over a drowned baby and if this fisherman finds her with the woman who left him at the altar, and her fully aware it's his child ...' He draws a breath, and Catherine understands the pain in his eyes. 'I'll go first thing tomorrow. Let's pray this mess untangles itself with no one harmed.'

Catherine will pray. Hard.

She doesn't mention Aaron again. What to do about

his presence here has been overtaken by this new, more urgent twist. Aaron and his propitious timing. Where might he wait out the night? To be sent on his way tomorrow without Hester ever having the chance to speak with him. That mustn't happen.

Will he be at The Ship? Possibly. Or possibly not.

Catherine's face flushes. She stares at the rug where cloud-dulled light tracks a path from the half-drawn curtains.

There is more she can do than pray. There are hours before full night falls.

Chapter Forty

ester cannot settle. Her thoughts tumble faster than a juggler's balls.

During the afternoon she resisted the muggy air for a time to dig dandelions from her flower beds, setting the roots aside for making tea. The bees clustered on their shaded hives, cooler outside than within the honeycombed space. The hens lay splayed under bushes, wings and legs spread crookedly. Drugged by the heat, Ellen and Rose slept, and after a time Hester lay on her bed too. She closed her eyes, hoping to nap until the babies woke. Sleep was evasive, however, preferring to avoid confrontation with Hester's confused emotions.

After a supper of bread and cheese, after feeding the girls and wiping their hot faces with a cold, wrung-out cloth, Hester has sought the comfort of the water. Hesitant to venture as far as the river, she kneels in the long grass on the bank of the stream. Her backside rests on her legs and Ellen balances against her, held steady by Hester's arm. Rose lies on a shawl on the grass. The river is close enough for Hester to hear the shouted cries of the midsummer evening's traffic. They are muted, wearied by the effort of wading through the viscous air.

Perspiration dampens her face. With her free hand, she lifts her long, dark braid from her neck to welcome a zephyr of coolness. Rose is awake, quiet and wide-eyed. Hester imagines the baby is listening for something, or someone. Her mother, no doubt. Hester sits Ellen on the shawl and picks Rose up to hold her close. Poor mite, never to bathe in a mother's love.

Even a love which sours. Hester saddens on her own behalf. She misses the mother she knew, wishes Father had not died and, with him, Mother's calm, practical contentment.

'I will be your mama, Rose,' she breathes into the baby's downy head. 'I'll love you.'

Sabrina's whispers weave through the muffled clamour from the river to join with Hester's.

Do what you have to do.

*

Aaron grows tired of waiting on the cliffs. The long daylight prods the undersides of the clouds, sending a white coruscation across the water. The fishermen's boats are pulled up high or tied to moorings while their owners seek supper or familiar drinking haunts. The barges rest alongside the wharf, waiting to be unloaded and reloaded. Only the ferry shows no sign of tiring, grinding its way across the darkening water on its great cables.

There are no secrets running in the swash of the river, nothing from the goddess.

Aaron walks slowly, heavily, to the cottage through the storm-pregnant twilight. The spirits gather as he enters the open door, their murmurs agitated, eager for something to happen. Marianne has gone. For now.

Legs stretched out, Aaron sits on a chair and tips his head to stare at the cobwebbed beams. His heavy-lidded eyes flutter, desperate to close. His head lolls forward – and straightens sharply at the soft rap on the door.

*

The faint, sweet smell of pale pink dog roses entwined in the hedge soothes Catherine's anxious mind. She is on a fool's mission. Overhanging brambles smother the track with deep shadows and the hard-baked earth gives up no secret hoof prints to tell her if another horse travelled here today. Papa will be furious. Nevertheless, Molly trots along, steady and sure.

Catherine pats the mare's neck. 'We need to do this, don't we?'

Molly lifts her head up, down. Catherine is comforted.

They round a corner and there it is. Her memory of the one visit to the cottage to collect Hester's few possessions, and the cat, has served her well. The stone building crouches beneath a tangle of untamed honeysuckle where pale, feeding moths flutter. Through the open, shrunken windows, candlelight flickers.

Catherine's relief is intense. She pushes herself from the saddle, pats Molly's neck.

'Let's meet Aaron.'

Chapter Forty One

The Bargeman is overstuffed with hot, thirsty drinkers. They overflow onto the road, elvers spilling from a barrel – sweaty, loud, their brains made sluggish by ale, cider and the weighty sultriness. The storm is garnering strength, accumulating heavy black clouds as once upon a time warring kings gathered armoured knights.

'For true I curses the day I said I'd woo this sister of your'n.' Jem Stokes slams his pint onto the wet bar and glares at Sim, perched on a stool beside him. He should send the boy on his way, reminder as he is of the witch and her evil ways. He won't, because he enjoys having the witch's brother close. There's a power in it, a justification knowing her own flesh and blood cast her aside like the devil's whore she is.

Sim nods with ponderous slowness.

Jem rolls his drink in his big hands, slopping beer onto the wet wood of the bar. 'Wish you and your mam had pushed her to set her witch's cap at some other victim. Witch, bitch.'

Sim screws up his eyes and nose. 'Not a witch,' he slurs.

Jem snorts and lifts the tankard. 'Too late to be thinking on her reputation.' He takes a gulp, waves the tankard close enough to Sim's head to clip the tip of his ear. Sim flinches. 'My Jane'd be alive, not drowned, and the babby too, if it weren't for your schemes and your devil-fornicating sister.'

Sim's brow creases, he opens his mouth. Is he going to deny it?

'Jem, Jem,' a high, excited voice cries at his back.

He jerks his arm from the tug on his sleeve, swivels on his stool ready to smack the idiot pulling at him. He frowns.

'Jenny? Whatcha doing here? No place for a girl. Get on home, afore I take you there and tell your mam to keep you better.'

'It's about the witch, Jem.'

'The witch?' Jem's frown deepens. 'What about her?'

'They told me to leave.' Jenny's eyes are hard. 'I knows they was talking about her so's I stayed in the hall and listened. She can't get away with what she done to Jane and–'

'Listened to wha'?' Sim pokes a sharp finger at Jenny.

Jenny swats the finger. Her eyes are on Jem. 'I knows where she is. And–' her grim smile purses into a mean pout.

'An' what?' Sim says, and gets a dig in his ribs from Jem who says, 'An' what?'

'The witch's got Rose.'

Jem's stupefaction lasts two thumping heartbeats before he rises from his stool and grabs Jenny's arms.

'Rose ain't drowned?'

The girl shakes her head, grinning. 'She got her out the water, somehow–'

'Somehow?' Jem bellows.

Every drinker halts, ale mugs halfway to mouths, slurred sentences ceased. They stare at him, mouths gaping.

'Somehow?' He shouts it to the smoke-fogged room.

'Witchcraft, devil's work.' He spits on the filthy floor, glares at Sim who huddles on his stool, eyes casting everywhere except at Jem. 'Gotta get my babby back, out of the witch's clutches. Doan't you reckon?'

Sim dares to catch Jem's eye. 'What you planning?'

The lad's pale beneath his river tan, his eyelids flicker. Jem raises his great fists, clenches them. Sim flinches. So he bloody should. Ain't it all the lad's fault, all of it, pimping his evil sister, throwing her at Jem?

Fury batters his ribs, would chew its way out like a fox in a trap if it had teeth. 'I'm planning'–he sprawls the word, savouring it–'to deal with the devil's witch once and for all.'

The silence holds and Jem throws his invitation out there with the conviction of a Methodist preacher labouring the horrors of hell.

'Who's coming with me? To get my babby back.'

The roar soothes his jilted manhood and stokes his lust for revenge.

*

The ledger is, at last, up to date. Cornelius sands the last entry, wipes his pen clean and places the lid on the inkpot. He wriggles his stiff shoulders to ease the tension and stretches his arms wide. He's hungry, and he prays, with no hope his prayer will be answered, his mother has eaten her supper hours ago and not waited for him. He slides off the stool, checks and locks the cast-iron safe in Mr Michaels' office. In the outer office, he shrugs into his coat and takes one last look around before extinguishing the oil lamp above his desk and exiting into the lane. The air assails him like a hot, wet towel.

As Cornelius locks the door, he becomes aware of shouts and cries. He glances along the cobbles to the far end where the lane meets the High Street. A flare of torches brightens the twilight and casts shadows on the stone walls.

Darkened warehouse windows reflect a shimmering yellow glow. He frowns.

His horse is stabled in the other direction. Cornelius walks quickly on, to fetch the animal. If there is trouble brewing and torches waving, best to take himself and his horse out of the way.

'Heard a lot of shouting,' he says to the farrier who's working on an emergency shoeing in the next stall. 'Something happening?'

The farrier keeps his attention on the horse's hoof. 'Larrikins no doubt, out for trouble. Full moon tonight. Midsummer too.'

Cornelius laughs, not with any conviction, saddles his horse and leads it outside.

'Good night,' he calls. He hefts himself into the saddle and sets off at a trot up the lane.

The shouts have moved on, the sounds and lights dimmed. Cornelius reaches the end of the lane, turns into the street and halts.

Ahead of him, a group of men carrying torches progress in a convoy down the hill to the river bank where the fishing boats are pulled up for the night. They are rowdy, milling about, jostling each other. A tall, wide man, hatless, sleeves rolled up, stomps along in front.

Cornelius' horse side steps when a young man, hair tousled, breathing hard, runs past in apparent pursuit of the group.

'Hey!' Cornelius calls. 'What's going on?'

The youth pivots on a heel, panting. 'Stokes is taking 'em to Barnley.' His eyes are black holes in a face made grey by the storm-laden light. 'Says he's gonna deal with her for good, get the babby.' He laughs a high-pitched giggle, stumbles, staggers upright, and is gone.

Cornelius' heart stops, restarts with a mighty thump.

He tugs the horse's head around so sharply the animal

snorts its disapproval, canters to the crest of the empty street, down the other side, leaps off when he reaches the Michaels' home, runs up the steps and bangs on the door. Twice.

Mr Michaels opens the door a fraction, then pulls it wide.

'Cornelius? What on earth?'

Cornelius stumbles into the hall.

'A mob sir, led by Stokes, heading on the river to Barnley, to Miss Williams.'

Miss Michaels, peering from the drawing room, gasps. Mrs Bryce, carrying a tea tray through the hall gives a muted shriek.

'Something about a baby.' Cornelius' eyes widen. 'Does he mean to steal Ellen?'

'How does he know about Barnley?' Joseph says. 'No, not Ellen. His own baby.' He shakes his head at Cornelius' frowning confusion. 'No time to explain. We need the constables urgently and someone to warn Miss Williams.'

He peers up the stairs.

'Is Catherine sleeping so soundly? Although I would rather she knew nothing of this—'

'Sleeping, sir?' Mrs Bryce purses her lips. 'She said something about needing air, took herself into the garden.' She frowns. 'That were not long after supper, and I don't remember her coming in.'

Mr Michaels' face pales in the gaslight. 'Not come in? For two hours? I thought she'd taken herself to bed, upset by what's happening. What the—' He looks to Miss Michaels. 'Lottie, please check her room. I'll check the garden.' He hurries down the hall, calling over his shoulder to Cornelius. 'See if Molly is in her stable.' His voice is taut.

Ten minutes later, Cornelius canters along the High Street, his horse's hooves striking the cobbles to awaken anyone not already disturbed by Jem Stokes' mob. At windows open to any coolness, curtains twitch in the wake of his path. At the township's end he uses what light remains to let the horse have its head. The animal responds, stretching powerful legs to eat up the distance to Barnley.

Cornelius' fear is a trapped bird fluttering, panicked, in the cage of his ribs.

The garden and Catherine's room were empty of Catherine. The stable was empty of Molly.

Catherine has gone to Hester. By herself, with darkness and a storm gathering.

Two storms.

*

Lydia opens the door to Joseph's urgent knocking.

'I know.' She runs a hand through her already untidy hair, turns into the parlour with Joseph following.

'How?'

'Sim came, distraught.' She sits heavily in one of the chairs beneath the window where the curtains have been drawn against the summer twilight, and curious passers-by. 'I didn't believe him at first.' She lifts her palms to her chin, presses them together in short bursts, looks to the ceiling and then to Joseph, fingers entwined. 'How naïve I was to think all this witch nonsense had gone away, folks had forgotten, we could get on with our lives.'

Joseph stands before the cold fireplace, twisting his hat. 'Where's Sim now?'

'Gone to Hester.' She releases her fingers, resumes her short, hard claps. 'She came here, with her child, last week. Wanting forgiveness. For the sake of the little girl, she said.'

'She told you where she lives?'

'Yes, thank the Lord, because it meant I could send Sim on his way and, God willing, he'll get there before Stokes finds them. If Will, my oldest, can't dissuade him first.' She looks up. 'He's at the river, trying to stop it all … if … if

… he's not too late.' Lydia stands abruptly, sways, steadies herself. 'What if …? No, I can't, won't think of it. And her and I estranged still …' Her voice drops to a whisper, a catch in it.

Joseph's heart aches. What if it was Catherine? Is he Christian enough to forgive, to love her, whatever her actions? He prays he is, although who can know until fully tested? The immediacy, however, is the danger Lydia's daughter and granddaughter are in.

'I'm so sorry, Lydia. I–'

She is sobbing quietly. With her arms hanging at her sides she looks for all the world like a repentant child. Joseph's full heart makes it hard to breathe. He takes a step forward, halts with his arms half-raised. Lydia lifts her head, and reveals a grief so deep, so clear that Joseph cannot help himself. He takes another step, gathers her to him and feels the rightness of her as she sobs against his chest.

*

Aaron jumps from his chair to throw open the door at the steady knock. Has Hester come to him?

A young woman stands before him, a horse softly snorts behind her. Where has she sprung from, in this isolated place, appearing at his door like a manifested spirit?

'Are you Aaron?' she says bluntly. 'Do you care for Hester?'

'Yes, and yes.'

He takes her outstretched hands. 'Where are they?'

'Barnley.' She stares into his eyes, as if judging Aaron's honesty. He holds her gaze. 'You need to go to her, immediately, show her you care for her.' She chews her bottom lip. 'You have to take her away, her and Ellen, before any harm comes to them.'

'Ellen. The baby?'

The young woman smiles with sweet tenderness and

Aaron's lips instinctively lift before he says, 'Harm? Who would wish them harm?'

He sits on a chair, urges her to the other and, having learned her name, listens to her hastily told tale of the jilted fisherman, his malicious slanders, and her horror of what might happen when he discovers Hester has Rose.

'Rose?'

Aaron raises an eyebrow at Catherine's brief explanation. 'The river nymphs brought her to Hester?'

'Yes.'

He gazes past his visitor and through the doorway in the direction of the river. 'Of course.'

Her explanation done, Catherine stands, slaps her gloves into her palm. 'It can't wait until morning.' She paces about the cottage. 'By then they will have forced her to give up Rose, word will be out and I'm terrified what that brute of a man might do.'

Aaron stays seated. He rubs his beard, emotions broiling as heavily as the clouds above the river. 'Hester might refuse to come with me.'

'She might.' Catherine steps close, stares down into his eyes. 'If you ever loved her, now is not the time to hesitate. Hester should have the choice, not Papa or Mrs Williams.'

Aaron wonders at the intensity in those pretty blue eyes.

'Nor you,' Catherine says. 'Only Hester.'

'I have to return you to Shiphaven first. It's not safe—'

No time.

Marianne is adamant.

'No time?' he murmurs. He closes his eyes, hears Mother Lovell's mutterings: 'The river witch, the goddess's darling. She will have her.'

He stirs himself. 'Are you able to ride with me?'

She juts out her chin in a way which reminds him of Hester.

'Of course, we need to go, now.'

*

Avoiding the long curve of the road, Aaron leads the way across a forest silenced by anticipation of the impending storm to go the shortest way to Barnley. Black clouds broil above the trees to goad the humid gloom into premature darkness. He looks up for the hundredth time, searching the gaps between the branches. The storm is near and when it arrives, God help those caught out in it. He peers around at Catherine. She leans forward in her side-saddle, following his hurrying lead. Her mare trots surefooted on the greenway, as confident as any deer. Nevertheless, Aaron huffs his worry into the shadows – a worry burdened with guilt over Hester.

From the time he allowed her into the cottage the midsummer eve she appeared unexpected, unwelcome, at his door, through to his willing surrender the night of All Hallows Eve, he has led her every step of the way to this bitter point. The knowledge burns him.

As do Mother Lovell's warnings, and the nymph's song below Shrewsbury bridge. His imagination cavorts with demonic images of fire, water steaming, waves slapping at flames.

The spirits have gathered, curious at what undertaking is afoot. Maybe they've been summoned by Marianne, whom Aaron senses at his shoulder.

Hurry, hurry, she begs him, mimicking Catherine's urgency.

Marianne is far from the cottage. What force carries her with them, to Hester, to the river?

*

They would have found her missing by now. Distress at the anguish she is causing battles Catherine's fierce belief in her mission. She keeps her eyes on Aaron's back, bouncing lightly in the saddle as they trot the greenways.

He tilts his head as if listening to someone, or something, and spurs his horse to a faster pace. Molly is tiring, falling further behind Aaron's gelding. She drank deeply at the last stream they crossed, the same one which flows past Hester's garden. Catherine comforts the mare with a pat and an encouraging, 'Not far now', and rides through a gap in a hedge.

Aaron is there, waiting, on the road from Shiphaven. He faces Barnley, which has hunkered down, few lights showing, waiting for the clouds to burst.

The sticky closeness weighs on Catherine's shoulders. Molly quivers beneath her, her determination to deal sturdily with the night's goings on, weakening.

'Which way?' Aaron says.

Catherine takes the lead and Molly gains her second wind, lifting her head and her pace as she recognises the High Street and the lane which will take them to Hester and Ellen.

Sudden doubt assails Catherine. Has she done the right thing? Shouldn't she have asked Hester first? No, for if she'd delayed by half a day, Papa would have persuaded Aaron to leave, this chance lost, never regained.

She dismounts at Hester's gate, runs to the door, bangs on it. 'Hester, Hester, open up, it's me. I need to talk to you.'

Catherine stands back as the door is unbolted and flung wide. Hester's worried gaze shifts from herself to Aaron, standing by the open gate. He has dismounted, but appears reluctant to step nearer. Wise man.

'Oh!' Hester's hand goes to her mouth as the rain finally cascades with a crack of lightning and a thunderous boom.

Chapter Forty Two

em pays no attention to the massing black clouds, drags the boat to the river. Enthusiastic hands push and pull, and when it becomes apparent one boat won't do, a drunken shout goes up: 'C'mon boys, we'll take two.'

Shouts of approval, of 'Fix the witch for good,' and 'Fetch the babby home,' galvanise Jem's hot hatred. It hammers his chest, wanting out, wanting to tear the devil's whore apart.

He ignores Will's strident pleas, begging for his wicked sister's life. The man's as guilty as his brother for insisting on him courting the witch. They must have known. Set him up for a fool. Jem smarts at the shame, whips around and snarls.

'Get outta here. Afore I lose my temper.'

Will rushes forward, arms swinging. Jem punches him in the side of the head, knocking him to the sand. He doesn't wait to see if he gets up, but wades into the water with his fellows around him and hauls himself into the boat.

He's on the river and the tide is turning. The water will

carry him, bending to his will as he demands, rewarding him as it's been forced to reward him all these years. Not with fish and brandy. Not this time.

Jem's the king of the river. The flare of the torches marks his triumphal procession.

Crack!

Lightning sizzles, blinding him. Jem's army, his righteous band, his soldiers of justice, jump. They swear. Jem blinks, growls at the sky where the clouds froth like a mad dog's spit. Rain attacks his uplifted face, sharp, stinging as if the clouds spat fish hooks.

'C'mon, let's get there and do this!' he screams.

'Yeah!'

'What's a bit of lightning?'

Jem grips the tiller, steering a course between the smooth warnings of sandbanks emerging from the outgoing tide. He sets no sail, not running downriver, not with the rising wind. Gusts tug at his shirt as if they would pluck it from his body. When they fail, they spiral, buffeting him from behind, from the side, whipping his hair across his eyes.

The river lifts to embrace the dank wind, swelling the waves which billow and collapse, billow and collapse. The boat surges, falls, and the water slap, slap, slaps the hull in a fury of its own. The wind howls its demonic mirth.

Jem is a fisherman. His soldiers are fishermen. They live with this river and her tempers. They toss their drenched torches aside, plant their legs, hold steady.

Lightning hurls its spears into the water.

Shouts carry through the wild, wet air from behind Jem's boat. Screams which diminish quickly, fall silent.

One boat will have to do.

Jem's soldier fishermen are quiet. He senses their bravado crumbling, filleted by the steel-edged rain and winds and the loss of their companions. He howls into the storm, cursing it, cursing the river – cursing the witch.

*

Hester pulls Catherine inside, out of the thundering rain, and curtly directs Aaron to a rough shelter behind the cottage where the horses will be sheltered and able to drink from an open barrel of clean water.

When he is gone, Hester faces Catherine across the rag rug decorating the stone flags of the tiny parlour.

'Where? How?' She folds her arms, and listens to Catherine's tale.

'Papa would insist he leave, tomorrow.' She wrings her hands, bare of her gloves which she has removed and placed on the low table. 'It's not right for him to do that, or to talk to your mother. It's your decision, Hester, it's for you to decide if you wish to see him. For an hour, a day, or forever.'

Hester snorts. 'Is he offering forever? I doubt it.'

The back door opens, bangs shut and Aaron appears in the kitchen doorway. His hat drips water. His coat is drenched. He makes no move to come into the room, but seeks Hester's eyes. His own are dark, their familiar gold glint dulled.

'I'm sorry. So very sorry, Hester.'

Hester searches for sincerity. She finds it, yet a search of her own heart yields little in the way of full forgiveness. She juts out her chin, waits.

'If I'd thought—'

'If you'd thought.' She's tart. A simple sorry can't undo the hurt, the loneliness, the shame. It certainly can't forgive the near loss of Ellen. Her breath catches. The drumming of the rain fills the silence.

*

Aaron removes his hat, holds it in his hands. He glances about the room with its pots of herbs, glass phials of potions, bowls of dried leaves. The mortar and pestle he gave her sits on a wooden shelf beside two heavy books. He is sure one is a Culpepper.

'You've made a life, a good life.' He offers a tiny smile. 'You've achieved your dream. Not many do that.'

'Perhaps,' Hester says and her voice retains its tartness, 'they're not willing to pay the price, to make the sacrifice.'

'Perhaps.'

Mother Lovell's words beat loudly in his head: 'The river witch, the goddess's darling. She will have her.'

Is there more sacrifice for Hester to make? He begins to form the sentence that will tell her why he is here when—

'Do you want to see her? Your daughter?'

He lifts his head. His heart thumps. He is being offered a gift, even if it's not forgiveness.

'May I?' He is humble.

Hester leads him into a tiny room. The storm has dimmed what remained of the evening light, yet there is enough for him to see the two sleeping babies, the older with an arm flung over the little one. He stands by the cot and gazes down. He wants to reach out a finger and caress the dark curls, gently stroke the white brow.

His child. His and Hester's. He's been an idiot. A self-obsessed coward. He clenches his jaw to stop from crying out his foolishness, begging forgiveness. He has no right.

Hester, beside him, isn't looking at the babies. Rather, he senses her eyes on him. He half turns, meets her gaze which is hard, and questioning.

'I'm sorry,' he says again. He wants her to respond because, for once, he cannot read her. Is there a softening of her look? He has no time to find out for two things happen at once.

*

Thunder rolls with a doomsday boom above the cottage roof.

Some drowned soul pounds on the front door which

shudders noisily.

Hester takes one moment to glance at the babies who stir, don't wake, before she runs from the bedroom to yank the handle. The opening blazes white with lightning and Sim staggers through to fall at her feet like a penitent before a priest.

She bends over him, hands reaching out.

He meets her hands with his. His wet hair streams across his puce face, his exhausted body quivers.

Aaron stares from the bedroom doorway.

'Hester, who's this?' Catherine says.

Hester tugs Sim upright. 'My brother, Simeon.'

'Stokes …' Sim stutters through his shivering. '…coming here, to find you, take the babby.'

'Take the baby? How can he know already?' Catherine draws a breath. 'Jenny.'

'The river.' Sim gags. 'They're on the river.'

A warm, familiar breath brushes Hester's ear. She twists about, there is no one there. Aaron, lines etched in his forehead has his head on one side as if listening.

The rain clatters on the cottage's stone tiles. The wind hurls itself at the windows to rattle the glass and provoke the frames into a thudding counter-attack. Through it all, Hester hears the whisper.

The river is our ally. We can do battle with Sabrina beside us.

'Battle?' Hester says it out loud, and Sim answers.

'He's threatening to deal with you for good. I told Ma …' He wraps his arms about his sodden body, his breathing slowing. 'She sent me.' He shakes his head. 'I'm sorry, Hester. Sorry about it all, and 'specially about Jem Stokes.'

Hester's sorry too, about it all. Mother knows, and cares? She hears again the soft click of the door behind herself and Ellen after what she'd considered a wasted visit. She walks to where Reuben's old coat hangs on a peg, lifts it and carries it to Sim. 'Wrap this around you. It'll save you from a chill.'

He throws the coat over his shoulders and pulls it close. 'Thanks.' His eyes are anxious, waiting.

Hester leans in, kisses his shiny wet cheek. 'It's what sisters do.' Forgiveness should start somewhere.

'And what are we do to about Stokes?' Aaron says. 'Does he know exactly where Hester is?'

'Not from me he don't,' Sim says, with a bare glance at Aaron. 'Won't take long to ferret it out the first house he happens along.' He reaches through the coat to touch Hester's arm. 'You have to leave.'

'Leave?'

Leave?

Hester squints at the tabby sitting upright on the hearth rug. The tabby squints back.

Not in this storm. I refuse to go into any sacks. And besides, what about them? She twitches her tail in the direction of the bedroom where the babies, miraculously, still sleep.

Catherine twists her fingers together, her knuckles digging into her chin. Her eyes beg Hester to leave.

A gentle heat touches Hester's ear.

I am fire, you are air. We battle this together.

And through the bang and crackle of the storm another voice carries, as it has done all Hester's life.

Be strong, Hester, take courage, do what you have to do.

The clutter in her head untangles, her leaping emotions settle.

'No,' she says to Sim. 'I won't leave.'

The lines in Aaron's forehead deepen. He rubs his wet beard. 'You have to. The danger …'

Hester throws out her arms. 'The river's strength is mine to call on. It's why she brought me Rose, to show me.' She walks to the hooks by the door, lifts her cloak. 'We'll be ready for them.' She throws the cloak over her shoulders, glares from Sim – who babbles she is mad, what is she talking about? – to Aaron, who stands stiffly, clenching and unclenching his fists in their sodden gloves.

'We won't fail,' Hester says. 'Sabrina won't deny me.'

*

Catherine's mind gallops, torn between what Papa would call simple common sense to leave, despite the storm, and a voice insisting her friend is right, that the nymphs have proven to be Hester's friends. If 'friends' is the correct word given what has happened. The river? Will it help or hinder?

Aaron argues. 'There are three of us. A mob is out there, driven by a drunk, furious man to attack you, and you want to carry the fight to them? On the river?' He rubs his hands together, eyes creased in frustrated worry, voice catching on the word *river* as if the water is the greater danger.

'Fire, air,' he mutters, and to himself, softly, 'You cannot fail this time.'

Catherine is given no time to decide which side she is on.

'You understand what you should do if we fail.' Hester stuffs her curls under a flat hat and tightens her cloak around her while she stares into Catherine's eyes.

'Don't—'

'I need your promise, if ever we were true sisters.' She takes hold of Catherine's hands. 'Your promise neither of my girls will be abandoned, including to the fisherman.'

Catherine wipes the dampness from her eyes and kisses Hester's cheek. 'You have it.'

A quick embrace and she is gone, with a reluctant, protective Aaron and a scowling Sim following her through the kitchen and into the storm. The tattoo of rain on the stone paths, the screeching of the wind around the chimney, ratchet up. The door bangs shut and the noise softens, like a curse withdrawn.

Catherine wraps her arms about her waist and walks to the room where the babies sleep. She lifts a corner of the cotton blanket and pulls it over Rose's gently undulating chest.

'It will come out right,' she soothes, while her heart drums a rhythmic panic in her chest to gainsay her assurances. Her thoughts fight each other, this way and that. She should have sided with Aaron. No, Hester is strong.

'The river is their friend,' she whispers. She strokes Rose's golden hair with tentative fingers. 'The river brought you here. It won't leave you motherless twice.'

How long before they reach the river? Has Stokes and his mob arrived there? Can the river be trusted? Hester might say Rose is proof of the river's alliance, yet all it has done is bring mighty trouble. Shouldn't they have sent Sim for the constables, waited? What magic is at work here, compelling Hester – and Aaron – to face Stokes on the stormy waters?

Catherine jumps at the thud of more heavy knocking at the front door. Her panic increases its tempo, it's hard to breathe.

Has Stokes abandoned the river and is here, outside, with his mob of ignorant fishermen? With only herself between him and Rose.

She leaves the babies, shutting the bedroom door after her, and moves cautiously to the window where the curtains are drawn. Twitching the material aside, she can see no mob, hear no shouting–

'Catherine, Catherine, are you there?'

'Cornelius?' Catherine unlatches the door and pulls it open.

He lurches inside, throws up his hands. 'Thank the dear Lord, you're here! And safe!'

Despite his sodden coat, his dripping hat and soaked gloves, he drags Catherine into a crushing embrace. Her panic flees, which doesn't slow the hammering of her heart. She wraps her arms about Cornelius' wet neck and buries her head in his chest.

It's Cornelius who moves first, kicking out his leg to close the door against the storm.

'I was frantic, your father and your aunt too, out in this,' he murmurs into her hair. He leans away to gaze at her, worry etched into his brow. 'It was your father suspected you'd come here, to tell your friend about the return of … of …'

'Hester's lover?' Catherine teases, smiling up into the depth of his brown eyes. She is floating, a summer breeze playing in a dazzling sky. 'Ellen's father?' She steps out of his wet embrace. 'I did come here, as you see.' Her smile widens. 'First, however, I needed to find Aaron – the lover, the father. I brought him here. He's with Hester.'

The reality of where Hester and Aaron are now, blows the breeze away in a frightened gust. Catherine's sudden happiness drops from her as easily as a loosely-worn shawl. She shivers.

'Where?' Cornelius peers around the empty room.

'The river. They've gone to the river. To stop Stokes.'

Cornelius doesn't ask how she knows about Stokes. 'Your father is fetching the constables.'

Catherine lets out a heavy sigh of relief.

Cornelius paces the room, dripping water onto the flags. 'Only two of them? Madness. How do they expect …?' He shakes his head, stands still. 'I have go to the river too, to help.'

Catherine places a hand on his sleeve. She is torn. To gain him at last and then possibly lose him, as well as Hester? She wants to clutch his coat, plead for him not to go, to stay away from danger. That won't do, though. Cornelius is no coward, and neither is she.

'Yes,' she says. Her voice is strong.

Lantern light shows through the curtains. The jangle of harness and barked orders carry above the wind. Thank God.

'And you will have company. It seems the constables have arrived.'

Chapter Forty Three

he rain stutters to a spattering halt. The waves mellow. Jem squints along the river where the blackness has lightened as the moon weaves between the clouds. He peers towards the bank where a cleft of darkness tells his experienced eyes a stream melds with the greater water. He judges the time since they left Shiphaven. He judges the river flow.

'We're here,' he says, and receives mumbled agreement.

It's the stream which flows through Barnley. Jem is certain of it. Hasn't he ridden this water for nigh on forty years?

He sets the tiller and the boat swings easily. There's no resistance. Rather, the river carries him steadily, surely, heading for the cleft of darkness.

Jem's triumph is resurgent. He can always beat this bastard of a river. She's just a rebellious woman who in the end is forced to accept her master.

'Hey, Jem.' One of his fishermen soldiers points, nudges Jem's arm. 'T'ain't them people on the bank?'

People? In this weather?

*

Sabrina carries the boat and its occupants to Hester, leading it along the newly emergent moon's silver path like a dog on a string. Faster the boat comes, devout with the zeal of purpose. There is no unfurled sail to catch a serendipitous wind, no oars dipping to force the vessel across the flow. Yet it sails on.

Hester glances at Sim, standing beside her, gaping at the silent scene on the water. This is not how the river works. It doesn't flow sideways. Hester knows he cannot see the arms, pearl in the moonlight, which reach from the water to guide the craft, nor the thick ropes of hair trailing behind in mockery of fishermen's nets.

A song rises from the waters. In this quiet calm, Hester doesn't have to strain to listen.

You are strong, Hester. You are wise. Do what you have to do.

The river nymphs call through the night in their high voices. 'Join us, swim with us, learn with us.'

The spirits gather on the riverbank. Their curious whispers cool the air around her. Has Aaron summoned them? Has she?

On Hester's other side, Aaron stands with his arms at his sides, fingers splayed against his trouser legs. He's given up trying to dissuade her, but his tension as they walked the muddy, slippery path to reach this spot silenced any talk. Anger? Fear? Determination? Whatever it is, Hester concedes – to herself – she is glad to have him with her. She thinks of his face, the plea for forgiveness clear, as he bent over Ellen earlier. Not asking, knowing it needs to be earned.

'This is your time, Marianne,' Aaron whispers, his voice tight. 'I will not fail twice.'

A familiar hot ghostly breath passes by Hester to stir Aaron's hair. She is glad for this too.

*

'We've been here before.' Aaron says it quietly, letting the memories rise unfettered, at last.

Dark curls hiding cheeks flushed from the fire, mutters of incantation, white flames curling around the simmering pot ...

'Drink this, Aaron.' Marianne had stretched her arm above the pot to push the silver cup at him. Her dark eyes were bright as wet belladonna berries. 'A potion to give us power.'

Aaron stepped away, palms held up in denial. Behind Marianne, below the stony cliffs, the silver-streaked river flowed to the sea. On the far bank, an All Hallows Eve fire the size of a small hill painted brush strokes of red and gold to brighten the hamlet's cottages. The faint sound of fiddles drifted above the few vessels on the water.

'You go too far,' Aaron said. 'Where will this lead?'

'There's no answer to that if we don't try.'

'Why can't you be content with what we have?'

Marianne ignored the question. 'If you won't drink with me, I'll drink alone.' She kept the cup held out, inviting him. Her red lips curled in a seductive smile. 'Sabrina wishes it. The river nymphs grow tired of calling me and I grow tired of refusing their call.'

'I ask a second time, where will this lead?'

'To power.' She lifted her head to the dark, cold night. 'To fly with the gulls.' She shook her curls. 'Mother Lovell never could make me a spell to fly. I can, Aaron. I have.'

'Could or would?'

Marianne spoke over him, her voice high with eagerness. 'I've imbued this with other magic, too. I've blended seeds and leaves, flowers and herbs, the fungi of the Forest to bring the spirits to us, to learn their secrets and to understand the minds of men and beasts and the fish that swim in the river.' She waved the cup. 'Will you soar with me, Aaron? My love?'

'No!' he cried as Marianne swallowed the hot liquid.

She pushed the cup into his hands. 'There's enough left,'

she said, and waited for him to drink, a child forced to take its medicine by a pitiless nanny.

And 'No!' he cried when Marianne ran to the cliff edge, lifted her arms to spread her cloak, and flew.

Higher she went, striving for the stars.

Sabrina called: *Be strong, be wise.*

The river nymphs beckoned: 'Join us, swim with us, learn with us.'

Aaron's stomach plummeted as Marianne's soar to the stars jolted to a halt. She hung, hair streaming. A heartbeat, two, and she fell, feet first, towards the water. Demonic shrieks, hellish as witches being flayed, rose on the windless night, their fury fierce at being summoned.

You'll do. Mother Lovell's words, her bony claws clamped to his twelve-year-old chin.

He had determined to prove her right, to be worthy. Despite his coward-filled chest which refused to take in air, he threw himself from the cliff, determined to battle the shrieking demons, to save Marianne. For one exalted moment he was power and weightlessness.

Marianne's plummet stalled. She swayed, head lolling like a hanged woman, held in space by God knew what, though Aaron doubted God was near.

The spirits pressed him in a swarm of sharp buzzing of angry wasps, fierce, attacking. Hellfire spumed from the river which churned and spat like a cornered cat to quell its own flames. The fire swelled, glowing red, hissing white hot steam, enfolding Marianne's unmoving form.

Aaron reached for her, through the flames. Her blank eyes were lit with red. Her dark curls shone, burnished with the heat which scorched Aaron's hair, his beard, his face. He reached again and again, grabbing at nothing.

He was not good enough.

Below him, the river nymphs had scattered. Sabrina battled the hellfire, the flames flickered and died. Aaron closed his eyes, waiting for his plunge into the river's cold embrace.

He had woken, shivering in the frostbitten dawn, near the cold white ashes which had boiled Marianne's false potion. His hair was singed, his hands blistered. His charred, wet clothes stank of greasy smoke.

In the darkness above the cleft, Aaron's fingers itch to clasp Hester's hand, to keep her beside him, to thwart whatever the river has in mind this time.

Sabrina will not be denied, not again.

The glee in Marianne's murmur sickens him. He fixes his gaze on the boat where the river nymphs bear Jem Stokes to the bank. Stokes has abandoned the tiller and balances at the prow, tall and broad. His fellows cluster behind him, heads shaking, bodies twisting, peering over the sides. Do the nymphs appear to them? He doubts it.

They are not far now. He senses Hester's fingers curl and uncurl, brushing his. She stares at the boat, a furrow of concentration on her brow.

He hears Marianne's delighted breaths: *They will not set one foot ashore. Come, Hester, come all, I need you.*

Hester must hear the call, for she raises her arms, spreads her cloak into black wings.

Aaron staggers as an unnatural, spirit-filled wind roars in his ears, buffets him with whirlwind strength. The spirit wind summons the exhausted rain to cascade once more. It whips the river into choppy waves to hurl at the oncoming boat. The nymphs dive below the vessel and up the other side, tossing their hanks of hair to splash the waves into a frothing frenzy, violently rocking the craft.

The men aboard cling to each other, shouting into the wind, crying out for help.

Except Stokes. The fisherman folds his arms across his chest and rocks with his vessel, as unyielding as the prow of a warship.

Beyond the boat, the moonlit river flows in an after-storm calm. Around the boat, the tempest flourishes as if all the wild horses of the bore have galloped to this one place to rear and toss their manes.

Fire, air, and water – we will conquer.

'What do you–?' Aaron asks of both Marianne and Hester, and receives this for an answer:

Noiseless, Hester rises on the wind. She is a gull in flight, her hair streaming. She flies into the storm.

'No!' Aaron's cry is pure grief.

He watches Hester fly above the seething river. He tightens his shoulders, draws on all his strength, all his experience. This time, for Hester, he will be good enough. The spirits bear him over the thrashing waters.

*

Jem instinctively shifts his weight in rhythm with the rocking boat. He grins, teeth bared to the squalling rain. He was right all along. The witch is showing her true colours, flying over the water. A black cloud of demons trails her.

He's crushed this bloody river, forced it to serve him as it should. He'll do the same with the witch. Crush her.

He might toss her to the river, scraps to a dog. Drown her the same way she drowned his stupid Jane. Or he'll smuggle her into the house by the King's Shilling, same way she smuggled his babby into her witch's hovel. He'll drag her in by her bloody curls, a pirate's booty to be used at will. At last. He's every right to her.

No leaving him at the altar this time. Won't give her the blessing of marriage. She's a whore, a witching demon whore, which is how he'll treat her. He exults in the triumph to come.

His soldier fishermen have gone coward. He hears them at his back, their whimpers strangled by the gusts, begging him to stop this, to row home to Shiphaven. He ignores their babbling nonsense. He's Jem Stokes, and he'll not be routed by any devil witch, nor any damn river.

*

Hester is face to face with the stinking, lumpen fisherman. The boat stills. The rapid, muttered prayers of Stokes' fellows carry to Hester over his shoulder. He humphs and smirks into her eyes. His arms are crossed.

'C'mon then,' he growls. 'Got something for yer.' He lays a hand on his crotch. 'Just what you need, devil fornicator.'

Eyes fixed on his, she lifts her arms and rises higher. The boat rocks, rights itself. Stokes grins.

The prow, where he stands, tips its nose upwards in a sudden, sharp movement.

Stokes' screaming comrades fall or throw themselves into the river, give themselves to its mercy. He is drenched with their frantic, drowning splashes.

'Murderer! Witch!'

Fury distorts his rain-slashed face. He snarls, bends forward, snatches at Hester and catches the edge of her cloak.

He tugs, and she spins like a child's toy, the cloak ravelling her into his body. They are nose to nose. Sabrina's waters rise and fall below them, choppy, uneven. The nymphs toss the boat in their wet arms, side to side. The wind pulls at Hester's hair, at Stokes' shirt. He splays his legs, stands firm, hatred blazing in his pale eyes.

Hester waits, unafraid.

'Gotcha. Whore.'

'Rot in hell.'

A hot, swift breath brushes Hester's cheek and the boat's rolling stern combusts into fierce flames. The fire roars, sucking the dampness from the wind and twirling it into a red and gold hurricane. Gleeful laughter mixes with the spit of the fire's lengthening tongues.

∗

Jem ignores the heat scorching his back. If he's to die, he'll take her with him to hell. He lifts his arms to crush her to him—

She is gone, unspun from his grip into the arms of a tall, dark-haired man. Gold flints reflect the fire's flames in the man's wild, black eyes.

The devil! The witch has conjured her demon lover to save her. He knew it! His righteous certainty goads his anger. The devil snatches the edge of the witch's cloak from Jem's wet, slippery clasp and he and the witch hover, side by side, daring him, provoking him. He roars with fury.

The black devil and the witch raise their hands in a sudden jerky movement. The prow of the boat surges higher, steep as the cliffs along the river.

Jem's proud stance falters. Arms flailing, he lifts one leg, searching for solidity and finding rain and wind, and the agonising pain of fire streaking his skin. He screams, falls, slowly, out over river, staring into the white-tipped waves. Golden sparks surround him, bite at his face, his arms, his body; a thousand wasps stinging, forcing him into the cursed waters.

Fright claws at his bowels. Twisting, naked arms reach for him. They tug him down into a coldness as searing as the flames. He fights, thrashes out. Thick ropes curl tight around his ribs, clamp his arms to his sides, bind his furiously kicking legs. He is dragged into the currents, his screams filled with icy water.

Mocking, burbling voices call.

'Join us, swim with us, learn from us.'

Chapter Forty Four

he wind has lost its brash squalling. It sings gently, ruffling the water where the stream gives itself to the river. The constables arrive with a young man with dark skin. Aaron whispers to Hester that this is Joseph Michaels' clerk and what is he doing here? Hester nods.

The constables, Cornelius, and a silent Sim drag wet, shaking, fishermen from the water. Their eyes are wary, or terrified, or blank, and they flick to Hester and Aaron and away again. They sit on the bank as far from the two of them as possible. Hester mourns the loss of her obscurity. Whatever the tabby says, her and the girls' future lies away from Barnley.

Stokes cannot be found, drowned or alive. When the tide ebbs and there is light, they will search the mudflats. Hester is certain it will be fruitless.

She stands beside Aaron, wrapped in her cloak. Her hand touches his. It is warm, smooth and Hester lets the images play in her mind. Aaron's long fingers hovering over jars of dried leaves, dark eyes questioning, 'which one do we use?'. Or scribbling in his journals, writing up her lessons, calculating quantities, noting time of year, locations where yarrow is most plentiful, where the belladonna thrives. His hands are as familiar to her as her own.

He half turns to her, the unspoken plea etched into the darkness of his eyes, into the set of his mouth. Hester wraps her fingers about his hand, and squeezes. He returns the squeeze, firm and strong. He doesn't let go, and Hester understands he will never do so again.

You are wise, you are strong.

The voice is clear in the warm night breeze. It's Sabrina's voice, yet not Sabrina.

Hester glances at Aaron. He stares at the rippling water, tears glistening.

'Be happy,' he murmurs.

Hester follows his gaze. Above the ripples a faint red-gold haze flares in the moonlight and is gone.

'Who is Marianne?' she says.

Thank you for reading *River Witch*.

Fantasy and history are my two writing joys, and this book gave me the chance to do both. It's been two years of hard work, but the reward I truly value is a happy reader. No point otherwise! It's the biggest buzz when people tell me how they couldn't put the story down, how they yelled at/ cried with/the characters, and how they felt they were there, in whatever setting the story takes place.

If *River Witch* made you feel any of this, or more, I would be very grateful if you took some time to write a review on Amazon or Goodreads, or just leave a rating – that's fine too.

We indie authors don't have the resources of publishing houses behind us to promote our books and therefore rely on reviews and word of mouth recommendations to spread the word.

And be assured that I read (devour) every review!

Tell a friend, post how much you enjoyed the book on social media, recommend *River Witch* to your book club, ask your local library to get it in.

THANK YOU

Acknowledgements

The idea to write *River Witch* came from a prosaic source. In 2020, I was asked to edit an article for the Forest of Dean's Local History Society's journal, *The New Regard*. The article had been researched and written by local historian Roger Deeks and was about Ellen Hayward, a 'wise woman' of the Forest tried for witchcraft in 1906. Ellen's story fascinated me, and I immediately decided to write an historical fiction novel based on her life. However, the story had aspects that made it difficult for me to make her a truly sympathetic heroine, so I turned to my first writing love of fantasy for rescue. And rescue came in the guise of combining local legends with the area's rich history to end up with the piece of historical fantasy you hold in your hands. I hope Roger approves the outcome, but in any case, my deep thanks to him for giving me the story.

Along every inch of the way, *River Witch* has benefitted from the considered and brilliant insights into everything from plot to commas, of my two critique partners, Paula and Jodi. I love you guys. Members of Dean Writers Circle's novel group also deserve heartfelt thanks for their ongoing contributions: thank you to Penny, James, Carol, Jean, Felicity and Patricia. I owe my beta readers much, for the consistency of their views on what worked and what didn't. I hope I've used your advice to best effect. I won't name them all, but I do want to give a special shout out to my wonderful friend and cheerleader, Lily, for her unstinting support through thick and thin.

My special thanks to Lauren Willmore for her gorgeous cover design.

Finally and mostly, my loving thanks to my patient, tolerant husband, David Harris, without whom this book would not exist.

Any spelling, grammatical or design flaws are entirely mine.

Cheryl Burman lives in the Forest of Dean, UK with her husband. She is the author of the fantasy trilogy, *Guardians of the Forest* and its prequel, *Legend of the Winged Lion*; and of *Keepers*, 1950s historical women's fiction set in her home country of Australia. Her flash fiction, short stories and bits of her novels have won various prizes, including being longlisted for the Historical Writers Association Short Story competition 2020 with a piece based on *River Witch*. Some of these stories are gathered into her slim collection, *Dragon Gift*.

Cheryl's monthly newsletter, By the Letter, keeps her readers up to date with her work, and offers short stories, bits of fascinating research, interviews with authors of interest, and local literary news. Sign up and receive a free eBook as a thank you gift.

All her books, including purchase links, can be found at her website cherylburman.com.